LOVE OR LOYALTY?

Lieutenant Jackson Vaughn was unlike any man Melissa had ever met. He excited her in a way she had never thought possible. She knew she would be sorry if she gave in to her passions, but she couldn't resist her handsome lover.

Night after night they secretly met in his bedroom. His tender kisses and soft caresses filled her with all-consuming desire. She anxiously waited for their hours together and when he proposed marriage, her heart eagerly responded.

But the war raged on and Jackson had to return to duty. Not knowing that Melissa's loyalties were with the Union, he pledged to kill every damn Yankee in sight. Meanwhile, Melissa silently thought of her brother—in a blue uniform. She dared not utter a word.

With her lover and her brother in battle—and on opposite sides—Melissa prayed that the war would end quickly . . . and that no one would discover the truth.

SENSATIONAL MISSISSIPPI SAGA

RIVER OF FORTUNE: THE PASSION (561, $2.50)
by Arthur Moore

When the beautiful Andrea Berlanger and her beloved Logan leave their homes to begin a new life together, they discover the true meaning of life and desire on a Mississippi riverboat and the great . . . RIVER OF FORTUNE.

RIVER OF FORTUNE: THE PAGANS (608, $2.50)
by Arthur Moore

When Andrea's life is threatened by her mean and evil stepmother, Lily Berlanger, Logan realizes that nothing is worth the gamble of losing the woman he loves and the life of passion and adventure they share on the great Mississippi River.

RIVER OF FORTUNE: THE PROUD (665, $2.50)
by Arthur Moore

Logan's dream finally comes true when he becomes the owner of a magnificent fleet of Mississippi steamers. He hopes for life-long happiness with the woman he loves, but soon realizes that Lily Berlanger—his ruthless and scheming rival—will stop at nothing to see him destroyed!

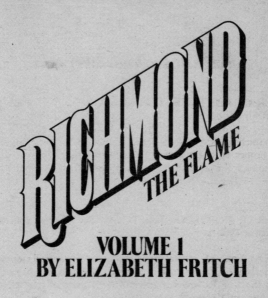

RICHMOND
THE FLAME

VOLUME 1
BY ELIZABETH FRITCH

ZEBRA BOOKS

KENSINGTON PUBLISHING CORP.

ZEBRA BOOKS

are published by

KENSINGTON PUBLISHING CORP.
21 East 40th Street
New York, N.Y. 10016

Printed in the United States of America

RICHMOND

THE FLAME

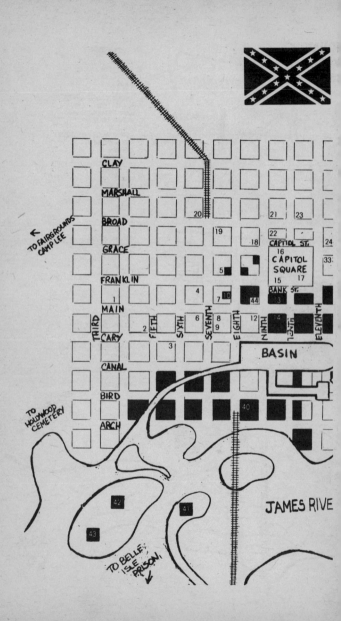

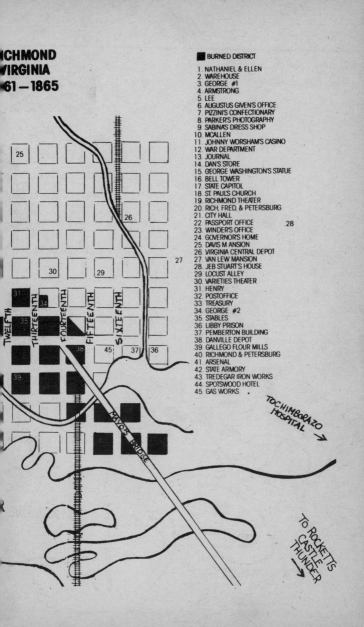

RICHMOND
VIRGINIA
1861 – 1865

■ BURNED DISTRICT

1. NATHANIEL & ELLEN
2. WAREHOUSE
3. GEORGE #1
4. ARMSTRONG
5. LEE
6. AUGUSTUS GIVEN'S OFFICE
7. PIZZINI'S CONFECTIONARY
8. PARKER'S PHOTOGRAPHY
9. SABINA'S DRESS SHOP
10. MCALLEN
11. JOHNNY WORSHAM'S CASINO
12. WAR DEPARTMENT
13. JOURNAL
14. DAN'S STORE
15. GEORGE WASHINGTON'S STATUE
16. BELL TOWER
17. STATE CAPITOL
18. ST. PAULS CHURCH
19. RICHMOND THEATER
20. RICH, FRED, & PETERSBURG
21. CITY HALL
22. PASSPORT OFFICE
23. WINDER'S OFFICE
24. GOVERNOR'S HOME
25. DAVIS MANSION
26. VIRGINIA CENTRAL DEPOT
27. VAN LEW MANSION
28. JEB STUART'S HOUSE
29. LOCUST ALLEY
30. VARIETIES THEATER
31. HENRY
32. POSTOFFICE
33. TREASURY
34. GEORGE #2
35. STABLES
36. LIBBY PRISON
37. PEMBERTON BUILDING
38. DANVILLE DEPOT
39. GALLEGO FLOUR MILLS
40. RICHMOND & PETERSBURG
41. ARSENAL
42. STATE ARMORY
43. TREDEGAR IRON WORKS
44. SPOTSWOOD HOTEL
45. GAS WORKS

One

It was a crisp autumn afternoon as Melissa Armstrong walked home through the hillsides of western Virginia. The slender, dark-haired girl glanced toward the Ohio River. She saw the billowy puffs of white coming from the smokestacks of the paddlewheeler, and she knew the *Allegheny Belle* was about to put in at the landing. She quickened her step, and the steamboat's whistle announced its arrival to the sleepy little town of Shady Run just as Melissa opened the door to her home.

"Jeremiah!" she gasped, out of breath. "They're here!"

Her younger brother looked up from packing his carpetbag. At seventeen, he was a handsome boy, with dark hair and a body strong from years of growing up outdoors. His dark eyes shone with anticipation and excitement. "I thought this day would never get here. I'd better hurry."

Melissa smiled fondly at her brother as she watched Jeremiah cram his belongings into his bag. She remembered the first time the *Allegheny Belle* had tied up at the landing, in 1855. It had been purely by chance that Sam McClelland had come to Shady Run when a piston rod on

11

the steamer had broken in two. The fresh and exuberant young engineer from Pittsburgh had come to Melissa's father's blacksmith shop for assistance, and an immediate friendship began. Shady Run became a regular stop for the steamboat, bringing news and small gifts. Then fourteen, Melissa had thought Sam the most vital and exciting man she had ever met.

Her recollections were interrupted by Jeremiah. "Did you fix anything good for Sam to eat? You know how he loves your cooking."

"Peach cobbler, with plenty of cinnamon—just the way he likes it. But I expect I'd best make a pot of coffee to go with it."

She went into the tiny kitchen, which was in reality just an extension of the parlor, and took the tin of coffee from the shelf, still thinking of Sam. He wasn't like the people in her own little town; he was full of tales of faraway places and free to go steamboating off to new adventures. The novelty of his way of life had been reason enough for Melissa to become hopelessly infatuated with him until, on one visit, he had told them of his marriage. She felt a wave of disappointment and bitterness. Finally it tempered as she realized that it had been Sam's independence and adventurous spirit that she had been captivated by, more than the man himself.

"Where's Papa?" she called to her brother.

"In his shop. You know how he feels about me going away."

"He'll get over it." She put the pot on the stove and returned to her brother. She pushed back a lock of his unruly hair. "Papa's very proud of you. You're the first in the family to continue your education."

"Cousin Andrew went to VMI," he reminded her.

12

"Oh, pooh! That doesn't count! He got expelled." She noticed the haphazard way in which Jeremiah was stuffing his clothes into his bag and took the shirt from his hands. "Lordy, Jeremiah, I hope you do better doctoring than you tend to your clothes."

Melissa thought of the trouble Jeremiah had had in convincing their father that he wanted to study medicine. The boy had never had much interest in becoming a blacksmith, and James Armstrong reluctantly agreed to allow his son to make the trip to Pittsburgh, where he would be under the tutelage of Dr. Jim White, Sam's brother-in-law.

She had watched Jeremiah's desire to become a doctor grow to a passion in the last year, for he wanted to learn medicine and then return home to take care of his friends and neighbors. The nearest doctor was in the next county: when he could be found at all, it was a long ride and often too late. There was a veterinarian in town, but he was of little value for measles or whooping cough. And, of course, there was Mama Louise, an old woman on a nearby plantation who many years ago had brought her herbs and magic from Africa to treat the sick.

It would be worth the separation from Jeremiah, she told herself, if it meant the fulfilling of his dreams.

Sam eased the steam off the engines as Captain Benjamin Reno guided the *Allegheny Belle* into the Shady Run landing. After checking the pressure gauges, he joined the captain in the wheelhouse. This was an unusual stop upriver, made solely for the purpose of picking up Jeremiah. Sam and Captain Reno had discussed the hazards involved in carrying Jeremiah to Pittsburgh, and they both decided it was worth the risk.

Jeremiah was bright, enthusiastic, and eager to learn, and neither Sam nor Ben had the heart to turn him down. But deep down inside, they both were worried.

Sam gazed out the window of the pilothouse at the quiet little town on the river and considered the situation. The Armstrongs had never voiced their opinion on the subject of slavery, one way or the other. He knew they owned no slaves, nor did many of the citizens of Shady Run. But there was a sizable reward to any informant who could show the *Allegheny Belle* to the authorities, caught with the goods, so to speak. The last trip from Cincinnati had been bad enough. When they stopped midstream several miles upriver to pick up their cargo, the rowboat had been fired upon from the bank. One of the crew had been grazed and the excitement caused one of their charges to go into premature labor.

"I'll stay aboard," Ben said, a worried look creasing his brow. "You go get the boy while I keep a lookout for anyone suspicious."

"I'll hurry. I didn't like the way that overseer from Dark Oaks was hanging around the dock in Cincinnati. He knows."

Ben nodded in agreement. "He knows. But he can't prove anything. If he could, he'd have made his move."

"Just the same, I'll hurry."

Melissa was just finishing helping her brother pack when Sam appeared at the door of the little house. In his middle twenties, he wore a leather cap tilted rakishly on his golden curls, and an engaging smile lit his handsome face.

"Are you all ready, Jeremiah?"

"I sure am," he beamed.

14

"I packed a hamper for you," Melissa told him, getting it from the kitchen table. She flashed a smile at Sam. "And I made peach cobbler especially for you, Mr. McClelland. Come sit down and have a piece."

"I'd love to, Melissa, but we can't tarry."

James Armstrong came in from his shop. "I expect you'll be needing this," he said, taking a box from his pocket and handing it to his son. The two resembled each other in stature only, for James's eyes were the same shade of sapphire as Melissa's, and his bristly hair, now threaded with gray, had once been fair. A solemn and quiet man nearing fifty, he possessed the contradictory attributes of both gentleness and physical strength.

Jeremiah opened the small leather-bound case, revealing a mother-of-pearl-handled straight razor. Melissa and Sam were peering at the contents as well.

"You'll need it pretty soon," Melissa observed, touching her brother's cheek lightly.

"I've been using Papa's already," Jeremiah confessed.

"I know," James smiled. "You always leave the blade dull." In a way, he was sorry that Jeremiah had decided to become a doctor instead of following his own trade as, years ago, he had followed his father's. But James had to admit that he was proud of his son. In a few years he would come home and take his place as one of the most respected men in the county.

Sam picked up the hamper. "We'd better be leaving."

Jeremiah took up his bag and turned to Melissa. She smoothed his collar, saying, "You remember to write."

"I will." Jeremiah hugged his sister and kissed her cheek. He then turned to his father. "I'll be the best doctor in the state."

"I know you will, son."

15

They shook hands, and Jeremiah joined Sam outside.

"Don't worry about him," Sam told them. "And I'll make sure he writes."

Jeremiah started to follow Sam, but then he suddenly put down his bag and ran back to embrace his father and sister. Then, gathering up his belongings, he hurried after Sam. Melissa blinked, hoping her brother wouldn't see her tears.

"Don't forget what I told you!" James called after him.

Jeremiah waved, and they disappeared around the corner.

"What aren't you supposed to forget?" Sam asked.

Jeremiah giggled. "Papa warned me to be careful of the—ah—women in Pittsburgh."

Sam laughed and put his arm around the boy's shoulder. "Jeremiah, my boy, you're in for quite an education!"

Once aboard the *Allegheny Belle*, Sam showed Jeremiah where to put his things and then went down to his engines. Jeremiah climbed back up to the pilothouse where Captain Reno's nephew, William, was conversing with his uncle. Sam told Jeremiah that William had come along this trip to help take care of the ledgers and learn more as a cub pilot. He was a little older than Jeremiah, tall and gangly. The two boys shook hands, and then William started out of the wheelhouse.

"I'm going to go check on the freight before we get under way," he called back.

Jeremiah was all eyes and ears as he gazed out the glass windows and heard the captain signal Sam with the bell.

"The river's riding easy today," Captain Reno remarked. A man in his early sixties, Benjamin Reno's

16

face and neck were leathery from the many years spent on the water, but his body was that of a man half his age. "Reckon you're in for a smooth trip the first time out."

Jeremiah felt the boat shudder and then sensed her moving, ever so slowly at first. Ben eased her out into the current and rang for more speed. Jeremiah was lost in his thoughts as he watched the green brush glide by on the shore; the few people watching waved as they passed.

As they rounded a bend some three miles out of Shady Run, Captain Reno picked up his glass and peered ahead at the straight stretch of water. He uttered a groan of frustration. "This is what I've been afraid of ever since we left Cincinnati."

"What?" Jeremiah asked.

Captain Reno handed him the glass. Ahead, Jeremiah could make out two barges secured together in the middle of the river at a narrow point. There were men on the barges—all armed.

"What is it?" Jeremiah asked, suddenly alarmed.

"Judgment day," Ben muttered. "Sit down on that bench and don't move."

Jeremiah did as he was told. Seated on the hard wooden bench, his hand gripped the polished brass rail below the window. Captain Reno rang for full speed ahead, and Sam answered him with steam power. The *Allegheny Belle* responded, plowed her prow into the water for a moment, then lifted it back out, skimming along the river like greased lightning. Jeremiah listened to the water churning under the paddle wheels and craned his neck to see outside. The barge loomed larger by the second. He wondered if the rest of the crew knew what was happening and hoped they were well prepared with arms of their own.

17

Jeremiah glanced back at the captain, standing with his feet planted squarely on the deck, gripping the helm tightly and staring straight ahead. The boy had no idea a steamboat could go this fast.

"You're going to crash right into them!" he cried.

"I hope to go right through them," Ben avowed, never taking his eyes off the target.

Down below, the heat from the boilers was oppressive as a giant of a black man shoveled coal as fast as he could into the gaping mouth of the furnace. Sam knew something was happening and had a pretty good idea why, but exactly what it was, he didn't know. He was too busy watching and listening for any telltale signs that his machinery was failing under the pressure.

Jeremiah heard a few random gunshots moments before he felt the crash. The impact jolted him off the bench and knocked him against the wheelhouse wall. He heard the shattering of the window and raised his arms protectively over his face as a shower of glass fell about him. He squeezed his eyes shut and listened to the pounding of the water, the crackling of splintering wood, and a few muffled cries.

Once the fragments of glass had settled, he scrambled to his knees and peeped over the jagged edge of the broken casement. In the river below, fragments of timber floated by, a barrel bobbed on the waves created by the paddles, and a man's body drifted aimlessly on the current. Grasping the railing, Jeremiah slowly raised himself to his feet, staring in fascinated horror at the red-checkered shirt in the water as it came to a halt against an overhanging limb on shore.

He didn't realize the *Allegheny Belle* had decreased her speed, until excited voices brought him back to reality.

18

Heavy feet clattering up the metal steps distracted him, and for the first time, he looked around the pilothouse. The deck was covered with slivers of glass, but Captain Reno was still standing firmly at the helm.

Sam burst through the door and viewed the scene. His face was grimy with soot, with dark lines in the creases of his neck where the perspiration had settled.

The captain gave him a broad grin. "We won't hear any more from that overseer today."

William appeared, out of breath. "No harm done to the freight." He looked at the shattered glass. "What a mess!"

Sam wiped his neck with his handkerchief. "Just what exactly happened?"

"We ran right through two barges," Ben told him. "For a minute there, I thought I might be joining my dear departed Martha. Any damage done to the engine?"

"None that I can see," Sam replied. "I'll check her again when she cools down some." He gave a sidelong glance at Jeremiah.

"Why don't you tell Nick to make a pot of coffee?" Ben suggested to Sam. "And get Jeremiah settled in his cabin. Matter of fact, why don't you tell Nick to just start supper as soon as he cleans up? I think we've got some explaining to do to Jeremiah. We can do it while we're eating."

Jeremiah straightened up. "I reckon I already know what you're going to tell me. I'm going down to my cabin now. I'll tell Nick about supper."

Sam and Ben watched Jeremiah leave the wheelhouse and then exchanged concerned looks. Would the boy understand the reasons why they were helping slaves escape from the South?

Jeremiah found his way along the companionway to his cabin and went in. He looked at the bunk with his carpetbag resting on top. A small table and chair were bolted to the floor. On the shelf under the porthole stood a washbasin and a cracked mirror hung on the back of the door. It was definitely not luxury, but he guessed it was not meant to be. The steamboat line was interested in profits, and there was more money to be made in hauling freight than passengers. The crew was small: Captain Ben Reno; Sam; Nick, who doubled as cook as well as second engineer; and a mate, Peter Emge, a German whom Jeremiah had only met once before and had difficulty understanding.

Going over to the basin, Jeremiah scooped up a handful of water and splashed his face. Then he grinned. "This might be quite an adventure!"

Jeremiah noticed the wooden panel below the bunk had evidently been jarred loose during the crash. When he bent down to put it back in place, he saw two eyes peeping out at him from a dark face. Leaving the panel as it was, Jeremiah straightened back up and laughed aloud. "Quite an adventure, indeed!"

Nick was working in the galley when Jeremiah entered, so he sat down at the table and watched the black man at the stove. Nick was in his thirties. His muscles bulged under his shirt and his big hands looked somewhat incongruous as he shaped biscuits.

"Where are you from, Nick?"

"Alabama."

"How'd you end up here?"

Nick's eyes met Jeremiah's for a moment, then went back to his biscuits, unsure what the boy was thinking after the day's escapade.

"I know what this boat is, Nick. This is part of what I've heard talk of—the Underground Railroad. We ran through those barges so they wouldn't find the runaway slaves on board."

"Yo' a right smart boy."

"Didn't take much to figure it out. But what are you doing here?"

"I asks myself dat very thing sometimes. But I feels I owes it to my people to help." He put his biscuits in the oven and the meat in the frying pan. He poured himself a cup of coffee and one for Jeremiah and sat down at the table. "It's like dis. . . . Eight years ago, I was pickin' cotton on a plantation. I didn't like it none, but I didn't know nothin' else. My woman, Pearl, an' me had enough to eat an' a roof over our heads. But den my masta sold Pearl to another plantation, an' dat made me right mad. So I lit out of dere one night an' went after her. We left in de middle of de night an' kept on goin'—nawth. Dat's all I knowed was to go nawth." He scooped a liberal amount of sugar into his coffee and Jeremiah watched him stir it, savoring the aroma.

"I figured if'n we kept goin', we'd find freedom somewheres. We'd been lucky, keepin' off'n de roads an' away from people, but after two days, a man in a wagon seen us. We was still lucky—he was de right man. He gave us food an' shelter an' took us, hid in his wagon, to another man. We must've ridden wif six or seven such men till we finally got to Cincinnati." Nick paused to take a long swallow of his coffee and settled back more comfortably in his chair. His black eyes mirrored his deep thoughts.

"Go on," Jeremiah prompted.

"Well, dat's when Cap'n Ben an' his brother picked us up an' took us to Pittsburgh. Dey wanted us to go on to Canada, but I made up my mind I wanted to stay an' do what I could to help my people. Cap'n Ben an' his brother took me on as cook, an' Pearl—we got married legal-like in Pittsburgh—she went to work fo' a family in town. In de winters, I worked in de shipyard, an' at night Pearl an' me learned to read an' write an' cipher. Now we got our own li'l house up in de Hill district. . . ."

Jeremiah had been thoughtfully tracing his finger over the chip in the cup. "Aren't you afraid to go back?"

"Sometimes. But it's a thing I got to do." Nick went over to the stove, turning the meat in the pan. "Yo' understands what I'm tryin' to say?"

"Yes," Jeremiah replied.

Sam had been standing quietly outside in the companionway. He stepped inside the galley. "So now you know."

"I think I knew a long time ago," Jeremiah said. "When you stopped at the landing, you never put in on your way back. After a while, I figured there was a reason. I think Papa knew too."

Sam sat down across from Jeremiah. "I'd really like to know how you feel about what we're doing."

"I don't think I really know yet. But I'm not going to turn you over to the law, if that's what you're thinking. I think what you're doing is right, but it's still illegal. All the same, it's not right for one man to own another. Papa said that many a time. He even lost a little bit of his trade for a while, until the folks realized they had to have a blacksmith now and then, and Papa was the only one nearby."

By the time the captain and Peter Emge had joined

them in the galley, Sam was sure Jeremiah would not betray them. God knows, enough people would, Sam thought, remembering some of the stories he had heard. The Fugitive Slave Law had become one of the most prolific causes of the continually growing controversies between upholders and opposers of the slave system. Seizures under the law were becoming more and more frequent, increasing in injustice and cruelty. The business of arresting men, women, and children to be sent back into slavery was carried on all over the free-labor states. By the law, every man was more or less compelled to become a slave hunter under certain conditions. Every kindhearted person caught giving a drink of water or shelter to a runaway was likely to be charged with a felony. The law had become a broad cover under which kidnapping of free persons of color was carried on. Scores of free-born men, women, and children were taken from their homes and consigned to slavery.

"William's at the wheel," Captain Reno said.

"I'll take my supper and his up and keep him company," Nick said.

"Did you have that little talk with our young friend yet?" Ben asked Sam.

Sam nodded, his mouth full of food.

"Can I ask you one thing?" Jeremiah inquired. "What would have happened to us if we'd been caught?"

"For us?" Peter laughed. "For us, vould be da gallows!"

Jeremiah's eyes widened. "Really?"

Ben laughed. "It's hard to say, lad."

"Don't let us scare you," Sam told him. "But it does have its risks. We've probably gotten out close to two hundred people in the last few years. And there's a man in Pittsburgh who believes in what we're doing so much, he's spent almost all his whole fortune organizing the escape routes. There might be thirty stations in Pittsburgh."

"Some of the folks back home wouldn't look too kindly on that," Jeremiah said, smiling. "And if they thought I was right here with you . . ." He began to laugh.

*　　*　　*

As Melissa hurried home to greet her friends from the *Allegheny Belle*, she realized how quickly the time had passed since Jeremiah first left for Pittsburgh. From the time they received his first letter, events had occurred at an amazing rate: the surprise nomination of Abraham Lincoln for the presidency and his even more surprising victory; the Secession Convention held at Montgomery, and the creation of the Confederate States of America; the election of Jefferson Davis of Mississippi as its president; and now this business about Fort Sumter, which had been going on for some time.

As she burst through the door, her father was pouring Sam a drink. She threw her arms around him and giggled as Sam lifted her off the floor and twirled her around. He set her back down and held her at arm's length.

"You get more beautiful every time I see you."

"Sam McClelland, what would Sarah think if she could hear you go on so!"

"She's too busy with the children to worry about me."

James handed Sam a glass, and the three of them sat down.

"Oh, Sam, it's so good to see you," Melissa said. "How are Sarah and the children?"

"Sarah's just fine. She has her hands full with Mary

24

and little Frank. I think she doesn't mind having me gone so much now with them to keep her company." He reached into his pocket and pulled out a thin leather case. Flipping the clasp with his thumb, he handed it to Melissa. It was a daguerreotype of a light-haired woman in her middle twenties, seated with a little boy and girl.

"Oh, they're beautiful!" she gasped. "Come look, Papa."

James joined Melissa beside the sofa and took the picture.

"I had it taken at Charles Kneeland's studio on Fifth Avenue this winter. I think Sarah was more afraid of all that newfangled equipment than the babies were." Once more Sam reached into his pocket and took out another presentation case. "And this is for you—from Jeremiah."

Melissa excitedly opened the case. "Oh, he's grown into such a handsome boy!" she exclaimed. "And would you look at his fancy clot' es!"

James had squatted down on his haunches and was leaning against the settee, peering at the photograph. "He's beginning to look like your grandpa."

While father and daughter were enjoying themselves with the pictures, Sam rose and walked over to the table, splashing a drop more whiskey into his glass. Glancing at the newspapers he had brought with him, he quietly folded them over to hide the headlines. He wondered if they knew; for that matter, if anyone knew in Shady Run. At best, communications were slow here. Except for the two-day-old papers the *Allegheny Belle* brought, James had said the news was usually a week old by the time it reached him. Granted, the town was on the Ohio River, but the traffic was mostly local farmers or shepherds passing through. He sighed and looked at the date on the *Pittsburgh Gazette*—April 13, 1861. Today was April 15.

"This must have cost him all his savings," James was saying, bringing Sam out of his reverie. "Is he still working at Mrs. Oliver's boarding house?"

"Yes. But Saturdays he's got a job tending bar at Fodie's Tavern."

Melissa laughed. "Wouldn't Mama have a fit if she knew that!" She took the presentation case of Sarah over to Sam. "We're having mutton tonight. Can't the captain and Nick come for supper too?"

"Ah—no. They'd like to, but the *Allegheny Belle*'s on a tight schedule. I should be getting back soon."

"Oh no, Sam! We've hardly had time to visit at all!" Melissa took his arm, leading him back to the sofa and sitting him down. "You can at least stay for a piece of crab-apple pie."

Sam grinned. "I expect I have time for that."

Melissa went into the kitchen, which was merely an extension of the parlor, and took last night's pie off the shelf.

"How's Jeremiah getting along with his studies?" James asked. "He don't say much about it in his letters."

"He's doing just fine, I hear. Sarah's brother has great hope for him. Says he'd make a fine surgeon—he's good with his hands and thinks fast when he has to."

Sam enjoyed his pie, savoring every bite, and after some more idle chatter, took his leave, clasping James's hand more firmly and embracing Melissa tighter than he ever had before.

"See you in a couple of months!" they called after him.

Sam waved and, stuffing his hands into his pockets,

26

walked back to the landing. "I wonder."

James decided not to go back to his shop in the afternoon. Melissa went about the business of preparing supper while her father settled himself comfortably in the rocker. He took out his pipe and picked up the *Wheeling Register* and the *Pittsburgh Gazette*. The headlines seemed to leap out at him:

"FORT SUMTER UNDER FIRE"

Two

Inside the fort at the entrance to Charleston Harbor was a company of artillerymen of the regular army, commanded by a Kentuckian named Robert Anderson. They had been sent there some months ago to stand guard over government property, a simple enough job in itself, but as 1861 progressed, a job of increasing tension.

The Southerners regarded the fort as an obstacle blocking the doorway to a great and romantic dream. Eager young men in gray uniforms lined the mud flats and sand dunes with cannons and sat by their stacked rifles waiting to see what would happen, and for a time there was an uneasy equilibrium.

As yet, there was no war. As far as Washington was concerned, the men in Fort Sumter had not an enemy in the world. Nevertheless, they were besieged. Major Anderson estimated that it would take all of the United States Army and Navy to rescue him. The men did what they could to make the place secure against possible attack, but it was a confusing predicament.

In March, a young black, thinking there might be a different set of rules in a place held by the Federal Army, stole a canoe and paddled out to the fort. Not wanting to add fuel to the fire, the officers sent him back to his owner in Charleston, unaware they had the first of the many thousands who would become known as Contrabands.

As the ring of gun emplacements grew on shore, the food supply dwindled inside the fort. The Confederate government sent an order instructing the major to take down the United States flag. The major sent back a message stating that he would obey no such order, but if the Confederates cared to be a little more patient, his men would be out of food in a few days and would have to give up then anyway.

Less than a week after Sam had left the papers, the normally quiet little town of Shady Run had turned into a hub of activity. Half the population leaned toward the Union, the other half toward the Confederacy. There were of course, a few fire-eaters who were ready to march straight to the White House and punch Abe Lincoln right in the nose.

After Fort Sumter had been evacuated, James Armstrong was suddenly deluged with work. Horses and mules needed good shoes, bits and harnesses needed repairing, and there were even a few calls for bayonets. About twenty of the young men were preparing to leave for the county seat to enlist in the Confederate Army. For some time they had been playing at soldier, just waiting for their opportunity. The dry-goods merchant had run out of gray cloth, but the soon-to-be soldiers crossed the Ohio into Cheshire one night, and, after threatening the merchant with their guns, took what gray cloth he had and left, swearing their allegiance to the South and cursing Abraham Lincoln.

Melissa could get very little teaching done with her students. The children were all too busy talking about war and occasionally fighting with one whose parents happened to be pro-Union. For in these early days, war was a glorious word. This was to be the grand experience. It looked to be an exciting vacation from the everyday life, to be financed and endorsed by the government.

Melissa looked up from the letter she was writing to Jeremiah. She couldn't find the words for what she wanted to say. Virginia had left the Union and joined the Confederacy. Did she dare suggest that he leave Pittsburgh and come home? Where were his loyalties now? For that matter, where were hers? James worked at his anvil from morning till dusk, never committing himself one way or another. Tomorrow morning, some of her friends were leaving, boys she had known all her life, and what would become of them? In the past three days alone, she had received two proposals of immediate marriage and two more if she would be willing to wait until the heroes had returned.

"You figuring on getting into the cavalry on this?" James asked, working on the left-rear hoof of a big black mare. Two of the would-be soldiers, Zebulon and Ethan Smith, were sitting on nail kegs in his shop. Both were big boys, well over six feet, with masses of tousled blond curls. Most people took them to be twins. "She's the most skittish critter I ever seen!"

"She's skittish," Zeb agreed. "But Ethan here can handle her."

"She's got good breeding," Ethan added.

"Breeding ain't everything," James mumbled, two nails stuck in the corner of his mouth.

"I wouldn't take her, only she won't pull a plow and Ma and the kids are going to need a plow horse."

"You reckon your ma can manage the place with you two gone?" James asked.

"Sure. Lem and Orville can take care of the place while we're gone. Besides, we'll whip them Yankees and be back here in a month."

James said nothing. He doubted it would be that fast. The Confederacy was full of great ideals but very little else.

"Least we won't have to worry about getting guns," Ethan grinned, removing a model 1849 Colt .31 caliber 5-shot revolver from his belt and admiring it. Zebulon had its twin.

Finished with the mare and glad of it, James walked over to the boy to examine the gun. "Is this your pa's gun?"

"One of 'em. I'm aiming to get me a lot of Yankees with this."

Ethan hated the Yankees more than the average Southerner did. His father, the first Ethan Smith, had joined the army to serve in the Mexican War back in 1846. Ironically, he had been a comrade of both Ulysses S. Grant and P. G. T. Beauregard. After the war, he had continued in the army, raising himself to the rank of major, when he was presented the two matching revolvers. However, his fondness for alcohol became such a problem that he was finally court-martialed for his beating of a fellow soldier to near death while in a drunken rage. He settled in Shady Run, purchasing a small farm with his savings, where he died of drink shortly after, leaving a wife, four sons, and a daughter. Ethan Jr. blamed the army for his father's failure as a farmer and his subsequent death.

Melissa poked her head into the darkness of the shop. "Papa, supper's soon ready."

Zebulon stood up, and Ethan touched the brim of his hat. "Afternoon, Melissa."

While Ethan was paying James, Zeb hurried out after Melissa.

"You sure you won't change your mind about marrying me before I leave?" he asked, walking beside her back to the house. "I won't be gone long, and you know I've always admired you more than the other girls around here."

Melissa had never felt either of the Smith boys were very promising prospects for husbands, even though they both had tried their hands at courting her throughout the past few years.

"I expect I'll still be here when you get back," she said.

"Does that mean you'll marry me then?"

"It doesn't mean anything but what it's supposed to mean. I'm not looking for a husband yet."

"Well, what are you waiting for? You're not getting any younger, you know!"

"I was just twenty last month!"

"Twenty! Shoot," he kicked at a stone. "You ought to have a batch of kids by now."

"If you keep talking that way, you'll make me feel like I'm too old for any man to want me."

Zeb took her arm. "Oh no, Melissa, I didn't mean nothing like that. You're the prettiest girl in the county." They had reached the door to her house, and Zeb pulled her a little closer. "Why don't I come in with you for a while, and you can say good-bye to me proper?"

Melissa looked up into his face and considered for a

moment. Zeb was rather good-looking in a coarse sort of way. There had been many a stolen kiss in the barn or at a church social between the two of them, and she did find Zeb amusing at times like that.

"I expect I could at least do that," she smiled, reaching for the doorknob. She stopped and peered past Zeb's shoulder. "Oh, fiddle! Here comes Papa and Ethan."

Zeb clenched his fist. "Now why couldn't Ethan be more talkative to your pa," he muttered. "He's in a big hurry to get over to the tavern tonight. The boys are going to have a little going-away party."

"Come on, Zeb!" Ethan called from the road.

"I'll be back soon, Melissa. You remember that," Zeb said.

"I'll remember. And you be careful."

"Did you get that letter to Jeremiah written?" James asked his daughter as they were sitting in the parlor after supper.

Melissa looked up from the shirt she was mending. "Not yet. Zeb says this war won't take long. What do you think?"

"I don't know, but I think the Confederacy bit off a mite more than it can chew. We don't have hardly any factories or anything, near as I can figure. And you can't go into battle with a shovel or a rake."

Three-quarters of the nation's wealth was produced in the North, which also contained sixty-five percent of the farm acreage and eighty-five percent of the factories. Most of the railroads and bank deposits were in the North, and of the South's population, one-third were slaves.

A letter had arrived that day from James's brother

33

Edward in Richmond. "Ned says I should come to Richmond," James remarked. "He says if the war lasts long, certain people can make a lot of money if they're smart. And Ned's managed to do that already."

Edward Armstrong, in his early fifties, had managed to prosper as a clerk for an exporting company, raising a family and living very well. To James's knowledge, clerks weren't usually as highly paid as his brother's life-style indicated in his letters. Perhaps it was just idle exaggeration. After all, he hadn't lived in splendor when they'd last seen each other ten years ago.

"You're not thinking of going there, are you?" Melissa asked.

"No, I've got all I need and want right here." James went over to his daughter and touched a tress of her hair. "You've been a great comfort to me since your mama died. She'd be right proud to see what a fine lady you've grown into."

Melissa set aside her mending and stood up, putting her arms around her father. "Oh, Papa, I wish Jeremiah was home."

"In a way, I'm glad he isn't. I wouldn't want him going off to war."

Melissa drew back and looked at her father. "Papa . . . what if he joins the Union Army?"

James smiled and patted her. "He won't, don't you fret."

Several gunshots and yelling from outside caused them to look up. There was hollering and whooping and a few more shots.

"What in tarnation?" James muttered. "Must be those boys all liquored up."

James opened the door and stepped outside on the

34

stoop, as many of the other neighbors had done. There was more yelling, accompanied by hoofbeats as five riders rounded the corner, waving their hats and pistols.

"Crazy fools," Melissa said to herself, returning to her mending.

As the big black mare thundered down the road, a dog leaped out of the shadows into its path. In the next instant, the mare had bolted and Ethan was falling drunkenly from the saddle, his finger unconsciously squeezing the trigger as he tried to regain his balance. After the shot went off, Melissa heard her father give a strangled cry. As she ran to him, she watched him slump against the door and sink to his knees.

"Papa!" she screamed, trying to catch him before he slumped all the way over. She was dimly aware of other hands helping her. She felt something warm and sticky with her hand and looked down to see that the left side of her father's shirt was covered with blood. "Papa!" she cried again.

James Armstrong coughed and looked at her, his eyes barely open. "You've made me proud, too, Melissa," he managed to say. "I want you to go to Ned now."

"No, Papa, I'll stay here with you!"

Melissa really didn't remember much after that. It all seemed so unreal—vague shadows and shapes carrying her father away; more shapes giving her whiskey, putting her to bed. She slept a deep and troubled sleep until the sound of that shot again woke her.

Mrs. Geary, the minister's wife, was making coffee when Melissa stumbled out of her bedroom the next morning.

"Then it wasn't a dream, was it?"

Mrs. Geary put her arms around Melissa. "No child, it wasn't a dream."

Melissa gave a little choked sound and then straightened up. "Where did they take Papa?"

"He's at the undertaking parlor, child. My Josephus is taking care of everything."

Melissa sank down on a chair at the kitchen table and began to cry again. Mrs. Geary patted her shoulder. "That's right, child, cry. Get it all out."

Immediately after the shooting, the townsfolk had held an informal hearing and unanimously declared it an accident: The horse bolted and the gun went off. Both brothers were thankful they were leaving in the morning, rather than having to face Melissa.

Melissa sat at the table and sobbed for nearly an hour. Mrs. Geary just left her to her tears. Then, just as suddenly as she had begun to cry, she ceased her weeping.

It's done now and there's nothing I can do about it and sitting here crying won't help. I've got to pull myself together and decide what to do now, she thought.

She turned around and looked at Mrs. Geary. "Is Reverend Geary arranging the funeral?"

"Yes, child. You don't need to worry about that. Now why don't you let me fix you something to eat?"

"No, I'm not hungry. When's the funeral to be?"

"Tomorrow morning. Is that all right with you?"

"I suppose so." Melissa stood up and went over to the coffeepot. "You've been very kind to stay here with me, but would you mind leaving now? I'd like to be alone for a little while."

"You're sure you'll be all right?"

"Yes, Mrs. Geary. I'm fine now."

Melissa watched the old woman go out the door, wishing she could do something other than sit in the house. If she were a man, she'd join the army—either army, at this point. She went into the bedroom and washed her face and combed her hair. After changing her dress, she found the box with her father's personal papers in it. There wasn't much: the deeds to the house and shop, another deed to a plot of land in the southern part of the county, a variety of bills and receipts, and ten newly printed fifty-dollar Confederate States treasury notes. There was no will, no instructions, nothing to tell her what to do.

"If I were to go to Uncle Edward in Richmond, what if Jeremiah came home in the meantime? On the other hand, maybe I ought to go to Pittsburgh. But I don't even know if I could get up there now, what with this silly old war on. No, I expect I'd better get to Richmond somehow, seeing as that's what Papa told me to do."

The funeral was held in the Presbyterian Church and conducted by the Reverend Josephus Geary. Melissa had managed to alter the black dress she had worn for her mother's funeral by lengthening the hem and letting out the bust line. She watched silently as her father's casket was lowered into the ground beside her mother and the brothers she had never known.

By afternoon, Melissa was glad she had made up her mind to leave. After endless friends and neighbors had given their condolences and left food, she was relieved to just sit in the rocker and be alone. One thing she could not abide was pity. Sympathy was one thing, but she knew she was receiving pity.

Her father had saved nearly $1,200 in gold over the years, tucked under his bed in a locked metal casket. Melissa decided not to sell the house or the shop. She didn't need the money, and perhaps someday Jeremiah would want it. It was as much his anyway. So was half the money, for that matter.

After fixing herself a cup of coffee and nibbling on a piece of cake someone had brought—about the first food she had eaten in the last thirty-six hours—she sat down at the table and began a letter to her brother, a letter she wished she didn't have to write.

A little while later, there was a knock at the door. It was a soldier in a gray uniform.

"'Scuse me for bothering you at a time like this, ma'am. The folks here told me about what happened, and I'm mighty sorry. But I'm out buying up equipment for the government. The folks here tell me your pa was a blacksmith. That right?"

"Yes."

The corporal was obviously nervous and embarrassed. "Well, if you'd be willing, seeing as how you ain't got no more use for it, maybe you'd sell us what's in your pa's shop."

"What do you mean? What things do you want?"

"Ma'am, the government needs everything—metal, tools, nails—everything we can gather."

"I see. You go on out and I'll fetch the key."

"Much obliged, ma'am."

The corporal disappeared, and Melissa took the key from the peg in the kitchen. There were two more soldiers with the corporal waiting by the double doors to the shop.

"Here's the key, Captain," she said, handing it to him.

"Thanks for the promotion, ma'am, but I'm just a corporal."

"Oh well, I don't know that much about the army."

Melissa watched as the three men prowled through the contents of the shop, obviously delighted with what they found. She decided to make it pay off if she could.

"Ma'am, we'll take everything you got if you want to sell it," the corporal said.

"How much?" she asked.

"I ain't sure yet. There's a lot of stuff in there, and it'll take some figuring. You got six kegs of nails, and they're worth four dollars a keg. And there's a lot of tack in there, too. And plenty of iron."

"How are you going to pay?"

"I got orders—half in Confederate bonds and half in gold. Unless you want it all in bonds."

"No. I'll take half in gold. You get it all figured out and write out a bill of sale. Then you come back to the house and see me." She started to walk away, but stopped and looked back at the corporal. "I suppose I can trust you to be fair?"

"Oh yes, ma'am. I wouldn't cheat a lady."

The corporal watched appreciatively the swing of Melissa's hips beneath the tight black dress as she walked back to the house. Shaking his head with a sigh, he turned back to the shop. His companions had been watching as well.

"All right, you two; let's get back to work."

Melissa spent the next day preparing for her trip. She

39

packed a trunk with clothes and a few family possessions: her father's watch, her mother's cameo and tortoiseshell hair comb, the family Bible, the daguerreotype of Jeremiah, and a quilt her grandmother had made in 1824. She cleaned her father's Kentucky rifle, and packed blankets and cooking utensils, not knowing where she would find shelter on her journey. She decided to take the wagon rather than the little trap the family rarely used. Her brother's roan was easier for her to ride than her father's gelding. Melissa was an excellent horsewoman, but since she had a choice, she took the roan.

She left the gelding in the care of the Gearys, along with money for its upkeep, the funds she had received from her sale to the soldiers.

"I don't know that I like the idea of you going off all alone," Mrs. Geary said. "What if the Yankees get you?"

Melissa smiled. "I'll be all right, Mrs. Geary. I can take care of myself." She had been riding for nearly as long as she had been walking, and could handle the rifle better than Jeremiah. "Now I've written down the address of my uncle in Richmond for you, and Jeremiah's address in Pittsburgh. But if Jeremiah should come back, you tell him what's happened and where I am."

"I still think it's not safe for a young girl to go all that way alone."

"I talked to that soldier who was here yesterday, and he said the roads are good. Don't worry about me."

"We'll pray for you," Reverend Geary told her, "and I'll keep the school going for you."

"You come over in the morning and have a big hot breakfast before you leave," Mrs. Geary told her.

Melissa finished packing the wagon and put in a

hamper of food before she left the house for the last time. She gathered up a large sack of oats from the barn, tossed it into the back of the wagon, and drove down the sleepy little road to the minister's house. She couldn't force herself to turn around and look at her home standing silent in the early-morning light.

Mrs. Geary had fixed a huge breakfast, which Melissa ate despite the fact that she wasn't particularly hungry.

"If the *Allegheny Belle* should stop on its way back to Pittsburgh, will you tell Sam what's happened?" she asked. "I wrote a letter to Jeremiah, but I'm going to wait till I get to a bigger town to post it."

With a sad wave to the Gearys, Melissa turned her wagon out of town and southeast toward Richmond.

Sam pushed back his chair from the table and dropped his napkin onto his empty plate. He gave a satisfied belch, which caused his four-year-old daughter to giggle.

"Do it again, Papa!"

Sam covered his face with his hands, peeking out between his fingers, swallowing air. When he removed his hands, he issued forth a loud resounding belch, causing Mary to go into gales of laughter and even little Frank to giggle and clap his hands.

Sarah looked helplessly at her mother, who was well used to her son-in-law's high spirits. Sam had returned home that afternoon unexpectedly from the river.

Sam, Jeremiah, and Sarah's brother Jim retired to the parlor after supper while Sarah and her mother took care of the plates and the children.

"So the steamboat company wants you to haul materials and men?" Jim asked.

"Yes. We didn't even get to Cincinnati this time. That

41

little packet overtook us and told us to come back here."

"How were Melissa and Papa taking the news of the war?" Jeremiah asked.

Sam cleared his throat. "I don't think they knew there was a war on when I saw them. And I didn't have the heart to tell them. I had an idea it might be the last time I'd see them. Looks like I was right."

Jim White stood up and walked over to the hearth and leaned against the mantel. He was tall and distinguished-looking, but prematurely graying at the temples, being in his late twenties. "Damn foolish business," he muttered.

"What do you think I should do?" Jeremiah asked. "Should I go home or stay here?"

"Why don't you wait and see?" Sam suggested. "That's what I aim to do—for a while, anyway. On the way home I couldn't make up my mind whether to join the army or not. Now I guess I'll do my duty by helping the army on the boat. 'Sides, Sarah would have a conniption fit if I joined the army."

"Pretty sure of yourself, aren't you?" Jim chided him.

"Oh, Sarah doesn't care about me," Sam laughed. "But a private in the army only gets paid sixteen dollars a month!"

Jeremiah laughed merely to be polite, but he was more concerned with his dilemma than with the McClellands' domestic affairs.

"I think I'll wait for a while before I go jumping into this too," Jim said. "There's plenty for me to do right here keeping up with my patients. And, Jeremiah, it might be wise for you to do the same. Keep on with your studies."

"Maybe you're right," he sighed.

Three

Melissa calculated she must have driven about sixty miles by noon the second day. So far, she hadn't met with any difficulties. The weather had been good, the roads were in fair condition, and she hadn't gotten lost. Her biggest problem had been her comfort. After several hours of bumpy, rutted roads, her bottom had begun to ache from bouncing on the hard wooden bench. She soon remedied the condition by folding up a blanket and using it as a cushion. She was wearing a floppy-brimmed old sunbonnet and a long-sleeved calico dress which managed to protect her from the sun.

She had spent the first night just outside of Willis, sleeping in the wagon with the rifle beside her. No one had bothered her, if indeed anyone had even noticed her. Travelers were not unusual, especially with men constantly striking out to join a regiment somewhere.

Upon entering Willis, she attempted to post her letter, but found the small town could not guarantee any mail. Mail delivery had been poor at best, but now it was even worse. She decided to keep the letter until she found a more promising place.

She passed many people, who generally called out a

greeting or an oath against either the Yankees or the Confederates. No one seemed to think it unusual for a young woman to be traveling alone. She had been able to pick up a paper dated April 20 in Willis, and she read that Lincoln had called for 75,000 troops and Jefferson Davis had in turn called for 100,000.

Melissa hadn't taken all of this very seriously until she scanned the paper as she drove along, letting the horse have its head. It had seemed remote to her, stuck away in the northwestern part of the state. The people there merely wanted to go on with their lives and leave politics out of it. True, there had been talk of that part of the state seceding from the rest of Virginia, but that had seemed very unlikely. You couldn't just divide a state. On the other hand, she thought, if you could divide a country . . . What was that she had read about a speech of Lincoln's talking about a house divided? Well, her house certainly was. Her brother was in Pittsburgh, her father dead, her uncle in Richmond, and she was right in the middle. When Virginia finally seceded, a Colonel Robert E. Lee resigned his post with the army and stayed with his home state, and Jefferson Davis had just recently made him commander of the Confederate Army.

Lincoln had ordered a blockade of all Southern ports, and Melissa wondered what effect this would have upon the exporting company for which her uncle worked.

The Confederacy had been a going concern since February and already had taken possession of some equipment and installations in the South. Besides Fort Sumter, there were Castle Pinckney and Fort Moultrie in Charleston Harbor, Fort Pulaski near Savannah, Fort Morgan at Mobile Bay, Forts Jackson and St. Philip below New Orleans, and the navy yard at Pensacola.

44

There had been riots in the Baltimore railroad stations. As the Sixth Massachusetts and the Twenty-sixth Pennsylvania were trying to board the train for Washington City, Confederate sympathizers attacked them. Four soldiers were killed and thirty wounded.

Melissa shuddered at all the grim stories which the newspaper contained and threw the paper into the back of the wagon.

She had reached the Gauley River by sundown and pulled off the road into the grass by the bridge. After building a small fire, she unharnessed and fed the horse while she was waiting for her coffee to boil. She ate what was left of the fried chicken she had brought from home and spread preserves on some rolls, listening to the sounds of the night, wishing she could take a bath somewhere to get the dust of the road off her skin. She settled down in the wagon under two heavy blankets, with the rifle beside her.

Melissa awoke with a start, aware that there was someone close by. She didn't think she had been asleep for very long, for the moon was still in about the same position as it had been before. She heard a twig snap and quietly felt for her rifle. As silently as possible, she threw off her covers and sat up, aiming her rifle at the dark shape bending over the embers of the campfire.

The intruder looked in her direction at the sound and froze at the sight of the gun.

"Don't shoot," a deep voice said, the figure straightening up. "I don't mean no harm."

Melissa was every bit as frightened of the stranger as he obviously was of her gun. "What do you want?"

"Nothin'. I mean, I was jes' hungry, dat's all. Please don' shoot me."

"Just stay where you are and don't move. I'm going to get out of this wagon now, and if you move, so help me, I'll shoot."

"I won't move."

Trying to keep her balance and hold on to the rifle as well, Melissa carefully climbed down from the wagon and took two timid steps toward the smoldering fire. The man was a tall, very thin black, and all she could see of his features were the huge whites of his eyes as he stared at the rifle.

"Where did you come from?" she asked.

"No place, ma'am. Jes' lemme go and I won't trouble yo' no mo'."

The man was terrified, and Melissa was beginning to feel a little braver. "Are you a runaway?"

"Please, ma'am. Jes' let me go."

She really was feeling sorry for him, cowering there like a trapped animal. "That coffee's still hot. Don't you want some?"

The man looked at her in surprise and disbelief.

"And I've got salt pork and biscuits in the wagon." Melissa turned around and walked to the back of the wagon, no longer pointing the gun, but ready lest he should make a move toward her. The man was still standing in the same place. "I might even have a cup myself."

"Y-Yes, ma'am," he muttered.

Melissa returned to the fire with a plate and two tin cups. She held out the food to him, and he took it cautiously.

"Thank yo' kindly, ma'am. Yo' kin put down dat gun

46

now. I ain't gonna do yo' no harm."

Melissa sat down, still a little wary of the man, and filled the two cups. "What's your name?"

"Corky, ma'am."

"Sit down, Corky, and eat."

"I can't do that, ma'am. Ain't allowed to sit wif de white folkses."

"It's dark. Pretend you can't see that I'm white and sit down. You make me nervous standing there."

Corky sat down gingerly.

"Where do you come from?" Melissa asked him. "You didn't tell me before. You are running, aren't you?"

Corky hung his head. "Is yo' gonna turn me in?"

"Should I? Who's your master?"

"Man by de name of Thomas. Lives down by Blue Stone Lake on a little farm. Jes' him and his wife and seven kids. He gits powerful mean sometimes. He don't need a slave—only has me dere to show his neighbors he ain't as po' as he really is. Every once in a while, he goes on a drunk, and dat's when he gits mean. Usually he beats me, but once he beat his wife and broke her arm. He got drunk yestiddy, so I jes' lit out."

"Where are you going?"

"North."

"North where?"

"Don't know. Jes' north."

"How good do you think your chances are of making it?"

Corky shrugged. "Not very good, ma'am. But I'm goin' to try anyway."

Melissa had been slowly forming an idea while Corky had been talking. "I have a letter I need to get up north— to Pittsburgh. And the mail is an awful mess right now. If

I were to help you, Corky, would you see that my letter got posted in the North?"

"Help me, ma'am? How?"

"Why I'll just write you out a pass saying that you're my slave and I'm sending you to Pittsburgh to deliver a very important message. Do you think that would work?"

"Don't know, ma'am, but it's worth a try."

Melissa stood up. "I'll go get the letter."

She found a pencil, but no paper. On the back of the envelope she wrote: "Permission given to Corky, my property, to deliver message to Pittsburgh. Melissa Armstrong. April 22, 1861." As an afterthought, she took out four half-dollars.

She returned to Corky and handed him the letter and the coins. "Now don't you lose that. It's as important to me as it is to you. That money should see you through."

"I'll hang on to it, don't yo' worry 'bout dat, ma'am. But how do yo' figure is de bestest way to get to dis here Pittsburgh?"

"You mean you're going all the way to Pittsburgh? I thought you'd post that letter once you got into Federal territory."

"If'n it's a free state, den it's as good a place as any, I reckon."

"It's free. And I know some people there. Maybe they could help you. Can you remember names well?"

"Oh yes, ma'am. I got me a good mem'ry."

"My brother's name and address are on that envelope. His name is Jeremiah Armstrong."

"Jeremiah Armstrong," Corky repeated.

"And Sam McClelland and Ben Reno. They work on a steamboat. Now I think if you follow the Kanawha River

48

here all the way up to Point Pleasant on the Ohio, you'll be in good shape."

"Yes, ma'am, I'll remember." Corky stood up. "I reckon I better git movin' now, ma'am. I got to ax yo'— why is yo' doin' dis fo' me?"

"I don't know. Because you're doing something for me in return. Or maybe because if I were in your place, I'd hope someone would help me. Good-bye, Corky. And good luck to you."

"Good-bye, ma'am."

The weather stayed warm as Melissa slowly made her way across the rolling hills. She spent the next night camped near White Sulphur Springs. With the morning came warm sunshine, and Melissa decided to take advantage of the water. No one was about, and the clear springs looked ever so inviting.

First checking the priming in the rifle, she leaned it against a tree near some bushes and put her clothes and a bar of soap on the bank of a secluded little cove. She tested the water with her foot and dove in, swimming underwater about twenty feet and then surfacing, her dark hair flowing about her. She swam back to the bank and picked up the soap. It felt so good to scrub away the dirt and dust of the road. She washed her hair and paddled around, luxuriating in the clear water and bright sunshine.

"Well now, ain't that right purty!"

Melissa jumped at the sound of a man's voice. She ducked under the water to her neck and looked frantically around her.

"At first I thought I was seeing things, but I reckon you're real enough," he said.

Melissa's eyes fell on the man. He was sitting near her clothes, grinning at her through a dark bushy beard. He was heavyset, and Melissa didn't like the looks of him at all.

"Now why don't you come on out of there?" he said.

Melissa couldn't speak. She was suddenly seized with a terrible feeling of panic.

When she made no move, the man stood up. "Come on out, girl. Or do I have to come in and get you?"

Melissa was trying to think of anything, any way she could possibly get to the rifle. It was half hidden by a bush. But the man was between her and the gun.

"I'm getting mad, girl. And you don't want to make a nice feller like me mad." He pulled a pistol from his belt and pointed it at her. "Now, do like I say and get out of the water."

Heart pounding, Melissa slowly made herself swim over to the bank and climb out, constantly trying to figure out how to make a break for the rifle. One look into the man's eyes and she felt her courage drain. A heavy hand clamped around her arm, and he pulled her closer to him. He smelled of sweat and stale whiskey, and Melissa felt faint for a moment.

"Now ain't I just lucky to come along when I did," he laughed, as his grinning face came closer to hers. At the first touch of his mouth, Melissa lifted her arm and struck the side of his face as hard as she could. He let the pistol drop to catch her wrist, twisting it viciously, and she gasped at the sudden pain. She drew her knee up to kick him, but he threw her off balance before she could make contact. She tried to scramble for his pistol, but he kicked it aside and dropped to his knees, pinning her arms down with his hands.

"Little lady, you might as well make up your mind to quit fighting me. I know what I want, and I aim to have it."

As he bent toward her once more, Melissa spat in his face.

"You little bitch!" he yelled, doubling up his fist.

Melissa felt something strike her jaw, knocking her senseless.

Melissa opened her eyes and blinked at the bright sun. She started to raise herself up and winced at a sharp pain. The memory suddenly flooded back to her, and she squeezed her eyes shut as if it could block out the horrible recollection. Then she heard a noise and turned her head. It was him, rummaging through the wagon, not fifty feet away. She turned her head the other way and there was the rifle, only a few feet from her reach. He mustn't have seen it. Feeling as if her insides were on fire, she slowly rolled over onto her stomach and inched toward the gun, keeping her eyes on the man. Her fingers touched the polished walnut stock and crept along the smooth wood. His back was to her now as he was going through the contents of her trunk. Her head pounding and body aching, she carefully got to her knees. Thankful that she had checked the priming earlier, her hand closed firmly around the rifle. The man was still engrossed in his scavenging and oblivious to the little moan that escaped Melissa's lips as she got to her feet. She took four steps toward the wagon, hefting the rifle to her shoulder and taking aim squarely between his shoulder blades. As filthy an animal as he was, Melissa couldn't bring herself to shoot him in the back.

The man held something up for his examination, and

the sunlight glinted on an object, shiny and gold. He started to put it into his pocket.

"That's my papa's watch!" Melissa screamed at him.

At the sound of her voice, the big man stood up and turned abruptly. He opened his mouth to speak, but at the sight of his face, Melissa's finger squeezed the trigger. The report echoed through the peaceful valley. A look of confusion appeared on the man's face before he toppled from the wagon. Melissa backed up a few steps, colliding with the tree. Startled, she turned around and then began to laugh almost hysterically. The laughter soon turned to sobs, shaking her whole body.

She looked at the man sprawled on his face in the grass, his one foot caught on the wagon wheel. She shivered suddenly, not from the cold but from her nerves, and realized she was still naked. She put down the gun and stepped over to her clothing, still where she had left it. Feeling as dirty on the inside as the mud and grass had made her outside, she stepped into the water once more and waded in waist-deep. The water stung and she winced. After dunking her head, she looked in the direction of the wagon again and decided she'd better hurry. She got out of the water and pulled her dress over her head, her body still wet and hair dripping. Picking up her shoes and drawers, she took them over and put them in the back of the wagon.

The man hadn't moved, didn't appear to be breathing. She picked up her father's watch and dropped it into her pocket. The horse was still standing quietly in his harness, cropping grass. Melissa briefly wondered why the shot hadn't frightened the animal. She fetched the rifle and put it in the wagon, noticing for the first time the man's horse tethered in the trees.

Swallowing her feeling of nausea, she pulled his foot free from the wheel, and it dropped on the ground with a sickening thud. She stood there, gazing at the lifeless body as if hypnotized, until the whinny of a horse in the distance brought her back to her senses.

Scrambling into the wagon, she snatched up the reins, and, whipping up the horse, drove off.

Melissa tried to keep her mind from straying back over the events of the last few hours. As the horse and wagon made the ascent of the Alleghenies, she tried to concentrate on the scenery, but to no avail. How could all these things have happened in such a short span of time since leaving her home? Helping a runaway slave was bad enough, but claiming him as her property to write out the pass was even worse. She had no idea what the consequences of that could be, and at this point she didn't really care. The fact that she had just shot and killed a man wasn't bothering her as much as the degradation of what he had done to her. This whole trip was turning into a nightmare. She couldn't imagine what else could possibly happen to her.

She made very slow progress that day, owing to her late start and uphill climb. The trip downhill the next day was uneventful until she decided to spend the night in the little town of Lowesville, where she was able to eat a hot meal and sleep in a relatively soft bed.

When she awoke in the morning, she found it very overcast. After collecting the horse and wagon at the livery stable, she struck out once more. By noon, the sky was dark with clouds, and shortly after stopping for her lunch, the heavens opened up. She threw a blanket over herself, but it afforded little protection from the rain.

53

Certain there would soon be a settlement somewhere, she kept on, the road becoming an oozing mass of mud. Soon she was hoping to just find a farmhouse—anything to give her shelter. Her hair and clothing were soaked and she felt as if she would never be dry again.

Just before she reached the James River, the wagon sank into a muddy bog hole and came to a stop. After several unsuccessful attempts to get the horse to pull it forward, Melissa got down from the seat, sinking in the mud up to her ankles, and tried leading the horse. The wheel was stuck too deep. She went around to the back of the wagon and pushed. The wheel moved slightly, but rolled back, and Melissa lost her footing, landing on her hands and knees. She held on to the wagon and pulled herself to her feet, uttering a few choice oaths she had heard used on occasion by some of her father's customers. She planted her feet as firmly as the mud would allow, preparing for another push when she heard a man's voice.

"We'll take care of that for you, miss."

She turned quickly at the sound, fearing the worst. She found herself staring into the face of a blue-uniformed soldier wearing a waterproof poncho. He was young and smiling kindly at her. He turned to one of the three men with him.

"Give the lady your poncho. Then let's get this wagon out of here."

Another man stepped toward her, removing his poncho and draping it around her shoulders. The first man turned back to her. "If you'll go over there, miss, and wait, we'll have this out of the mud in no time."

Silently, Melissa made her way over to the side of the road, pulling the poncho over her head. As she stood back under a tree to shelter her a little, she watched the four men through a curtain of driving rain. With three pushing and one leading the horse, the wagon was finally freed from the mire.

While one of the men led the horse and wagon toward the trees, the man she took to be an officer of some sort returned to her. "This is no weather for you to be out in, miss. We have a little camp back in the trees a ways. You can take shelter there until the storm passes."

Melissa looked at him suspiciously. He gave a little laugh and held up his hand. "On my honor, miss. You have nothing to fear from me or my men."

"Then I thank you kindly."

The soldier took her arm and led her a few hundred yards into the trees, the other men and the wagon a little ahead. There were four small tents and two men with rifles, protected under their ponchos, standing guard.

The soldier pointed to the second tent. "Go on in there, miss, and try to keep warm. There are blankets in there. I'll fetch you some coffee."

Melissa ducked under the tent flap and let the poncho drop to the ground. She wiped the rain from her face with her hand and gazed around, bending slightly so as not to bump her head. The rain beat a steady rhythm above her as she scanned the contents of the dark little canvas house. There were two bedrolls, two knapsacks, a small folding stool, some cooking utensils, and maps.

"I got the coffee, miss," the soldier said from outside the tent.

"Come in."

Melissa moved farther back into the tent to accommodate the soldier. He set down the coffeepot and a cup on the tarpaulin covering the ground. He handed her a bundle of clothing.

"Miss, you really should get out of those wet clothes. We're traveling kind of light, but I was able to find you some dry clothes."

"But you don't have to . . ."

"Please, miss, I don't want to see you took sick. I'll go on out now."

"Don't you want some coffee?"

"Why, yes, miss, I would. You just call me when you're decent."

After the soldier had backed out of the tent, Melissa started to remove her dress and then stopped. After yesterday, she wasn't sure what she should do. She didn't want to put herself in a compromising position. But she was soaked to the skin, and the soldier had been very solicitous. Shrugging her shoulders in an unconscious mannerism, she took off her dress and put on the baggy trousers and jacket. At least they were dry. After folding her wet dress up, she put it in the corner and called to the soldier.

"You can come in now."

The tent flap opened, and the dark-eyed man came in. He took one look at her standing there in the voluminous uniform with her wet hair streaming over her forehead, and he began to laugh. She glanced down at herself, the sleeves covering her hands, and began to chuckle too.

"I must look a sight!"

He looked at her face and saw the laughter in her blue eyes. "Now, that's better. I like you more when you're smiling. How's about that coffee?" He sat down on the floor and gestured for her to do the same, which she did. He had brought another cup, and poured coffee for both of them. Melissa took hers and drank it gratefully.

"I'm Sergeant Archibald Fleener of Indiana."

"I'm Melissa Armstrong."

"I had one of the men throw a canvas over your wagon. I'm afraid it's too late to do much good. You feeling better now?"

"Yes, thank you."

"Where were you bound for in this storm, if you don't mind my asking?"

"Oh, it's a long story," she sighed. "I'm on my way to Richmond."

Archibald thought she looked very sad, but very lovely, even though sitting there she did resemble a half-drowned kitten. How nice it would be to spend the day in this tent alone with her, he thought. His face flushed as he remembered his new bride back in Indiana.

"We won't be going anywhere in this rain," he said. "And I like long stories."

Her eyes met his for a moment, and she felt very grateful to this man. After all her troubles in the past few days, here was a man who was kind and solicitous. So she began to tell him about her father's death and her decision to make the journey to Richmond, omitting the incident at White Sulphur Springs.

"You've got gumption, miss, I'll say that. Why, all sorts of things could've happened to you."

She stared into her coffee cup. "Yes, I know."

"You say your brother's in Pittsburgh?"

She nodded.

"What if—what if he goes Union and joins the army?"

"He won't. I'm sure he won't join. He wants to become a doctor more than anything. Soldiering wouldn't interest him."

"Didn't particularly interest me either."

A voice came from outside the tent. "Sergeant, I got supper here for you and the lady."

Archibald stood up and opened the flap. Another soldier stuck his head inside. "Afternoon, miss." He set the two plates on the floor of the tent. "Rain's let up some. I don't think supper got too wet."

"Thank you," Melissa said.

"Call me for guard duty at eight," Archibald told the soldier as he left.

Melissa eyed the beans, bacon, and hardtack hungrily. She hadn't realized what an appetite she had built up. Archibald sat down and poured them each more coffee.

"Eat up, miss. It's not too fancy, but it's nourishing."

"It really looks very good to me right now."

The two of them ate in silence, and Melissa found it to be one of the best meals she had eaten in a long time. She leaned back on her hands and stretched.

"Sergeant, what are you and your men doing here?"

"I don't know that I should tell you, miss, you being a Virginian and all."

She laughed. "Why, Sergeant, I'm no Secesh spy. I'm just curious."

"I allow you are, miss. The general sent us down here to see what's going on, that's all."

"Just you few men?"

"Oh, no, miss. There's another eight men a little farther east of here. We split up."

"Aren't you afraid? I mean, you are in enemy country now."

Archibald smiled. "I'm afraid. But right now I think we're pretty safe. We've been keeping low. And this here war hasn't had much chance to get off the ground yet."

"Were you in the army before?"

"Oh, no, miss. I'm a farmer. Got a little place up near Beanblossom. Know where that is?" Melissa shook her head, and he continued. "It's really just a little place at the edge of my pa's farm. I been building it for a year so's I could get married. I finished it last February. It was right hard work in all that snow, but I wanted to get it done by spring."

"Did you get married?"

"Oh, yes, indeed, I surely did. I'm hoping when I get back my wife'll tell me I'm going to be a father. Lord knows, we were trying hard enough."

He suddenly blushed, and Melissa smiled. "I'm sure she's a lovely girl, and very lucky."

"Thank you," he mumbled, still embarrassed.

"Are there a lot of men joining the army?"

"They surely are. Why, some counties had more men turn out than they needed. One group raised such a ruckus about being sent home, the governor had to change the regulations and arrange for more regiments. The railroad's carrying all soldiers for free."

"I've seen a lot of men on their way to volunteer down here, but nothing like that. 'Course, where I came from, our sentiments were mixed."

"I guess I know how you feel about this, seeing as how you helped that runaway slave."

"I haven't made up my mind yet. But as I understand it, slavery isn't the only issue."

"No, miss. I'm not an educated man. I don't understand any of it—only that them Rebels fired on our flag."

"Well, I expect when I get to Richmond, I'll hear nothing but the other side of it. All I want now is to settle down somewhere." She yawned. "Excuse me."

Archibald stood up. "I allow you're tired, miss. I'll go on out and let you get some sleep. It's about time for my duty now anyway."

He gathered up the plates and coffeepot.

"Thank you, Sergeant. You've been very kind."

He nodded and pulled the tent flap down as he left.

Before crawling under the blanket, Melissa draped her dress over the tent pole, hoping it would dry during the night. The rain had tapered off considerably, and the soft patter on the canvas lulled her to sleep almost immediately.

When Melissa awoke in the little tent, she had forgotten where she was and looked around in surprise. She yawned and sat up. Her dress felt nearly dry, and she put it on. Her shoes, she remembered, were still in the wagon where she had left them before she had tried to free the wheel from the mud. She peeked out the tent flap and saw two men by a small fire. The sun was shining and the sky was cloudless. She felt very uncomfortable after drinking all that coffee the night before.

Sergeant Fleener came over to her as she stepped out of the tent. "'Morning, miss. Did you sleep well?"

"Yes, thank you."

"Breakfast is ready."

"Oh." She glanced around, blushing. "Do you think I could join you in a minute?"

"Sure. How come?"

She turned even redder and pointed off to the trees. "I—uh . . ."

Archibald blushed this time. "Oh, yes, miss. Go right ahead."

Melissa hurried off into the woods, and Archibald

60

ambled back to the campfire. The other three tents had been struck, and he told one of the men to take down the last one.

"You might hitch up her horse for her, too."

Melissa returned to the fire to find Archibald scraping eggs out of a pan and onto a plate. "Help yourself to coffee," he told her.

She poured herself a cup and sat down. Archibald handed her the plate of food.

"Aren't you going to eat?" she wondered.

"Oh, I already ate." He sat down with a cup of coffee.

"You're breaking camp," she observed.

He nodded. "Can't stay in one place for very long. I didn't like staying here as long as we did, but that rain was too much for us. We're going to head back now. General McClellan will be wanting our reports."

Melissa nearly dropped her plate. "Did you say McClelland?"

"Yes, miss. He's in charge of the army out here."

"Not Sam McClelland?"

"No. His name's George, I believe."

"Is he from Pittsburgh, do you know?"

"I believe he's from Ohio. Why?"

"I have a friend named Sam McClelland. For a minute there, I thought he might be your commander. I wonder if they're related?"

"I wouldn't know. But the men surely do like him. He's a West Pointer, and Lincoln sets great store in him. He commands everything along the Ohio River."

One of the men came over to Melissa, carrying her shoes and rifle. "Here's your shoes, miss. And your rifle—it's a real beauty. I'm afraid it got pretty wet. I'd be glad to clean it up for you while you're eating."

"Why, thank you. That's very kind of you."

Melissa was amazed at how polite these farm boys were, as she watched the young private take the rifle over to where his kit was lying on the ground.

"You still planning on going on to Richmond today?" Archibald asked her.

"Yes. I hope to make it by tomorrow or the next day. I want to get started soon."

"You finish your meal. You'll have to excuse me. I have some things I have to do."

Melissa watched the men breaking their small camp, wondering how these boys would fare if it ever came to battle.

She left the campfire and went over to Sergeant Fleener, who was saddling his horse.

"I want to thank you for everything, Sergeant," she said. "You and your men have been very good to me."

"Our pleasure. Truth to tell, things had been kind of dull till we ran into you." He held out his hand for her to shake, but on impulse she stood on tiptoe and placed a kiss on his cheek. He blushed furiously while the other men chuckled.

The little private stepped forward to assist her into the wagon. "That's a right fine gun, miss. You take good care of it."

"I will, thank you." She picked up the reins.

"You take care in Richmond, now," Archibald told her.

"I will. And thank you all again—and God bless you."

Melissa flicked the reins, and the horse started off. She turned around once and waved at the little band of blue-clad farmboys from Indiana.

*   *   *

A cloud of cigar smoke hovered over the four men sitting around a table. A tall, elegantly dressed man lifted a glass to his companions.

"Gentlemen, to our new venture. May it prove prosperous to us all."

A murmur of agreement followed as the men drank the contents of their glasses. This was the board of directors of the Tidewater Nail Company, newly formed that morning. After buying out various concerns, these four gentlemen now controlled ninety-five per cent of the South's entire supply of nails.

"We should see the profits very soon," a beady-eyed man remarked.

"Very soon, Augustus," the tall man smiled. He had piercing blue eyes set deeply in his handsome face. His silver hair was combed back, resembling a flowing mane. He put down his glass. "You must excuse me now, gentlemen. We are expecting guests tonight, and Nancy doesn't like me to be late."

Another man, short and stocky, stood up and accompanied the silver-haired man to the door. "I'll work up something, Edward, and put an announcement in the *Journal*. You'll get word to the Ordnance Department?"

"That's my supper guest."

Edward Armstrong stepped out of the dingy little lawyer's office and onto the street. He pulled out his watch and checked the time: three-thirty. He had enough time to stop at the barber shop before returning home. As he walked along the street, he smiled at his good fortune. The war was going to make him a rich man. Since the Union blockade had been put into effect, his job as a clerk at the exporting company loo ed bad. The warehouse was full of all sorts of things waiting to be shipped out. Then this opportunity to invest in the nail company had come along, and he considered his options.

In the fourteen years he had been clerking for the export company, he had quietly siphoned off some $20,000 undetected by the owners, two doddering old men in their seventies who had always had the utmost faith in Edward Armstrong. He was a pillar of the community, and attended church regularly. Married to a fine wife and raising three bright children, until recently he had lived in a moderately comfortable home. He didn't drink or gamble excessively, apparently didn't do any womanizing, and was a model of efficiency in the office.

He had invested $5,000 in the Tidewater Nail Company, but with the war, the demand for nails was bound to rise, and with the demand, the price would rise. The other stockholders of the Tidewater Nail Company Edward had known for some time: Lewis McAllen, the owner and editor of the Richmond *Journal*, not in the class of the *Examiner* or the *Dispatch*, but it enjoyed a good circulation; John Denny, a clerk like himself at the Tredegar Iron Works; and Augustus Given, the fat little lawyer.

Edward turned down Ninth Street and thought of his family. His shrewd head for finances would leave them very well off indeed, he was sure. His wife Nancy would be able to continue living an easy life. It hadn't always been that way, but since he had begun working for the export company and making good money, she had been able to enjoy life. She was accepted in society, belonged to various organizations and charities, dressed in the best clothes, and even had three servants. Andrew, his only son, had gone to the finest schools and attended VMI until he was expelled for cheating on an examination. He had his father's blood, only he wasn't as clever. Margaret, his oldest daughter, had married into a well-respected family, the Boones of Fairfax County. She had always been a homebody, and insisted that she and her husband Joseph live in Richmond with her parents. Edward didn't much care for Joseph. He spent more time reading poetry and daydreaming than anything else. But Margaret was expecting now, after four years of marriage, and Edward looked forward to becoming a grandfather. His youngest daughter, Mahaley, was his favorite. She was a little spitfire, reminding him a great deal of himself as he had been when he was young. She was a beauty too, attracting the attentions of scores of men, now that she was nearly seventeen.

Edward felt fine about the world as he opened the door to the barber shop.

Four

The streets of Richmond were teeming with humanity as Melissa drove her wagon into town late on the afternoon of April 28: horse-drawn vehicles of all descriptions, men on horseback, vendors selling produce, slaves running about on errands for their masters, women strolling along the sidewalks, children playing, and soldiers. Soldiers from all places in the South— Zouaves in their bright colors and baggy trousers, dragoons in their splendid Napoleonic uniforms and plumed shakos, Virginia Military cadets, artillerymen with their red caps, backwoods riflemen in their buckskins.

Melissa was tired and hot and dirty. Her back hurt from bending over the reins, her bottom hurt despite the improvised cushioned seat. Checking the numbers along Franklin Street, she finally came to a halt in front of an elegant three-story brick-house. She took her uncle's letter from her pocket and double-checked the address. Yes, this was it, but such a house! Feeling self-conscious about her somewhat disheveled appearance, she stepped through the little wrought-iron gate and went up on the porch.

A young black girl opened the door in answer to Melissa's knock.

"Yes, ma'am?" she asked, eyeing Melissa's attire with suspicion.

"Is this the house of Edward Armstrong?"

"Yessum."

"I'm his niece."

The girl's eyes widened.

Melissa was becoming impatient with the girl. "Is my uncle in? Or my aunt? Or any of my cousins?"

"Yessum."

Before Melissa had a chance to lose her temper completely, she heard a woman's voice from inside. "Who is it, Cindy?"

The servant had no chance to answer, for Melissa pushed by her and into the entry hall, coming face to face with Nancy Armstrong. She was an attractive woman in her early forties, short and slightly plump. A high-strung person, she gestured frequently, waving her hands in the air. Had it not been for the threading of gray in her blond hair, her attractive face would have belied her age.

"Aunt Nancy!"

"Melissa?"

Suddenly overwhelmed by fatigue and nerves, Melissa fell into her aunt's arms. "Oh, Aunt Nancy!"

Confused, Nancy comforted her. "Dear Melissa, what's wrong? What are you doing here?"

"Papa was killed and Jeremiah's in Pittsburgh, and I didn't know where else to go."

Nancy patted her. "There, there . . . you poor thing. Come sit down."

Melissa straightened up and sniffed, brushing back a stray wisp of hair. "I'll be all right. I'm just so tired."

"I'm sure you are. Why don't I get you settled in your room and you can rest?" Melissa nodded. "How did you get here?"

"In the wagon."

Nancy turned to the servant, who was gaping at the stranger. "Cindy, tell Bobo to take the wagon around back and bring in the luggage."

"Yessum." And the girl disappeared.

"I can show you to your room now, or would you maybe like a drop of sherry first?" Nancy asked.

"Are you sure I'm not intruding?"

"Of course you're not intruding! Don't be a goose! Come have some sherry." Nancy took Melissa's arm and guided her into the parlor. "Sit down. Edward's going to be so upset when he hears about this."

Melissa was gazing around the room and thought it looked like pictures of fine houses she had seen in magazines. Nancy handed her a crystal glass of sherry.

"Now drink this and you'll feel better. I always do. Edward should be home in another hour. Margaret's upstairs taking a nap. She's expecting, you know. And Mahaley's off somewhere—probably shopping."

"Is everyone well?"

"As well as can be expected with those horrid Yankees sitting on our doorstep. You know, it's a good thing you came here. Why, you being all alone, if the Yankees came, Lord knows what might have happened to you."

Melissa was about to mention the Indiana scouts but thought better of it.

"Aunt Nancy, do you think it would be all right if I went to my room now? I really am very tired and I'd like to get cleaned up."

"Of course, dear. I do go on when I get excited."

Melissa followed her aunt upstairs and along a carpeted hallway to her new bedroom.

"I see Bobo's already brought your things up," Nancy said. "Would you like to take a bath?"

"Could I?"

"I'll have Cindy bring you hot water and attend to your things. She can show you where everything is. And if you want anything, just ask for it."

"Thank you, Aunt Nancy."

After her aunt had left, Melissa sat down on the large bed and took off her shoes, wiggling her toes. She felt a little ashamed for being relieved that Nancy had gone out, but the woman's constant nervous chatter made her tense. She couldn't help being a little awed by the splendor in which her uncle lived. He must have done very well in his business.

There was a tap on the door, and Cindy entered with two pails of hot water.

"Here's your bathwater, missy. De tub behind de screen. You want me to fill it?"

"Yes, please."

"I'll unpack and hang up your clothes for you, too. You got anything what needs washing?"

"Yes, but I can do it in the morning."

"You can't do dat! Mistress Nancy, she be right put out at dat." Cindy returned from behind the big screen. "Towels and soap back dere, too."

"Thank you, Cindy."

The copper tub was steaming when Melissa went behind the screen and she thought she detected the scent of jasmine. She took off her travel-stained dress, hung it over the screen, and pinned her hair up on top of her head.

Cindy was unpacking Melissa's things, shaking her head and clucking her tongue, thinking "Dis mus' be de po' relations."

Mahaley rolled over and threw off the blanket, the shaft of sunlight filtering through the torn window shade, picking up the dancing dust motes. She sat up and brushed her tangled golden curls away from her face.

"I have to go, Johnny. I've spent too much time here already."

Receiving no answer, she glanced over her shoulder and saw that Johnny was sleeping soundly. Perturbed at his rudeness, she was about to smack him to wake him up when her eyes fell on the gold-braided jacket and hat draped over the bedpost. She sighed and decided not to wake him. A soldier needed to get as much rest and pleasure as possible before leaving to fight for the cause. Padding across the floorboards on bare feet, Mahaley was pleased with her decision to help the Confederacy in the only way in which she knew. Being a woman and unable to join a regiment, she could at least make the fine young men who were about to go forth to battle as happy as she could. Her father had said many times how everyone should do their part to help their new country.

She studied her petite, well-formed body in the mirror and twirled in a pirouette. She approved of her looks completely, from the small upturned nose to her graceful ankles. Leaning closer to the glass, she allowed her full, expressive mouth to break into a mischievous grin. I must admit, Mahaley Armstrong, she thought, you are most definitely sending the boys off to battle with something to remember.

*   *   *

Andrew had returned home from his job as proof-reader and advertising copywriter for the *Journal*. He poured himself a strong whiskey and sprawled in a chair in the parlor. At twenty-two, Andrew had accomplished very little in his life. He worked only because it was expected of him, spending as little time at it as possible. He was a handsome man, with dark hair and a bushy mustache, which he constantly toyed with. He had some of his mother's tendency to nervousness, but instead of expending this nervous energy on work, he spent it on the minor vices of the time.

"Oh, Andrew, I didn't know you were here," his mother said, bustling over to him. "You look tired, dear."

"I'm fine, Mother."

"I was just out in the kitchen telling Tunia she'll be setting an extra place for meals now."

"Why?"

"Oh, that's right, you don't know. Your cousin Melissa has come to stay. It's the saddest thing—her father died."

"Uncle James is dead?"

"Killed. Probably by Yankees. Oh, I don't know. She didn't tell me any details. The poor little thing. She looked so exhausted."

"Sit down, Mother."

"I think I heard your father's carriage." She hurried out into the hall and peeked out the curtains of one of the windows which were on either side of the front door. Edward was getting out of the carriage and Mahaley was with him. Nancy opened the door.

"Hello, Nancy," her husband greeted her, placing a perfunctory kiss on her cheek. "I saw Mahaley walking home, so here we are."

"Hello, Mother."

"Edward, do come in. I have so much to tell you."

Placing his hat on the hall tree, he sighed, "Yes, Nancy?"

"Edward, I don't know how to begin. It's been the strangest day. Melissa—she just appeared this afternoon. I'm afraid James is dead."

"Dead?" Edward gasped and reached for the liquor decanter. Even though the brothers were not close in adulthood, as children they had been inseparable. James had followed his older brother everywhere, and Edward had taught him to swim and shoot and ride a horse while their father was busy with the blacksmith shop. Their mother had died giving birth to a stillborn daughter when James was six.

He poured a glass of whiskey and raised it to his lips, hoping to numb his sense of loss. He thought of when he'd turned seventeen and gone to Charleston, where he worked at various jobs. James had stayed on with their father.

Edward drained his glass and refilled it. His father had died of a heart attack in 1836. Edward was twenty-five at the time, newly married and living in Lynchburg, moving later to Richmond. James had remained at home and continued the operation of the blacksmith shop. Despite the distance, they had always maintained a warm relationship.

"How did it happen?" Edward asked.

"I don't know. The child was so tired when she got here, I had Cindy get her settled in her room."

Melissa studied her meager wardrobe, thinking she

must look like a back-country bumpkin, which she had to admit she was, in a way. She took down her best dress, which she usually saved for church, and slipped it over her head. Both she and her mother had bought hoops and dresses when they visited Richmond before, but they were sure to be out of style by now, and that would look even worse than no hoops at all. Besides, the hoops were still packed away in the attic in the house at Shady Run. After stepping into her shoes and giving her hair a final brush, she left the room. Her only concern about her clothes was the fact that she wouldn't want to embarrass her family by her rustic appearance. She decided to use some of her money to go shopping, and the idea cheered her.

Hearing voices in the parlor, she hesitated a moment before entering. Edward noticed her and hurried over to her, gathering her in his arms.

"Melissa, my dear. Such a terrible thing. How did it happen?"

Before Melissa could answer, the cook called them for supper. Edward walked with his arm around Melissa into the large dining room. After the delayed greetings to her cousins and Nancy's announcement that Margaret was having a tray in her room, Edward urged Melissa to fill him in on the details of her father's death.

"Well, it all happened so quickly." Melissa swallowed hard. "Papa and I were in the house one evening, and we heard all this commotion in the street. Some of the boys were celebrating before leaving for their regiment in the morning. Papa stepped outside to take a look, and one of the boys' horses reared and his gun went off and hit Papa."

"Then it wasn't Yankees," Nancy observed.

"No, of course it wasn't Yankees. It was just an accident," Melissa said, wiping a tear. "A horrible accident."

"He didn't suffer long, then?" Edward asked.

"No. He was just conscious for a couple of minutes. He told me to come here."

"And he was right. You know you're welcome here," Edward said, patting her hand. "You and Jeremiah are my only other family."

"What about Jeremiah?" Andrew asked.

"He's still in Pittsburgh, I guess. I sent a letter with . . . I sent him a letter." Melissa found herself wondering again if Corky had made the journey safely.

"He's coming back, of course?"

"I don't know. Papa and I were talking about that just before he . . . just before the accident."

"He'll be back," Edward said. "He probably packed his bag the day we took Fort Sumter."

"I don't know. He wants to become a doctor awfully bad."

"Well, he can come home and once this nasty business is all over with, he can go to school here. There are many fine schools in the South—the Medical College of Virginia is right here in the city."

Conversation faded while Tunia the cook took away the soup plates and served the second course. She was a big, heavyset middle-aged woman.

"Where's Joseph tonight?" Mahaley wondered.

"He probably fell asleep at his telegraph key," Edward muttered.

"Maybe if he were to join the army, he'd become a little more ambitious," Mahaley suggested.

Andrew was about to speak, but held his tongue,

feeling that now was not the proper time to make his announcement.

Nancy turned to Melissa. "You haven't met Joseph yet. He's Margaret's husband, you know. He's nice enough, but he just can't seem to get interested in anything."

Melissa nodded, wondering if Margaret was still as strong-willed and temperamental as she had been as a girl.

"Did you sell the house and shop?" Edward asked her.

"No. Some soldiers came by and bought most of the equipment and supplies from the shop for the government. I kept the house and shop in case either Jeremiah or I decide to go back."

"You don't want to go back until we put those Yankees in their place," Nancy said.

"It'll be so much fun with you here now," Mahaley told Melissa. "Why don't we go shopping tomorrow?"

"I thought that's where you went today," Nancy said.

"Oh, you know me. I'll use any excuse to go shopping."

"You'd better buy all your fancies before the blockade gets any worse," Andrew smiled.

"Oh, we'll never run out of things," Edward said. "The prices may go a little higher, that's all."

Andrew and Edward retired to the study after supper.

"Father, I realize this is a bad time to bring this up, but I've enlisted in the army."

"The army! That's wonderful! I've been hoping you'd join. The Confederacy needs more men like you. What regiment?"

"The Twelfth Virginia. It's not as glamorous as the

cavalry or as messy as the artillery."

"Who's your commander?"

"I don't know yet. There's talk we may go in under Longstreet," Andrew said. "I didn't like to bring the subject up at the supper table, what with Melissa here and all. I was afraid Mother might get upset."

Edward laughed. "Don't think she won't worry about you, but she'll be so happy. She'll be the proudest mother this side of the Potomac." Edward poured them each a drink from the brandy decanter. "Now we have a double celebration. Today would be a very happy day if it wasn't for James."

"Yes," Andrew sighed, sipping his brandy. "I always liked Uncle James. Melissa's turned into quite a beauty."

"Indeed."

"Half my friends will be around as soon as they hear about her."

"You can just tell your kind of friends to keep their distance where Melissa is concerned. I plan to keep an eye on her the same as I do Mahaley, and Margaret before."

"Yes, Father. I'll warn them all—Melissa's to be treated like a lady," Andrew laughed. "You said double celebration. What was the other thing?"

"I was talking to some people today, and the chances are very good that I may be able to get a job working for the government when they move the capital here. From the looks of things, the export company doesn't have long to last."

"Who knows anymore?" Andrew finished his brandy and set down the glass. "I'm off."

"Where to?"

"I don't know. But there's bound to be something to

o tonight."

When Melissa got downstairs in the morning, refreshed from a good night's sleep, Edward and another man, whom she assumed was Joseph, were sitting at the table drinking coffee. Both men stood up when she entered the room.

"Ah, Melissa. You're up bright and early," Edward told her. "This is Joseph Boone, Margaret's husband."

"How do you do?" Joseph said.

"Fine, thank you," Melissa smiled.

"This is a pleasant surprise," Edward remarked. "Usually Joseph and I have to take breakfast alone. The women in this household are known for sleeping late. Sometimes Andrew makes it, but Lewis doesn't expect him at the paper early."

Joseph poured a cup of coffee for Melissa and then sat down, peering at her over the top of his spectacles. He was tall and thin with sharp features and a rather downtrodden expression. "I'm sorry to hear about your father."

"Thank you," she murmured.

Edward decided to change the subject. "So you and Mahaley are going shopping today. Do you need any money?"

"Oh, no. I have some. And I was thinking I might like to get some sort of employment. I taught school back in Shady Run."

"Well, I can inquire around. But there's no need."

"You're very kind, Uncle Edward, but it's not just the money. I like to be doing something. I can't stand to be idle."

Edward shot a glance at Joseph. He was pushing egg

77

around on his plate and gazing at Melissa, completely enchanted with her beauty. Edward frowned. "How's Margaret this morning, Joseph? I didn't see her yesterday at all."

"Better, I think."

Tunia brought a plate for Melissa just as Andrew appeared, looking as if he had had very little sleep.

"Good morning, all. No breakfast for me, Tunia."

"You look like you were out late last night," Edward remarked.

Andrew nodded, pouring himself a cup of coffee. His eyes fell on the plate of ham and eggs, and his stomach turned over. He seated himself beside Melissa and avoided looking in the direction of her food. He rubbed his temples.

Edward smiled. "Doing a little celebrating?"

"Something like that. Did you tell Mother?"

"I surely did. I thought she was going to start singing 'The Bonnie Blue Flag' from the bedroom window."

Melissa and Joseph exchanged bewildered glances.

"Andrew has joined the army," Edward explained.

Both Joseph and Melissa echoed a subdued "Oh."

"You don't sound very pleased."

"Yes, I suppose I am," Melissa said. "It's just very hard for me to understand all this."

"That's because you've been stuck out there in Shady Run," Edward said. "You don't get the true story out there. After a little time here, you'll come around."

"You're lucky you left when you did," Andrew told her. "There's talk now of western Virginia seceding from the rest of the state."

"What would it be then? A whole new country?"

"Union."

78

Melissa drank her coffee to hide her consternation. Maybe the move to Richmond was made too soon. Her feelings still were very mixed, although her sympathies were more with the Union. Not so much for any political reasons as for the fact that she felt it was wrong for a country to split itself apart.

"I did read something about that, now that you mention it," she said. "But I thought it was all talk."

"It may be," Edward agreed. "President Davis is going to try to nip it in the bud."

"When will you be leaving?" Joseph asked Andrew.

"As soon as I get my uniform."

Mahaley entered the room. "Uniform? What uniform?"

"You're brother's a soldier now," Edward told her.

"Oh, Andrew!" she squealed, hugging him. He was sure his head was going to fall off. "I'm so proud of you!"

He disengaged her arms and stood up. "Thank you. I have to be leaving now."

Joseph stood also. "I'll walk with you. Good day, all."

Mahaley sat down at the table. "Oh, that's wonderful," she said. "He might even become a general."

Edward smiled. "Don't get your hopes up too high. I should be leaving too. You two ladies are going shopping?"

"Yes," Mahaley replied, picking up her napkin so the cook could set her plate down. "I'm so glad Melissa's here."

"So am I," Edward said, placing a kiss on each girl's head. "Have a good time today. I'll see you this evening."

After Edward had left, Mahaley ate a few bites of breakfast, and Melissa helped herself to more coffee.

"I was thinking after I got into bed last night,"

Mahaley began. "It may take a while before your dresses are ready. Oh, I'm sure we could get something thrown together in a hurry, but why waste money on a poorly made outfit? You're about the same size as Margaret, and she's got a closet-full of things she can't wear right now. You could wear some of her things until yours are ready."

"Oh, I couldn't do that."

"Yes, you can. She won't mind. All she can think about right now is this baby."

"She wants one very badly?"

"Oh, yes," Mahaley chuckled. "I sometimes think she wishes it had a different father, though."

"Why? Don't she and Joseph get along?"

"Oh, I don't know. She wants a baby and likes the idea of having a husband, but I don't think she exactly likes being married, if you know what I mean."

"I'm afraid I don't."

"Oh, it's hard for me to explain. It's just a feeling I have. Margaret was always afraid of being an old maid. It's not that she isn't attractive, but her temper sent the beaus packing after a while. I was still very young then, but I can remember. All her friends were getting married, and Margaret didn't even have an offer, so she started to panic. Then Joseph came along, and she snatched him up before he even knew what was happening. Poor Joseph. He's really very sweet, but such a dreamer. I do feel sorry for him, though. Margaret pushes him around a great deal. Besides that, I don't think they get along very well in bed."

Melissa was about to swallow some coffee, but choked on it instead.

"It's hot. Be careful," Mahaley told her.

80

After breakfast, Melissa and Mahaley trooped back upstairs and knocked on Margaret's door. Margaret was sitting in bed, propped against her pillows, knitting.

"Melissa dear," she smiled, holding out her hand. "How nice it is to see you. I only wish it were under more pleasant circumstances. How well you look."

"You're looking well yourself. When's the baby due?"

"In another six weeks or so. I'd been feeling fit as a fiddle until this past week."

At twenty-five, Margaret looked a great deal like Nancy must have at that age, Melissa thought. She was no great beauty, with her mousy brown hair and dark eyes, but she was attractive enough.

"Margaret, I had a wonderful idea," Mahaley began, and explained about the dresses.

"Yes. Help yourself. Lord knows, I can't get into anything now."

"Are you sure?" Melissa asked her.

"Go ahead."

Melissa selected two dresses, promising to be very careful of them and to return them as soon as hers were ready. When she put one of them on, she found the bodice a little snug and the waist a little too roomy, but it was acceptable. Her own stockings were of lisle and had a patch at the heel, but nobody would see that. She found walking difficult in the wide crinoline skirts she was unused to, and practiced walking around the room several times. The idea of how she must look struck her funny, and she began to laugh. She took her little metal box of money from her trunk and counted out fifty dollars from her share. Before leaving home, she had divided the money in half—part for herself and part for Jeremiah. She had never dreamed of splurging this much money and felt rather guilty about it, but after all, it was her money. And she had always wanted to have nice things. Tucking the box away in the trunk, she put the money in her reticule and started downstairs. By concentrating very hard and holding on to the banister, she managed to get down without a mishap.

Bobo was waiting with the carriage, and the two girls left the house. They stopped at a little shop, and Mahaley told Bobo to pick them up at the Colonial House at four o'clock.

A bell tinkled as they entered the dress shop. A friendly-looking woman in her thirties greeted Mahaley.

"Sabina, this is my cousin Melissa," Mahaley said. "She's going to be staying with us from now on."

Melissa and Sabina exchanged greetings.

"Isn't that a dress I made for Margaret?" Sabina asked.

Mahaley laughed. "It is. That's why we're here."

"I lived in the country and haven't any proper city clothes," Melissa explained. "I expect I need just about everything."

"Oh dear," Sabina sighed. "That's not going to be easy."

"Why?" Mahaley asked. "The blockade?"

"No. That hasn't affected me yet. But I've got all my girls working around the clock making uniforms."

Mahaley clapped her hand to her mouth. "That's right! Oh, I forgot all about that."

Melissa had been running her fingers over a bolt of blue silk. "This is lovely."

Sabina came over to her. "It is. And some of the finest material we've had in a long while. It would set off your eyes."

"Oh, it's so beautiful. Don't you think you could make

me something soon?"

Sabina smiled. "Come into the back and we'll get your measurements."

When they had finished, Melissa realized she had only enough money to leave a deposit. The rest of the bill would have to be paid when she came in for her final fitting. Sabina promised to hurry since she had made such a good sale.

Melissa was quite pleased with herself as she and Mahaley sat at a table in the Colonial House, her parcels placed beside her on the floor.

"We've found that by going to Sabina, we can get just as good if not better workmanship than by going to the bigger, more well-known dressmakers. They're known for their name and not their abilities," Mahaley said. "Besides, she's cheaper."

"I wouldn't call that cheap."

Mahaley smiled. "Then it's as well we didn't go to Madame Regina's. She charges twice as much, and most of that's simply so you'll have her name sewn into the garment. Mother had her do a ball gown once, and its seams split on the dance floor."

This struck Melissa funny. "What did she do?"

"She had Father dance her over to the door, get their wraps, and they left. What are you going to eat?"

"I don't know. Everything on the menu looks so tempting." And expensive, Melissa thought. "What do you suggest?" Upon receiving no reply, Melissa followed Mahaley's gaze. She was watching two cavalrymen laughing and talking at a table in the corner. "Do you know them?"

"No. But I'd like to. I wish they'd look this way."

Melissa glanced back in the direction of the men. At the same time, the dark-haired soldier looked directly at Melissa. She flushed and turned back to study the menu. He had said something to his companion, who was now looking in their direction. Mahaley gave a little wave and then returned to the menu.

"They'll be over in a little while," she told Melissa quietly.

"How do you know?"

"I just know. You wait and see."

After receiving their meal, Melissa and Mahaley ate in comparative silence. Melissa was amazed at Mahaley's boldness. She peeked in the direction of the corner table. The men were still there, and the bearded man was telling the other a very animated story. They were both having a fine time.

The girls were just finishing their meal when the two men approached the table.

"Ladies," the bearded man greeted. "My friend and I were wondering if you'd care to join us for an ice cream?"

"Oh, why Colonel, that would be very nice," Mahaley said.

Melissa flushed again and shot Mahaley a concerned look as the men pulled up two chairs. The waiter came to remove the plates.

"Four ice creams, please," the bearded man said. He looked at Melissa and smiled. "Permit me to introduce us. This is Lieutenant Jackson Vaughn, and I'm Colonel James Ewell Brown Stuart. My friends call me Jeb."

"I'm Mahaley Armstrong, and this is my cousin, Melissa Armstrong."

"My pleasure, ladies."

Jackson smiled at Melissa, causing the corners of his

mustache to turn up slightly.

"Melissa's new in town," Mahaley announced.

"And where might you be from?" Jackson asked her.

"Mason County," she murmured, still a little flustered at all this. "It's on the Ohio River."

"That's might pretty country out there."

"Oh, do you know it?"

"Yes, miss, I do indeed. My father was a traveling preacher, and that was one of his favorite places. He said the country was so peaceful, it just naturally had to make people closer to God."

"I imagine it does."

Melissa found herself warming to this big, rugged-looking man a little. He hardly looked like a preacher's son, with his strong hands and suntanned face.

"You've just moved here recently?" Jeb asked her.

"Yes. Very recently."

"I imagine you find the city a little less peaceful than your home."

"Quite a bit," she replied.

Mahaley was beginning to feel put out at all the attention Melissa was receiving. "I've lived here all my life."

"Have you?"

"Yes."

The ice cream arrived, and Melissa looked at the frosty mound with delight.

"Ooh, this is a treat," she said. "I haven't eaten ice cream in ever so long. And it's one of my favorite things."

Melissa put a spoonful in her mouth, the coldness making her teeth tingle, and let it melt over her tongue, savoring it all.

Jackson had been watching her intently. "Good?"

She grinned at him. "Delicious."

"It looks as if you ladies have been doing some shopping," Jeb remarked.

"Yes. We've been to the dressmaker's," Mahaley replied.

"Which one?"

"Sabina's, on Seventh Street."

"Are you satisfied with the work?"

"Oh, yes; very."

"Then I shall have to tell my wife. She's thoroughly disgusted with the things she's been getting lately."

Mahaley's face fell. A wife! What poor luck!

"Do you and your wife live here in the city?"

"Just outside."

"Are you married too, Lieutenant Vaughn?" Mahaley asked.

"No," he smiled. "I haven't been fortunate enough to meet the right girl yet." He looked directly at Melissa, and icy fingers seemed to be running up and down her spine.

It was soon time for the girls to be leaving, and the men carried their bundles outside for them. Bobo hopped down from his box on the carriage to put the parcels inside.

"Thank you very much for the ice cream," Melissa said, extending her hand for Jackson to shake.

"My pleasure. I wonder if I might be allowed to call on you sometime?"

"Why—ah . . ." She looked into his almost black eyes and felt those icy fingers on her spine again. "Yes, you may, Lieutenant Vaughn."

He grinned, showing even white teeth. "Thank you.

Some afternoon very soon, I hope." He assisted her into the carriage, and she thought he gave her hand an extra squeeze. "Good day, Miss Armstrong."

"Good day, Lieutenant Vaughn, Colonel Stuart."

Mahaley was very quiet on the drive home. She wasn't sure she liked all this attention Melissa was getting.

Several evenings later, the Armstrongs were entertaining a dinner guest, Edward's friend Lewis McAllen, the newspaper publisher. A bachelor in his early forties, he seemed completely delighted with Melissa. One of her new dresses had been completed and she looked exceptionally beautiful. And indeed, the blue silk did enhance her eyes.

The talk was mostly in praise of the brave South. Melissa found it tiresome, and the descriptions of Yankees most definitely did not jibe with what she knew of her friends in Pittsburgh. But she kept her opinions to herself. In the time that she had been living in Richmond, she had discovered her family to be ardent secessionists.

"We'll be sorry to see Andrew leave us," Lewis was saying. "But under the circumstances, I'm happy to let him go."

Seated beside the guest, Melissa turned to him. "Mr. McAllen, do you have anyone yet to replace Andrew?"

"No. Not yet."

"Do you have anyone in mind for the job?"

"As a matter of fact, I don't."

Melissa took a deep breath, gathering her courage. "Would you consider hiring a woman?"

"A woman?"

"Yes—me."

"Well . . . I . . . ah . . ." he stammered.

"Melissa!" Margaret gasped. "It's unheard of!"

"It isn't unheard of. Why, I can read and write and spell as well as any man—perhaps better!" She turned back to Lewis. "Would you consider me?"

"Well, I don't know. You'll be around cigar-smoking men who don't use the most pleasant language all the time."

"Oh, fiddle! Cigar smoke doesn't bother me. And simply because I don't use that kind of language doesn't mean I haven't heard it all before. I've grown up with men cussing in my papa's blacksmith shop."

Lewis glanced questioningly at Edward, who was smiling. Just now he could see in Melissa the strong-minded woman his mother had been.

"I think Melissa's right," Nancy finally said. All eyes turned with amazement to her. "The women should free our men from tasks so they can go out and fight for the Confederacy."

Lewis looked around the table helplessly. He turned back to Melissa. "You come down to the newspaper in the morning, and I'll show you around. Then we'll see."

"Oh, thank you, Mr. McAllen!"

"I haven't hired you yet."

"I know."

Looking at her youthful innocence and enthusiasm, Lewis wished he had the nerve to suggest some other arrangement for Melissa. Perhaps if he was nice to her, something like that might develop. He glanced at Edward, who was frowning at him as if to say, "I know you too well, Lewis. We'll have none of that."

Immediately after breakfast, Melissa and Joseph

walked the four blocks to the newspaper office. It smelled strongly of ink and stale cigar smoke. The place was extremely quiet except for a towheaded boy sitting at the telegraph key, and a beefy, red-faced man setting type.

"Good morning, Bruce . . . Abner," Joseph said.

The beefy man merely waved in the air, but the boy stood up.

"Quiet night," he told Joseph, eyeing Melissa. "Nothin' come over the wire. I ain't never been so bored. You're welcome to it, Joseph."

"Abner, this is my wife's cousin, Miss Armstrong."

"Hello, Abner."

"Pleased to meet you, ma'am."

"Abner takes over the telegraph key at night. Is McAllen in?"

"He's in his office."

Joseph tapped on the door at the back of the building.

"Good luck," he smiled, as Melissa went in.

Lewis McAllen looked up from behind piles of papers on his desk.

"Ah, Miss Armstrong. I see you haven't changed your mind."

"Did you think I would?"

He smiled, showing a wide gap between his front teeth. "No, I didn't really think you would."

"It's very quiet here. I always thought a newspaper office would be a busy place."

"It is. Give it another half an hour. Perhaps I should take this opportunity to show you around and explain things."

Melissa followed Lewis all over the building, taking in all the equipment and operations. Her duties would be to read the copy and correct spelling errors, and calculate the cost for advertising and write the actual advertisement.

"I think I may have Joseph teach you to use the telegraph. I'd like to have more than one person who can operate it in the daytime, in case an emergency comes up. I have to tell you, Miss Armstrong, the policy of this paper is completely in sympathy with the South. We support the Confederacy and the president to the utmost. Would you abide by that policy?"

"Mr. McAllen, I was born and bred a Virginian."

"Can you make a good pot of coffee?"

"Why, yes. Papa always said it was the best he'd ever drunk."

"In that case, Miss Armstrong, you're hired."

"Oh thank you, Mr. McAllen!" she exclaimed. She had an urge to hug him but settled for shaking his hand vigorously instead. "You won't regret it."

"You'll start tomorrow morning. I'll pay you seventy-five cents a day."

Happy and excited, Melissa returned home. Nancy was waiting in the parlor for her, anxious to learn how she did.

"I start tomorrow."

"Oh, I'm so glad. It's time we women started making a little noise. If you're capable, why shouldn't you work? Oh, I nearly forgot. A message came for you while you were out. It's there on the table."

Melissa picked up the envelope and turned it over, examining the unfamiliar handwriting. It wasn't Jeremiah's.

"Where did it come from?"

"A little colored boy brought it."

Melissa opened the envelope and unfolded the paper.

Dear Miss Armstrong:

I hope you have not forgotten me nor your kind permission to allow me to call on you. Unfortunately, I must leave the city for several weeks on military matters. My unit has been called to Montgomery to escort the president to Richmond. It is my sincere hope that I will have the honor of calling on you when I return. I trust you are in good health.

Respectfully,
Lt. Jackson Vaughn

Five

Wending his way around to the back of the two-story building, the thin black man stepped up on the porch and knocked on the door. After some time, an elderly woman opened it a small crack.

"Yes?"

"Ma'am, I'm lookin' fo' Jeremiah Armstrong. Do he live here?"

"Yes. But he's not in at the moment."

"He be back soon, ma'am? I come a long way to give him a letter from his sister."

"His sister? Oh, he's been so worried about her and his father. Let me see the letter. I'll give it to him."

"Beggin' yo' pardon, ma'am. I ain't about to let go of dis till I give it to him personal. I come too far fo' to lose it now."

After following the directions Mrs. Oliver had given him, Corky found himself on another back porch, knocking on the door. This time, a man answered.

"Yes?"

"Can I find Jeremiah Armstrong here, suh?"

"Yes."

Corky breathed a sigh of relief. "I gots a letter for him,

uh. Can I see him?"

"Come in." Sam opened the door wider, and Corky tepped inside the small but clean kitchen.

"Who is it, Sam?" a woman's voice called from nother room.

"It's a man with a letter for Jeremiah." Sam looked at he blurred ink on the envelope Corky was clutching. "It's from Melissa."

They heard a thud as if a chair had been knocked over, nd Jeremiah dashed into the kitchen.

"Where is it?"

Corky proudly handed the envelope over to him, leased with his accomplishment.

Ripping the envelope open, Jeremiah walked back into he other room, followed by Sam. Bewildered, Corky hifted his weight from foot to foot, waiting to be told vhat to do.

Jim, Sam, and Sarah gathered around Jeremiah while ıe read the letter aloud, learning for the first time of his ather's death. Sam poured him a drink and set it down on he table, noticing the pencil scratchings on the back of he envelope. He picked it up and examined it.

"Well, I'll be damned," he muttered to himself. He walked into the kitchen where Corky was still waiting. "You're a runaway?"

"No, suh. I free now—ain't I?"

Sam laughed out loud. "Come on inside. You ıungry?"

"Yessuh."

"Come on, then. I'll have Sarah fix you something."

"In de house, suh?"

Sam patted his shoulder. "In the house. You're free ıow, remember?"

"Yessuh!"

Looking very pale, Jeremiah was rereading the letter. He looked up as Corky entered. "Why did she send this with you?" he asked.

"De mail, suh. She don't trust it."

Sam had sent Sarah to the kitchen to get Corky some supper.

"Sit down—ah—what's your name?"

"Corky, suh."

"Sit down, Corky."

Nervously, Corky sat down at the table. He had never sat at a table where white people took their meals. In fact, he had seldom sat at all in the presence of whites.

The dark-haired boy looked at him, his eyes moist. "You saw my sister?"

"Yessuh. She give me some food and some money and said if'n I was goin' nawth, would I take dis to yo'?"

"I'm so confused. I don't understand any of this."

"I think I do a little," Sam ventured. "Corky was a runaway slave, and he ran into Melissa someplace. Is that right, Corky?"

"Yessuh."

"Tell us about it," Sam urged.

Corky launched into an explanation of his encounter with Melissa in the woods. Sarah set down a steaming bowl of stew and dumplings as he was ending his tale.

"Lordy," Sarah said. "She's going all that way in just a wagon—all by herself! How far is that?"

"Almost three hundred miles, I think," Jeremiah replied.

His mouth watering, Corky was inhaling the aroma of the stew.

"Eat while it's hot, Corky," Sam told him.

"I just don't know," Jeremiah muttered. "I can't think. What should I do? I think maybe I should go to her."

"I think the first thing to do is to consider everything," Jim spoke for the first time. "First of all, Melissa will have a home in Richmond with your uncle, am I right?"

"Yes, of course."

"And here you are, a promising young doctor—almost. At a time when the country is going to need all the doctors it can get."

"But I could finish my schooling in Richmond."

Jim raised his eyebrows. "Now? Feeling the way you do about things?"

"I wouldn't fight for the South. Maybe I should send for Melissa, bring her to Pittsburgh. Oh, I don't even know if she got to Richmond safely!"

Sarah moved beside his chair, smoothing his hair. "Why don't you sleep on it, Jeremiah? Think things out."

"Do you have a place to stay, Corky?"

"No, suh."

"Well, you can sleep here on the sofa for tonight. Then we'll see about what we can do with you tomorrow."

"I've already thought about that," Jim said. "With so many boys joining the army, the hospital is short of help. I'm sure I can find some job for you there, Corky."

Corky grinned. "Thank you, suh. I think I gonna like dis bein' free jus' fine."

One of the first things Jeremiah did in the morning was to inquire at the post office how well mail was moving

95

into the South. Very slowly, if at all, was the reply.

Sighing, Jeremiah started on his way to Dr. White's offices, where he was serving as his assistant. He had decided on writing Melissa, telling her that he was going to stay in Pittsburgh. His loyalty to the Union would not allow him to return to Virginia now with a clear conscience. It was for her to decide whether she wanted to stay with Uncle Edward or come to Pittsburgh.

Dr. Jim White's office was full of men when Jeremiah entered. His dental practice had swelled enormously of late. One of the army's prerequisites was healthy teeth. One had to tear open a cartridge with one's teeth, not to mention the difficulty in eating hardtack.

Jeremiah put on his smock and washed his hands, something which he always did, even though most doctors thought it a waste of time. His first patient entered the examining room, a light brown-haired man with a Vandyke beard. He was thin, of medium height, and walked with a cane, although he was only in his middle twenties.

"Good morning, Henry," he said. "How's the leg today?"

"Better, I think. It doesn't hurt anymore like it used to, but it's stiff as hell."

"Take off your trousers, and we'll have a look."

"You look worried about something, Jeremiah."

"I guess I am. I had a letter from my sister. She's in Richmond. Our father died."

"Oh, I'm sorry to hear it."

"Thank you. But my problem now is trying to get a letter back to her. The mails are terrible."

"I know."

Jeremiah examined the healing stitches along the back

96

of Henry's left calf. The ligaments and muscles had been torn badly in an accident.

"It's healing nicely."

"But they still won't let me in the army."

"No. Not with that. You'll always have a limp, and you'd never make a good soldier with a gimpy leg."

"I may be able to serve my country in another way," Henry smiled. "If you say I'm fit enough to travel."

"Travel how?"

"By train."

"No, I don't think you'll have any trouble. Just don't run any races. And use your cane."

"That's all I wanted to know, Doc. By the way, if you're interested in getting a letter to your sister, I may be able to help. I'll get back to you about it—tomorrow at the latest."

The mysterious patient left the office.

Henry Walkenfeldt was a young German-born newspaper reporter. Any chance of his enlisting in the army had been thwarted a month before, when his leg got caught in some machinery while he was covering a coal-mining accident in Mifflin Township. He had been bitterly disappointed when he was rejected by the army without any hope of ever being accepted, for he deeply believed in the preservation of the Union. However, owing to his uncanny ability to ferret out information, he had been recently approached by several agents of Allan Pinkerton, the noted detective. He now saw an opportunity to serve his country.

He passed Allegheny City Park where the regimental band of the Thirteenth Pennsylvania Volunteers was practicing and turned into an office building, his cane tapping his progress up the stairs. He entered the tiny

97

office of Jonathon Clark, the Pinkerton man.

"Sit down, Mr. Walkenfeldt. What do the doctors say? Are you ready to travel?"

"I am."

"And you're sure you want this assignment?"

"Yes, sir."

The man smiled. "Excellent. We've been making all the arrangements. You'll leave in two days, on May 20. You'll have forged papers and letters, establishing you as a newspaperman from California. Did you read all that information I gave you about California?"

"Yes, and studied it very carefully. I feel as if I've just come from there. How exactly am I to get into Richmond?"

"I'm coming to that. You'll take the train to Philadelphia, then on to Washington City, where you'll contact another of our men. From there, you'll be taken to Arlington and then to Alexandria. We have a good many troops in that area at the moment. From Alexandria, it should be no problem to get to Richmond. We'll leave it to you to get established there. We've gone over that all before. Once you're settled in, you'll be contacted by one of our agents."

"Are there many agents in Richmond?"

"Very few right now. Are you still game?"

"I'm game. It seems to be the only game I can play now."

Richmond was becoming a very busy city. Its population was growing constantly. Nancy had joined with a group of other women to form one of the many sewing circles, where they gave up the more frivolous lace hankies for uniforms. Mahaley and some of her friends were also busy scraping lint and rolling bandages.

Andrew went daily for his training to the Central Fair Grounds, about a mile out of the city, which was used for the camp of instruction. There he was drilled in military exercises by Colonel Smith and his corps of cadets from the Virginia Military Institute at Lexington. A Colonel Gillam was placed in command of the camp, and from the raw recruits, he sent out many regiments of well-trained soldiers. Virginians were not a military people, and everything pertaining to war had to be learned.

The railroad brought in soldiers from all the Confederacy, and the white tents of the camps dotted the landscapes surrounding Richmond. The populace turned out at the depots to greet the soldiers, and they bore the appearance of guests at a holiday festival. The evening dress parades attracted admiring crowds of ladies, to whom every soldier seemed a hero.

All the states of the South were represented in and around the camps of Richmond, and the striking characteristics of the people of each state were plainly distinguishable: the glowing enthusiasm of the South Carolinian; the cool determination of the Virginian; the fiery impetuosity of the Louisianian; the steady courage of the Arkansas man; the wild ardor of the Mississippian; the active energy of the Tennessean. The Kentuckian, the Georgian, the North Carolinian, the Missourian, and of course the Texan, each had his distinctive characteristics.

On May 20, President Jefferson Davis arrived in Richmond, to the cheers of the populace. In honor of his arrival, almost every house in the city was decorated with the Stars and Bars, including the Armstrong residence. The president's entourage, including his favorite aide,

General Wigfall, and Secretary of State Robert Toombs, had been greeted with enthusiasm at every stop on their journey. At every railroad station, men, women, and children turned out to cheer the chief of state. At Richmond, Davis was received with equal élan, and he addressed the crowds at the fairgrounds. "We have now reached the point," he said, "where, arguments being exhausted, it only remains for us to stand by our weapons."

A suite of rooms was ready at the Spotswood Hotel for the president's use until the executive mansion was finished. His wife, Varina Howell Davis, and their three children would join him in Richmond in a week, and a ball was being planned in her honor.

Melissa had been in the office of the *Journal* when the presidential party arrived. Her ever-increasing anxiety over her feelings was beginning to wear on her nerves. She was surrounded by zealous southerners, yet she felt herself becoming more and more in favor of the Union. Edward had landed a job as a clerk in the War Department, and supper conversations centered on that topic.

Andrew was soon to leave for Manassas, about thirty miles from the city, where the Confederate forces were gathering under General Beauregard. Melissa had to admit Andrew looked splendid in his new uniform, even more handsome than usual. He had been mustered in as a sergeant, partly owing to the fact that he had once attended VMI and partly to his family's good name, but because of his education, he would most likely receive a promotion before he ever saw action. His uniform trousers were of light blue with a dark-blue stripe, he wore a double-breasted gray frock coat with two rows of seven buttons, and light-blue facing and piping. A hunting horn on the brass infantry badge was worn on top of his kepi with his regimental number on the front of the cap. His father had presented him with a brand new US rifle musket, .58-caliber 1855 Harper's Ferry model, complete with bayonet and black leather cartridge pouch, and a bone-handled Bowie knife with his name carved into it. His mother had given him a small testament to carry in his knapsack, while Mahaley had sewn him a sash to match the blue facings on his jacket. Margaret, in her late stages of pregnancy, had knitted him three pairs of socks. Joining in the spirit of things, Melissa had supplied him with a "housewife," a small leather case containing needles, thread, thimble, and extra buttons.

Andrew loved all the attention he was getting—not only from his family, but from every lady in the city, it seemed. The men in uniform were flattered and praised and flirted with by practically every female in Richmond. He was certainly glad he had never settled down to one girl before, for now he had his choice of any belle in the city.

As Melissa returned home in the afternoon from her day at the paper, she was distressed about the latest developments. While Union troops were taking over Alexandria, a young New Yorker, Colonel Elmer Ellsworth, had been shot by the proprietor of a tavern from which he was taking down the Confederate flag. The tavern owner was promptly bayoneted, and now both North and South had their first martyrs.

A message was awaiting her from Lieutenant Vaughn. He had returned and requested to escort her to the President's Ball on May 27. She was thrilled with the idea. Even if she didn't believe in the causes of the

Confederacy, this was an honor indeed.

She ran upstairs and looked through her clothes. The four dresses Sabina had made were lovely, but definitely not appropriate for a ball. "Lordy, it's only two days away!" she muttered. "Sabina could never fix me up with anything in that time!"

She hurried back downstairs and into the kitchen. Bobo was sitting at the table watching Tunia make doughnuts.

"Oh, Bobo, I'm so glad you're here. I was going to look for you. Could you drive me to Sabina's dress shop now?"

"Yessum, Miss Melissa. I be glad to. Masta Edward, he say fo' me to fetch him at his work at five."

"You can drop me off and then go get him and pick me up on your way back. I'll go get my things and be right out."

"Yessum, Miss Melissa."

After Melissa had left the kitchen, Tunia turned to Bobo. "I likes dat girl. She don't order us to do sompin she ax us if'n we kin do it."

Bobo grabbed a doughnut before Tunia had a chance to stop him.

"Put dat back!" she yelled after him as he went out the door.

Melissa gathered up her reticule and put on her bonnet and cloak. Bobo assisted her into the carriage and drove her to Sabina's. When Melissa entered the shop, Sabina was almost ready to go home for the night.

"Oh, Sabina, I know this is very short notice, but I've been invited to the President's Ball, and I haven't anything to wear."

"The President's Ball! How exciting! However did you do that?"

"I met an officer—a Lieutenant Vaughn. He asked me. Can you help me?"

"I think you may be in luck. Just this morning a woman came in and canceled an order on a gown. Her husband joined the army, and she doesn't want to spend the extra money right now. The gown's nearly completed, and if you like it, I can have it altered to fit you and finished in time."

"Oh Sabina, you're an angel!"

One look at the gown and Melissa fell in love with it. It was peach-colored satin. The bodice was decidedly more daring than anything she had ever worn, but she rather liked the way her figure looked in it.

"Oh Melissa, you'll truly be the belle of the ball in this," Sabina said. "It's almost a perfect fit. A few alterations here and there . . ."

"Can you have it ready in time?"

"I'll make the time—if you promise to tell me all about the ball and who all was there and what they were doing."

The bell on the door tinkled, and Sabina peeked out the curtain from the back room.

"It's your uncle."

Melissa stuck her head out from the curtain. "I'll be right out, Uncle Edward."

"No hurry, Melissa."

By the time Melissa and Sabina appeared, Edward had stacked a dozen bolts of material on the counter.

"I think I'll take these home."

"What for, Uncle Edward?"

"Just as a precaution. If the blockade gets any tighter, wouldn't want my women running around in rags."

"Shall I put them on your account, Mr. Armstrong?" Sabina asked.

"No, I'll pay you cash."

"Uncle Edward, I've been invited to the President Ball."

"Why, Melissa, that's wonderful. I've been trying wangle an invitation for myself and Nancy."

"Mahaley and I met two cavalry officers—Lieutena Vaughn and Colonel Stuart."

"Not J. E. B. Stuart?"

"Yes."

"I've heard about him. They have great plans for him But isn't he a married man?"

"Yes. I believe he is. I was asked by Lieutenar Vaughn. It's all right for me to go, isn't it?"

"Of course it is. Why don't you see how this pair c white kid gloves fits, and I'll make you a present c them."

"Oh, Uncle Edward, you don't need to do that."

"But, I want to. Besides, it won't hurt my career any t have my niece attend the President's Ball. Let's just sa those gloves are a business investment."

Edward gathered up his parcels, and Sabina tol Melissa to come in early the morning of the twenty seventh for a final fitting. Edward helped Melissa into th carriage and they started on their way home.

"I'll have to send Lieutenant Vaughn a note tellin him that I accept his invitation," she said. "Do you thin I could ask Bobo to deliver it tonight?"

"Bobo, as well as Cindy and Tunia, are at you disposal, my dear. I want you to stop behaving like guest. You're family. I consider you one of my ow children."

Melissa leaned over and kissed his cheek. "Thank you, Uncle Edward. You've made all of this much easier for me. I only wish I knew how Jeremiah was, and if he got my letter."

"I know. I wish there was some way we could rely on the mails. Perhaps this Lieutenant Vaughn could suggest something?"

"Well, I've been doing some thinking, ever since Joseph has been teaching me to operate the telegraph. Do you think Mr. McAllen would let me send a message that way?"

"By God, Melissa, why didn't I think of that!"

"I've been afraid to ask Mr. McAllen. He acts kind of— well, I don't know, like he doesn't like me very much. He hasn't complained about my work, but he's so—well, short with me all the time."

Edward laughed. "Lewis and I had lunch together last week, and he's delighted with your work. You'll have to understand that he's been a bachelor all his life, and he isn't used to women doing anything but sipping tea and making conversation." Edward also had a feeling Lewis was quite taken with Melissa. In fact, he might even go so far as to say he had fallen in love with her.

Melissa had time to compose an acceptance note to Lieutenant Vaughn, asking him to come an hour earlier so her family could meet him, as Edward had suggested. She gave the note to Bobo, telling him to deliver it in person after he had eaten his supper.

At the table that evening, she spent a good bit of time describing her dress to Mahaley and Nancy. Mahaley's earlier envy had abated, for she had her fair share of beaus.

"I have a lovely string of pearls I'd be happy to let you

105

wear," Nancy told her.

"Thank you, Aunt Nancy, but I have my mother's cameo. I know it's not very big, but I'd like to wear it, just the same. I thought I'd fasten it to a velvet ribbon and wear it at my throat."

"Black velvet," Nancy smiled. "Most definitely black, if the dress is peach."

"But my gloves are white."

"That doesn't matter," Mahaley told her. "And you can borrow my lace shawl. The evenings aren't too chilly now, and it would look lovely."

"Ladies," Edward interrupted. "Joseph and I have had quite enough of our lesson on females' fashions for tonight."

Melissa crawled into bed that night and found it difficult to get to sleep for thinking of the lovely gown and the exciting evening ahead.

She awoke with a start to the sound of hurried footsteps and muffled voices in the hall. It was still dark as she sat up, trying to make out the words. Something about Margaret. Margaret must be having the baby.

Melissa threw her feet over the edge of the bed and found her slippers. Her wrapper was still lying at the foot of the bed, and, slipping into it, she stepped out into the hall. She was greeted with an agonizing moan coming from Margaret's room. Mahaley opened her bedroom door just then, and the two girls exchanged glances.

"Do you think there's anything we can do?" Melissa wondered.

"I'll go see."

Mahaley entered the bedroom to find Nancy and Joseph hovering over the bed. Margaret looked white as a sheet.

"Is there anything I can do to help?" she asked, just as Tunia bustled into the room.

The big black woman went over to the bed and touched Margaret's forehead. "I's here, honey. Tunia'll look out fo' you till de doctor get here." She turned to Joseph. "Yo' Mas' Joseph, kin get out, if'n yo' please. Dis ain't no place fo' menfolk."

"But . . ." he began to protest.

Margaret looked at him. "Get out, Joseph."

Mahaley was startled at the tone of her sister's voice. She took Joseph by the hand, leading him out into the hallway.

"Come on, Joseph. Tunia's right. Has anyone gone for the doctor?"

"Yes. Edward went down to send Bobo. I feel like I should be doing something."

"There's nothing you can do."

Melissa joined them and looked questioningly at Mahaley, who shrugged.

"Why don't we go downstairs, and I'll make some coffee?" Melissa suggested.

"That's a good idea. I'll stay up here for a while—till Dr. Cartright gets here," Mahaley said.

Joseph seemed to be in a little bit of a daze about everything.

Melissa felt so sorry for Joseph. After living in the same house with them for a month, she felt Mahaley's assessment of the marriage was correct. Margaret cared very little for her husband.

"Nothing's going to happen to her," she told him. "She's just frightened. She's never had a baby before. She'll be all right."

107

The gas lamps were lit in the parlor, and Edward was standing by the hearth, gazing into the empty fireplace. Andrew was sprawled on the couch.

"How is she doing?" Edward asked.

"I'm sure she's doing fine," Melissa said. "I thought I'd make us some coffee."

Leaving the men, Melissa went into the kitchen to find Cindy sitting at the little table.

"I'm going to make some coffee, Cindy. Why don't you put out some of Tunia's doughnuts? I expect we might be up most of the night."

When Melissa returned to the parlor, followed by Cindy carrying the silver coffee service, Mahaley had joined the men. The doctor had arrived and was upstairs with Margaret. Even though the bedroom door was closed, an occasional cry from Margaret could be heard. Joseph was a nervous wreck, and Andrew finally put a generous measure of brandy in his brother-in-law's coffee.

After more than three hours, Mahaley decided this business of giving birth was more harrowing than she had thought it to be, and gave a silent prayer, hoping that she wouldn't find herself in that situation.

Melissa finally went back upstairs to see how things were coming along. Nancy stuck her head out the door in answer to her knock.

"Everyone is so concerned," Melissa said. "It's been such a long time. How's she doing?"

Just then they heard the doctor say, "It's coming."

Nancy shut the door and went back inside the room. Melissa leaned against the wall and sighed, wondering if having babies was worth all the trouble. Of course it is, she chided herself. After a few minutes, she heard a

108

baby's wail. She sighed again.

The door opened and Tunia came out with a bunch of towels.

"It's a boy!" she announced. "A li'l pink baby boy!"

After the congratulations, back-patting, and hugging were through, Melissa went back to her room. She finally drifted off to sleep, but it was nearly morning by then.

Melissa peeked in at the baby before leaving for the paper. Joseph was so exhausted that he decided to stay home. She was rather tired herself, and now she was going to have to do Joseph's job as well as her own.

She found herself staring at the telegraph key for some time, contemplating sending a wire to Pittsburgh. She asked permission from Lewis McAllen, and he fumed and fussed, but finally relented. She made it short and to the point, hoping the message would get through.

As the train bringing President Davis's wife and children pulled into the station, Henry Walkenfeldt stood among the crowd, watching as the family got into their carriage and drove away. He squinted into the sunshine and smiled. He had arrived only an hour earlier. Picking up his bag, he left the depot to find lodgings, which was no simple task in this already crowded city. It was after sundown when he finally located a small room by the waterfront. After a glass of beer and a sandwich in the tavern, he picked up several newspapers and returned to his room. Tomorrow he would have to look for a job.

Before he was twenty-four hours old, young Jefferson Davis Boone had already become the center of attention in the Armstrong household. Joseph was the father, but one would never guess it by Margaret's actions.

The day promised to be a pleasant one as Melissa awoke. It was Saturday, the day of the ball. After a hurried breakfast, she left for Sabina's and her final fitting. Only a few darts needed to be changed, and by noon Melissa was once again home. She dropped her change into the money box, wondering if her father would approve of her spending so much on clothes . . . and using Confederate notes to do so. Edward and the majority of the inhabitants of Richmond had complete faith in the Confederate treasury, but Melissa wasn't so sure. She preferred the feel of coins to paper, and was glad any change she got back from her purchases was in US currency.

After bathing and washing her hair, she worked on fastening her mother's cameo to the black velvet ribbon. Her hair still damp, she went down to the kitchen to get a bite to eat. Tunia was also eating at the table.

She stood up. "Yo' want fo' me to fix yo' sompin', missy?"

"No thank you, Tunia. I'll find something. You sit down and finish your meal."

Tunia rolled her eyes and sat back down. By now, she had learned that Melissa was a different breed from the majority of whites she had known.

"Miss Melissa, kin I ax yo' sompin'?"

"What is it?"

"Did yo' folks own slaves where yo' come from?"

"No we didn't. Not very many people around there did. We didn't need to. Why?"

"Just wonderin'. Yo' don't treat us like we slaves."

"I'd rather think of you as a friend."

110

Melissa sat down with a piece of cold chicken and a glass of milk, well aware that Edward wouldn't like her eating in the kitchen.

"Dese Yankees I hearin' about all de time . . ." Tunia began.

"Yes?"

"Is it true dey wants to make us free?"

Melissa was in a dilemma. She wanted to speak honestly to Tunia, but the war was something you didn't discuss with slaves. People were afraid they would run away or become surly. And Melissa didn't want to cause problems in the household.

"The Yankees want to do a lot of things. Tell me, Tunia, what do you think of little Jeff?"

"Oh, dat baby!" Tunia laughed, revealing several missing teeth. "He de cutest li'l thing. He gonna be a big boy when he grow up." She shook her head sadly. "Po' Mas' Joseph. I jus' don' undastan' dat Margaret. She act like he ain't even de father. And I knows he is. She hardly let him touch her, let alone any otha' man." Tunia clapped her big hand over her mouth. "I reckon I should keep my big mouth shut."

Melissa smiled. "It's all right, Tunia. Mahaley said something like that before. And I've noticed how she is with Joseph."

"I expect some gals jus' don't know when dey's well off."

Mahaley returned from her afternoon with one of the South Carolina boys to get ready for Melissa's caller. She wanted to make an impression, hoping Lieutenant Vaughn might have a friend. Melissa had Cindy help her

111

into her gown and do her hair. When she looked at herself in the full-length mirror, she hardly recognized the country girl from Shady Run.

Edward was in the parlor with Joseph and Nancy.

"Melissa, you're absolutely gorgeous!" Nancy exclaimed.

"You'll be the most beautiful girl there tonight," Edward agreed. "I only wish your father could see you."

At the sound of a carriage outside, Melissa peeked out the window. "Lordy, it's him! It must be later than I thought."

Cindy escorted the soldier into the parlor. He stood for a moment at the doorway, where Melissa got the full effect of his handsome figure in his cavalry uniform: his gray frock coat with yellow collar, cuffs, and piping; a yellow silk sash encircling his waist. His trousers were light blue, tucked into shiny black boots. A saber dangled from black leather slings at his waist.

Melissa felt a rush of excitement as he stepped into the room.

Edward approached him, offering his hand. "I'm Edward Armstrong, Melissa's uncle."

"My honor, sir."

Edward made the introductions and bade him sit down. Jackson sat on one side of the settee, and Melissa on the other. She smiled at him shyly.

"Would you care for some sherry, Lieutenant Vaughn?" Edward asked. "Or something a bit stronger, perhaps?"

"Whiskey, if you please."

"Ladies, how about you?"

"Sherry would be fine, Edward," Nancy told him, Melissa nodding agreement.

As Edward was dispensing the spirits, Mahaley appeared.

"Hello, Lieutenant Vaughn."

"Hello, Miss Armstrong. It's nice to see you again."

After Edward served the libations, Melissa turned to Jackson. "How was your trip from Montgomery?"

"Very interesting. We were kept very busy with the president. He was so mobbed with well-wishers at every stop, it was hard to keep an eye on him."

"Is it true there have been threats on his life?" Nancy asked.

"Oh yes. But he expects that sort of thing. He says he can't let it scare him. He has a job to do."

"Then you must know the president quite well?" Edward asked.

"I know him. I wouldn't say well though." He looked at Melissa. "I did think if we left a little earlier, I might have an opportunity to introduce you to him before all the guests arrive."

"Oh, I'd like that very much."

Edward smiled again. Something like this might be used to his advantage.

"I take it you were in the military before the war?" Edward asked him.

"Yes. I entered West Point back in fifty-two. Jeb and I helped Bob Lee with that John Brown business."

"What kind of a man is this Lee?"

"He's a brilliant soldier. I personally feel if anyone can lick the Yankees, it's going to be him."

"You don't for a moment doubt that we can, do you?" Nancy asked.

"No, ma'am. They aren't any more ready than we are, only we've got the will to fight."

113

"Here! Here!" Nancy applauded. "I think we should have another sherry to that."

Jackson stood up. "There's nothing I'd like better, ma'am, but if we want to talk to the president, I think we should be on our way." He turned to Melissa. "Are you ready?"

"Yes."

Jackson helped Melissa with her shawl, and, after fastening his own cloak and picking up his plumed hat, ushered her out the door. He assisted her into the carriage and then got in beside her.

"Is this your carriage?" she asked.

"No. I hired it for tonight." He put his hand over hers. "Miss Armstrong, may I say I think you're the loveliest girl I've ever met in my life?"

"Why, Lieutenant . . ."

"I mean it. I've thought about you ever since that day we met. I hope you won't think me forward, but I don't know how much time I may have before I leave."

"Leave for where?"

"Probably up toward Manassas. I'm not a forward man, Miss Armstrong, but these times make a man speak his mind sooner than he normally would."

"I understand."

"Then you're not offended?"

"No, I'm not offended. I'm very flattered."

"That's a great relief to me. I was afraid you might think me too brash."

"You're very brash, Lieutenant Vaughn. But under the circumstances, it can be excused."

In the fading light inside the carriage, she looked into his dark eyes, and they seemed to be looking straight into her soul. As his face neared hers, she began to lean

114

oward him, but then she realized how bold she must
appear to him. She drew back and settled herself more
comfortably on the seat of the carriage.

"Tell me about yourself, Lieutenant Vaughn."

He cleared his throat. "What would you like to
now?"

"Oh, I don't know. You said you went to West Point."

"Yes. My brother John and I both did, when our papa
lied. My mama died when I was a boy. Papa didn't have
any money, and we didn't have any kind of trade. I was
sixteen and John was fifteen."

"Is he in the army now too?"

"Yes. He's a major with the Union Army."

"The Union Army!"

"Yes. He got married and lives with his wife and
children in Washington City. She's somehow distantly
related to Secretary Seward. He decided to stay. I
resigned my commission and went with Virginia when
he left the Union. I grew up here. It's my home."

"It must be very difficult for you."

"I'm not unique. I'm sure there are a lot of others in
my position."

"Perhaps. In a way, I'm in the same situation myself.
My brother's in Pittsburgh."

"Is he with the army?"

"I certainly hope not. I don't really think so. He went
up there several years ago to study medicine."

The carriage came to a halt in front of an elegant
mansion on Clay Street. Jackson and Melissa were met by
a liveried servant who took their wraps. Melissa gazed
about at all the opulent furnishings as they entered the
large room already full of mingling people.

115

Jeb hurried over to greet them.

"Miss Armstrong, what a surprise!"

"How are you, Colonel Stuart?"

"Delighted to see you again, indeed. May I say Jackson, you're a very fortunate man. I hope you'll le me have at least one dance with her?"

"Perhaps just one," Jackson smiled.

"Isn't your wife with you, Colonel Stuart?" Melissa asked him.

"No, I'm afraid not. She's still at our home."

Jackson took Melissa's elbow. "I think now would be a good time to visit with Mr. Davis. There aren't too many people around them now."

"Will you excuse us, Colonel Stuart?"

"Only for a little while, Miss Armstrong."

Melissa didn't feel as nervous as she thought she woul be as Jackson steered her across the room. Jefferson Davis was a slight man, not appearing to weigh more than one hundred pounds, but his bearing was very erect making him his full six feet. He was very neatly dressed with piercing gray-blue eyes, even though a severe attack of glaucoma in 1858 had left him blind in one of them

"Ah, Lieutenant Vaughn, how good it is you could join us," Jefferson Davis smiled, shaking his hand.

"It's my honor, Mr. President. May I present my companion, Miss Melissa Armstrong?"

Davis smiled warmly and took her hand. "A pleasure my dear. You're not related to the Armstrongs of Amelia County, are you?"

"No, sir. I'm from Mason County, out west. My uncl lives here in the city, though. Edward Armstrong."

"I'm afraid I don't know him. My wife noticed you the minute you came in. Remarked on the color of you gown." He touched his wife's arm. She turned her attention away from the man with whom she had been speaking. "Varina, this is Miss Melissa Armstrong. The young lady you remarked about."

"How happy I am to meet you," Mrs. Davis said, taking Melissa's hand. "Your gown caught my eye the minute you walked in. It's exquisite."

"Thank you, Mrs. Davis."

Varina Howell Davis, twenty years her husband's junior, was a tall, commanding figure with dark hair, eyes, and complexion; and a full and expressive mouth. She was a handsome woman, but not one normally termed as pretty. Melissa felt at ease with her at once.

"This is Lieutenant Vaughn," Davis told his wife. "He was with me on the trip from Montgomery."

A servant came by with a tray of glasses. Jackson did the honors, handing the first glass to the president, then serving Mrs. Davis, Melissa, and himself.

"May I propose a toast to you, sir," he said.

"I would rather we drink to the success of the Confederacy and all that it stands for."

Putting aside her political feelings for the moment, Melissa drank the sparkling liquid. It tickled all the way down her throat.

"Excellent champagne," Davis remarked.

So this is champagne, Melissa thought. Why, I rather like it.

"You must tell me where you had that gown made," Varina told her. "Is it from Paris?"

"Oh no, ma'am. I had it done right here in the city. At Sabina's."

"I'll have to look into that."

Melissa took another drink of champagne, laughing to

117

herself as she pictured the look on Sabina's face when the first lady of the Confederacy walked into her shop.

Several more people joined them, and Jackson felt it was time to move on.

"If you'll excuse us," he nodded to the president and Mrs. Davis.

Jackson and Melissa spoke to several other guests and it was soon time for the buffet supper to be served.

"Shall I fix you a plate?" he asked her.

"Please."

"I'll tell you what. . . . You see that settee over there in that corner? Why don't you get us two glasses of wine and save us a place over there?"

Melissa had no sooner sat down with the wine when she was joined by Mrs. Davis.

"Oh, I'm so glad to get a chance to sit down," Varina told her. "I saw you over here in this quiet little corner and decided this was a good place to avoid all the guests. I do love people, but tonight I'm still a little tired from my journey. You don't mind, do you?"

"No, not at all."

"I imagine your young lieutenant will be joining you?"

"Yes. He's gone to get us something to eat."

"He's very good-looking. Have you known him long?"

"Not very. I've just been in the city for a month."

"Oh really? Where are you from originally?"

"Mason County. I moved here after my father died. I'm living with my uncle and his family."

Jackson reappeared with two heaping plates of food. Despite the fact that she was the president's wife, he wished Varina had picked someplace else to sit. He wanted to be alone with Melissa, if one could consider it eing alone in a room full of people.

"Oh, here you are, Lieutenant," Varina said. "Oh, at looks delicious. I wonder if I could impose on you nd ask you to fix me a plate?"

"I'd be happy to. As a matter of fact, why don't you ke this one and I'll just go and get myself another one."

Melissa watched Jackson move away through the owd and then turned back to Mrs. Davis.

"My cousin had her first baby the other night, and ey named him in honor of your husband—Jefferson avis Boone."

Varina laughed. "That's wonderful. Let us hope he ows up to be a free citizen of the Confederate States of merica."

"Yes," Melissa murmured.

Jackson returned with his plate and another glass of ine and seated himself on the floor at Melissa's feet.

They never did have any time alone together until they ached the dance floor. Melissa was surprised at what a od dancer Jackson was, for his rugged appearance idn't suggest an aptitude for gracefulness. She did feel e was holding her a little closer than was necessary, but, khilarated with the wine and the gaiety, she didn't mind the least. In fact, she rather liked it.

She danced the Virginia reel with Jeb Stuart, and was tonished when Jefferson Davis asked her for a waltz.

On the way back to the house in the carriage, Jackson id Melissa were discussing the events of the evening.

"The regimental band is giving a concert at Metropoli-n Hall next Friday evening," Jackson told her. "It's not ing to be anything like a symphony of the classics, ind you, just patriotic songs and popular tunes. I

119

wonder if you'd care to go with me?"

"Yes, I'd like that very much."

"Perhaps we could have a late supper afterwar
Hopefully, I might be able to reserve a bottle
champagne. You liked that, didn't you?"

"Yes. I've never had it before. But isn't it terribl
expensive?"

"I can't think of anything or anybody I'd rather spen
my money on than you. Besides, we might as well tak
advantage of it while it's available. I'm not sure ho
much will be getting through the blockade."

Jackson escorted Melissa to the door. She fumble
with the lock for several minutes until Jackson took th
key from her and opened the door on the first try. H
stepped inside the hall with her and handed her the ke

"Thank you very much, Lieutenant Vaughn. I had
wonderful time."

"Did you really?"

"Yes."

"I'm glad. I enjoyed it too." He stepped closer to he
placing his hands lightly on either side of her face. "
enjoyed being with you. What happened the rest of th
evening, I didn't care about." His thumbs were gentl
stroking her face. "You're beautiful, do you know that?
Suddenly his lips were upon hers, warm and soft, h
mustache scratching her ever so lightly. He drew bac
and smiled at her. "I'll look forward to next Friday, Mis
Armstrong—Melissa. Good night."

"Good night," she murmured, watching him as h
went out the door. She stood there for a moment, tryir
to regain her composure. She didn't know quite what ha
happened to her when Jackson had kissed her. She ha
had an urge to throw her arms around his neck and spen

120

the rest of the evening in his arms. She turned around and slowly went up the stairs, never before having been so physically attracted to any man.

She was surprised to find Cindy dozing in a chair in her room.

"What are you doing here?" she asked the girl.

"I's waitin' to help you get outten yo' dress." Cindy came over to unfasten the hooks at the back of the gown. "Mas' Edward, he mighty happy 'bout you goin' to dis party."

"Why?"

"Don't know. Yo' wants waked fo' church in de mawnin'?"

"Yes, Cindy."

Melissa sent Cindy on her way once the unreachable hooks had been taken care of and the corset lacings undone. She couldn't get used to having another person help her dress.

The breakfast table conversation centered around Melissa's evening.

"The president danced with you?" Nancy exclaimed. "Oh, what an honor!"

"He's very nice," Melissa told her. "Very polite and courteous. He doesn't really seem like I imagined a president should be."

"How exciting!" Nancy laughed.

"And Lieutenant Vaughn. Did you have a good time with him?" Mahaley queried.

"Yes. He's quite charming. He asked me to attend a concert next Friday evening. Is that all right with you, Uncle Edward?"

"Whatever you like. You're a grown woman now. You

don't need to ask my permission. I only ask that you and Mahaley use good judgment in the company you keep. I'm sure I don't need to warn you to keep away from those Louisiana Zouaves."

Andrew laughed. "I even keep away from them. I hope they don't get sent along with my unit."

"I wish you weren't leaving tomorrow, dear," Nancy sighed.

"Mother, if I'm to be a soldier, I have to go where I'm sent. I can't just sit around in my uniform. Besides, it's only up to Harper's Ferry."

"I know. But I can't help worrying."

Bobo brought the carriage around for the ladies, while Andrew and Edward rode their horses. It was only a short distance to St. Paul's, but Edward liked the appearance they presented.

Immediately, they noticed a section had been reserved, and soon after they settled in their pew, the Davis family entered the church—Jefferson, Varina, Jefferson, Jr., Maggie, and Joseph. Mrs. Davis recognized Melissa as she passed and smiled pleasantly.

After the service, Varina Davis took her family over to Melissa's where introductions were made.

"I see you have a soldier in the family," Davis remarked.

"Yes, sir," Andrew replied. "I leave for Harper's Ferry tomorrow under General Johnston."

"I wish you Godspeed," Davis told them. "This war will be fought on Virginia's soil, I know that now. What happens here will determine the fate of the Confederacy."

Six

Melissa was working on the paper, correcting spelling on an article about arms. When the Harper's Ferry arsenal had been taken over by the Confederate Government, it contained thousands of flintlock rifles. Now they were being converted into Minie muskets by substituting a percussion lock for the flintlock, grooving the barrel, and adding a sight at the breech—all for the cost of $1.50 per gun.

The door opened and in stepped a young man with a cane. The office was relatively empty, for most of the employees were lined up waiting for the president's parade.

"May I help you?" questioned Melissa.

"I'd like to speak with the owner of the paper. Is he in?"

"I believe so. I'll see. Who shall I say is calling?"

"My name is Henry Walkenfeldt."

Melissa tapped on the door at the rear of the office and entered. "Excuse me, Mr. McAllen. There's a gentleman who would like to see you. His name is Henry Walkenfeldt."

"Henry who? I don't know him. What's he want?"

"I don't know—I didn't ask him."

Lewis muttered under his breath. "Oh all right. Send him in."

Melissa returned to the young man and opened the wooden gate for him to enter. Pointing toward the back she said, "You may go in."

"Thank you." Henry took two steps and then turned to Melissa, asking quietly, "By the way, what's his name?"

"Lewis McAllen—and he's grumpy as an old bear."

"Thank you."

Henry entered the tiny office and introduced himself.

"I don't have much time to spare," Lewis said. "I'm very busy. Half of my decent men have gone off and joined the army."

"Then perhaps I came to the right place. I'm a journalist. I've been in California for the past six years. I came to Richmond hoping to find a job reporting the true facts about the Confederacy. I'm a firm believer in the South. I'd join the army myself, only I've got a bad leg."

"You say you were a reporter in California?"

"Yes. In San Francisco and Sacramento. Would you care to see my credentials?" Henry produced an envelope from his breast pocket.

Lewis waved it away. "No need. Why did you come to this paper?"

"I already stopped at the *Examiner*. Mr. Daniel said he didn't need anyone right now."

"Oh, that Daniel!" Lewis grumbled. "We don't see eye to eye anyway. He says I sensationalize the news. I say bullshit to that. I print what people like to read." Lewis leaned back and studied the young man a little more carefully. "You say you believe in the cause,

124

Mr.—ah . . . ?"

"Walkenfeldt. Yes, I definitely believe in the cause."

"I'll tell you what. I'll put you on for a week. You write me something interesting I like, and we'll talk on a more permanent basis. We'll talk salary then too."

"Very well." Henry stood up and shook hands with Lewis. "Thank you, Mr. McAllen."

As Henry left Lewis's office, he paused at Melissa's desk.

"I'm going to be working on the paper from now on. My name's Henry Walkenfeldt."

She accepted his outstretched hand. "Yes, I know. You told me. That's not an easy name to forget. Mine's Melissa Armstrong."

Henry was momentarily shaken. She must be the one I brought the letter for, he thought. I wonder—could it be? Yes, I can see a little of Jeremiah there.

"I'm happy to meet you," she was saying. "Where are you from? You don't talk like a Southerner."

"I've been in California."

"In the gold mines?"

Henry smiled. "I don't look that old, do I? But you're right. I was up around there."

"Well, I'm very glad you'll be working here. Maybe now things will be a little more cheery around here."

"I'll do my best, Miss Armstrong. Good day."

Henry wandered over to watch the parade; Jefferson Davis was on his gray Arab, and Robert E. Lee rode at his side.

"Henry, how good to run into you," a man said, slapping his back.

Startled, Henry turned to look at the stranger.

"Why don't we go over to the Swan Tavern and have a

125

drink?" the man suggested. "And talk about our mutual friend, Jonathon Clark."

The Pinkerton man had found him.

Edward came into the *Journal's* office near closing time. He let himself through the little wooden gate. "Hello, Melissa. I have to talk to Lewis for a while. I'll walk home with you." He took an envelope from his pocket and gave it to her. "This was at the post office for you."

"Thank you, Uncle Edward."

Edward went on back to Lewis's office while Melissa hurriedly opened the letter from Jeremiah, not noticing it was postmarked from Richmond.

"Edward," Lewis greeted. "Sorry I couldn't make it for lunch today. I've been having a hell of a time with all my boys off in the army. Like a drink?"

"I wouldn't mind."

While Lewis was taking a bottle from his bottom desk drawer, Edward took another envelope from his pocket, this one much thicker.

"Augustus says this is only the beginning," Edward said, accepting the glass. "There's five hundred in bonds there—all profit, once our initial expenses are deducted. He says he figured we'd be running in the red for a few months, but we're not, as you can see. The price of nails has already gone from $4.00 to $6.50 a keg."

"That's good news. The best I've had in a long time. I'm afraid this paper's going to be running in the red."

"Problems?"

"Oh, yes and no. The writers I've got now are all the bottom of the barrel—or the bottle, whichever. I did hire a new fellow today. I hope he works out. People want

126

something more than we've been giving them."

"How's Melissa working out?"

"Melissa? Oh, she's a peach. If I wasn't so strapped financially, I might even give her a raise. We've gotten three more advertisers last week alone because of her." Lewis swallowed his whiskey and smacked his lips. "You know, I had my doubts about hiring a woman, but I'm beginning to think it was the wisest move I've made in a long time. I don't need to worry about her drinking or whoring around. Besides, she makes a damned good pot of coffee."

"Perhaps you should tell her how much you appreciate her?"

"Why?"

"She thinks you don't like her."

"That's nonsense. I just don't feel I should hand out praise merely because she's a woman."

Melissa was waiting for Edward when he came out of the office.

"The letter was from Jeremiah," she told him, as they left the paper. "He got my letter and, of course, he was very upset about Papa. He's going to stay in Pittsburgh to finish his schooling."

"He hasn't turned into a little Yankee, has he?"

Melissa didn't answer her uncle directly. "He's doing very well and he feels if he came here, his training would be disrupted. He's not going to join the army or anything. I can't say I blame him. Things are in an uproar here now. He says it's my decision where I want to live. And I think I'll stay here."

"That's the spirit. This'll all be over with soon, and then we'll all get together as a family again."

"I don't think President Davis thinks it'll be over soon."

Three days later, Melissa was working in the office when Jackson came in.

"Good afternoon, Lieutenant Vaughn. What brings you in here?"

"I wanted to remind you about tomorrow evening. I'll call for you at six. I made reservations at the Ballard House for supper at ten. Can you wait that long, or will you starve?"

She giggled. "I'll survive."

"They're holding a bottle of champagne too."

Henry came in, and Melissa introduced the two men.

"What happened to your leg?" Jackson asked.

"I got caught in a mining accident," Henry replied; then bit his tongue for his slip.

"Yes," Melissa explained. "Mr. Walkenfeldt spent a lot of time in the California gold country."

Henry relaxed, silently blessing Melissa for that plausible explanation.

"What's your unit?" Henry asked him.

"Stuart's cavalry."

"I've heard good things about them."

"He's a fine soldier. I've known him since we were in West Point together. We'll be leaving for Manassas Sunday, to join General Beauregard. I think he's planning to invade Washington City."

Henry nodded.

Jackson and Melissa seated themselves in their seats at Metropolitan Hall. The theater was full of people, including several government officials in the balcony boxes. Jackson was enjoying himself immensely, surreptitiously peeking at Melissa's cleavage.

The band played several ballads, then broke into a chain of patriotic songs including "The Southern Chaunt of Defiance," "The Bonnie Blue Flag," "I'm a Good Old Rebel," "The Jeff Davis Quickstep," "The Confederate March," and, of course, "Dixie."

At the Ballard House, Jackson had reserved a quiet little table in the corner of the dining room. The waiter brought the champagne, and after turning the bottle in the silver tub of ice, popped the cork. Melissa was fascinated by this little rite, watching the bubbles crash into one another as Jackson passed the glass to her. The waiter departed and Melissa wondered for a moment if Jackson had forgotten about supper, for she was very hungry.

Jackson lifted his glass to her. "Now, what shall we drink to?"

"I don't know. I'm not very well versed in proposing toasts."

"Could I suggest we drink to us?"

"Us?"

"Yes. You and me, and whatever the future may hold for either of us."

When Melissa looked into the dark recesses of Jackson's eyes, she once again felt that sensation of warmth course through her body. She smiled. "Very well, Lieutenant. To us."

Jackson gazed at her over his glass as he drained its contents. Melissa found her glass nearly empty when she put it down on the table.

"That's good," she grinned.

Jackson thought at that moment she looked like a little girl, a very innocent little girl, and he felt a pang of guilt for the thoughts he had been entertaining.

"Miss Armstrong . . . May I call you Melissa?"

"Please do, if I may call you Jackson?"

"I'd like nothing better." He took the bottle from the ice and refilled their glasses.

"How did you get a name like Jackson?"

"My papa was a great admirer of Andrew Jackson. I was born while he was President."

"How old are you, if you don't mind my asking?"

"Twenty-seven. I was born in 1834." He took another sip of his champagne. "Now, may I ask you a question?"

Melissa nodded.

"Why aren't you married? I can't imagine why no one has claimed you yet."

She smiled. "I don't think I really like that term—of being claimed. It sounds like I'm a piece of property waiting to be picked up at the pawn shop."

"Then, let me rephrase it. . . ."

"Never mind," she laughed. "I know what you mean." Her stomach growled. "When are we going to order supper?"

"I've already done that. I came by this afternoon and told the chef what I wanted. I hope you don't mind."

"No." She was a little awed by all this sophistication, and she hoped her unpolished edges weren't too apparent.

"You never answered my question," he reminded her.

"About why I'm not married? It's very simple. I believe you said you hadn't found the right girl? Well, I've never found the right man."

"You mean you never met anyone you thought you'd

like to marry?"

"Well, once maybe," she admitted. "But I was only fourteen at the time."

"And he didn't wait for you to get a little older?"

"I'm afraid not. But he's very happily married now and has two children."

"But you must have had some proposals."

"Oh, yes. I've had proposals, but I didn't consider any of them seriously. They were from boys I'd known all my life—and they came just before they joined the army."

"I hope you don't feel that way about me?"

"What way?"

"That I'm not serious. I don't want you to think that I'm desperately trying to win your affections merely because I'm a soldier."

"Why, Jackson, I didn't know you were trying to win my affections."

Before the conversation could be carried any farther, their supper arrived. Melissa gasped at the plate in front of her when the waiter lifted the domed silver top.

"Why, it's a tiny chicken!"

Jackson had to stifle a laugh. "It's a Cornish game hen."

"What's that?"

"A tiny chicken," he teased.

Melissa enjoyed her meal thoroughly, but found herself growing a little tipsy from the champagne and the wine marinating the food. She was relieved that the meal had come to interrupt their conversation. She found Jackson terribly attractive, but she wasn't sure she wanted to get involved with anyone right now, not in these uncertain times. She liked him well enough, but the only feelings she had for him were purely physical, and

131

that bothered her. Well, it didn't exactly bother her, but she had never experienced it before, at least not to this extent. As she sipped her champagne, she found herself thinking things that she had been told nice young ladies weren't supposed to think about.

"You're very pensive," Jackson told her. "What are you thinking about?"

Melissa reddened. "Oh, nothing."

"You know what I was just thinking?"

"No, what?"

"How much I've enjoyed this evening. And I'll have the memory to take with me when I leave on Sunday."

In the carriage, Jackson touched Melissa's cheek with his fingers. She turned her face and looked into his eyes for a moment, then found his lips in the darkness. She was surprised at the passion with which she kissed him, her fingers twining themselves in his thick black hair. He nuzzled his face against her neck, his lips touching her earlobe. She shivered.

"Melissa," he murmured. "I need you so much. I've never wanted any woman as I want you." He looked into her face. "Come home with me tonight."

"Jackson, I . . ."

His mouth covered hers once more, and as his hand found her breast, she felt her resistance fading.

"Jackson, please, you mustn't ask this of me."

"Why? You want me, I know you do."

"Yes, I do. But not now, not yet. I ask you to respect my wishes."

He kissed her forehead lightly. "I understand. I had no right to suggest such a thing in the first place." He smiled. "Besides, now perhaps I'll have something to look forward to when I return."

"I'm sorry, Jackson."

"Don't be. I'm not."

The carriage came to a stop, and the two of them walked to the porch.

"Will you write me?" he asked.

"Yes. But where will you be?"

"Just send it to Stuart's cavalry. It'll find me."

"When will you be back?"

"I don't know. Very soon, I hope. I might even be able to send you a postcard from Washington City."

Seven

During the months of June and early July, Richmond underwent a series of changes. The effects of the blockade were beginning to be felt. Imported articles such as wines and rich silks could still be found, but only at a highly inflated price. The demand for books such as "The Trooper's Manual," "The Skirmisher's Drill and Bayonet Exercises," and "Instructions in Field Artillery" was high, and the booksellers sold out immediately. Some church basements had become workshops where sewing machines hummed from morning until night, turning out clothing, bedding for hospital wards, haversacks, and tents. The women sewing the heavy tents of cumbersome sailcloth and the thick material for jackets and overcoats soon found themselves with stiff, swollen, bleeding fingers. Basements of other churches were cleared and turned into hospital facilities, with cots set up and the cushions of the pews turned into mattresses.

Social life underwent some changes as well, and it was rare to find a young man on the streets in civilian clothes. The citizens were awakened every morning to the reveille of the drum which called the soldiers to duty. Martial music could be heard in various parts of the city all day. Nothing was seen, nothing was thought of, nothing was talked about but the war which involved them all.

On July 21, Melissa noticed Jefferson Davis was conspicuously absent from the family pew in church. From all outward appearances, no one would have supposed anything unusual had occurred. St. Paul's was filled as usual, but the number of females greatly outnumbered the males. President Davis had left that morning, along with his staff, to visit Manassas.

All that day it was quiet, and a calmness pervaded the city. The citizens knew there was a battle going on, but no word had been received for twenty-four hours.

What happened at the little stream of Bull Run had never been equaled before or since. Nothing went the way it had been planned. For Union and Confederate forces alike, it turned into simply a matter of sending untrained troops into the firing line and hoping for the best. Many of the men lost heart and ran away at the first crack of rifle fire. But many more stayed on and fought with great courage. These men knew so little of what they were about, many of them were shot by their own comrades in the confusion.

When it appeared Union victory was assured, the Federal forces paused for breath and to regroup. But, during this pause, the Confederates began to stiffen their resistance. They were reinforced by the arrival of Johnston's troops from the Shenandoah Valley under General Jubal T. Early.

Among these reinforcements was Second Lieutenant Andrew Armstrong. The dust was so thick and the noise so loud, he blundered blindly along with his comrades. As he watched men fall all around him, he wondered why they made no sounds. He realized that a man didn't groan or cry when hit, he merely sank down silently to the ground or crawled away if he could. A horse gave out shrieks when struck, but the rider was silent. The only sounds on the battlefield he heard were the crash of muskets, the roar of the cannons, the shriek of shells, and the Rebel whoop.

Andrew, like most of his troop, had not tasted food in the last thirty-six hours, and their rations had been scanty before the fight had begun. He was hot, his throat dry, and his feet ached in his boots. So far, he had not fired a shot. As he approached the scene of the fiercest fighting, a shell exploded nearby, and the concussion knocked him down. He scrambled into a ditch by a small creek branch, trying to catch his breath. As he looked up, he saw a man shot in the neck. Instead of falling, the man reached down and scooped up a handful of mud, pressed it against the bullet hole, and continued on fighting. Andrew stumbled out of the ditch and into the fray, wondering what had become of the man.

Union General Irvin McDowell soon realized his big effort had failed, and he called a retreat. This turned out to be a disorganized flight, crowds of men going in all directions.

That evening, the stretcher-bearers began their dreary work, collecting the wounded and carrying them to the field hospitals. Under the cover of a tree, staring at the stars, lay Lieutenant Jackson Vaughn. He had been lying there for about forty-five minutes, listening to the cries and moans and screams of the wounded. He had been given a drink of whiskey and water from a canteen, and now he lay waiting his turn inside the hospital tent. He was glad it was night, glad it was dark. He didn't want to look at his arm. He and his horse had been shot just before the Union retreat. The horse had fallen on him, pinning him under its weight for some two hours before he was found.

He must have lost consciousness for a while, for the next thing he knew, he was being carried into the tent. The sickening sweet odor of fresh blood assailed his nostrils, and as he looked around him, he saw blood everywhere. He was laid on a table and his jacket was cut away from him. The surgeon's apron was also stained with blood as he bent over his wound, and Jackson cried out as his arm was examined.

"It's got to come off."

"*No!*" Jackson screamed, trying to sit up. Hands on his shoulders restrained him.

"I'm sorry," the surgeon said. "There's no saving it."

"I won't allow you to cut off my arm."

"You probably won't live if it stays."

"I'll take my chances, doctor. I'd rather be dead than spend the rest of my life as a one-armed cripple."

The surgeon shrugged and waved for two men. "Get this man out of here and on the first train South."

By Sunday evening, Richmond knew of the Confederate victory at Manassas. There was a deepening conviction in the hearts of thousands in the belief of the Confederacy. Men, women, and children cheered, drunk with glory, filling themselves with joy and pride. But with the victory, came the realization that war was not a grand holiday. The lives of many young men from both North and South had been lost, and war became the grim reality of death and destruction.

The first train bearing fifty Federal prisoners had

arrived that afternoon. For lack of a better place to put them, they were housed in the Libby warehouse. People crowded the pavements outside, hoping for a chance to see the Yankees.

The next day brought rain, which was a great relief to those wounded still on the field. The trains began bringing the wounded into the city. Being unmarried, Mahaley was unacceptable for nursing duties, but Nancy went immediately to volunteer her services. It would give her something to occupy her mind until she received word of Andrew. She went to the Soldier's Rest, a refuge for the sick and wounded located on Clay Street, not far from the parade grounds. It had been a three-room schoolhouse which had been transformed, with whitewashed walls and cots covered with clean linen sheets. The schoolroom proper contained about thirty beds, another room was reserved for patients who might need special attention, and another room set aside for preparing meals.

Hospital accommodations in Richmond were poor, and the citizens opened their homes to the wounded. But if the hospitals were inadequate, the prison facilities were nonexistent. The buildings used for this purpose proved insufficient and unfit for the many men.

Melissa was poring over the lists of the wounded and killed in the newspaper office. Most of these reports were incomplete, but when she came across the list of the Twelfth Virginia and found no mention of Andrew, she felt he was safe.

Henry had been at the train depot all morning and watched the arrival of the bodies of Generals Bernard Bee and Francis Bartow. They were taken to the Senate Room where they would lie in state.

Stopping at various vendors on his return to the paper, he picked up a variety of things for his lunch, buying enough in the hope that Melissa would share it with him. In the time he had been in Richmond, he had been friendly, but not overly so. He lived in fear that he might make that one fatal error, mentioning his acquaintance with her brother.

Henry entered the office and closed the door behind him against the elements, his cloak and hat dripping from the rain.

Melissa looked up from her desk and smiled. "Get very wet?"

"Not too. Where is everybody?"

"Out trying to get information."

Henry deposited his purchases on his desk, across the aisle from Melissa. "I brought some lunch for you, if you're hungry."

"Why thank you, Mr. Walkenfeldt. That's very thoughtful. I didn't have time this morning to pack anything, and I didn't really want to go out in all of this."

"It's nothing fancy," Henry grinned.

"I'll go get us some coffee."

Melissa went to the little stove tucked away in the corner, with its chimney stuck out the window. She imagined the opening would make the office very cold in the winter. When she returned, Henry had divided up the cheese, bread, and peaches. Peaches were something new Henry had discovered, owing to their absence in Pittsburgh.

"What's the depot like?" Melissa asked.

"It's pretty frightening. So many wounded."

"I know. I just don't understand it. It's all so senseless."

"I agree. And there's talk afoot now about the hospitals' facilities being so bad. I don't know what they'll do with the wounded. Did you hear anything about your cousin?"

"Not really. But there was a fairly complete list. He wasn't on it. You heard President Davis's speech last night, didn't you?"

"It wasn't really a speech. He just spoke to the people from the steps of the Spotswood."

"Did he mention Stuart's cavalry?"

"Oh, that's right, your gentleman friend— What's his name?"

"Jackson Vaughn. I know he was going up to Manassas. I'm a little concerned."

"I'll ask around and see if anyone knows anything about it."

Melissa bit into her peach, causing juice to run down her chin.

Henry gave her his handkerchief. "I have the same trouble. Only it gets in my beard." He took out a pocketknife and handed it to her. "Try cutting it in half."

Melissa sliced the peach and set the open knife on the desk, when her eye caught the manufacturer's name on the blade. Picking it up again, she examined it: Brown and Tetley, Pittsburgh, Pa.

"Pittsburgh. Have you ever been in Pittsburgh, Mr. Walkenfeldt?"

"Why no, I haven't."

"Oh," she sighed. "I hope my friends weren't involved in any of that Manassas business."

"Your brother?"

"Yes. And some other friends. They used to stop at our landing on the steamboat. They're very nice. Actually, all the Yankees I've ever met have been very nice. But don't you tell Mr. McAllen I said so. Did I ever tell you about the soldiers from Indiana who helped me when I was coming to Richmond?"

Nancy found her first day at the hospital a little more harrowing than she had anticipated. When she got home, she had Cindy fix her bath and bring a bowl of soup to her room.

Edward came home from his office in the War Department and hurried upstairs to the bedroom.

"Nancy? Where are you?"

"In the tub, Edward."

He stuck his head around the Chinese screen. Nancy reached to cover herself with the towel.

"Oh, for God's sake, Nancy. After twenty-five years of marriage, you have nothing to hide from me."

"Please, Edward."

"Very well," he grumbled, going over to the dresser, thinking that he had to admit she no longer looked like she did twenty-five years ago. "I got word of Andrew. He's unhurt."

"Oh, thank heaven, Edward. I'm so happy. I've been worried to death all day. Those poor boys. So much pain and suffering. If Andrew had come into that hospital like that, I just don't know what I would've done."

Melissa, Mahaley, Margaret, and Edward ate alone that evening. Joseph hadn't come home from work yet. In fact, he had been home very little for the past week.

There was an undercurrent of tension between him and Margaret, one which everyone was aware of, but no one mentioned.

Andrew arrived home two days later, full of tales of the battle. He also had a message for Melissa from Jeb Stuart.

"He told me to tell you that Jackson Vaughn had been wounded and sent to Richmond."

"Where?"

"I don't know. Stuart didn't know either. He didn't even know how badly hurt he was."

"Oh, how sad," Nancy sighed. "He hasn't been brought to the Soldier's Rest, I know."

"Do you think Mr. McAllen would give me the day off to go search for him, Uncle Edward?"

"I'll go if you like," Mahaley offered. "I'm tired of rolling bandages, and this would be every bit as worthwhile."

Mahaley found Jackson late the next afternoon in a makeshift hospital in a partially vacant warehouse, where she inquired of the matron in charge of the patients and found his name on the list.

"Lieutenant Vaughn. He was brought in Monday morning," the woman told her.

"What's wrong with him?"

"It just says gunshot wound."

"Is he all right?"

"I really don't know, miss. I don't have that information. Are you a relative?"

"No. I don't believe he has any relatives. He's a friend of the family."

"I'll see if I can find a doctor you can talk to—when he's not busy."

Mahaley sat down to wait, staring at her gloomy surroundings.

After nearly an hour had elapsed, a doctor appeared. He was young and slightly built with sandy hair and beard.

"You wished to speak with a doctor, miss?"

Mahaley stood up. "Yes. You have a soldier here—Lieutenant Vaughn. I want to know of his condition."

"I've seen so many men the last few days. . . ."

"Please, doctor. I've waited here for a long time. Could I see him?"

"I'm sorry. I can't permit you . . ." He looked at the distress on Mahaley's face and relented. "Very well. Follow me."

After checking a list to find out which bed the patient was in, the doctor motioned for Mahaley to follow him. She felt a wave of nausea as she passed the rows of cots. Noticing her expression, the doctor took her arm to steady her.

"It's not a very pleasant sight, is it, miss?"

Mahaley didn't answer, for they had stopped in front of a cot. Jackson was either sleeping or unconscious, his chest and left arm wrapped with stained bandages.

"Ah, this one," the doctor said, shaking his head. "I'm afraid he's in a very bad way. Is he a relative of yours?"

"No."

"Your affianced?"

"No. Just a family friend. What's wrong with him? He looks so . . . so . . ."

"Infection. He was shot in the arm, evidently with a rifled musket. Those balls are very bad—they shatter the bone in hundreds of pieces usually, not a clean wound at all. By all rights, the arm should have been amputated,

143

but the man refused. Apparently on the field and again here as well. It's his right to refuse amputation, but, in this case, I'm afraid it was the wrong choice. I removed the bullet and patched him up as well as I could, but he's hardly been conscious at all since. He's running a very high fever from the infection."

"Is he going to die?"

"I don't know. Most likely. Unfortunately, there aren't enough doctors and nurses to give him the kind of care he needs. Like that dressing—it should be changed every few hours. And his forehead should be bathed with ice packs to keep down the fever."

"Could he be moved?"

"Moved where?"

"To a private home, where he would get constant attention and be more comfortable."

"I'm afraid that's the only chance he's got right now."

"Then in that case, I'll go home now and have a carriage brought for him as soon as possible. Thank you Doctor—?"

"Aldrich. Nathaniel Aldrich."

Mahaley hurried home in time to find Edward just getting out of the carriage in front of the house.

"Mahaley, what's wrong? You look very upset."

"Oh, Father, it's Lieutenant Vaughn. He's very badly hurt—almost dead. The doctor says they don't have enough doctors to go around. Can we bring him here?"

"Here?" Edward asked in amazement. He told Bobo not to put away the carriage and took Mahaley's arm. "Come into the house and we'll talk about it."

When he and Mahaley entered the house, Edward sent Cindy to round up the rest of the family.

"Now, come into the drawing room and sit down. This is something I believe the entire household should be consulted about."

Nancy and Melissa came downstairs at the same time Andrew strolled out of the kitchen, munching on a sweet roll. When Melissa walked into the room, Mahaley went over to her and took Melissa's hands in her own.

"Melissa, I found Lieutenant Vaughn."

From the look on her cousin's face, Melissa knew the situation was serious. "Is he hurt very badly?"

Mahaley nodded.

"Mahaley has proposed we bring this man into our home for his recovery," Edward told them. "I felt we should consider this carefully, all of us."

"Why Edward, I'm surprised at you," Nancy said. "If the man needs attention, he shall certainly be welcome to make his recovery here."

"What happened to him?" Melissa asked.

"He was shot in the arm. The doctor said he refused to have it amputated, so now it's infected. He's got a fever and he's unconscious most of the time."

"Does he have much of a chance?" Andrew asked.

"No. Not unless he's brought here."

"That settles it," Nancy said. "Although the matter was settled with me as soon as I heard about it. Andrew, I think you should have Bobo put blankets and pillows in the carriage. We can put him in the spare bedroom."

"Aunt Nancy," Melissa interrupted. "I feel the same way as you do, but it's such an inconvenience. I don't know what to say. I won't be here during the day to take care of him."

"It doesn't matter. Mahaley and Margaret and Cindy and Tunia are available. I don't need to spend quite so much time at the Soldier's Rest. We'll manage. And after all, it's the least we can do for this brave son of the South."

With that declaration, Nancy bustled out of the room to find the servants. Andrew glanced at his father who said, "I left Bobo out front with the carriage. You'd better tell him to get the blankets."

After Andrew had gone, Melissa looked around helplessly for a moment. She agreed that if Jackson's only chance lay in being moved here, it was the thing to do, but she felt she was causing a terrible imposition. After all, he was more or less her beau.

"I'll go get my cloak," she finally said.

"I think Andrew should go with you," Edward told her.

Mahaley followed Melissa and squeezed her arm gently. "I hope he'll be all right."

"Why, thank you, Mahaley."

"The doctor I spoke to was Nathaniel Aldrich."

Andrew and Melissa drove along the crowded streets in the twilight.

"Andrew, did you see many wounded men when you were at Manassas?"

"Many. Some of them did amazing things."

"But did many of them live?"

"I don't know. I avoided the field hospitals. Melissa, just how serious are you about this fellow? I got the impression from Mahaley that you two were practically engaged."

"I got that impression too. I saw him several times and we exchanged a few letters, but I didn't feel it was serious at all. At least not on my part."

146

"Oh well, don't let it worry you," he smiled, patting her hand. "Mahaley's at a very impressionable age. I think she finds a man in a uniform the most exciting and romantic thing in the world."

Andrew and Melissa found Dr. Aldrich drinking coffee and eating a sandwich by the matron's desk when they entered.

"We're looking for Dr. Aldrich," Andrew said.

"I'm Dr. Aldrich. What can I do for you?"

"My sister spoke to you earlier about moving a Lieutenant Vaughn from here. We've brought a carriage to take him home with us."

Dr. Aldrich put his sandwich and coffee on the desk. "I'll need you to sign him out. He's unable to do so himself. I'll write down a list of things you'll need to do and supplies you'll need to have on hand."

"I'll go get our coachman," Andrew said. "He'll help us get him moved out."

Dr. Aldrich was scratching some instructions on a sheet of paper. "This man is very sick, miss. It's a big responsibility and I can't assure you of the outcome."

"I understand," Melissa nodded.

"I hope you're not the squeamish type."

"I don't know if I am or not."

"That young lady I spoke to this afternoon?"

"My cousin Mahaley?"

"She seems very capable and very concerned. Does she have a husband or beau in the army?"

"No. She . . ."

Just then Andrew returned with Bobo.

"If you'll just sign this . . ." Dr. Aldrich pushed a paper across the desk toward Andrew.

*　　*　　*

Bobo and Andrew carried an unconscious Jackson Vaughn out to the carriage and settled him as comfortably as possible, lying down on the seat. Melissa sat across from him, making sure he was jostled as little as the road would allow. Andrew rode beside Bobo on the box. Jackson moaned once, and Melissa bent over him.

"Jackson, it's all right. You're going to be all right."

Jackson had been carried upstairs to the extra bedroom on an improvised litter made from a storm shutter, and Nancy and Cindy tried to settle him in bed.

"Andrew, I believe you could spare a few pairs of your linen drawers," Nancy said. "There's no sense in his wearing a nightshirt when we have to change his dressings so often."

Jackson was clad only in his torn, dirty uniform trousers. Melissa had carried his boots.

By now, Margaret had appeared to look in on the patient.

"Oh, Margaret, I'm glad you're here," Nancy said. "As soon as Andrew comes back with his drawers, you can help me put them on Lieutenant Vaughn."

"What!" Edward exclaimed.

"Well, really, Edward. I can't have either Melissa or Mahaley help me. Margaret's a married woman."

Edward left the room, shaking his head and wondering if he would ever get his supper this night.

When Andrew returned with his drawers, Nancy shooed everyone out of the room except Margaret, who was a rather unwilling accomplice.

"I'm going to see if Tunia's done anything about supper," Mahaley said.

148

Melissa took the first watch that evening, trying to keep his forehead bathed with cold towels as much as possible. Tomorrow, Andrew would go in search of ice and the other supplies. Mahaley relieved Melissa at ten, and Cindy took over at two.

Before leaving for the hospital in the morning, Nancy had Cindy help her bathe Jackson and change his dressings. His fever hadn't subsided, and his breathing was very shallow. She hoped she could find out a little more about his treatment from the doctors at the Soldier's Rest.

Andrew managed to purchase some spirits of camphor, yellow jasmine, morphine, and quinine, along with some sponges. Mahaley cut up some sheets and rolled bandages while Margaret watched over the patient.

When Mahaley came up to the room with a basket of clean bandages, Jackson regained consciousness for a moment. He opened his eyes and stared blankly at the two women.

"Water," he murmured.

Margaret held a cup to his lips while Mahaley managed to raise his head slightly.

"Is that a good sign?" Margaret wondered.

"I don't know. I guess so." Mahaley bent over him. "Lieutenant Vaughn, can you hear me?"

But Jackson had lapsed back into unconsciousness.

For eighteen days, Jackson drifted in and out of consciousness, unaware of his surroundings or who was with him. The liquid he drank was a brew made from the yellow jasmine leaves to help control the fever. There was no more ice to be obtained at any price after the first supply Andrew had found. The family doctor had been called twice to examine the gunshot wound. The infection had not spread nor had it become gangrenous, but it wasn't going away either.

On the nineteenth evening, Melissa had just replaced a cold compress on Jackson's forehead and was nodding in her chair by the window. The lamp by the bedside was dimly lit.

"Melissa."

She awakened with a start. Jackson's head was turned on the pillow, and he was looking at her. She hurried over to the bed. The glassy look that had been in his eyes was gone.

"Jackson, do you know me?"

"Melissa," he repeated weakly.

"Oh, thank God!" She took his hand and felt his pulse. It was much stronger, and his brow felt cooler.

"Are you really here, Melissa?"

"Of course I'm here. And you're going to get better now. I know it."

In the next week, Jackson lost his fever completely, but his wound was not draining as it should have. Dr. Cartright, the family physician, was again summoned, and he inserted a rubber tube into Jackson's arm to facilitate the drainage. He still slept a great deal, spoke little, and ate little besides broth or porridge.

For a while, Margaret had begun to feel very useful, sharing the vigil with the others. But as Jackson improved, her duties subsided. She had little Jeff to take care of, but he was a good baby and demanded little of her attention. Things were worsening between her and Joseph. After her recovery from the birth of their son,

Margaret had refused to let Joseph make love to her. She told him it was because she still was not feeling well enough, and he accepted this at first. Joseph had never been very demanding with his husbandly rights anyway, but she knew he was becoming impatient. At first he spent his evenings out, but now he just sat around and stared at her. It wasn't a fear of pregnancy. She loved little Jeff and hadn't had too hard a time with the delivery compared with many other women. The plain and simple truth of the matter was that she didn't like sex. Margaret found no pleasure in it at all and felt it was totally unnecessary. The only reason she had put up with it before was to get pregnant, and she supposed when she wanted another baby, she would put up with it again.

Mrs. Davis always visited with Melissa and her family after church services, and shortly after the first family had moved into the new Executive Mansion, she invited the Armstrong women to tea. The ladies dressed themselves as nicely as they could and left Jackson in the care of Tunia and Cindy.

The Confederate White House was located at Twelfth and Clay Streets, once the Brookenbrough Estate. It was on a little hill overlooking a landscape of romantic beauty. Large and stately, it was luxuriously furnished.

The Armstrongs were met by a liveried servant who ushered them into the drawing room. Melissa gazed about at the massive marble fireplace mantel and the many tropical plants placed about the room.

Varina came over to greet them, as ever a kind and graceful woman. "Ladies, I'm so happy you could come." She turned to Nancy who was wearing a new pink silk dress made from the material Edward had stockpiled.

151

"That gown is absolutely stunning, Mrs. Armstrong . . . or would you mind if I called you Nancy?"

"I'd be most happy if you would."

"Then you must call me Varina," she said, taking in the girls with her glance as well. "All of you."

The afternoon was spent chatting over tea and cakes, along with the more prominent women of Richmond society in 1861: Mrs. Angela Mallory, wife of Secretary of the Navy Stephen Mallory; Mary Memminger, wife of Secretary of the Treasury Christopher Memminger; Mrs. Elvira Reagan, wife of Postmaster General John H. Reagan; Mrs. Natalie Benjamin, wife of Attorney General Judah P. Benjamin; Margaret Howell, sister of the president's wife. Their ages and backgrounds varied widely, but all were coiffured and gowned to perfection, each trying to outdo the other.

"I think your husband has done a wonderful job with our postal system, Elvira," Varina told her. "I'm sure the people don't mind paying two cents more for a letter if they're assured of getting it where they want it to go." She went on to say that on June 1, the first Confederate stamps were issued, a likeness of Jefferson Davis, which was the only postal stamp in American history to portray a living man. The prewar rate for half-ounce letters had been three cents, but the Confederates raised it to five cents for a 500-mile delivery zone. Anything farther than that was ten cents. A crew of experts from New York had come to Richmond where they formed a new company and made the first Confederate stamps.

Melissa didn't ask Mrs. Reagan if she had any influence in getting the mail to Pittsburgh. She was surrounded by the fair ladies of the Confederacy, and she didn't want to give any indications of where her true feelings lay. Besides, she rather liked all these women. They talked mostly of their husbands and sons and brothers who were doing everything they could for the war effort.

"Everyone's so optimistic these days," Nancy said. "You can feel it everywhere. Everything's been going right for us lately."

"I agree," Varina said. "Jefferson's quite pleased except for that business in the western part of the state."

Melissa looked around, wondering to what new business she was referring.

"Last night's meeting lasted until the wee hours of the morning," Eliza Walker remarked. "And Leroy never tells me anything."

"I feel fortunate," Varina said. "Jefferson confides in me a lot. I believe last night they discussed the possibilities of some action against the Federals in the West in the near future. Lee's going out there around Cheat Mountain sometime next month to see about putting the Yankees in their place."

"And high time," Mrs. Benjamin agreed. "They're absolute pests."

"How's your patient doing?" Varina asked Melissa.

"A little better. But he's still very weak."

"Those poor boys," Varina sighed. "I just don't know what would have become of them if private citizens hadn't opened their homes. I do hope all of you ladies are working on your projects for the bazaar."

A bazaar was to be held September 20 to raise funds to build a large military hospital in Richmond. Chimborazo Hill had been chosen by Surgeon General Moore as the site, and construction was set to begin soon.

*   *   *

When Melissa returned home, she went to check on Jackson. Instead of Cindy sitting with him, she found Andrew, apparently in the midst of a bawdy story. All she heard when she entered was something about a midget.

"I see our patient is doing much better," she observed.

Both men sobered. "Much better," Jackson said, smiling through the full beard he had sprouted.

"I guess I'll be going," Andrew said.

"Why don't you stay a few minutes longer?" Melissa suggested. "I'd like to change my clothes. And you can finish your story."

Melissa prepared Jackson's medicine and took it in to him. They were both chuckling, so evidently Andrew's story had been a good one. After Andrew left, Melissa gave Jackson the bitter-tasting liquid and checked his arm.

"Did you have a nice time this afternoon?" he wondered.

"Oh, yes. Mrs. Davis asked after your health. How are you feeling? Really, I mean."

"Oh, I don't know. My arm hurts—aches, you know. But the thing I feel worst about is putting all you people to so much trouble."

"Don't feel bad about that. If it hadn't been you, it might have been another soldier. That's why we need more hospitals. We're having a bazaar next month to raise money for one. That's something I wanted to talk to you about. What do men most need in the field—little things, I mean."

"Wait," he said. "There's something I have to talk to you about first. It's been bothering me for a while."

"What is it?"

"Well, Cindy's been taking care of me lately for

154

things—like giving me a bath, you know. I asked her if she'd always done that for me, and she said no. I didn't ask her any more about it. I guess I was embarrassed. But now I've got to know. Who did it when I first got here? Was it you?"

Melissa laughed and shook her head. "Oh, Jackson."

"It wasn't you then?"

"No. It was Margaret and Aunt Nancy."

Jackson digested this information; then turned beet red underneath his beard. Melissa had to go over and look out the window in order to keep from laughing out loud at the expression on his face.

She finally turned around and looked at him. "Are you getting hungry?"

"Yes."

"That's a good sign. But I still don't think you should have anything heavy. How about some eggs tonight?"

"That sounds good to me."

Melissa went downstairs to tell Tunia and found Edward going through the pantry, making a list.

"What are you doing, Uncle Edward?"

He straightened up and looked at her, somewhat startled. "Oh, Melissa. I'm taking inventory. I don't know how long we'll be able to get certain things. I'm going shopping on Saturday. Is there anything you can think of that we might need?"

"I can't think of anything."

"Can I borrow your wagon? Ours isn't as big."

"Of course. As a matter of fact, I was thinking of selling it. Naturally, I'll keep Jeremiah's horse."

"Don't sell the wagon. We may need it sometime."

"Uncle Edward, are things really going to be that bad?"

"Of course not," Edward smiled. "I'm merely taking precautions. I have the money now, so why not be on the safe side?"

Melissa took a tray upstairs for Jackson and herself. After helping him to sit up, she propped two pillows behind his back.

"You're just having eggs too?" he asked.

"I'm not very hungry. I had some cakes at the Davises'. Here's some toasted bread with a little jam on it."

Jackson seemed to enjoy his meal, but it tired him. He went to sleep immediately after he had eaten.

The next day, Melissa found she had accumulated a great deal of work. She had been surprised when Lewis had told her she could have yesterday off to attend the Davises' tea party.

Henry came in late in the day and sat down at his desk to copy an article.

"Where were you yesterday?" he asked her.

"I had tea with Mrs. Davis."

"Really? Say, that might make an interesting article. Would you mind telling me about it?"

Melissa described the mansion and told him what the women discussed.

"He's sending Lee to western Virginia?" Henry asked. "When?"

"I don't know."

"Did she say whereabouts exactly?"

"Cheat Mountain."

Henry wanted to pursue it further but decided it wouldn't be wise. Besides, Melissa probably didn't know any more.

"By the way, I met a man who might be able to get mail up past the lines," he said.

"You did? Who is he?"

"Oh, just a man. If you'd like, I could give him a letter for your brother."

"Oh, thank you, Mr. Walkenfeldt. I'll bring it to you Monday."

"Ah . . . Miss Armstrong," he said quietly. "Could I ask you not to mention this to anyone? I wouldn't want to get this man into any trouble."

Melissa studied Henry's face for a moment and had a very strange feeling all of a sudden. His blue eyes betrayed nothing. She had always been a good judge of people, but Henry was one person she hadn't been able to figure out.

"Of course, Mr. Walkenfeldt."

Edward and Bobo left early Saturday morning on their rounds to purchase the supplies. After a few stops, Edward realized he was doing the right thing. Provisions were more difficult to obtain than he had imagined. By midafternoon, they returned home with the wagon loaded down with coffee, tea, brandy, flour, sugar, salt, spices, jellies, hams, lard, vinegar, molasses, hominy, rice, and dry goods. He felt they would be well supplied for a while and he possibly had avoided paying even higher prices. As it was, the price of salt alone had already risen from one cent to five cents a pound.

Andrew was leaving once again with General Joe Johnston on Monday. He had bought a sturdy pair of shoes to replace his boots. Perhaps boots looked better, but they definitely weren't comfortable for walking long distances.

After seeing what had happened at Manassas, the family was more reluctant to let him go, and he was more reluctant to leave as well.

Two days after Andrew had left, Margaret found Joseph alone in the drawing room one evening.

"Joseph, there's something I wish you to do for me."

"What is it?"

"Now that we again have a spare bedroom, I would like you to move into it."

"What!"

"I don't want you sleeping in the same bed with me."

Joseph stood up and, going over to her, put his hands on her shoulders, turning her around to look at him. "Margaret, what have I done to make you hate me so?"

"I don't hate you, Joseph. Don't think that. I just would rather you moved into Andrew's room."

"But I'm your husband!"

"Shhh! Lower your voice!"

"All right. I'll keep my voice down. But would you kindly tell me what this is going to look like to your family?"

"I hadn't thought of that."

"Well, you'd better think of it. We're supposed to be happily married."

"We are happily married."

"Are we?"

"Why, Joseph, I've been a good wife to you."

"Have you—really? Listen, Margaret, I've been a very patient man with you. So far, I've done everything the way you want. I've lived in this house with your family, I went to work at your father's friend's paper, I've given you whatever you asked for, and I've held back my

158

desires as much as any man could. But this is asking too much."

"It won't be forever, Joseph. In another year or two when I want another child . . ."

"In a year or two! And what am I supposed to do in the meantime?"

"Joseph, I said lower your voice."

"Very well." Joseph sighed and turned toward the door. "If it will make you happy, I'll move out."

Joseph went upstairs to gather up his toilet articles and nightshirt. He didn't understand Margaret. For that matter, he didn't understand himself. If he were a different type of man, he would probably go out and find himself another woman. Lord knew, there were plenty of them around Richmond these days. But he didn't really want another woman. He didn't really want Margaret all that much either. It was the principle of the matter. Margaret had been anxious enough on the first night of their honeymoon, but ever since that night, she had been a different woman. He knew she didn't enjoy sex from her passive indifference, so he tried to curtail his lovemaking to as little as possible. He felt he had always been very considerate of her sexually, and now she was thanking him by turning him out of his own bed.

Nancy was sitting alone at the table when Cindy passed by with a tray for Jackson's breakfast.

"Good morning, Cindy."

"Mawnin', Miss Nancy." She hesitated for a moment, uncertain whether to speak.

"Did you want to say something, Cindy?"

"I ain't sure, Miss Nancy. Maybe it ain't my place."

Nancy sighed. "What is it, Cindy?"

"It's Masta Joseph. When I come along de hall dis mawnin', I seed him comin' outten Masta Andrew's room. Later, I went in to see, and de bed been slept in and Masta Joseph's shavin' stuff was in dere."

"Thank you Cindy. That will be all. You'd better take the lieutenant his breakfast before it gets cold."

"Yessum."

After Cindy had gone, Nancy shook her head sadly. "I just don't understand that girl."

"What girl, Mother?" Mahaley asked, flouncing in and plopping herself down at the table. She was fresh and bright, a sharp contrast to her mother's present downcast mood.

"Your sister."

"Margaret? What's she done now?"

"Yes, what have I done?" Margaret came into the room and took her place at the table. She unfolded her napkin and scowled at her plate.

"Cindy tells me Joseph slept in Andrew's room last night," Nancy said.

Mahaley raised her eyebrows and hitched her chair a little closer to the table.

"I asked him to," Margaret told her mother.

"Would you mind telling me why? Did you and Joseph have an argument?"

"No. We didn't have an argument." Margaret poured a cup of coffee, lacing it liberally with cream.

"I'm waiting for an explanation," Nancy told her.

"Mother, I don't feel it's any of your concern."

"What concerns you, concerns me." Nancy glanced at Mahaley. "Perhaps we should discuss this when we're alone."

Mahaley's face fell.

"There's no need," Margaret said. "If you must have an explanation, I simply don't want to have another baby right away."

"Margaret, that's no reason to put him out of your bed. You know, there are ways that can be avoided. Perhaps I should have your father speak to Joseph. . . ."

"Mother! I will not have you discussing my personal life like you were discussing the weather!"

Margaret stood up, nearly bumping into Tunia, who had come in with the breakfast. Mahaley watched her sister storm out of the room.

"Miss Margaret upset 'bout sompin'?" Tunia wondered, already well aware of what had taken place last night. Slaves, she mused, had an uncanny way of learning things about the household even before their masters knew. They generally were the repositories of the family secrets, confidants in everything. Often their masters' best friends, they laughed and sorrowed right along with them. By this afternoon, all the neighbors' slaves would also know that Margaret and Joseph Boone were sleeping in separate bedrooms.

Eight

Jeremiah had spent the last four months working constantly at the offices of Dr. White or helping out in the hospitals. In the evenings, he sat in his room at Mrs. Oliver's boardinghouse, studying his medical books. His progress since coming to Pittsburgh had been remarkable. He even surprised himself with his aptitude for learning. And he loved it. When he helped to alleviate someone's suffering, his pride swelled. When he could do nothing for a patient, he tried to give them a cheerful smile anyway.

Usually on Sunday evenings, he took supper at the McClellands' whether Sam was at home or not. Lately, Sam had been home very little, for the government had contracted the *Allegheny Belle* as a supply ship.

Other than the fact that the Allegheny Arsenal was busy day and night and the military parades marched along the streets, Pittsburgh bore no resemblance to Richmond. The citizens were detached, the struggle was going on far away. There was no lack of supplies, no fear of invasion, no armed camps in the vicinity. The average citizen only heard about the war, but Jim White, Sarah, and Jeremiah saw it the day the first casualties were brought in from Big Bethel, Phillipi, Rich Mountain, and Bull Run. Sarah had gone with her brother daily to the hospital to help care for the wounded, leaving the children in the care of her mother.

Jeremiah was mightily relieved when he received another letter from Melissa. She told him how she had met President Davis and his family and attended several social affairs with them, how Edward was now a clerk in the War Department, how Nancy helped at the Soldier's Rest, and about the wounded cavalryman who was staying in their home. She inquired about Corky, hoping he had found a new life for himself.

One Sunday evening in mid-September, Jeremiah was having his weekly supper with the McClellands, relating his sister's news.

"She's met Jefferson Davis?" Sarah remarked. "I thought all along her sympathies were with the Union."

"They are. She hasn't written it in so many words, but I can feel it. I know my sister."

"Regardless where your sympathies lie, meeting any presiden* .s quite an honor," Sarah's mother remarked. "When my father was a boy back in England, he worked as a groom. One day he had to deliver a horse to John Adams. He wasn't president at the time, but I can remember my father telling that story like it was the proudest day in his life."

Dr. White smiled. "I wonder if Mr. Adams gave him a tip?"

Jeremiah and Sarah laughed. "It's a shame Sam can't be here," Sarah sighed. "I wish he'd get this fool notion about joining the navy out of his head."

"The same as you think it's a fool notion I want to join the army," Dr. White said. "Sarah, we're at war. You've

163

seen that at the hospital. If there had been adequate surgeons on the field, many of those men wouldn't be in the shape they're in. Besides, I haven't made up my mind yet, and neither has Sam."

Jeremiah looked sadly at Sarah, feeling sorry for her and all the other women who had to stay home while their men went off to war.

The next morning, Jeremiah had a call at the office from the Pinkerton man, Jonathon Clark. Without identifying himself, he informed Jeremiah that if he wished to get mail through to Richmond, he could leave it at a certain address. Henry had written a note to the man, requesting that he help his friends, assuring him they would ask no questions. During the infancy of the United States Secret Service, a great deal was based on trust, and a great many errors were made because of this trust. But Jeremiah was happy enough with this news to let it pass.

Over mountains considered impassable to bodies of troops, beset with a raging storm, General Robert E. Lee reached his destination of Cheat Mountain. On the summit was the outpost of the Fourteenth and Seventeenth Indiana and the Twenty-fourth Ohio. Aware of Lee's movements, the Union soldiers had been waiting for him, surprised that he had even reached this far. He had already been repulsed once at Elkwater, and after three days of waiting out the Federals unsuccessfully, Lee withdrew to Big Sewell Mountain, where he joined General John B. Floyd. The plan that had been so carefully worked out to cut off the Federal communications line from the western Alleghenies to the Shenandoah Valley had been a disaster, resulting in some eighty Confederate casualties. With twice as many men as the

164

Federals, the Confederates had failed.

Somehow, the Union Army knew ahead of time of Lee's movements.

Melissa was working at her desk when the newspaper received word of Lee's defeat on a mission which few were aware was even taking place. That she had ever heard it mentioned had slipped her mind until that moment. Henry was working quietly at his desk, and she shot a glance across at him. A little smile turned up the corners of his mouth.

It couldn't be, she thought. "Why, Henry Walkenfeldt couldn't possibly be a spy." She studied him a little harder. "He doesn't look like a spy. I always thought spies went slinking around dark alleys listening at people's doors. Why, Lordy, I'm the one who told him in the first place."

While the newspaper office was atwitter with excitement, Melissa sat staring at Henry. He finally looked over at her.

"Have you got all your things ready for the bazaar next Saturday?" he asked her.

"Ah—oh, yes. Most everything."

"Good. I hope we have a good turnout. Now with the news of this defeat, we'll need to cheer up the morale of our boys."

Melissa nodded dumbly, thinking, I must have been wrong.

Crime was rampant in Richmond. With the influx of people to the capital also came its share of bad characters. Robberies and murders were on the rise. The provost marshal in Richmond was John H. Winder, and it was his job to police the city. The force which had been adequate in the easygoing days before the war, when people seldom bothered to lock their doors in the daytime, was now totally ineffectual. Winder gathered a force of secret-service men who began to deal with the problem a little more satisfactorily. The two prisons, Castle Thunder and Castle Godwin, were soon full of unsavory characters.

Otherwise, things were going well. Business was booming. The air was smoky from the chimneys of the foundries, new shops were opening, merchandise was moving. The packets for Scottsville left daily, and for Lexington three times a week. The trip to Jamestown and other points was made on Monday, Wednesday, and Friday by the steamer *Curtis Peck*. The Richmond and Petersburg mail train left at five every morning for points farther south, while the Virginia Central left daily for Staunton at 7:30.

Melissa was happy now that she had found a way to get mail through to her brother, and he, in turn, had sent her letters. The methods with which this was accomplished, she didn't care to speculate upon.

The Armstrong women gathered up their items for the bazaar and drove to the Richmond Hall. They found booths had been set up, and a band was tuning up in the corner. All the women hurried to set up their wares and get ready for the crowds. Melissa had baked tarts until she felt she could never again look at another tart. She and Mahaley, who had baked cookies, watched the people gathering from their section of the baked goods department.

Henry came by and bought quite a bit, asking Melissa if she would put it aside for him until he was ready to leave.

"I hope they let us out of here so we can dance," Mahaley sighed.

"Pretty soon we won't have anything left to sell if it keeps going like this," Melissa remarked.

"Was that the man you work with?" Mahaley asked, after Henry had moved on.

"Yes."

"He's kind of nice looking. But he'd be much better looking in a uniform."

After their wares had sold out, Melissa took their money to John Denny, who was in charge of collecting all the funds raised. He had been to the house for supper several times, and Melissa didn't like him very much. When she thought about it, she had to admit she liked few of Edward's friends.

After stopping by to see how Nancy was doing with her handkerchiefs, which bore a small embroidered Confederate flag in the corner, she stopped to see Margaret selling combs.

"Is Joseph coming?"

"I don't know," Margaret replied.

Melissa wandered away, thinking about what a disaster that situation had turned into. She knew Joseph was drinking—not a great deal, but he had seldom touched liquor before.

Her thoughts were broken when Jeb Stuart approached her. "Miss Armstrong, I'm so glad to see you. I just got into town last night. Did you hear anything about Jackson?"

"You mean you don't know? He's staying at our house."

"How is he?"

"He's getting better every day. He was near death when we found him. You must come see him. He speaks of you often. By the way, congratulations on your promotion, General."

The band struck up a lively tune, and Jeb whirled Melissa around the dance floor.

Mahaley had wandered over to the refreshments and was sipping some punch.

"Excuse me, aren't you Miss Armstrong?"

Mahaley turned but didn't recognize the man who had addressed her, although he looked vaguely familiar, as he smiled shyly at her beneath his sandy-colored beard. His green eyes sparkled merrily. "Yes, I'm Mahaley Armstrong."

"I don't think you'll probably remember me. I'm Dr. Nathaniel Aldrich. We met at the hospital shortly after Manassas."

"Oh, yes, doctor. I remember you."

"How have you been?"

"Very well, thank you. And you?"

"I'll be much relieved when we get some decent hospital facilities built here. That friend who was so badly wounded. How did he fare?"

"He's improving. We had an awful time with him at first, until his fever went away."

"Then he didn't die?"

"No. He's quite alive. Our family doctor said you performed a miracle in saving his arm."

"The saving of the arm wasn't so difficult—it was the saving of the life afterward that was the trick. That we owe to you and your family."

A very plain but lovely girl came over to them. "Oh, here you are, Nathaniel," she said, linking her arm through his. "I thought I'd lost you."

Mahaley felt a wave of resentment and jealousy, even though she hardly knew the man.

"Miss Armstrong, may I present my sister Ellen?" Nathaniel said. "Ellen, this is Miss Mahaley Armstrong."

"How very nice to meet you," Ellen smiled.

Mahaley smiled back. "It must be very exciting to have a doctor for a brother."

"It keeps him very busy. I hardly ever see him."

Melissa had been dancing quite a bit, and finally got away to the refreshments. By this time, Henry had also joined the table.

"You've been getting quite a workout," Henry smiled at her. "I've been watching you."

"I'm so thirsty," she said.

While Henry was getting her a cup of punch, Mahaley introduced her to the Aldriches.

Melissa thought Mahaley seemed more effusive than usual with Dr. Aldrich, and she remarked on it to Henry after the others had left them.

"Your cousin seems rather effusive anyway," Henry remarked.

"Yes, that she is," Melissa agreed.

Melissa noticed the braided rosette of palmetto on his lapel.

"I see you're wearing a Secession Badge," she observed.

"Yes. There's a woman over there selling them. I'm really looking forward to getting home and sampling those tarts of yours. They look delicious."

"I hope you enjoy them. You must get awfully tired of eating alone."

169

Henry shrugged. "One gets used to it. They're playing a waltz. I think I can probably manage that, if you'd care to dance?"

"Why, yes, I would."

Putting down their punch cups, Henry and Melissa made their way over to the dance floor.

Edward and Lewis were standing off to one side, talking with John Denny.

"Isn't that your man dancing with Melissa?" Edward asked Lewis.

Lewis studied the dancers for a moment. "Walkenfeldt? I didn't think he could dance with that limp of his."

"I've read some of his work."

"He's a good man. The readers like him. He paints a very pretty picture of the government and the people."

"Let's just hope he doesn't get hold of the books on the Tidewater Nail Company," John smiled.

Edward laughed. "When I look at my bank account, I could almost shake Abe Lincoln's hand for starting this."

Back on the dance floor, Melissa found she rather enjoyed dancing with Henry.

"You know, Mr. Walkenfeldt, you're really a very good dancer."

"Thank you. I wasn't sure how I'd fare. I haven't danced for a long time."

"Did you leave a sweetheart back in California?"

"No. The ones who weren't married were hardly the sort you'd want to bring home to mother."

Henry was surprised at how easily the lie came out. If he kept telling it over and over enough, he might really begin to believe he had lived in California. He had to smile to himself, thinking of the difference between a San

170

Francisco dance-hall girl and the gay young girls he knew from the German-American social functions he had attended back in Pittsburgh.

As the dance ended, Melissa's attention was caught by Mrs. Davis, who was waving at her, motioning her to join her.

"Would you like to meet the president, Mr. Walkenfeldt?" Melissa asked him.

"What?"

"Come along." Slipping her arm through this, she led Henry over to Varina Davis.

"Melissa, how nice to see you. And who is this gentleman?"

"Mrs. Davis, may I present Henry Walkenfeldt."

Turning away from his friends, Jefferson Davis smiled at Melissa. "Miss Armstrong, one of my favorite ladies. How are you, my dear?"

Melissa made the introductions, and Henry shook hands with the president.

"Walkenfeldt? The writer for the *Journal?*"

"Yes, sir."

"I've enjoyed your work."

While Henry was chatting with the president, Melissa noticed a tall officer with slate-gray hair and beard talking to Jeb Stuart. Jefferson touched the gold-braided sleeve of the man, "Bob, I'd like you to meet Henry Walkenfeldt. I was just reading his story on your efforts out West. One of the few stories giving the facts of your statistics and equipment difficulties. Mr. Walkenfeldt, I'd like you to meet General Robert Lee."

Henry felt a twinge of guilt and shame as he shook the solemn-faced man's hand.

"It's nice to know that someone understands the

171

problems of an undersupplied army," Lee said. "Were you a soldier once, Mr. Walkenfeldt?"

"No, sir. I just like to consider the human side of things."

Mahaley had been spending most of the afternoon with Dr. Aldrich, dancing and talking.

"Do you think I could come see the lieutenant?" he asked her. "I'd like to check on his condition." He was interested in his former patient, but what he really wanted was an excuse to see Mahaley again.

"Yes, anytime."

"How about tomorrow?"

"Tomorrow's Sunday."

"I know. Is that inconvenient?"

"No. But I didn't think you'd want to work on Sunday."

Nathaniel smiled. "I work every day. I'll make my rounds at the hospital in the morning, and I could be by around two. Would that be all right?"

"Yes. We'll be back from church by then."

In the following weeks, Mahaley saw Dr. Aldrich occasionally. She couldn't exactly figure him out. He was a different type of man from the others she had known. He was a gentleman.

Jeb visited Jackson at least twice a week, and there was usually much laughter coming from the bedroom. Jackson was anxious to get back to the cavalry and hoped after the new year, he would be able to do so. The infection which had nearly killed him had left him weak and slow to mend.

By Thanksgiving, Jackson was able to dress and come

downstairs for dinner. The family had gone to church services in the morning, and Tunia had cooked up a fine meal. Besides Jackson and the family, there was Lewis McAllen, and Melissa had invited Henry to share dinner with them, as she knew he would otherwise be alone. Mahaley had asked Ellen and Nathaniel Aldrich.

Melissa was seated between Jackson and Henry, but she could see Joseph tipping the wine bottle frequently at the end of the table. Lewis didn't miss it either, for several times in the recent past he had upbraided him for coming into work late with a hangover.

After Edward said grace, the food was passed around the table, likely the last meal like this any family in Richmond would see in some time: turkey with all the trimmings, fresh-cooked peas, rice, cranberry sauce, sweet potatoes, corn, and pie.

"I wonder what kind of Thanksgiving dinner Andrew is having?" Nancy sighed.

"He's a smart boy," Edward smiled. "I'm sure he found the mess with the best food."

"Have you heard when he'll be home?" Lewis asked.

"In his last letter he says he hopes to be home for Christmas," Nancy said. "He's not doing anything right now."

"The whole army doesn't seem to be doing anything right now," Edward muttered.

"Jeb told me he's leaving this week. They plan some action up around Washington City," Jackson told them. "That skirmish they had with the First Pennsylvania Cavalry up around Dranesville was poorly planned. He says it's hoped they can make another try at it before Christmas."

"All the Yankees are mad at McClellan now anyway,"

Lewis remarked. "Now would be a good time to strike."

"From a physician's point of view, I wish this whole thing would be ended soon," Nathaniel said.

"I think it will be in a few months," Edward observed. "President Davis says by February, England will be so starved for cotton, they'll have to come in and help us. After we join forces with the English, we'll have the upper hand."

"Let's not talk of war anymore," Melissa suggested. "Let's talk about something else. After all, it's Thanksgiving."

"We sent a lot of food over to the prisoners at Libby," Ellen said. Ellen was a clerk at the Commissary Department.

"I hope the Yankees are as kind to our boys," Nancy sighed.

Melissa gave Henry a sidelong glance. Apparently, the topic of war couldn't be avoided.

As soon as the guests had left, Jackson went upstairs to his room. The day had tired him out more than he had imagined possible. With his left arm in its sling, he still managed to remove his shoes and socks. After taking off his trousers and jacket, his problems began. His cravat got tangled in his sling, and in the process of trying to get out of that, he found himself helplessly twisted up in his shirt.

Passing his door, Melissa heard Jackson's "Damnit!"

She tapped on the door. "Jackson, are you all right?"

"Well, not really."

"Is there something I can do to help?"

"Yes. But I'm not dressed."

"Oh."

"I've got my drawers on at least. I don't mind if you don't mind."

"Well . . ." She hesitated for a moment and then went in. At the sight of Jackson all tangled up in his shirt, she began to giggle. And he began to laugh too, until he winced at the pain in his arm. She hurried over to him and began to straighten him out.

"You see? I told you you should have worn your shirt sleeve over your sling," she scolded.

"It was bad enough having my jacket sleeve hanging loose."

Melissa finally extricated him from his shirt and sling. "Now you see? All this horseplay's started your wound leaking again. Now get in bed and let me change your dressings."

"Yes, ma'am," he grinned, saluting her.

While Jackson crawled under his covers, Melissa gathered up the sponge, clean bandages, and salve. The first time she had looked upon the oozing, gaping wounded arm, she thought she was going to either faint or vomit, or both. Now she was used to it. Besides, it didn't look nearly so bad now—just one stubborn little patch which didn't want to close.

"There now," she said. "That's better. Did you hurt it very much?"

"It'll be all right."

"Do you want some laudanum?"

"After that meal tonight? I always sleep well on a full stomach." He reached up with his good arm and touched a tress of her hair. "Do you know something?"

"What?"

"In all this time I've been here, I've never once

175

kissed you."

"You were hardly in any condition to do any kissing—
or even thinking about kissing."

"Yes. But I've been thinking a lot about it lately."

"Have you?"

"Uh-huh," he grinned, gently drawing her face down
to his. "And I'm tired of just thinking about it."

Melissa's lips found Jackson's as she leaned over him,
her fingers curling around the thick hair of his chest.

Joseph followed Margaret up the stairs and along the
hall.

"Is the baby asleep?" he asked.

"I don't know. Cindy's been up several times to check
on him."

"May I come in and see him for a while?"

"Why, of course, Joseph. He's your son too."

Joseph bent over the wicker cradle, one of Edward's
presents. Jeff was sleeping quietly. Joseph touched the
small hand, and it closed around his father's finger.

Margaret peered into the cradle. "He's such a good
little boy. You should spend more time with him."

"I didn't think you wanted me around."

"Joseph, now you know that isn't true."

"Margaret, can't we be a family again?"

Margaret went over to her dressing table and, sitting
down, began to remove her hairpins.

"Margaret?" he asked again.

"We've been all through this before."

"I haven't mentioned it. I've tried to abide by your
wishes. But it's been over three months."

"I know."

Joseph disengaged his finger from the baby's grasp and

walked over to the dressing table. "I'm only thirty-one years old," he said. "I haven't dried up completely yet."

"Don't be vulgar."

"I'm not being vulgar. I'm being honest with you. Why can't you be honest with me?"

"I have been."

"No you haven't. If you'd tell me what it is exactly that you don't like, perhaps we could do something about it."

"What do you mean?"

"If we could just sit down and discuss your problems, it might help." As each hairpin came out, another curl of hair fell about her shoulders, and Joseph felt a stirring of excitement. He reached down and crushed some of her hair in his hand. "You haven't always been like this Margaret. When I was courting you, you were— well . . ."

"I was what?" she asked indignantly.

"Well—eager, I guess would be the best way to put it."

"Joseph, I made you wait until we were married."

"I know. But we're married now, and I shouldn't have to wait." He bent down and buried his face in her hair. "Margaret, I need you. Don't turn me out tonight."

"We made an agreement."

"I want to break that agreement."

Margaret stood up and went over to the cradle. Joseph followed and pulled her against him.

"I'm your husband, Margaret."

"Joseph, stop it!" He was kissing her neck, fumbling with the hooks on her gown. "Stop it!" She felt the material tear and pushed him away. He stumbled backward into the bedpost.

The baby had started to cry, and Margaret picked him up, trying to quiet him. Joseph stood staring at her.

"Get out of here, Joseph."

"Margaret, I . . ."

"Get out, I said. And don't ever come back into this bedroom again."

In the other bedroom, Melissa was bending over Jackson's bed, the lamplight making the few auburn highlights in her hair shine. "I'd better go," she murmured, moving away.

He reached for her again, but she gently pushed him back against the pillow.

"Come back tonight. After everyone's asleep."

"Jackson!"

"Please. I want you near me. Just to hold you close."

"But . . ."

"Nothing will happen." He grinned and nodded toward his arm. "I'm still an invalid, remember?"

Melissa grinned back at him. "I'll think about it."

After gathering up the dirty bandages and bowl of water, she left the room. Joseph was just coming out of Margaret's bedroom. He was heading for the stairs, so Melissa hurried after him.

"Joseph, are you going downstairs?"

He stopped and looked at her. She thought his face looked a little flushed, and his spectacles were a little crooked.

"Would you take this down for me?" she asked him.

"Of course."

She handed him the bowl and thanked him.

Joseph left the bowl on the table by the back door for Tunia or Cindy to do whatever they did with such things. He started for the study and Edward's liquor cabinet. He

178

was feeling sorry for himself and not a little ashamed of what he had been thinking when Melissa stopped him in the upstairs hallway. After lighting a lamp and pouring himself a large brandy, he took the decanter with him and sat down in Edward's overstuffed chair. The house was quiet except for an occasional thump above him as the household settled down to bed. The clock was ticking on the mantel, and he squinted to see the time. Ten o'clock. The chimes confirmed this, and Joseph swallowed his brandy. He poured himself another.

Margaret made him very angry. He imagined Melissa wouldn't behave like that. Melissa was warm and generous and caring. Margaret was cold and selfish. He wondered where Margaret got it from. Mahaley certainly wasn't like that. In fact, he had had his suspicions about Mahaley's activities for some time. Nancy was sympathetic and kind, even if she was a little flighty. Andrew was self-centered but not selfish. So was Edward, and Edward liked to have his own way. So did Margaret. And she had had her own way up until now. But, by God, not anymore.

After getting into her nightclothes, Melissa glanced at her bed, which Cindy had turned down earlier, when she had put in the warming pan. She giggled and put on her robe, turning off the lamp. She peeked out the door to make sure no one was about and tiptoed down the hall to Jackson's room. She opened the door and stepped in, quickly closing it behind her.

"Jackson," she whispered.

"I'm still here."

She made her way over to the bed. "I shouldn't be here, you know."

"Yes, you should. Get in. I made a warm place for you."

Melissa took off her robe and slipped in beside him under the covers. Jackson put his right arm around her, and she cuddled up to him.

"If Aunt Nancy knew about this, she'd probably throw me out of the house."

"Don't worry about it." He stroked her hair. "It's nice like this, isn't it?"

"Yes."

They were both quiet for a while until Jackson finally spoke. "What are you thinking about?"

"Oh, I don't know. About being here like this with you. I've never been in bed with a man before."

"I'm glad," he said. "You know, I've been happy here. This is the first real home I've ever lived in." He rolled over on his side, facing her. "And I'm even happier now," he whispered, kissing her.

Weaving along the darkened hallway, Joseph stopped in front of Margaret's door. He reached down and found the knob. Locked. "Damn her anyway!"

He knocked.

Margaret wearily got out of bed and went over to the door. "Is that you, Joseph?"

"Unlock this door, Margaret."

"Go away, Joseph. It's no use."

"Unlock it, damn you! Or I'll break it down!"

"Joseph, you're drunk. I won't let you in."

"You *will!*"

Joseph threw his shoulder against the door, but it didn't give. Margaret moved back from the door at the sound. Raising his leg, Joseph kicked as hard as he could,

180

and the flimsy lock gave way.

"Joseph, you're crazy! Get out of here!"

"Crazy, am I?"

Melissa jumped out of bed at the sound of the crash and grabbed her robe.

"What the hell's going on?" Jackson wondered.

Melissa opened the door in time to see Edward running into Margaret's room. Joseph was yelling, and the baby was crying. Mahaley dashed past her and met Nancy in the hall.

"Father, get him out of here!" Margaret cried.

Joseph was knocking over furniture and calling Margaret all sorts of names. Edward tried to drag him out by the arm, but Joseph continued in his frenzy.

"She's my wife! I have a right to be in here!"

Cindy had gone for Bobo, and he came dashing into the room. Between Edward and Bobo, they got Joseph out of the room and into the hall. Mahaley and Nancy went in to comfort Margaret, and Melissa picked up the baby.

"You drunken fool!" Edward exclaimed.

"Leave me alone!" Joseph pulled free and ran for the stairs. "Leave me alone—all of you!"

"Go see where he's gone, Bobo," Edward said.

By this time Margaret was practically hysterical.

"There, there, dear. It'll be all right now," Nancy was saying.

After struggling into his robe, Jackson appeared at Margaret's door. With the baby in her arms, Melissa went over to him.

"Is there anything I can do?" he asked.

"I don't think so," she replied. She glanced over her shoulder at Margaret then, turning back to Jackson, said

"Why don't you fetch that bottle of laudanum from your room?"

Jackson nodded and left. When Melissa turned around again, Mahaley was looking at her with an expression that was a combination of surprise and amusement. Melissa paled as she realized Mahaley must have seen her coming out of Jackson's room. It must look much different than it really was.

Bobo came to the door. "Masta Joseph, he done gone out de front do'."

Edward joined Melissa and Bobo. "Well, there's no sense going after him," he sighed. "I think we've done about all we can do tonight. I want you to fix this door tomorrow, Bobo."

"Yessuh."

Jackson reappeared with the laudanum.

"That's a good idea," Edward said. "Melissa, why don't you keep the baby in your room tonight?"

Bobo carried the cradle down to Melissa's room, and soon the house was quiet again. But there was an unspoken sympathy for Joseph among everyone. He had behaved badly, to say the least, but no one could really blame him for wanting what was rightfully his.

After leaving the house last night, Joseph had sat on a bench in Capitol Square for a long time, thinking. There was nothing left for him here. Margaret would never forgive him, and she would undoubtedly raise their son as a stranger to him. As he looked at the Stars and Bars hanging limply on the flagpole, he got up and walked slowly to the *Journal*, letting himself in with his key. He wrote a letter to Margaret and his resignation for Lewis, and then he slept for a few hours until daybreak. He then left the paper to find the recruiting office.

When Melissa arrived at the paper, she found an envelope with Margaret's name on it along with a note to her on her desk. The note was from Joseph, asking her to give the letter to Margaret.

After Lewis McAllen came in and read Joseph's resignation, he blustered around the office.

"The damn fool! Now what am I going to do? Everyone's leaving me. He didn't say anything about it to me yesterday. Miss Armstrong, did you know anything about this?"

"About what, Mr. McAllen?"

"Joseph. He's gone off to join the army."

Melissa shook her head sadly. "I didn't know."

"Well, until I can find someone else to replace him, you'll have to take care of the telegraph. Starting today, your wages are $1.25 a day."

Still spouting off, Lewis went back to his office and slammed the door. Melissa was stunned—poor Joseph. She took a nickel out of her reticule and went over to Ish, the little black errand boy.

"Here's a nickel, Ish. I want you to take this letter to my house. Do you know where that is?"

"Yessum," he grinned, inspecting the nickel. "I gone dere a lot fo' Masta Lewis."

Melissa sat down wearily at her desk and tried to concentrate on her work.

By nightfall, Joseph found himself at Camp Lee on the outskirts of Richmond, a corporal and telegraph operator for General Beauregard's staff.

Nine

Andrew arrived home December 20, in time for the Christmas festivities. He was full of tales again, mostly of camp life. The inclement weather had held military action to a minimum, and he was happy to once again be in the city. The vain, good-looking Andrew intended to pay close attention to all the ladies of Richmond.

Jackson had recovered completely and planned to rejoin his unit after Christmas. Sabina had made him a new uniform, and he had managed to procure a new horse, saber, and revolver. Once again, he presented the appearance of the robust cavalier, for the care and food he had received had put flesh back on his lanky frame and returned the sparkle to his smile.

At Nancy's insistence, he had stayed on at the Armstrong house. He had considered proposing marriage to Melissa, but after some thought on the matter, decided it wouldn't be practical. He knew as well as anyone how uncertain his life would be once he returned to the cavalry. So he left his feelings unspoken.

When Margaret first learned of Joseph's joining the army, her first reaction had been one of good riddance. But since then, she had mellowed and hoped he was all right.

No one had heard a word from him since he had left. At Melissa's request, Henry had been able to find out to which unit Joseph belonged.

Henry had grown very fond of Melissa. For his own sake, he had kept close friendships in Richmond to a minimum. He knew many people but none of them well, except perhaps Melissa. And he really didn't know her all that well. His journalistic talents had earned him a name for himself in Richmond, and he was well respected by the people, the politicians, and the army.

Edward was amassing quite a tidy little sum from the Tidewater Nail Company. As he had predicted, the prices had risen, and now nails were selling for ten dollars a keg.

The people's hearts were not as full of merriment as in past holiday seasons, and the weather did nothing to dispel this feeling. It was snowy and rainy, never extremely cold, but it was an unhealthy and uncomfortable time. Instead of the usual round of parties and receptions, the women stayed at home in the evenings to knit scarves and socks for the soldiers' Christmas bags.

The first family was doing no entertaining, for Mrs. Davis had given birth to little William Howell Davis a few days before.

Melissa had embroidered Jackson's name on each of a pair of white leather gauntlets as her gift to him. She had had to work on them in the evenings in her room, so that he wouldn't be apt to walk in on her while she was embroidering. She felt she should have a gift for Henry, so she bought him a warm wool muffler.

On the evening after Andrew's return, Melissa was in her room just finishing Jackson's gloves when Mahaley tapped on the door.

"You do neat work," Mahaley remarked, examining

Melissa's handiwork.

"Thank you."

"I had a wonderful idea," Mahaley began. "With Andrew home now, we have to make sure he's at home when we decorate the tree."

"I'm sure he'll want to be."

"Oh, I don't know. If I know my brother, he'd rather spend his time in a brothel."

"Mahaley, what a thing to say!"

"Oh, don't be such a prude." She plumped herself down on the bed and pushed her golden curls away from her face. "It's true, you know. Besides, I know what's been going on with you and Jackson."

"Nothing's been going on," Melissa said. And it was true, to some extent. At least, she thought, "that" hadn't happened yet.

"Oh, well, it doesn't matter anyway. What I came in to tell you is that I think Ellen and Andrew would make a nice couple. After all, I like Nathaniel, so why shouldn't my brother like his sister?"

"But they don't even know each other."

"I know that," Mahaley said. "That's why we have to make sure Andrew's here."

"Well, I don't see how we can make sure he'll stay home. Besides, maybe Ellen wouldn't care for him. Some people don't appreciate matchmakers."

"Well, it won't hurt to introduce them."

"I'll try to think of something."

"Good. And I'll mention it to Jackson tomorrow when we go to get the tree," Mahaley said. "Good night."

After Mahaley had gone, Melissa smiled to herself. She had never known anybody who was so fascinated with the subject of romance. She wondered if Mahaley had been

186

trying to make her jealous by that remark about going to get the Christmas tree with Jackson. If she had, it hadn't worked. Melissa wasn't jealous because she wasn't emotionally involved with Jackson. She liked him well enough, and they did their share of fooling around, but to get serious with a soldier now was complete idiocy in her mind. Jackson was always very attentive to Melissa's every wish, and for this she was very grateful. Besides, she knew Jackson wasn't interested in Mahaley. He had even referred to her as a "scatterbrained female" on more than one occasion.

After bundling up in their warmest coats and collecting the ax and saw from Bobo, Jackson and Mahaley started out of town in the wagon in search of a Christmas tree. The wagon bumped along over the thin, crusted ice and muddy chuckholes. Jackson soon found himself tiring of Mahaley's endless chatter and he was mightily relieved when they found a group of promising-looking trees.

Mahaley studied Jackson's lean and athletic figure appreciatively, clad in a pair of her brother's snug-fitting trousers.

"How big?" he asked.

Her fantasies interrupted, Mahaley was briefly taken aback by his question.

"What?"

"How big a tree do you want?"

"Oh, I don't know. Bigger than you, I guess," she smiled.

After selecting an eight-foot pine, Jackson began to chop. He was pleased with the way his arm was reacting to the exertion, but he was winded by the time he had finished.

"I'm out of shape," he remarked, as he settled the tree in the wagon.

"You look pretty good to me," Mahaley smiled. "How's your arm?"

"Not too bad. Now, how many branches do you want?"

"Just a couple."

Jackson sawed off three branches from another tree, which, he had been told, would decorate the front door. A light snow started to fall as he climbed back into the wagon.

"Let's go, before this gets any worse," he said.

"You know, I was telling Melissa I think we should get Andrew and Ellen together," Mahaley said.

"Oh?"

"Yes. But I'm afraid Andrew won't be home Sunday night. You know how soldiers are on leave."

"Yes, I know," he smiled. "But it's Christmas Eve. Surely he'll want to be with his family. I know I would."

"That's sweet."

Jackson's eyes widened, for all of a sudden, Mahaley's mittened hand was on his thigh.

"You're a very nice man, Jackson. You know, you're not at all like I had imagined you'd be when we first met."

"I'm not?" He was wondering what to do or say next, for Mahaley's hand was slowly creeping up his thigh.

"No. I thought you'd be just like all the other soldiers."

"How's that?"

"Oh, you know," she giggled. "But you're not like that at all. You're almost kind of shy."

Jackson looked at her out of the corner of his eye.

"Well, you're surely not."

Mahaley flashed him an inviting smile, and for an instant, Jackson was tempted to give in to this invitation. But as he looked at Mahaley's face and saw the strange combination of sensuality and innocence, he thought of what the consequences of a dalliance with Melissa's cousin might be like. Ashamed and embarrassed at his physical reaction, he gently pushed Mahaley's hand away.

She looked questioningly at him and all he could say was "This is neither the time nor the place for such things."

Bobo was waiting to help unload the Christmas tree. Jackson saw that Mahaley was waiting around for him so he offered to give Bobo a hand. If she thought he was about to make any advances toward her, she was sadly mistaken. If Edward ever got wind of any shenanigans, he would never hear the end of it. Melissa would probably never forgive him either, and it was Melissa he wanted.

Disappointed, Mahaley went into the house.

Margaret was in the kitchen supervising the packing up of food to be distributed to the soldiers in the hospitals. There was baked ham, fruitcake, and Tunia was spooning cooked sweet potatoes into glass jars.

"Did you get the tree?" Margaret asked.

"Yes," Mahaley grumbled, hurrying out of the kitchen and upstairs.

That evening, everyone was gathered in the drawing room except Andrew. Margaret and Nancy were still busy knitting for the soldiers, Edward was reading the paper, Mahaley and Melissa were sitting on the floor fashioning bows and tying them onto the pine bough, and Jackson was watching them.

"Oh, I forgot to tell you, Jackson," Melissa said. "A message came through at the paper today about Jeb."

"Not bad news, I hope?" Nancy asked.

"Yes and no. He's not hurt or anything, but I guess that little expedition up at Dranesville failed."

"Failed? How?" Jackson wondered. "It had been worked out so carefully."

A group of Pennsylvania infantry and artillery led by General Ord had been lying in wait for Jeb Stuart and his band of Confederate foragers. Stuart's force, comprised mostly of infantry, had been severely routed.

"I think our military information is getting up to the Yankees," Edward said. "President Davis should tell his men to keep their mouths shut better. Anybody with half a brain could figure out what our army's planning, the way everybody talks so freely."

Melissa swallowed and continued working with the ribbons. More and more, her suspicions about Henry were growing. She frankly didn't care one way or the other what he was, but she wouldn't like to see him get caught if he were a spy.

"Were there any casualties?" Jackson asked her.

"Yes. About forty killed and over one hundred wounded. There weren't any names yet."

"How about the Yankees?" Nancy asked.

"There weren't any figures. Their losses were less, though."

"I hope it wasn't any of my friends," Jackson sighed. "I think I'll go on upstairs now. Good night, all."

Jackson had purchased several yards of red velvet

190

ribbon from Sabina to tie around his Christmas gifts. While in the drawing room. he had been studying how Melissa was making her bows for the pine spray, but after forty-five minutes, all he had was a tangled mess. Gathering up his presents and the ribbon, he first checked the hall to make sure no one was about, and then he hurried down to Melissa's room. He tapped on the door.

Melissa was soaking in the tub. "Who is it?"

"Jackson."

"Oh, Jackson, come back in about ten minutes."

At the same time Melissa was answering him, Jackson heard Nancy and Mahaley coming up the stairs, laughing and talking. Not having enough time to get back to his own room to hide the presents, he opened the door and stepped into Melissa's room. He looked around but didn't see her, but he heard the water sloshing behind the screen.

Melissa had just been stepping out of the tub when she heard the door shut. "Is that you, Jackson?"

"Yes." He set down his bundles on a chair.

"Didn't you hear me say to come back later?" she asked, peering over the top of the screen. With her hair tied on top of her head, the water glistened on her bare shoulders and neck.

"I'm sorry. I wanted you to put ribbons on my Christmas gifts," he said. "I got caught out in the hall with your aunt and Mahaley coming. I didn't want them to see the presents, so I came in here."

"Well, just a minute then. Let me get dried off and put on my robe." She looked around and discovered she had forgotten to hang her robe over the screen. "Oh, fiddle! Do you see my robe out there anyplace?"

Jackson glanced around until his eyes fell on the pink robe on the chair, buried under the presents. "This pink thing?" he asked her.

"Yes. Would you hand it to me, please?"

Jackson looked at the arm extended out from behind the screen and then at the robe. Biting his lip, he reached out and caught Melissa's wrist, giving it a gentle tug. Lest she lose her balance, Melissa stepped out from the screen, clutching the towel in front of her.

"Jackson," she complained, half smiling. "What do you think you're doing?"

"This," he whispered, enfolding her in his arms and kissing her. Jackson pulled the ribbon, releasing her hair to cascade over her shoulders. Melissa allowed her hands to creep up to his neck, leaving the towel to stay wedged in between them.

A tap on the door startled them. "It's me, Miss Melissa," Cindy called. "I brung de wawmin' pan."

Melissa looked into Jackson's face and smiled. "Never mind, Cindy. I won't be needing it tonight."

She turned back to Jackson, and their eyes met meaningfully for an instant before she allowed herself to be swept up into his arms and carried to the waiting bed.

Jeremiah sat back on his haunches and studied his workmanship. Yes, it was a fine train. Every spare moment for more than a month, he had been working on it. He gave the rope a slight tug, and the wooden engine rolled a few inches, followed by a wooden coal car and lastly the open freight car. Little Mary and Frank McClelland would love it. He had to admit, his woodcarving had turned out much better than he had ever hoped for. His biggest problem had been the cow

192

catcher, for it had needed to be attached separately and didn't want to stay. But one of his patients had been a carpenter, and Jeremiah gave him free medical treatment in return for helping him with the train.

For Sam and Sarah, he had purchased a small chiming mantel clock, for Sarah had often complained about not having a clock. For Grandma White, as he had come to call Sarah's mother, he had a decorated silver thimble, and for Jim he had a new watch fob with his name engraved on it. He bought a slate for Corky to practice his reading and writing lessons upon, and a china teapot for Nick and Pearl. His present for Captain Reno was a new pipe.

When he looked at the pile of Christmas gifts on the table, he wondered how he had let himself get so extravagant with his money. The reason was simple, he knew. These people were now his family. Melissa was far away in Richmond, the capital of the Confederacy. As far as Jeremiah was concerned, she might as well be on the moon. Granted, the correspondence was steady, and for this he was grateful, but he wanted to see her again. He had talked to a government man about securing a pass to go south for a visit, but it was difficult to do and risky to undertake. Besides, he really didn't feel he should take the time off from his work and studies.

After changing his clothes and shaving, he gathered up some of his gifts and started for the McClellands'. He had outgrown his first heavy winter coat and had to invest in a new one. He had grown a lot in the time he had been in Pittsburgh. His features were strong, as his father's had been, but a certain resemblance to his mother softened the sharp planes of his face. He had sprouted a few inches taller and filled out, and, at nineteen, he cut a fine figure.

Sam had evidently shoveled the walk recently, for, as Jeremiah stepped up to the porch, it was one of the few places that was clear of snow.

Sam opened the door with a big grin on his face. "Merry Christmas!"

"Merry Christmas," Jeremiah smiled, kicking the snow off his boots and stepping inside.

Jeremiah set his presents down, and Sam took his coat and scarf. Sarah came out of the parlor to greet him.

"Oh Jeremiah, come in and warm yourself," she welcomed him, taking his arm. "You must be frozen stiff."

"It is a little nippy out there," he admitted.

Dr. White handed him a cup of eggnog. "That should take the chill out of your bones."

Captain Ben had been entertaining the children with a tale. Frank and Mary left him to run over to Jeremiah, hugging him around the knees. Both blond like their parents, their sturdy little bodies radiated good health and a loving home.

"Santa Claus comes tonight!" Frank squealed.

"I know. Have you been a good boy all year?"

"Sort of," he said reluctantly.

Jeremiah set down his eggnog and picked up four-year-old Mary. "And what do you want Santa to bring you?"

"A new baby."

"Oh," Jeremiah said, trying to keep a straight face. He glanced at Sarah, who shrugged her shoulders.

"I want a pony," Frank announced.

"Don't you think you're a little too small for a pony?"

"Not if it's a little pony."

Sarah came over to them and picked Frank up. "I think it's time you two went to bed. I promised you could wait for Jeremiah, and now that you've seen him, it's bedtime."

"But . . ."

"You want to be asleep when Santa comes, don't you?" Sam said. "Come on, I'll go up and tuck you in."

The children said good night to Jeremiah and Ben. Sam and Sarah carried them upstairs to the little bedroom Frank and Mary shared with their grandmother.

"When will Santa Claus get here?" Frank asked, as Sarah tucked the covers around him.

"Not for a while yet. He has lots of stops to make," Sarah replied.

"Does he visit those Rebs?" Frank asked.

"Yes. I'm sure he visits all little children," Sarah said.

"Even in the South," Sam added.

"Is he gonna bring me a new baby?" Mary wondered.

"Hush now," Sarah said, kissing both their foreheads. "Go to sleep."

Sam bent down to kiss his children and then followed Sarah out of the room. He put his arm around her waist and gave her a gentle squeeze.

"Maybe we ought to see about that new baby," he smiled. "I allow it won't be here for Christmas, but . . ."

"Why, Sam McClelland!" Sarah giggled.

He winked at her. "I think maybe we ought to look into that this very night."

Sam had another reason for his sentimental mood. Unknown to Sarah, he had joined the navy. He wouldn't be on the regular warships, but all the same, it was the navy. The hospital steamer USS *Madison* was ready to go, and after the new year, she was heading for the Mississippi with Lieutenant Sam McClelland at the engines.

*   *   *

Andrew had just finished pouring the contents of two bottles of brandy into the eggnog in the huge cut-crystal bowl. After stirring it with the ladle, he filled a cup and sampled the mixture.

"Wow," he murmured, smacking his lips, as Mahaley came in.

She eyed the empty bottles. "What do you want to do—get everybody drunk?"

"Might be rather fun. At least it would liven up the party."

"Then you're going to stay?"

"For a while anyway. It's always the same: we'll trim the tree, then Mother will play the piano while we sing Christmas carols, and then we'll exchange presents."

"So? What's wrong with that?"

Bobo had put the tree in the corner earlier, and it stood bare, waiting for its trimmings. The candles had been hard to find, but ever-resourceful Edward had come up with some. The bows and small candies were waiting in a basket by the tree.

Jackson had taken his gifts into Edward's study when Melissa came in with hers. She was wearing a red velvet gown with white lace at the bodice and cuffs.

"You look lovely," he smiled.

"Thank you."

He set his gifts down and took her in his arms. "I'm the luckiest man in the world," he said. "This is going to be the best Christmas I've ever had."

Melissa smiled, but he saw a touch of sadness in her eyes.

He touched her chin with his fingertips. "What's wrong?"

"Oh, I don't know. I've been thinking all day today, this is my first Christmas without either Papa or Jeremiah."

"I know. I've been thinking about my brother too."

Melissa had been very successful in keeping her mind off her father until that afternoon when they went to deliver the food to the hospitals. Lying in a cot with both his legs gone had been Ethan Smith, wounded at Buffalo Mountain. She could feel no animosity toward him—only pity.

She looked at Jackson and smiled. "We'll just have to make the best of it. Come on, let's go sample that eggnog before the guests arrive."

When Melissa and Jackson went into the dining room, they found Lewis McAllen talking to Edward.

"Miss Armstrong, how beautiful you look tonight," Lewis said.

"Why, thank you, Mr. McAllen."

"Is there any mistletoe hanging someplace I might lure you under?"

Melissa blushed and looked a little surprised.

"I knew there was something we forgot," Edward remarked.

Tunia brought a plate of little cakes out of the kitchen and set them on the table. While Lewis was examining the food, Jackson ladled some eggnog for Melissa and himself.

"I understand you'll be rejoining the cavalry, Lieutenant Vaughn," Lewis said.

"On the twenty-sixth."

"I hope you can prod them into a little action. This doing nothing makes me nervous."

"It's near impossible to move men and horses and

equipment over roads in weather like this. The Yankees are in the same fix."

Tunia returned with more food just as the large brass knocker on the door announced another caller. Cindy was upstairs, still helping Nancy and Margaret to dress.

"I'll get it, Tunia," Melissa said, taking her eggnog with her.

Henry was waiting on the porch as she opened the door.

"Merry Christmas, Miss Armstrong."

"Merry Christmas. Please come in."

Henry stepped inside with several parcels. He handed a small box to her. "This is for you," he said. "And this other is for the family."

She examined the box while Henry took off his coat and hat and hung them on the wall tree.

"You look very nice tonight, Miss Armstrong."

"Thank you. But could I ask you to do me a great favor?"

"Anything."

"Would you please call me Melissa?"

Nancy and Margaret came down the stairs, followed by Cindy.

"Mr. Walkenfeldt, I'm so happy you could come tonight," Nancy said.

"Thank you, Mrs. Armstrong. It was very good of you to invite me." He handed her the package of brown paper. "Merry Christmas."

"Oh, can I open it now?" she asked. "I just love surprises, and I haven't been able to open anything yet. My husband's very strict about that."

"Open it whenever you like."

"Why don't we go in to the others, and Henry can have

198

some eggnog?" Melissa suggested. Before anyone could move, there was another knock at the door.

It was Ellen and Nathaniel Aldrich. After the seasonal greetings and removing their wraps, everyone went into the dining room.

"I believe everyone knows everyone else," Nancy said.

"I don't," Andrew smiled, stepping over to the newcomers.

"Oh, that's right, dear," Nancy said, and made the introductions. "Mr. Walkenfeldt brought me a present, and I'm going to open it right now."

While everyone watched, Nancy unwrapped the package to discover two pounds of butter, a necessity which was rapidly becoming a luxury.

"Thank you, Mr. Walkenfeldt. This is something we can use probably better than most anything else we might get." She handed it to Mahaley. "Take this out to the kitchen, dear, and give it to Tunia."

Everyone filled their cups with Andrew's potent eggnog and retired into the drawing room. Mahaley stopped on the way to refill her cup a third time.

"Are we going to trim the tree now?" Mahaley asked. "Father, you always put the star on the top first."

Edward pulled the piano stool over and climbed upon it, attaching the tin star to the top of the tree. He then sat back down to watch the younger people do the decorating. Besides remarks on the tree, the conversation centered on the political situation, as usual.

"Where did you ever find that butter?" Ellen asked Henry. "We're having trouble getting enough at the Commissary Department."

"A woman in the building where I live makes

her own."

"That's a good idea," Melissa remarked.

"We don't know anything about making butter," Mahaley giggled.

"I do," Melissa said. "It's easy. All we need is a butter churn."

After Jackson had hung the decorations on the uppermost branches of the tree, he sat down to drink his eggnog. The more he thought about Melissa's talents and abilities, the more he wished he were free to marry her. He was almost beginning to wish he wasn't in the cavalry.

Lewis and Edward had gotten into a rather heated discussion about the government's failure to regulate the printing of currency and the hated "shinplasters" which were appearing everywhere. Due to the lack of small bills issued by the treasury, some towns, counties, and private bankers had printed bills in the denominations of one dollar, fifty cents, and twenty-five cents to meet the shortage. Their backing by gold was questionable, and they were becoming a glut on the market.

"Is Augustus all ready to leave on Wednesday?" Lewis asked him.

"Where's Augustus going?" Nancy wondered.

"That, my dear, is a little surprise I have for you," Edward smiled. "A little business venture I've decided to undertake with Augustus, Lewis, and John."

"What is it?"

"You mean you haven't told her yet?" Lewis asked him.

"I thought I'd wait, but now that the subject's come up . . . We're going to buy a ship."

"A ship? Father, what do you want with a ship?" Margaret asked.

"Not just an ordinary ship—a blockade runner, designed especially for getting past those damnable Yankee patrols."

"Edward, do you think it's wise?" Nancy asked.

"Only time will tell. We've been in contact with a firm in Liverpool for some months now. Augustus is going over to make the final arrangements. I'd go myself, but I can't take the time off from work. She's a beauty, according to the builders."

"I think it's wonderful!" Mahaley exclaimed.

"I hope you'll be bringing in medicines," Nathaniel said. "We need them very badly."

"Medicines, arms, clothing . . . whatever."

"I wish I'd known before I signed up for another three years," Andrew muttered. "I might like to do that instead."

"You don't know anything about ships," Mahaley told him.

"I didn't know anything about soldiering before, either."

Melissa stood back to admire the nearly completed tree. "I think I'll go get another eggnog," she said. "Can I get some for anyone else?"

Four empty cups were immediately thrust in her direction.

"I'll help you," Henry smiled.

The two of them went into the dining room.

"I can't imagine old McAllen risking his money on an investment like that," Henry laughed. "He's so tight with his money."

"I know. And Uncle Edward too. I don't mean he's a pennypincher. He's very generous. But I didn't think he was the type to get involved in something like this."

"It might pay off handsomely."

She looked directly at Henry over the punch bowl. "Perhaps you'll think I'm crazy, and if you don't understand what I'm going to say, then just forget that I ever said it. But as long as my uncle's involved in this, please don't say anything to anyone about the boat. I don't want my uncle to get hurt in any way. He's been very good to me."

"Why would I want to tell anyone?"

"That's something only you can answer, Henry."

At that moment, looking into Melissa's blue eyes and solemn face, Henry knew that she knew. Or if she didn't know for sure, she suspected strongly. He didn't know how to react. Could he expect a visit from the provost marshal, or could he trust her?

Henry's normally cool composure was momentarily shaken, and Melissa saw this. If her suspicions were right, she wanted to reassure him. But if they were wrong, she didn't want to say anything more that might indicate her true feelings.

A chord from the piano brought them both out of their thoughts.

"Come on," she smiled. "Let's go back and join the party."

Cindy stuck her head out the kitchen door.

"Cindy, why don't you take these cakes into the drawing room so everybody won't forget about them?" Melissa suggested. "And then fix some eggnog for yourself and Bobo and Tunia."

"Fo' us, Miss Melissa?" she asked, incredulous.

"Of course. It's Christmas for you too, you know."

Andrew had forgotten about his earlier plans to leave the party. Ellen hadn't shown any particular interest in him, nor had he in her, but they were both taking each other's measure. He found her to be rather pretty and very sweet, and possibly very vulnerable.

After a few songs and more eggnog and food, Mahaley and Melissa distributed the gifts. Mahaley was becoming a little tipsy, but no one thought anything about it.

Lewis took two small packages from his pocket and handed one each to Melissa and Henry. "Those are just a little insurance that neither of you will leave the paper for a while."

The gifts proved to be a wooden nameplate for each of their desks. Next, Margaret opened her gift from Jackson—a box of bonbons. Melissa gave Andrew an oilcloth map case, and Andrew gave the entire family a large gilt-framed daguerreotype of himself in his uniform. Both Jackson and Henry were appreciative of their gifts from Melissa, and she received from Henry a painted porcelain ink bottle, and an inlaid rosewood trinket box from Jackson. Nancy and Edward gave her a fur muff. Mahaley gave Jackson a plume for his new hat, and a fine shaving brush to Nathaniel.

After the rest of the gifts had been opened and the last of the eggnog drunk, the guests prepared to leave.

Andrew caught Mahaley's arm. "Are Ellen and Nathaniel coming tomorrow for dinner?" he whispered.

"Yes."

At the door, Andrew took Ellen's hand in his. "It was a pleasure meeting you, Miss Aldrich. I'll look forward to seeing you tomorrow."

"Thank you."

Mahaley poked Melissa. "See? I told you."

The weather didn't deter the family from attending the

Christmas church services at St. Paul's. The usual greetings were accompanied by inquiries of boys in the field or being held prisoner in the North.

Tunia had prepared a buffet, and when the family returned from church, the servants were given their presents and the rest of the day to do as they pleased. Bobo received a new coat, actually one of Andrew's old ones. Tunia got a new apron and kerchief and Cindy got a new dress.

Jackson was rather quiet all day long, for he didn't want to leave the next day. This family had become very important to him, and he dreaded leaving. They had more or less adopted him as one of their own. When Edward had presented him with a fine pair of field glasses, he had been deeply touched. His melancholy increased as he lay in bed with Melissa nestled in his arms that night.

His thoughts were interrupted as Melissa spoke. "When do you think we'll see each other again?"

"The next time I get into town, I expect," he sighed, stroking her soft hair. "And that'll be as soon as possible, if I have any say-so."

"Don't go trying to be a hero. I'd like you back in one piece next time."

"Will you miss me?"

"Of course I will."

He leaned over her, resting on his elbow, and studied her face in the moonlight.

"Will you do something for me while I'm gone?" he asked.

"What?"

"Would you go down to the photography studio and have your picture taken for me? I don't know why I didn't think of it before. I'd like to have it now to take ack with me, but I'll just have to wait. Would you do ?"

"Of course. If I'd known you wanted one, I could've ad it for your Christmas present."

"The gauntlets are just fine. Besides, the way I really vant to remember you is just the way you are now," he vhispered, kissing her.

The city seemed a little more quiet the following week vith many of the soldiers having gone back to their espective camps. Melissa felt a little sorry to see Jackson o, and the miserable weather did nothing to help. Iowever, New Year's Day dawned crisp and bright for iovernor Letcher's reception. Owing to the blockade, he usual champagne had to be replaced by steaming hot oddy, but the affair was as ever full of the good-humored ospitality and dignified courtesy for which his func-ions were famous. Melissa was a little surprised to see Irs. Davis up and about so soon after the birth of her on.

Melissa found Henry once more being complimented or his writing and involved in discussions with the noted oliticians. There were many complaints about the nactivity of the army.

"We're going to work out west," Davis said. "That's he only place the weather will permit the troops to do nything. Beauregard, Van Dorn, and Price are working n something right now."

"The Mississippi?" Henry asked him.

"It's the only place, like I said. But I can't say any nore right now. I just don't know any more."

Three weeks later, Melissa discovered a folded piece of

205

paper lying on the floor by Henry's desk after he had gone home for the day. He was usually meticulously neat, so she picked it up and unfolded it. Scrawled upon the paper was: "Springfield. Van Dorn—18,000. Price—15,000. McCulloch—Indians. Mid-February."

Carefully refolding the paper, she slipped it into her reticule. After finishing her work for the day, she went home, pondering the information contained in Henry's note. She had planned to throw it away and not involve herself until she read Jeremiah's letter, which Edward had picked up at the post office. Sam was in the navy, on a hospital ship stationed at Cairo, not from from Springfield. If Henry's information could prevent Sam from being in danger, then she was determined to help.

After supper, she put on her cloak and bonnet and had Bobo drive her to Henry's boardinghouse. It was not the nicest of neighborhoods, but the inside appeared clean as she climbed the stairs to the second floor.

Henry had spent the last two hours in a panic. After discovering the note missing from his pocket, he went back to the paper and searched everywhere. When he returned to his room, he checked to make sure his pistol was loaded and then packed his bags. If the note had been found at the paper, its writer would be known. If he had lost it elsewhere, he might go undetected. But he could take no chances. He cursed himself for being so foolish as to have written down the information in the first place.

He was just packing away the last of his possessions when there was a tap at the door. Even if he had had two good legs, he wouldn't have considered going out the window. Picking up his pepperbox pistol, he went over to the door.

"Who's there?" he called.

"Melissa."

He opened the door a crack and peered out. "What are you doing here?"

"If you'll let me come in, I'll tell you."

Henry stood back and allowed her to enter. Melissa gazed at the suitcase and then at the pistol in Henry's hand as he locked the door.

"Are you planning to shoot me?" she smiled.

"What?" He looked at the gun and then laid it on top of the bureau. "What are you doing here?"

"I have something of yours." She reached into her reticule and took out the note, handing it to him. "You dropped this in the office."

"Did you read it?"

"Yes."

"Did anyone else see it?"

"No."

He stared at her for a long moment, trying to decide what to do or say next.

"It's all right, Henry. I know what you are. I'm on your side. I want to help if I can."

Henry was so relieved, he felt like crying. In all his life, he had never known such fear as he had experienced in the last two hours. "Oh, Melissa," he mumbled, putting his arms around her and hugging her. "You don't know what a relief it is—what I've been going through since I lost this."

"I know. That's why I came as soon as I could. Appparently it was just in time."

Henry realized he was holding her in his arms and backed away. "Forgive me. I didn't mean to be so personal."

"It's all right."

"You really are for the Union?"

"Yes. But nobody knows."

"That makes two of us then." He smiled, then he began to laugh. "Oh, Melissa, you don't know how happy I am right now. I feel like celebrating. My landlady made some blackberry wine. Would you join me for a glass?"

"I'd love to."

Henry poured the wine into two glasses from a big glass jar. "Please sit down," he said, taking his coat off the only chair in the room. He handed her the glass. "I think I feel much better about things right now." He sat down on the bed. "It's been very hard not being able to confide in anyone."

"I can imagine."

"I've always felt you were Union, but I didn't dare say anything. Your family doesn't suspect me, do they?"

"No. You're quite a hero, really. Your writing is very convincing."

"It's meant to be. Since we have no more secrets, I may as well tell you that I knew your brother in Pittsburgh."

"You did?" Melissa's heart began to pound as the joy of realization that Henry was acquainted with Jeremiah began to sink in.

"When did you see him last?"

"In the spring. He fixed my leg."

"Then you weren't hurt in California?"

Henry laughed. "I've never been in California in my life."

"Henry Walkenfeldt, you amaze me. Now, tell me all about Jeremiah."

"Oh, I didn't know him very well at all. He seemed like a very capable doctor when he took care of me. He

208

mentioned about the mails, and so I said I might be able to help him out, never dreaming I'd run into you. He never said what you looked like, but as soon as I saw you, I could see a resemblance."

"He actually performed an operation on you?" She swelled with pride in remembering her brother who once had cried for hours because their setter's broken leg could not be mended.

"I was in very capable hands," Henry smiled.

"I guess it's a small world, after all," she laughed. "I'll have to write him about this."

"I'd rather you didn't."

"Oh, that's right. Well, tell me what I can do to help."

"Nothing."

"But, Henry, I want to."

"It's too dangerous, Melissa."

"Oh, fiddle! Henry Walkenfeldt, I've already given you information, although I didn't know it at the time."

"I know that. But if you were caught, do you know what would happen to you?"

"Castle Thunder?"

"A noose, more likely."

Melissa's eyes widened. "Then why do you do it?"

"I believe in the Union. Besides, somebody has to do it, and so far, I've been able to pass myself off as a confirmed Secessionist." He stood up and put his glass down. "Now, as much as I enjoy your company, I think it's time for you to leave. If anyone saw you come up here, it might not help your reputation."

"I suppose you're right. Although I told Uncle Edward I was coming here. Don't worry," she smiled, standing up. "I told him you left some papers at the office for a story you were working on, and I knew you planned to

209

use them tonight."

"Why didn't he just have your man deliver them?"

"Margaret had been acting ornery all through supper, and she was still at it when I left. Uncle Edward told me he didn't blame me for wanting to get out for a while."

"Well, I thank you for your help."

"I plan to do more, Henry. You can't overlook the fact that I have access to information. My uncle works in the War Department, and the Davis family seems very fond of me. And don't forget my correspondence with Jackson, or Andrew's letters. When nobody suspects you, they tell you all kinds of things. If I knew what to look for, I could be a wealth of information."

"I know, Melissa. But please let's just leave it this way for now."

"Very well," she sighed. "Good night, Henry."

"Good night, Melissa."

After Melissa got into bed that night, she couldn't sleep for thinking about her position. Her lover and her cousin and Joseph were wearing the gray. She didn't want to do anything to endanger their lives. On the other hand, her brother and Sam were for the Union, and they believed in the same principles in which she believed. Jeremiah was all she had left, and Sam was like a brother. Andrew, she felt, wasn't the type of man to put himself in a position of peril. Jackson was a trained soldier and a member of the finest cavalry units in the South. His injury had been a consequence of the ridiculous debacle which took place in Manassas. Joseph was only a telegraph operator.

Castle Thunder wouldn't be a pretty place to sit out the war, and the thought of hanging terrified her. Yet how or why would anyone possibly suspect her? For one thing, she was a woman, and, as yet, no female spies had come into prominence. Another reason for her immunity from suspicion was her family. Certainly no one would ever doubt the loyalty of the niece of Edward Armstrong, for wasn't he one of the biggest contributors to the war effort?

Melissa rolled over and punched her pillow, satisfied with her decision to help her friend Henry. She felt fairly confident in her safety, and all her instincts, which had usually been right, told her to assist him to get as much information as she could. Perhaps she could even help end this terrible destructive war sooner.

Melissa found Henry sitting at his desk when she arrived at the paper. She was usually the first one in besides the press operators and typesetters.

"I guess I better put the coffee on before Mr. McAllen gets here," she said.

The coffee left in the canister was all there was. She would have to remind Lewis to get in some more, if any could be found for sale. When she returned to her desk, she started sorting through her work.

"You know, Henry, I was thinking last night . . ."

"Hummm?"

"I thought perhaps Uncle Edward could get his friend John Denny to let you take a tour of the Tredegar Iron Works so you could write a story about it."

"That's ridiculous, Melissa. They don't let just anybody in there."

Lewis came in the front door. "What's ridiculous?"

"Melissa had an idea," Henry said.

"Melissa's ideas are usually pretty good. What is it?"

"Thank you, Mr. McAllen. As I was saying, if John Denny could arrange for Henry to take a tour of the Tredegar Iron Works and write a story about it . . ." Before either of the men could object, she continued, "I don't mean about what's being built inside. I mean about the morale of the factory workers, their patriotic spirit, how they feel about their contributions to the cause."

"That's positively brilliant!" Lewis exclaimed. "Miss Armstrong, you're a wonder. I'll get in touch with John today."

After Lewis had gone, Melissa smiled smugly at Henry. He grinned back at her.

Ten

Instead of the Mississippi River, Sam found himself
tied up outside Paducah, Kentucky waiting for orders to
follow the fleet of Flag Officer Andrew H. Foote down the
Tennessee River to Fort Henry. It was the morning of
February 3, and Sam was nervous. Even though his ship
would be bringing up the rear, he didn't know what to
expect.

The land troops under generals U. S. Grant and C. F.
Smith were already embarking from transports a few
miles below the fort. The Confederates were led by
Beauregard. The river below the fort was full of floating
mines, but most of these had been fished out of the water
and found to be useless because water had leaked inside
and wet the powder.

As the hospital steamer crept along, Sam heard the
pounding of the guns from the shore batteries. Before
long he was ordered to halt. One of the sailors rushed
down to the engine room, laughing.

"Them crazy Rebs just gave up!" he exclaimed.
"Didn't even give the army time to help us out."

"They surrendered?"

"Yep. The Reb commander came out in a rowboat and

gave the whole damned place to us."

Sam was amazed. This might be easier than he had anticipated. After the few wounded were taken aboard, the *Madison* started back toward the Ohio.

The reconnaissance reports were heartening, and Grant decided to take Fort Donelson, so once more Sam found himself following the fleet down the Cumberland River. The land troops had been reorganized, and it had taken Grant longer than he wished to get everything ready. But by the thirteenth, he was ready to move. The men who had camped out during the overland march from Fort Henry were not in the best of shape. They had slept without tents or fires and had insufficient food and clothing. Grant urged General Lew Wallace for reinforcements, and on the fourteenth, they made their rendezvous, and the flotilla arrived that afternoon.

Sam once more heard the pounding of the naval guns, and left his post to climb up on deck to watch. Foote was having troubles, for at close range, his gunners constantly overshot, while the Confederate gunners found their targets and did considerable damage. Foote, badly wounded himself, finally had to withdraw, leaving two boats disabled, two others damaged, and scores of dead and wounded.

Sam started up the engines, this time with a full load of wounded, and headed toward Cairo. By the time the ship was unloaded and ready to be sent back down to the fort, word arrived that it also had surrendered on the sixteenth.

Despite the surrender, the engagement had been a costly one for the Union, with 446 killed and 1,735 wounded. But the waterways to Alabama were open, the Memphis and Charleston railroad was in Union hands, and the North had its first real victory and a new public figure—Ulysses Simpson Grant.

The morning of February 23 dawned with a terrible rainstorm. However, that wasn't to deter Nancy, Mahaley, and Margaret from going to Capitol Square for the inauguration of Jefferson Davis. They left earlier than necessary to let Bobo get a spot close by to park the carriage, and even at that, they were none too soon. Within the hour, the crowds grew: some in carriages, some huddled under umbrellas or dripping hats, cloaks, blankets, oilcloths—anything that could be put to use as shelter from the driving rain. Boots were covered with muck, and skirts trailed in the mud, but still the people gathered.

A covered platform had been erected next to the bronze statue of George Washington where the dignitaries assembled for the ceremonies. Through sheets of rain, Bishop Johns opened the ceremony with a prayer. Then Judge J. D. Halyburton of the Confederate Circuit Court administered the oath of office to President Davis and Vice President Stephens, after which Jefferson Davis delivered his speech.

Even though few could hear anything that was said, the crowds cheered their president, for now the permanent Confederate government was officially established in Richmond. A party was held for the cabinet members and their families in the Virginia State Library, which was conveniently housed in the Capitol.

"I'm disappointed," Margaret sighed. "I didn't hear anything. Why couldn't they have waited until spring?"

"I think it was carried off very well, under the circumstances," Nancy said. "Besides, his speech will be in the paper tomorrow."

"Does anyone mind if I have Bobo and the carriage for a while this afternoon?" Mahaley wondered.

"I don't mind," Nancy said. "But surely you don't want to go out again in this?"

"I have an appointment for tea."

"Tea!" Margaret laughed. "That's funny! Not one restaurant in town serves tea anymore."

"You know what I mean," Mahaley said. "It doesn't sound very good to say one has an appointment for boiled sage leaves!"

Except for the very rich or those who, like Edward, had had the foresight to stockpile, coffee and tea had practically disappeared from the market. People were beginning to experiment with different substitutions for coffee—rye, corn, and sweet potatoes. The leaves of blackberry, sage, and currant were used in place of tea, while molasses and sorghum replaced sugar as a sweetener.

Mahaley hurried off for her "tea," which was really a meeting with a Mississippi sharpshooter.

Melissa and Edward got home from work and took off their dripping wraps.

"When will this dreadful weather ever stop?" Melissa sighed. "I don't believe we've had two successive nice days since the first of the year."

"Just between you and me, I'm glad I had to work today," Edward smiled. "Inauguration or not, I'd rather stay dry. Would you like some sherry to warm you up?"

"Oh, thank you, Uncle Edward, but I don't think so. I want to get ready for the reception. Henry is coming at seven."

"Melissa, perhaps this is none of my business, but your friendship with Henry . . . Don't get me wrong, I like Henry, but what about Lieutenant Vaughn?"

"Major Vaughn now," she reminded, smiling. "I haven't forgotten about him. I'm very fond of him. But I like Henry too. Henry and I are just friends."

"I didn't mean to pry."

"It's all right, Uncle Edward. But I'll tell you the same thing I've told myself a hundred times. As long as we're at war, I'm not going to allow myself to become serious with any man. I don't want to get hurt. Perhaps I'm selfish, but that's the way I feel."

"You're a smart girl. I wish my own daughters had your good sense. Margaret throwing away her marriage, and Mahaley . . ."

"What about Mahaley?"

"Oh, I don't know. It's just a gut feeling. When I see her around the soldiers at different functions, I worry about her. She's a little flirt. I wouldn't want her to get herself into any trouble. That young doctor seems a good influence on her, but if he's not around, she starts acting up."

"Oh, I'm sure it's nothing. I don't blame her for wanting attention. All girls do. And all the soldiers are more than willing to give it."

"I guess that's it," he smiled. "Her mother used to be the same way."

Melissa went up to her room and started to dress for the evening. She worried about Mahaley herself. She knew these soldiers well enough to know that when they came to town on a brief furlough, the majority wanted more than an innocent flirtation. It wasn't any of her affair, though. Melissa's opinion wouldn't be appreciated.

Besides, she was hardly in a position to speak, after her last three nights with Jackson. She hated to admit it, but those nights were what she missed most about Jackson.

She wondered if her photograph had reached him safely. She enjoyed her afternoon at Parker's Photography Studio so much that she was thinking about going back. She had sent a copy of her picture to Jeremiah, but now she was sorry she didn't have the whole family to send to him. Besides, she wasn't sure how much longer Mr. Parker would be in business. He mentioned he might be going out in the field with the army, as Matthew Brady was doing for the North.

The carriage was crowded on the way to the president's mansion, and all were glad it was a short drive. The gas lamps were glowing brightly, welcoming the guests to the warmth inside.

However, once the Armstrongs entered, they found few guests had arrived yet. The orchestra was playing to a nearly empty room, and the president and his wife were chatting to a few friends.

"Lordy, where is everybody?" Mahaley wondered. "What did he say in that speech today?"

"Hush!" Margaret warned, poking her sister in the side.

The president broke away from the group and came toward Edward, smiling, his hand outstretched. "Mr. Armstrong, how good of you to come."

"It's a privilege, sir," Edward said.

"And your charming ladies," Davis smiled. He then turned to Henry. "Mr. Walkenfeldt, I wish to compliment you again on your talents."

"Thank you, sir."

"Come. Join our little group." Davis linked his arm through Nancy's and patted her hand as they strolled across the room. "Mrs. Armstrong, you look lovely, as always."

"Why, thank you, Mr. Davis."

Nancy looked about her and noticed the admiring glances of the guests as she strolled the room on the president's arm. Thinking back to the time when she had married Edward at the age of seventeen and their restless wanderings with two small children in tow, her pleasure and pride at this triumphant moment were unmatched.

Gathered around Mrs. Davis were Attorney General Judah P. Benjamin and his wife; Vice President Alexander H. Stephens; Surgeon General Samuel P. Moore; and Senator Louis Wigfall and his wife, Louise. After introductions were made, glasses of punch were placed in the newcomers' hands.

"Isn't this weather just awful," Varina remarked. "I don't really blame the people for staying home."

"The fewer people, the more punch for us, eh?" Benjamin laughed.

"Isn't it a shame, of all occasions, to serve punch instead of champagne," Varina sighed. "The few bottles we could find, we put in the punch, but it just isn't the same."

"I think it's quite tasty," Margaret said. "What's in it?"

"Blackberry wine, some oranges, and of course, the champagne."

"Perhaps we should call it Rebel Punch," Henry smiled.

"That's very good," Davis laughed. "Just what we intend to do to the Yankees."

Melissa noticed Davis's attempt at levity seemed strained. He didn't look at all happy, as if something were bothering him—and indeed it was. The fall of Fort Donelson had been quite a blow to him. It had been the basis for the whole defense scheme of the West. And in the days following the surrender, the South had had to abandon Nashville and Fort Columbus as well.

"Mr. Walkenfeldt, I want to congratulate you on that wonderful story you did on the workers in the factories," Wigfall said.

"In my last communication with General Jackson, he mentioned your article," Davis told him. "When the men in the camps read your piece, it did wonders for their morale. He said they seemed to cheer up, knowing the factory workers were behind them so much."

Henry began to redden. "I'm glad. Anything that can brighten up our boys' spirits."

"You know, Walkenfeldt," Benjamin said, "we were talking the other day about starting up a little portrait gallery in the Capitol to honor the men who help the cause—not soldiers or politicians, but the others."

"And women too," Varina chided. "Don't forget the women."

Davis gave his wife an indulgent smile.

"Would you consider being one of our rogues' gallery, so to speak?" Benjamin asked Henry.

"I'd be honored, sir."

"Splendid." He turned to Wigfall. "Louis, I think you can bring it up to your committee."

Several more people arrived, so Henry took the opportunity to ask Melissa to dance.

Once they were out on the dance floor, Melissa gave him a mischievous smile. "Aren't you ashamed of yourself?"

"Yes and no."

"What's that supposed to mean?"

"Unfortunately, I like these people."

"So do I."

"Then you know how I feel."

As the evening progressed, more guests began to arrive. Upon entering the room, Nathaniel spotted Mahaley and went over to her.

"Oh, Nathaniel, I wondered what happened to you."

"I had to work late at the hospital."

Edward was talking to Samuel Moore, so Mahaley took Nathaniel over to them. The surgeon general was an elderly man, his thin face partially hidden by great white sideburns.

"Ah, Nathaniel, I see you finally got here," Edward said. "I'd like to present you to Surgeon General Moore. Dr. Moore, this is Dr. Nathaniel Aldrich."

The two men shook hands. "I'm very glad to meet you, sir," Nathaniel said. "I'd like to tell you how much I admire and respect you, especially what you've been doing to build up our hospital facilities."

"Where are you serving?"

"Right now I'm at Richmond General."

"You're very busy now."

"Yes sir. Fifty more men came in today—mostly pneumonia."

"I've been trying to persuade the army to get better supplies out to those soldiers. I was telling President Davis earlier. Those boys can't possibly be fit to fight come spring if conditions aren't made better."

"What's wrong?" Mahaley asked.

"This dreadful weather," Moore explained. "They

haven't enough shelter and warm clothing. They're suffering terribly from exposure: pneumonia, pleurisy, rheumatism, catarrhal fevers, lung diseases. And there's nothing we doctors can do about it until they're better supplied."

"One man who came in today told me he'd lie down to sleep in a dry spot, and wake up almost submerged in a puddle," Nathaniel remarked.

"Can't something be done?" Edward asked. "Surely the army must have the equipment."

Moore shook his head sadly. "I'm afraid not. That's why the medical department has to rely so strongly on the success of the blockade runners."

Edward nodded, making a mental note to order plenty of medicine, blankets, and clothing when, and if, his ship arrived. He could make his money well enough on satins and lace. Let the soldiers get the things they needed without his turning a profit.

"I think we ought to take up a collection of blankets and things," Mahaley suggested. "Certainly we have some to spare. And I'm sure most everyone does."

It was some time before Mahaley could get Nathaniel away from the surgeon general and out onto the dance floor.

"Nathaniel, do you like me?" she asked.

"Why, yes, of course I do. What a thing to ask."

"Do you think I'm pretty?"

"Yes. Very pretty."

She smiled at him, "And how long have we known each other?"

"Why, just since after Manassas, last summer. Why?"

"Then why haven't you ever kissed me?"

"I have kissed you—Christmas Day."

"On the cheek!" she exclaimed, pouting a little.

"Well . . ."

"I just wondered if there was something wrong with me? A girl likes to feel attractive."

"You are attractive."

"Then what are you waiting for?"

"Why, Mahaley, a gentleman doesn't kiss a lady right away. It's just not done."

"Oh, pooh! How much longer do we have to know each other? Besides," she smiled, tossing her golden curls, "what makes you think I'm a lady?"

"Because you just are."

Out in the field, Jackson spent the wet winter months camped near Manassas. The only things that brightened his days were Melissa's photograph and letters, and the new harmonica Jeb had given him for Christmas. As the snow and sleet piled up around them, Stuart's men entertained themselves by singing along with Jackson's harmonica and Sweeny's banjo.

In the meantime, Andrew was camped up on the Peninsula. Among the troops was a general feeling of weariness and discontent. Many of the men were sick, and some had to be sent to Richmond. Orders had been issued against gambling and liquor, but Andrew and some of his industrious comrades had set up a still in the woods. The wild blackberries and gooseberries they gathered went into the making of their brew, and they became quite popular among the men. An effort had been made to bolster their morale with religion, but moonshine and cards were preferred to the regimental chaplains.

Andrew's regiment was a little better off than some. The ones who had money could bribe their officers for leaves or furloughs, and go into the surrounding towns to avail themselves of whatever pleasures there were to be found. Discipline suffered, and insubordination was common.

Joseph was faring a little better. Camped near Corinth, the climate was healthier, the food was better, and he kept busy on his telegraph. The companionship and camaraderie he shared with his fellow soldiers made Joseph feel good. His superiors were pleased with his work, and for the first time in a long while, Joseph felt needed and appreciated, and most of all, he was happy.

The early part of March was not a good time for the South. The battle of Pea Ridge in Arkansas had been lost, and, with it, went the whole state of Missouri.

Richmond was full of soldiers on leave or en route to their camps. They filled themselves with bad whiskey and were too poor to pay the highly inflated hotel rates. Many slept on the sidewalks or in alleys, causing the respectable citizens to raise their voices in protest.

On March 5, General Winder ordered the city under martial law. The Union sentiment in the city was under observation, and the detectives made a number of arrests. It became necessary to obtain a passport to leave the city. However, the Passport Office and its employees were even worse than the muggers and thieves roaming the streets. Located at Ninth and Broad Streets, the office was a filthy place. The rowdy clerks harassed the applicants, and the place smelled from the thousands of old uniforms stored in the basement.

All the saloons and distilleries in the city and for a

radius of ten miles were ordered closed, and the only way liquor could be obtained was by a doctor's prescription. With their fondness for alcohol, Winder's men forged prescriptions and then turned around and arrested the unfortunate apothecary who sold it to them.

Winder also tried to regulate the prices of food. Groceries, liquor, or articles from abroad were exempted, which left the markets nearly empty. Butter and eggs disappeared altogether, and most of the meat was not fit to eat. Fish became the staple protein, but in order to get it, one had to go down to the market at the break of day and fight the crowds haggling over prices.

Nancy became one of the members of the newly formed Ladies' Defense Association, and their first task was to raise funds to build an ironclad steamer to patrol the James River.

Standing on the bridge of the blockade runner *Grasshopper* was George Ainsworth, supercargo. He had been employed by Augustus Given as seagoing clerk, to keep an eye on cargo, captain, pilot, and crew. He had been working at his desk in the Crown Shipping Company in Liverpool when he had been approached by the Virginia lawyer. He immediately accepted the job, hoping for a chance at adventure and riches. He was tall and lean, in his early thirties, and, right now, very tense.

The *Grasshopper* had been built especially for running the blockade, one of the first of its kind. She had been designed from the mistakes of the earlier blockade runners. With graceful lines, she was a two-funneled paddle steamer of 210 tons, made of steel, 196 feet, with an eighteen-foot beam. The two masts were the only equipage aloft. She rode only eight feet above the water and was painted entirely dull gray so that she would be nearly impossible to see on a dark night.

The crew was entirely English except for the pilot, Jacob Coonfield, a South Carolinian who knew the coast like the palm of his hand. The captain was Will Bubb, daring and quick to act in an emergency. Ernest Llewellyn was the chief engineer, who kept his engines purring.

They were laden with cargo, and, having left Nassau a few days earlier, were now nearing the coast of Virginia. There was no moon, and not a light showed anywhere on board. Smoking on deck was forbidden, the engine-room hatches were covered with tarpaulins, and even the dimly lighted compass was temporarily covered.

On the bridge, George, Will, and Augustus peered into the darkness, expecting at any moment to see the flash of Yankee guns.

"There's one of them," Will said, pointing.

Off to the starboard was a long, low object, a Federal cruiser, lying perfectly still. An order was sent down, and the engines were cut. The silence was overpowering. Even though they passed within a hundred yards of the Yankee boat, they were not seen. But before they could breathe any easier from getting clear of the boat, another cruiser appeared straight ahead, moving across the *Grasshopper*'s bow.

Once more the engineer received the order, and the engines were stopped altogether. The enemy passed by, disappearing into the darkness.

The engines started up, and once more they began heading toward land. On their first trip out, both Augustus and George were holding their breath.

"We're almost home free," Will Bubb said. "See that

hill on the coast there? It means we're close to Fort Monroe."

"Do you mean we don't need to worry anymore?" Augustus asked.

"Not at all. But the waiting will soon be over."

Fortunately, no more Federal patrols were spotted that night and within half an hour, the *Grasshopper* was safely over the bar and on to Norfolk.

Captain Bubb didn't particularly favor Norfolk, for its position was not as favorable as Savannah or Wilmington. But he wasn't one to quibble with his employers when the money was as good as this. He just didn't want to sit out the rest of the war in a Federal jail up North. But he felt that with his top-notch crew, they wouldn't be apt to make any costly mistakes.

Augustus was pleased at the size of the warehouse John Denny had been able to rent. After arranging for the goods to be unloaded, he paid off the crew. The final arrangements for transporting and disposing of the cargo were to be made in Richmond, as well as seeing about the return cargo.

George and Augustus took a packet up the James, after telling the twenty-seven crew members to enjoy a short vacation.

It was late afternoon when the two men reached Richmond, where they split up, agreeing to meet at the lawyer's office at 7:30 that evening.

George found a hack and told the driver to take him to a hotel. To his chagrin, the Spotswood had not one vacant room. He then tried the Exchange and found the situation there was the same. Muttering to himself, he stepped up to the clerk at the American Hotel.

"Do you have a room?" he asked.

"It's nothing fancy," the clerk replied, eyeing George's natty attire.

"I'm not fussy."

After signing the register, George followed a little black boy up the stairs. He gazed out the window to the street below and the adjacent factory belching smoke.

"Yo' wants anything else, suh?" the boy asked.

"Is there some way I might have a bath?"

"Yessuh. I be back wif de water and de tub, suh."

George sighed. So this was glorious America, where his great grandfather had lost the sight of his right eye at Brandywine so many years ago. This dingy little hotel room, when he had dreams of being regaled as a friend and savior of the beleaguered South. He smiled. Well, at least he had a new suit of clothes, and he had to admit this room was better than the cramped lodgings in which he had lived over the Lion's Head Pub.

After receiving word that the *Grasshopper* had arrived and there was a meeting scheduled, Edward was sorry he would not be able to spend the entire evening at home for Melissa's birthday. He decided to make up for it by stopping at Pizzini's on his way home and buying a gallon of ice cream, packed in ice.

The best present Melissa could have wanted was actually not a present at all. In the past few months, she had been hard pressed to do all her work at the paper, with the increased volume. To make it even more difficult, she had to watch the telegraph as well. Adding to the problems was the paper shortage, which had forced Lewis to print on only a half sheet, and she had to condense everything. The advertisements depressed her

228

too, emphasizing the hard times that were upon them. A beverage called dandelion coffee was toasted to be the equal to the best java; great cloth suited for military purposes was advertised as very cheap for the times; a druggist explained his low stock by saying his usual channels of supplies had been closed. Lewis had hired a man to take over the telegraph. He was a former soldier who had lost an arm at Belmont, Missouri back in November. Now, at least, she could devote all her energies and concentration to that for which she had been originally hired.

She had urged her family not to make a fuss, but Edward presented her with a silver hairbrush with her name engraved on it.

"Oh, Uncle Edward, you shouldn't have."

"Nonsense. What are birthdays for? But I warn you, don't eat too big a supper."

"Why?"

"I have another little surprise in the kitchen," he smiled. "It's to make up for my absence the rest of the evening."

"Where are you going?" Nancy asked him.

"I have a meeting at Augustus's office. The ship docked last night, safe and sound. We have some details to work out."

"Oh, Father, I'd love to see the ship!" Mahaley exclaimed. "Where is it?"

"Norfolk. I'd kind of like to see her myself. Perhaps it can be arranged. A little holiday might do us all good."

"That would be wonderful, Father," Margaret said. "I've been feeling so stifled here all winter. I'd like to get the baby out someplace different."

"Then it's settled. Today is Thursday. We'll go down

on Saturday morning and spend the night. I'll have to arrange for passports, though. But that should be no problem. I might even be able to get them through the office."

Melissa savored every mouthful of her ice cream, and insisted that Tunia, Cindy, and Bobo be allowed to have some as well. The coldness seemed to frighten little Jeff at first, but he soon began to enjoy it.

Edward was the last to arrive at Augustus's office, and he was introduced to George, who had all the ledgers and manifests spread all over the desk.

"All her papers are in order," Augustus explained. "We needed to employ a British captain who held a Board of Trade certificate to clear her, and the crew is all in accordance with the Merchant Shipping Act. She's sailing under a British flag for obvious reasons."

"Then this is completely legal?" John asked, somewhat surprised.

"As far as anybody but the United States is concerned," Augustus smiled.

"I've got all the bills of lading in that envelope there," George said. "The shipment cost you approximately $7,500."

"And what did we get for all that?" Lewis asked.

George opened his ledger to the correct page and read aloud: "Four thousand Enfield rifles; eight thousand pounds of cannon powder; fifty cases of morphine; twenty-four cases of brandy; six thousand woolen blankets; one thousand pairs of shoes; ten cases of champagne; twenty bolts of English chintz; forty bolts of gray broadcloth; and twenty-four boxes of Havana cigars."

Edward smiled. "Thank you, Mr. Ainsworth, and may I venture to say you'll be a very rich man on your next return."

"I certainly hope so."

"I've arranged with a broker to ship back six hundred bales of cotton," Edward said. "He's holding it in his warehouse in Norfolk. How do you propose the best way to get our cargo here to Richmond?"

"By train," John replied. "I think the Norfolk and Petersburg, and then the Richmond and Petersburg."

"I plan to take the family down to Norfolk Saturday for a little outing. I'll make the arrangements then," Edward said.

After the evening's business had been concluded, late into the night, Edward asked George to come to supper the next evening. George was delighted to accept, for the cook on the *Grasshopper* was not much of a culinary genius.

Melissa was rather excited about her upcoming trip to Norfolk, and she wondered what the Englishman who was coming to supper would be like.

Henry came into the paper late in the afternoon.

"Where have you been all day?" Melissa asked him.

"I was just talking to General Lee," he smiled. "He nearly ran me down with that damned horse of his."

"Did you find out anything interesting?" Melissa wondered.

"No. He says he's mostly trying to get his troops better supplied."

"Speaking of supplies, Uncle Edward's investment arrived from England."

"The ship?"

"Yes. But I'm not sure if he wants it generally known."

"That's very interesting."

"Henry, you promised you wouldn't do anything about it."

"I know. And I keep my promises. Besides, that part of it's none of my affair."

"You're very dressed up today."

"I had my picture taken."

"Is Mr. Parker still here?"

"No. He's gone off to follow the army. His wife's taken over the business for him."

The other women were still dressing when Melissa went downstairs that evening. She could hear Tunia scolding little Jeff in the kitchen, so she went out to investigate. He had evidently toddled over to the table and pulled the ham off onto the floor.

"Dis ham's ruined!" Tunia wailed. "I can't serve no ham what's been on de flo'!"

Melissa carefully inspected the meat. "Go ahead, Tunia. I don't see anything on it. You always keep the floor clean. Besides, even if it did pick up something, a little dirt never hurt anybody."

Tunia grinned at her. "Don' yo' tell Miss Nancy."

"I won't. And I'll take Jeff with me so he can't cause any more problems."

Melissa picked up the baby and carried him into the drawing room, where she found one of Mahaley's old rag dolls with which he had been playing. Now that Jeff was beginning to walk, Edward had had Bobo put up a gate at the top of the stairway.

"You look just like your papa," Melissa told him,

wondering what Joseph would think of his son. She was sure he would pay more attention to the child than Margaret. For as much as she doted on him immediately after his birth, she certainly didn't bother much with him now. His companions were most generally Cindy or Tunia, and sometimes even Bobo.

There was a knock at the door, and, knowing Cindy and Tunia were both busy, Melissa answered it.

George was somewhat surprised to find this lovely young woman open the door, expecting some old darkie instead.

"You must be Mr. Ainsworth," Melissa said.

"Yes."

"Please come in," she smiled, standing aside. "I'm Melissa, Edward's niece."

"It's a pleasure," George said, shaking her hand and thinking: Such eyes.

Jeff toddled out of the drawing room, and Melissa picked him up. "And this is little Jeff."

"Yours?"

"No," she smiled. "He's my cousin's. Please take off your coat and then we can go into the drawing room."

While he was hanging his coat on the hall tree, Melissa studied him thoughtfully. He was thin but not frail, and his complexion had the healthy glow of a man who had just been out in the sea air and wind. His brown hair and mustache shone with coppery highlights and, as he turned back to her, Melissa thought his hazel eyes were the kindest she had ever seen.

Nancy bustled down the stairs, tucking a loose lock of grayish-blond hair into its comb.

"Aunt Nancy, this is George Ainsworth."

Melissa took Jeff upstairs while Nancy entertained

George in the drawing room.

"What's he look like?" Mahaley asked Melissa, as they walked down the stairs together.

"Oh, I don't know. All right, I guess. He's awfully skinny, though."

Nancy was asking George about his home in England when Mahaley and Melissa appeared. George stood up as Mahaley was introduced to him. She decided right away that he was too old for her.

"Would you care for something to drink, Mr. Ainsworth?" Nancy asked.

"Why, yes. Thank you."

"I'll get it," Mahaley said. "What would you like?"

"Whatever you have," he smiled.

While Mahaley was pouring a whiskey for George and sherry for the rest, Margaret entered. George was beginning to feel a little uncomfortable with all these women as he sipped his whiskey.

"What do you think of America?" Margaret asked him.

"To tell you the truth, I haven't made up my mind. I really haven't seen much of it yet."

"Did you have any trouble finding a place to stay?"

"Yes, I did. I was thinking, as long as I'm going to be coming to the city from time to time, it might be a good idea to take a room here."

"That's a very good idea," Nancy agreed. "If many more people move into the city, I don't know where we'll put them all."

"I thought I'd ask Mr. Given to look 'round for me."

"Are you going back to England right away?" Margaret asked.

"I don't think so. I believe we're just going to Nassau."

234

Edward came in and shook George's hand. "I'm sorry I'm late," he said. "I trust my ladies have been entertaining you?"

"Yes."

Edward took an envelope from his pocket. "I had to stay later to arrange for our passports," he explained. "As long as none of us are Union spies," he smiled.

Nancy laughed. "Oh, Edward, that's funny!"

Melissa stared into her sherry.

Edward refilled George's glass and fixed himself a drink. "I'll make the arrangements to have the goods sent up here tomorrow. I hope you don't mind having a little company on the way to Norfolk?"

"Not at all."

"Do you think you could bring in some corduroy, Mr. Ainsworth?" Margaret asked. "I've been all over looking for some this week. I wanted to have a little suit made for my son."

"I'll see what I can do."

"And perfume," Nancy said. "I'm almost out of perfume."

"Don't forget scented soap," Mahaley said.

"Ladies," Edward smiled, holding up his hand. "Don't bother our guest with that now. I'll make out a list. Although that isn't a bad idea. Those things will bring in a nice profit."

"I hope you have medicine on that list," Melissa said.

George looked at Melissa with new interest. His brief encounters with these southern women had given him the opinion that they were all frivolous and self-centered. This one might be different.

"That's most definitely on the list," George told her. "Morphine, quinine, and chloroform."

"What about laudanum?"

George glanced at Edward, who nodded. "We'll add laudanum."

Tunia announced supper, and the group went into the dining room.

"I'm so excited about our trip tomorrow," Mahaley said. "When are we leaving, Father?"

"Very early. So I want none of your dawdling in the morning."

"Are you married, Mr. Ainsworth?" Nancy asked.

"I was."

"Were?"

"My wife died." George found that easier to say than to admit she had run off with a whiskey drummer from Livesy nearly ten years ago.

"Oh, I'm sorry."

"Thank you. It was a long time ago." He felt uncomfortable. "This is a very good meal."

"Yes, it is," Nancy agreed. Tunia was just leaving the room when Nancy stopped her. "Tunia, did you do something different to the ham tonight? It's excellent."

Tunia glanced at Melissa. "Why, no, ma'am. Jes' must be dem cloves."

Melissa stifled a giggle and stabbed at a piece of meat.

"My son's in the army," Edward told George. "And so is Margaret's husband."

"And Melissa's beau," Mahaley added.

Even before the sun rose, the Armstrong family was up and about. The packet left for Norfolk at seven, but Edward wanted everyone there in plenty of time. With the exception of Melissa, the women were fussing and stewing, trying to decide what to wear and what to pack.

236

Cindy was every bit as excited as the others, for she was going along to attend the ladies and keep an eye on the baby.

When George saw the carriage, laden with boxes, arrive at the dock, he wondered just how long these people planned to stay in Norfolk. From the glimpse he had of it, the town looked more like a sailor's refuge than a social center. Edward had taken a small cabin for the ladies to stay out of the sun and to have a place to keep the child.

Melissa stood on the deck and watched the shoreline pass by as they headed down the James. It was a clear, sunny morning, and she found the sea air and strange smells exhilarating. At the first movement of the boat, Margaret felt her stomach churning, and spent the entire trip in the cabin.

They settled themselves in their rooms at the Norfolk Hotel and then met in the dining room for something to eat. Margaret decided to forego the tour of the *Grasshopper*.

Mahaley was quite interested in all the sailors they passed on their way to the dock and thought it might be fun to widen her scope of the branches of the service in which she had furthered her own little cause. But she didn't quite know how she would go about it, for she was sharing a room with Melissa.

Some of the cotton had been loaded aboard, and it was fortunate not all of it had been, or else not much of the *Grasshopper* could be seen.

"She's a real beauty," Edward remarked.

The family was introduced to Captain Bubb and Pilot Coonfield, who offered to take the ladies on a tour.

"I'd like to talk to you, Mr. Armstrong," the captain

said. "I've been talking to the men here, and I'm inclined to agree with them from my past experiences. I think it would be a good idea to mount a couple of guns fore and aft."

"Do you think that's really necessary?"

"I do. Speaking for myself and the rest of the crew, if it came to fighting it out with a patrol boat that was our match or spending the rest of the war in a bloody Yankee prison, we'd rather take our chances with the guns."

"I don't know," Edward sighed.

"It's for your own benefit, Mr. Armstrong. If we're taken, you'll lose everything anyway. We won't go fighting it out with the whole fleet. If our chances are good, the guns might save the ship, not to mention a considerable amount of money."

"Very well. I'll leave it to you then."

"Yes, sir. I'll see to it in Nassau."

"One thing I wanted to bring up," Edward said. "I think it best if Mr. Ainsworth accompany the cargo by train to Richmond each trip. It would only mean a day or two delay."

"That's fine with me, Mr. Armstrong," Will grinned. "The lads can find plenty to do here in town. Now, if you'd like to follow me, I'll take you down and show you the engines."

Melissa went up on deck to get some fresh air. She felt all right actually, but seeing the boat made her think of Sam. She hadn't heard from her brother in a while, and she was beginning to worry. The last she had heard Sam was to be on a hospital ship, and that didn't guarantee his safety. Thinking about the good times they all used to have when the *Allegheny Belle* stopped at the Shady Run

238

landing, she remembered her father and Jeremiah and felt sad. How everything had changed in a year!

"Enjoying the view?"

She turned and found George standing beside her, munching on a piece of candy.

"Yes. But the ocean's so big," she said. "I've never seen the ocean before. Aren't you afraid? I mean, what if the boat sprang a leak?"

"Then I'd have a very long swim," he smiled.

"I'm serious."

"So am I. I'm not a sailor. I don't know anything about boats—only what goes in their cargo holds."

"Then why are you doing this? Do you believe so much in the Confederacy?"

"No. I believe in . . ."

Just then the engines started, and the boat gave a sudden jolt, knocking Melissa off balance and against George. In the instant she was near him, she caught the scent of bay rum and peppermint. He caught her by the shoulders and gazed into her face for a moment before steadying her.

"Excuse me," she murmured.

"It's quite all right."

She regained her composure. "Now what was it you were saying?"

"I don't know. Oh, yes, I do. It was just that I'm doing this because I was sick of sitting in the same stuffy little office every day, doing the same things over and over. Besides, I was tired of being poor."

In one of the cabins below, Mahaley was in the arms of young Joe Majors, the first mate. The two had slipped away from the rest of the family for a moment.

239

"We'd better get back to the others before they come looking for us," Mahaley sighed.

"Do you have to be with them all day?" he asked. "Could you get back to the ship at all?"

"Why, what are you suggesting?" she teased, fluttering her long lashes coyly.

"You know what I'm suggesting."

"I'll have to think of something. Are you free all day?"

"Till about six, when I go on duty."

"What about the other sailors? I wouldn't want this to get around."

"They'll be envious."

She giggled. "You know what I mean. Will they tell I was in your cabin?"

"Who would they tell? Besides, they'll be too busy to notice."

"All right. I've got an idea. Come on. Let's go find the others."

The group was gathered up on deck when Mahaley and Joe arrived.

"Father, this young man has asked me to accompany him on a little tour of the town this afternoon," Mahaley said.

"Oh? We'd planned to have the captain and pilot join us for supper tonight at the hotel," Edward told her.

"I'll have her back in plenty of time, sir," Joe said. "I have to be on duty at six."

Edward studied the young man. He was harmless-looking, but one could never tell. He shot a glance at the captain, whose expression told him nothing.

"Very well," Edward said. "But I want you back at the hotel by five. Perhaps Melissa would like to join you?"

Mahaley's look shot daggers at her cousin.

"Oh, I don't think so, Uncle Edward," Melissa said. "I'm a little tired."

When Mahaley returned to the hotel, Melissa was not in their room. She was thankful, for she had a feeling Melissa knew what had been going on.

Melissa was sitting on the sofa in the lobby, sipping some sort of frosty concoction with George.

"This is very good. What is it?" she asked.

"I don't know what it's called. I had one at the home of the shipping agent in Nassau. I found out what's in it, though."

"And you just told the man here how to make it?"

"Yes. I'm glad you like it."

"I really shouldn't be drinking it. Women don't usually imbibe anything stronger than wine."

"But you do like it, though?"

"Yes. Besides, I'm not a very conventional sort of woman, anyway. My employer, Mr. McAllen, you know him, don't you?"

"Yes. I didn't know he was your employer. What do you do?"

"I work at his newspaper. He was downright against hiring a woman in the first place, but now he's used to me. But he says I'm the most headstrong woman he's ever met. Headstrong Armstrong, he calls me sometimes."

George laughed. "I shall have to remember that."

"Mr. Ainsworth, I wonder if you could do me a favor while you're in Nassau?"

"What?"

"Could you find out for me what kind of mail service there is to the North?"

"Very good, I understand."

"Really?"

"I believe so. The islands aren't at war with the United States."

"That's so good to hear. You see, my brother is living up North, and he's going to have a birthday in June. I'd like to send him a present, because I missed Christmas altogether. But what I had in mind is too big to be slipped through the lines here."

"Well, anything I can do . . ."

At about ten o'clock that evening, the family gathered on the dock to watch the *Grasshopper* sail for Nassau. Or at least they attempted to watch. The night was perfect for her departure, the clouds hid the stars, and the moon was a mere sliver. The ship blended in so perfectly with the night, she was nearly impossible to see.

"They're all good men, and they know what they're about," Edward remarked. "We should see Mr. Ainsworth again in a few weeks."

Andrew received a furlough of five days in the early part of April. One of the first things he did was to visit one of the local brothels, and then he went to see Ellen. With the coming of spring, the business of prostitution was booming in Richmond. The provost marshal was being swamped by complaints, especially by the president of the Young Men's Christian Association hospital. An enterprising madam had opened her establishment directly across the street from the hospital, and the convalescent patients were being lured over to the other side before they had completely recuperated. Several luxuriant gambling establishments had been recently opened on Main Street, where, despite the shortages, caviar and champagne could still be found.

While Andrew was enjoying life in the city, Joseph had been camped near Corinth. He was now following the rest of some 40,000 men to Pittsburgh Landing in Tennessee, where they hoped to surprise the Union Army. Expecting no action, the unseasoned Federal troops didn't bother to make any entrenchments, deploying themselves in a haphazard fashion.

The Confederate troops were just as green, for the most part. They were forever tangling themselves into traffic jams, making the march a ragged disorder. They shot squirrels, fought mock battles, and ate their five days' ration in three days. General Beauregard was sure the Federals would hear them coming and wanted to turn back, but General Albert Sidney Johnston would not hear of it.

Late in the afternoon of April 5, they finally reached their destination, two miles from Pittsburgh Landing. Joseph went about setting up his instruments in the telegrapher's tent, while the men strung the wires. One of his friends shot a deer, and Joseph shared the feast with his messmates.

Joseph had just finished his supper when a message came over the wire. After copying it down, he went over to the headquarters tent, where Generals Beauregard, Johnston, Polk, Hardee, and Bragg were having a conference.

Joseph entered and saluted. "A wire from the president, sir."

"Read it, Corporal."

Joseph adjusted his glasses. "To General Albert Sidney

243

Johnston, CSA: I hope you will be able to close with the enemy before his two columns unite. I anticipate a victory."

"I would fight them if they were a million," Johnston remarked. "Gentlemen, we shall attack at daylight tomorrow."

Beauregard stepped outside the tent with Joseph. "Corporal Boone, you're a good man. Stay by that wire tomorrow."

"Yes, sir."

Beauregard took a flask from his pocket and offered it to Joseph. "I don't like this at all, Corporal. We made too much noise and took too long getting here. I thought I'd just about convinced them to give it up when that wire came from the president. By tomorrow night, we'll know who was right."

"Yes, sir."

Sunday morning, Johnston struck. The Yankees were either still in bed or making their way to breakfast, the victims of complete surprise. They scurried out of their tents, half dressed, grabbing their rifles and trying to arouse their comrades. Grant himself was several miles away with half of his division with him. Sherman had his men gathered around Shiloh Church, and the rest of the divisions were scattered all around.

The Confederates fought desperately, trying to erase the embarrassment of Fort Donelson. The Union lines were hurled back to the river in total confusion, and the partially trained and disciplined troops would not rally.

The Confederate soldiers scavenged among the discards of the Yankees for new rifles and food.

Johnston had been up front all day, and as he rode into a peach orchard, he was shot in the leg, severing an artery. But despite the loss of their general, the Confederates carried the day.

Beauregard was both amazed and delighted with the victory. That evening, in the midst of a thunderstorm, he ordered Joseph to wire the president, informing him of assured victory and the sad news of General Johnston's death.

Sitting alone in the tent, after eating his fill of captured Union rations, Joseph began the tedious task of sending off the names of the dead. While he was working, he was thinking about his son. He had thought about him a lot in the past few days, as he heard other men speaking of their families. When the opportunity arose, he planned to go home to Richmond to see his son. He didn't want the child to grow up thinking of his father as a stranger. Margaret had won. He wanted no part of their marriage, only to see his son. Perhaps when this engagement was over, he would see about getting a furlough.

While the Confederates were basking in their glory, Grant was busy. He ordered the wooden gunboats *Tyler* and *Lexington* to take positions opposite the landing. His reinforcements arrived, some 7,000 men, led by General Lew Wallace. Units of General Don Carlos Buell's command crossed the river. When dawn broke, the Yankees took the offensive.

An orderly rushed into the telegrapher's tent. "General Beauregard says to send a message—we're retreating! Then pack up and get the hell out of here!"

Joseph tapped out the message and then cut the lines. He put his equipment in its case, grabbed his haversack, and started out of the tent. Before he had even stepped outside, a mortar shell exploded less than three feet away.

That evening as the straggling defeated Confederates were burying their dead, Joseph Boone was among them—never to see his son again.

Eleven

Margaret had received the news of Joseph's death with genuine sorrow. She blamed herself silently for causing him to join the army in the first place. She had written a note to his parents, telling them the news and even though his body would not be there, they were going to have a stone erected at the cemetery for him.

When George arrived in Richmond, he found the black wreath of mourning hung upon the Armstrongs' door. It was Saturday afternoon when Cindy ushered him into the house.

"Is Mr. Armstrong in?" he asked.

"Yessuh. He in de study. I tells him yo' is here."

Edward welcomed him into his study and offered him a drink.

"The mourning wreath on the door . . ." George began.

"My son-in-law. Killed at Shiloh."

"I'm sorry to hear it."

"It was a shock to all of us."

"The cotton fetched a nice bit of money. The cargo is being moved to Mr. Given's warehouse now."

"No problems on the voyage?"

"None."

Edward smiled. "I'm very happy with our arrangement, Mr. Ainsworth. That last load you brought in has taken care of our initial investment."

"That's very good to hear. Did you find some lodgings for me?"

"Yes." Edward took a key from his desk drawer and handed it to George. "It's not very elegant, but there isn't much available right now."

"I'm sure it's fine. I don't need much since I won't be in town for very long periods of time."

George and Edward discussed business a little more until they were interrupted by Andrew. Edward introduced his son to George.

"Father, I'm sorry to disturb you, but I was wondering if I could have some money?"

"What are you doing with your army pay?"

"Oh, you know—it goes. Eleven dollars a month doesn't last very long. And I wanted to take Ellen to the theater and to supper tonight. It's my last night, remember?"

"Very well." Edward took a locked metal box from his desk.

"Are you going back to your unit tomorrow?" George asked.

"Yes. We're heading for Yorktown," Andrew replied.

Edward gave his son some Confederate notes. "While you're here, Andrew, I'd like your opinion on something."

"What?"

"We've been hearing a lot of rumors about an invasion on the peninsula. What do you think?"

Andrew chuckled. "As you well know, I'm no military strategist."

At this remark, Edward had to laugh. "Nevertheless . . ."

"Well, I would say something's happening. Otherwise, why is Joe Johnston moving all his troops to that area? And McClellan does have a number of men at Newport News."

"How safe would you say Norfolk is?"

"I don't know."

Andrew put his money into his pocket and poured himself a drink, lounging against the mantel.

"Lewis and I were discussing all this the other day," Edward said. "If, by chance, we should lose Norfolk, what shall we do?"

"I'd like to know that myself," George smiled. "I'd hate to dock next trip and be greeted by the Yankees."

"My point exactly," Edward said. "I fear Captain Bubb was right when he suggested landing in Wilmington. I think we should switch our base of operations. I hate the delay in moving the cargo up from there, but I don't know what else to do."

"So what do you want me to do?" George asked.

"Tell the captain to land in Wilmington next time. I'll get in touch with a couple of cotton brokers I know down there. I'm sure they will be glad to do business. I don't know what to do about you, though. I hate for you not to accompany the shipment on the train, but I don't like to waste all that time."

"I don't know what to suggest," George said.

"Why not go every other trip?" Andrew suggested. "That way, you'll be able to take care of the books. And I'm sure you could hire somebody to ride the train with the goods, when you don't go. There's lots of cripples who need work."

"How does that sound to you, Mr. Ainsworth?" Edward asked.

"It's fine with me."

Melissa came into the room, wearing one of her old country dresses she had brought with her from Shady Run, and George thought she looked as fresh as a spring flower in the printed calico. She was surprised to discover George, for she had been looking for Andrew.

George stood up. "Good afternoon, Miss Armstrong."

"Oh, hello, Mr. Ainsworth. I didn't know you were here."

"We got in last night."

She turned to Andrew. "I got the marzipan you wanted."

"Thank you. I know Ellen will love it."

"Say, why don't you take Mr. Ainsworth with you tonight?" Edward suggested. "Show him a little bit of the city."

"Oh, that's not necessary."

"Of course it is. Perhaps Melissa would go too?"

"Uncle Edward . . ."

"Andrew won't mind, will you Andrew? Unless you had other plans, Mr. Ainsworth?"

"No. I had no plans."

"Good. Then it's all settled."

Melissa and Andrew rode along the streets in the carriage, the box of marzipan on the seat between them. She pulled her cloak more closely about her, for the early spring air was chilly.

"I'm sorry, Andrew. I'm sure you wanted to be alone with Ellen. But your father practically insisted."

"It's all right," he smiled.

"How are things progressing between you two? Or is that none of my business?"

"It's a strange thing. You know, Ellen's the first girl I've ever treated well. That's an awful thing to say, but it's true. I like Ellen. I respect her."

"Do you love her?"

"I don't know."

"She's a very sweet person."

"Yes. I think so. She's the kind of girl you marry. The others . . . well . . ."

They picked up George and then drove on to the little boardinghouse where Ellen and Nathaniel lived. Andrew took the candy and went to fetch her, while the other two waited in the carriage.

"Did you leave any family back in England, Mr. Ainsworth?"

"My parents and two brothers."

"What do they think of your new career?"

"I haven't told them exactly what it is I'm doing," he admitted. "I wouldn't want to worry my mother. I'm the youngest, and she still thinks of me as her little boy, despite the fact that I'm past thirty. But I know they'll be happy to get the money I send them. You never told me why you're living with your uncle."

Melissa recounted the story of Jeremiah going away and her father being shot by Ethan Smith. By the time she had finished, Ellen and Andrew had arrived, and they all left for Metropolitan Hall.

"The Richmond Theater burned down in January," Andrew told George. "But they're rebuilding."

"It's nearly done," Melissa said. "I put an ad in the paper the other day announcing the program for the

251

grand opening."

"I personally think the money that's being spent on the theater could be put to better uses," Ellen remarked.

The play was a Shakespearean tragedy, and Melissa found it to be very dull. Even though she had seen few dramatic performances, she thought the actors a bunch of rank amateurs, and she was glad when it was over. The group went to the Spotswood Hotel, and were ushered to the table Andrew had reserved.

"Order anything you like," Andrew told them. "I've got to go back to hardtack and salt beef tomorrow, so I intend to gorge myself tonight."

Melissa noticed the prices had been scratched out and changed twice. If one had the money, food was still plentiful, and Andrew ordered a bottle of Madeira wine. George was amazed at the cost of food, compared to what he would pay in Nassau.

"Did you really only get hardtack and salt beef in camp, Andrew?" Ellen asked. "We've got a pretty good supply at the Commissary Department."

"It depended. Sometimes we got bacon or ham. And we did pretty well with game. What I missed most were fresh vegetables. You can't very well grow those in snow."

"What kind of game did you shoot?" George asked him.

"Squirrels mostly. Once in a while we got a deer."

Melissa looked up and saw Robert E. Lee approaching the table.

"Miss Armstrong, isn't it?"

"Yes, General. How good of you to remember me." She made the introductions.

"A soldier, eh? What unit?" he asked Andrew.

"The Twelfth Virginia. I'm leaving for the Peninsula tomorrow."

"What's your division?"

"General Huger—Second Brigade."

Lee made no comment. Instead, he turned to George. "I take it you're a visitor to our country?"

"Yes. I'm here on business."

"Mr. Ainsworth is helping us fight the blockade," Ellen announced. She was very much in favor of George's work.

"Is that so?" Lee smiled. "Then let me wish you all the best of luck."

"Thank you, sir."

Lee looked at Melissa. "I wanted to tell you to thank Mr. Walkenfeldt again if you should see him, for all the fine things he's written. He has remarkable insight."

"Why—yes. I'll be happy to tell him."

The waiter appeared with their meal.

"Well, I see your supper has arrived," Lee said. "I won't keep you any longer. And good luck to both of you gentlemen."

George noticed Melissa's mysterious little smile all during their dinner and he wondered at its reason. He had no way of knowing that she was thinking about General Lee's praise of Henry and how pleased she was at the agent's brilliant duplicity.

Melissa was working on a notice to be put in the paper asking for women to volunteer to sew up sandbags for the fortifications around Yorktown. The entire office was buzzing over the conviction of the Union spy. Timothy Webster had been tried and found guilty of espionage and was sentenced to hang.

Lincoln had authorized his secretary of war, Edwin M.

Stanton, to communicate with Jefferson Davis. The administration told the Confederates that so far they had been lenient in dealing with southern agents. If they were to go through with the execution, there might be reprisals.

Melissa had only that morning relayed Robert E. Lee's message to Henry. She was frightened for him now.

"Henry, I must talk to you," she said quietly. "Could we meet someplace tonight? Perhaps your place?"

"I know what you're going to say. Don't fret about me."

"But . . ."

"Hush!"

Melissa's fears for Henry's safety all but disappeared when Jackson strolled through the newspaper's office door. He saw her busily working at her desk, and he stood just outside the wooden gate, staring at her. A few moments passed until she finally looked up.

"Jackson!" she squealed, getting up.

Everyone in the office stopped what they were doing to see what had caused Melissa's outburst. She looked around, embarrassed. She went through the gate and took his hands, a smile on her face, her eyes sparkling. He thought at that moment, she was the most beautiful thing in the world.

"Let's step outside for a minute," she said, still aware that everyone was watching her. The two of them walked out into the sunshine. "Jackson, what are you doing here?"

"Just passing through," he smiled, squeezing her hands. "It's so good to see you. Jeb came into town to see Flora and his family, so I figured if he could do it, so could I."

"I'm glad you did. How long will you be here?"

"Just till tomorrow. Oh, Melissa, each time I see you, you get more beautiful, and I didn't think that was possible. How have you been?"

"I've been fine. Did you hear about Joseph?"

"No. What about him?"

"He was killed at Shiloh."

"Oh, I'm sorry. I liked Joseph."

"So did I." She brightened up again. "But everyone else is fine. And they'll be so glad to see you. I'll see if Mr. McAllen will let me go home a little early. You'll stay at our house tonight, won't you?"

"I was hoping you'd ask me," he smiled, meeting her eyes with his.

She grinned back at him. "I can't stay out here too long or Mr. McAllen will have a fit. Why don't you go on home and get settled?"

"Are you sure it's all right?"

"Of course."

"All right." He squeezed her hands again. "I'll see you later."

Nancy was almost as excited to see Jackson as Melissa had been.

"I hope it's not an inconvenience," he said.

"Nonsense, Lieutenant Vaughn—I mean, Major Vaughn."

"Why don't we just dispense with the formalities altogether? Please call me Jackson."

"Very well."

"Melissa told me about Joseph. I'm very sorry. I hope my being here won't bring any painful reminders to Margaret."

"She's taking it very well—outwardly. Although I suspect she's doing a great deal of brooding on the inside. But a little excitement around here always helps. Andrew just left this morning."

When Melissa finally got home from the office, she found everyone but Margaret in the drawing room, drinking some of Edward's blockade-run wine.

"I'm sorry I couldn't get away any sooner," she said. "The place is in an absolute mess with all these troops passing through."

"I feel very fortunate and grateful to have a place to sleep tonight," Jackson said.

"You know you're welcome here anytime," Edward said. "Sit down, Melissa, and let me get you some wine."

Melissa seated herself beside Jackson on the settee. "How's your arm?" she asked him.

"Oh, fine. No problems at all," Jackson said, extending his arm and pumping his fist. "The only thing is my grip. It's not as strong as it used to be."

"Do you need much of a grip?" Mahaley asked. "I mean, all you do is hold your reins, don't you?"

"My saber."

"Before you leave tomorrow, I'd like to know what the cavalry's lacking," Edward told him.

"What do you mean?"

"My blockade-runner. I'd like to order the supplies you might need."

"Oh, that's right. You were talking about it when I was here before. Has she come in yet?"

"Twice. She's a beauty," Edward beamed.

"The crew is very nice too," Mahaley said. "Aren't they, Melissa?"

Melissa gave her cousin a dirty look, but she was saved from further comment when Margaret entered with the baby.

"Hello, Major Vaughn."

Jackson stood up and extended his hand. "Hello, Margaret. May I tell you how sorry I am."

"Thank you."

She sat down, and Jeff toddled over to Jackson, attracted by his brass buttons, which were now rather tarnished.

"Hello, Jeff," Jackson said, bending down. "You're getting to be a big boy."

Jeff was reaching for the buttons, so Jackson picked him up and put him on his lap.

"He's getting into everything, now that he's walking," Margaret said.

Jeff examined the buttons, and then drew back. Sniffing, he wrinkled up his nose.

"I know, Jeff," Jackson smiled embarrassedly. "My uniform needs laundering."

Jeff scrambled down off Jackson's lap and went back to his mother. "I think I'll take him out to the kitchen for his supper."

"Tunia could probably wash your uniform tonight," Melissa suggested.

"That's a good idea," Nancy agreed. "She can hang it in the kitchen close to the stove, and it should be dry by morning."

"Thank you," Jackson said. "Soap is a little hard to come by out there."

"I'll remember that," Edward remarked.

"Actually, I'd like to have another uniform made. And a couple of extra shirts." Jackson turned to Melissa. "If I

257

give you some money, do you think you could have that woman make me another?"

"Sabina?"

"Yes."

"I suppose so. If she can get any cloth."

"Don't worry about that," Edward said. "I have a couple of bolts in the attic, just in case we needed it for Andrew."

"I appreciate all this," Jackson said.

"Don't think anything of it," Nancy told him. "If it weren't for all you young men, there wouldn't even be a Confederacy."

After supper, Edward talked to Jackson for a while in the study, and then he finally got away to go upstairs. He put on one of Andrew's robes and gave his dirty clothes to Cindy.

As she lay under the covers of her bed, Melissa was quite put out at Mahaley. More than once she had referred to the fact that Henry had been her escort to different social affairs, and she managed to allude to her evening with George Ainsworth. She had begun to feel very uncomfortable at the table. Even though it was all perfectly innocent, it might not appear that way to Jackson. She wouldn't want him to get mad, for she was genuinely fond of him.

She heard the door open and turned in that direction. Jackson's form was silhouetted against the dim lights of the hall. He closed the door, and the room was dark once more.

"It's just me," he whispered, reaching for the covers.

"I know. I didn't really expect General Grant."

"I wouldn't worry so much about Grant right now," he

258

said, taking off his robe. "It's McClellan you better watch out for."

"In my bed?"

"No, you silly little thing," he laughed, getting into bed beside her. He put his arms around her and kissed her gently. "I've missed you."

"I've missed you too."

"Then show me," he whispered.

Jackson covered Melissa's mouth with his own, and as he rolled her over onto her back, his hands caressed her soft body with urgency. "Oh, Melissa," he murmured. "It's been such a long time."

Edward had been going over his lists for the next shipment order when he remembered something he had forgotten to ask Jackson. Hoping to find him still awake, he went upstairs and tapped on the door. He waited for a few minutes, receiving no answer. "Must be asleep," Edward thought, going back down the hall. "Probably the first soft bed he's slept in for some time."

Nestled in Jackson's arms, Melissa felt there couldn't possibly be a war going on. "I wish you didn't have to leave so soon," she said.

"So do I. I really shouldn't even have taken the time to come here for one day."

"I'm glad you did."

"I am too. What was all that Mahaley was saying?"

"Oh, you know Mahaley."

"If you've been seeing other men . . ."

"Only Henry. And he's just a friend. And that man from the *Grasshopper*—that was Uncle Edward's doing."

"What I was trying to say is that if you want to see

other men, it's all right with me. I can't hold you to anything. It's not fair. I might not be home for months— who knows? And I don't expect you to shut yourself away. You're too full of life to spend your time waiting around. That's why it's hard for me to tell you the things I want to."

"What things?"

"Like how much I love you."

Melissa raised up on her elbow and kissed him. "Thank you, Jackson."

"For loving you? I can't help but love you. But I don't want you to say you love me, even if you do. I couldn't bear going away then. I'd like to leave things as they are now, with you knowing how I feel. When the war's over, then we can think about what we want to do."

"All right."

"Just don't forget me while I'm gone."

"Oh, I could never do that."

Jackson left the next morning with a clean uniform, its buttons shining once again; several cakes of soap; and three bottles of Madeira from Edward. From the porch, Melissa watched him as he mounted his horse and waved before nudging Gypsy into a trot. She thought of his declaration of love the previous night and tried to weigh her own feelings. She truly cared for him, but, as she watched his muscular body in the gray uniform turn the corner, she wondered how much was genuine and how much was her physical desire for him.

For the people of Richmond, life went on as usual. President Davis was growing thinner and becoming more worried-looking. Briarfield, his Mississippi plantation, had been sacked and looted by the Federals. On April 16, the congress passed the first Confederate Conscription Act, making all white males between the ages of eighteen and thirty-five subject to call by the president. However, there were many shortcomings to this act, and the press was very eager to editorialize on the subject. What they called the "Twenty-Nigger Law" enabled any male owning more than twenty slaves to stay home.

The city was full of soldiers. Officers on short leaves or on official business had time for a little social relaxation. The common soldier passed through on his way to the Peninsula, patched and ragged, smeared with the dirt of half a dozen counties on his uniform. Typhoid was rampant, and the hospitals were full of sick men.

The women were busily engaged in making sandbags for the fortifications of Yorktown. One group of ladies made 30,000 in thirty hours.

On April 25, came the news of the fall of New Orleans, and with it went the military stores, the guns and the garrisons of the forts, and the command of navigation of the Mississippi. The price of sugar and salt skyrocketed.

Lewis informed Henry that he wished him to cover the execution of Timothy Webster, the Union spy. Swallowing his fear and distaste, Henry agreed, not wanting to appear any less than the ardent Confederate everyone believed him to be.

Before sunrise on April 29, Henry found himself at Camp Lee, once Richmond's fairgrounds. A large crowd was gathering to watch the show. Notebook in hand, Henry gazed at the massive wooden scaffold. Henry, like everyone else, knew all about the man who was about to die. In reality, Timothy Webster *had* been a Union spy, working for Allan Pinkerton. But he had been posing as a Confederate agent, giving away information that looked valuable on the surface.

As the day brightened, the prisoner was escorted past the waiting coffin, the minister trying to comfort him. The crowd hurled oaths at Webster as he made his way up the steps of the gallows. His hands were tied behind him, his feet bound, and a black hood placed over his face.

Henry felt his heart must be beating as loudly as the rolling drums of the guard. The executioner released the drop, and the wooden frame creaked as the body fell through the opening. But, to everyone's astonishment, Webster fell all the way down and landed with a thud on the ground. The knot had slipped.

Several soldiers rushed forward and helped Webster to his feet, leading him to the stairs. To assure that the same thing wouldn't happen again, the hangman tied the rope too tightly.

Henry heard Webster mumble from behind his mask, "You'll choke me to death this time."

The trap was sprung again, and this time the body fell through. Henry heard the snap of the man's neck and watched as if hypnotized, the body swinging back and forth at the end of the rope.

On his way back to the paper, Henry paused in an alley and vomited.

For nearly a month, the Confederates had held back General McClellan's men on the Peninsula. With one-quarter as many men, General John G. Magruder had done it by deception. He kept marching troops back and forth to make them look triple their number, and by setting up logs to resemble artillery pieces, known as

Quaker guns.

Many companies of artillery were never relieved during the siege of Yorktown. It rained incessantly, and the trenches were filled with water. The weather was unseasonably cold, and no fires were allowed. The constant sound of enemy artillery got on their nerves. The men subsisted on flour and salt meat in reduced quantities, but their patriotism made them indifferent to suffering.

Johnston held out as long as he could, but on May 3, he evacuated Yorktown. It was past midnight as Jeb Stuart's little band of cavalry followed the last division of infantry. The deep mud delayed their trek to Williamsburg; the roads were almost impassable. Guns, wagons, and marching men were all jammed together.

When Johnston abandoned Yorktown, he also left a number of subterranean shells with trip wires attached to discourage Yankee patrols. His own associate, General Longstreet, condemned it as barbarous.

The troops sloshed on through the mud, finding nowhere to camp except sodden fields. It began to rain again, and Jackson, like the others, was extremely uncomfortable. Then, to top it all off, his horse threw a shoe.

The farriers being much ahead of Stuart's men, Jackson decided to pull out of the line of march. He dismounted and stopped one of his comrades. "My horse threw a shoe. I'm going over to that farmhouse on that little rise over there and see if they've got any blacksmith equipment. Tell Jeb I'll catch up with you."

Upon arriving at the farm, Jackson was informed that he would have to travel a mile west to get equipment. Realizing he would never catch up with the brigade at this rate, he went on to the other farm, using the farmer's forge and partaking of a bowl of stew from his generous wife. It wasn't until he heard the crack of rifle fire and the booming of artillery that he knew what was happening.

After thanking the farmer and his wife, Jackson jumped on his horse and hurried toward the Williamsburg road. There were blue uniforms swarming all over the place, so he had to take a long route around.

It was twilight by the time he reached his unit, and by that time, the fighting was all over.

"What the hell happened?" he asked, gazing around at the wounded and exhausted men.

"McClellan's men caught us," Jeb said. "You picked a mighty convenient time to go hunting a blacksmith."

"Now just a minute!" Jackson exclaimed. "You don't for a minute think that I . . ."

"Calm down," Jeb grinned, holding up his hand. "You'll bust a blood vessel puffing out like that. I didn't mean anything. I know you didn't run out on us."

"All right then," Jackson muttered, still a little mad. "I'll go see if I can help with the wounded."

Andrew had been listening to the cannon fire in the distance and wondering what they were going to do. So far, he had been waiting around Norfolk, anticipating some sort of fight. At the sight of Yankee warships and transports on the York River, Secretary Mallory ordered that the ship *Virginia* be blown up. Huger ordered evacuation, and Andrew followed his troop toward Petersburg.

The weather was rainy during the days with thunderstorms at night. In the next week, the walking wounded began to arrive in Richmond from Williamsburg, and once more the women got busy in the hospitals. Winder Hospital was filled to overflowing, and the generous families of the city sent their dinners to the railroad station to feed the wounded lying on cornstalk leaves in the boxcars.

After the evacuation of Norfolk, the Confederate Congress adjourned on May 10. The city was so dangerously menaced, many of the members decided to leave. The legislature passed a resolution declaring the intention to burn the city and reduce it to ashes rather than permit it to fall into the hands of the enemy or to suffer the terror of destruction and bombardment. An appropriation was made for the removal of women, children, and the indigent citizens.

Some of the archives were being taken out of the Capitol to be transported to Columbia, South Carolina. Mrs. Davis and her children left for Raleigh.

The entire city was in an uproar.

Melissa got up from her desk at the paper and went over to the doorway to stand beside Henry and Lewis. People were leaving the city by the hundreds, in all directions. Every manner of conveyance had been pressed into service, and houses were left deserted. Baggage wagons, heaped with trunks, boxes, and baskets rattled down the street past the office of the *Journal*.

"Where will they all go?" Melissa wondered.

"I don't know," Lewis said. "Perhaps to the country— plantations of relatives or friends."

"I've never seen anything like it," Henry remarked. "Are people really so afraid of the Yankees? They're not savages, after all."

"I have to agree with you there, Walkenfeldt. If the city does fall, we're not all going to be murdered. The worst that could happen would be if McClellan turned out to be another Butler."

Melissa giggled. "I can just see Aunt Nancy arrested as a prostitute."

The two men chuckled along with her. She was referring to General Benjamin Butler's infamous Order #28. When the Federals occupied New Orleans, they were subject to much abuse by the women of the city. To put an end to it, General Butler issued an order stating that any female who was not respectful to a Union soldier would be arrested as a prostitute.

"The man should be shot," Lewis grumbled.

The only hope for holding the enemy at bay was Drewry's Bluff. But the fort there was only half finished, with just four guns to impede the *Monitor* and the other Union gunboats. There were a few torpedoes in the channel, but they could not be relied upon to do the job.

Melissa awoke on the morning of May 13 to the sound of booming artillery. She got out of bed and looked out the window. It was too cloudy to see anything. She dressed quickly and went downstairs to breakfast. Edward was just coming in the front door.

"What's going on, Uncle Edward?"

"I was just out trying to get some information. Apparently the Yankees are attacking the fort at Drewry's Bluff."

"What does it all mean?"

"It means the Yankees are knocking at our back door," he smiled. "But cheer up, my dear. We'll keep them out."

Melissa wasn't so sure as she walked to work that day. The citizens were in even more of a panic than they had been before. This was the first time actual sounds of hostile action could be heard in Richmond.

Once again, the mayor pledged himself not to surrender the city, but the statement wasn't necessary. By nightfall, the Federal flotilla was in retreat, after coming to the conclusion that it was impractical to strike at Richmond from the water.

On May 20, Henry met Mahaley at the top of Hospital Hill. He, like many others, had gone to watch the Federal observation balloons hovering over the city. The smoke from the campfires of the Yankees could be seen in the distance. McClellan was in Williamsburg.

"Hello, Mr. Walkenfeldt," Mahaley said.

"Oh, hello, Miss Armstrong."

"Call me Mahaley, please."

"All right. If you'll call me Henry."

"The Yankees are awfully close."

"I know," Henry replied.

"Why don't the soldiers shoot holes in those balloons?"

"They're too high. The guns won't reach that far."

"What are you doing here?"

"Watching. The same as everybody else."

Mahaley noticed Henry had his cane. Sometimes he used it, and sometimes he didn't. She peered at him out of the corner of her eye. He was really a very attractive man. And even though he wasn't in uniform, he was certainly doing a great service to the Confederacy. She gave the idea of sleeping with him a little consideration, but finally rejected it. He knew the family, and she didn't know how discreet he might be. Besides, he seemed only to have eyes for Melissa. She sighed and wished Nathaniel would liven up a little.

Fifty more cases of typhoid had come in from Ashland, and Nathaniel was undoubtedly busy. Not wanting to subject the patients already in the hospitals to the disease, a problem arose as to where to put them. Finally, a merchant at Fourth and Broad Streets offered to put them in his empty dry-goods store.

By evening, Stuart's scouts reported that Union General Irvin McDowell was falling back toward Fredericksburg, and the people of Richmond slept a little easier.

Andrew had reached Petersburg on the fifteenth, and after waiting another week, moved up toward Richmond.

General Johnston was ready to attack the Federals at Fair Oaks at the Seven Pines Road. It began to look like a Confederate victory, but due to General Huger's incompetency in following orders, the battle was considered a draw. General Johnston was wounded and brought to Richmond. He was replaced by Robert E. Lee, who retained command of the Army of Northern Virginia from then on. The only good thing which had come of the battle was the capture of abandoned Federal equipment when the Yankees had retreated. There were 6,700 muskets and rifles; medical, commissary, and quartermaster stores; tents; and a sutler's stock of preserved fruits and brandies.

The hospitals had been cleaned and aired in preparation for the onslaught of wounded. The ambulance corps was swamped by the wounded. The vans of the Southern Express Company were impressed into service to carry the men. Despite the preparations, the hospitals in Richmond were still inadequate. Most of the men had been wounded above the waist because of the thick brush in which they had been fighting. Warehouses and stores on Main Street opened up to accommodate the thousands of men. Along with the wounded came the summer sun, and with it, the endless flies to disturb the already miserable men.

Nancy was surprised to find that Margaret wished to offer her services at the hospitals. Mahaley supervised Tunia in making gallons of soup to be taken around to the various hospitals.

On one particularly warm day, Melissa was very uncomfortable working in the office. Two of the windows were now stuck that had been shut tight for the winter, and no one had bothered to fix them. Henry was warm himself. Besides, he wanted an excuse to walk across the street.

"Melissa, why don't we walk over to Dan's store and see if he's got something cool to drink?" he suggested.

"Oh, I'd love to," she said, putting her pen back into the inkwell. She stood up and brushed back a lock of damp hair from her forehead. Picking up her reticule, she joined Henry at the door. "When Mr. McAllen gets back, I'm going to ask him to have somebody get those windows open."

"If he'll do it for anyone, it'd be you."

"Mr. McAllen?" She began to laugh. "He hardly gives me the time of day. He's always complaining about something to me."

"But he doesn't complain *about* you, does he?"

She thought for a moment as they stepped up onto the

sidewalk in front of Dan's general store. "No . . . I guess not."

"He confides in you."

"But that doesn't mean he's sweet on me."

"I'm a man, Melissa. Take my word for it. McAllen's sweet on you."

Melissa giggled. "He's old enough to be my father! Uncle Edward wouldn't think too much of that."

Henry opened the door, and Melissa stepped inside the little store. The shelves weren't as full as they had been a year ago. A woman was just paying for a gallon of molasses when they entered.

"Hello Henry," Dan greeted.

"Hello Dan."

Melissa had only been in the store a few times. She didn't know Dan very well, but he seemed to be a pleasant enough person, a balding, middle-aged man.

"Hot enough for you?" Dan smiled. He gave the women her change, thanking her, and she left.

Henry watched her go; then turned back to Dan. "Dan, this is Miss Armstrong."

"Hello," she smiled.

"I've seen you in here before. Didn't know your name, though. You work at the paper, don't you?"

"Yes."

Dan chuckled. "This whole block was talking when McAllen first hired you. Now it ain't so unusual for a woman to be working. What can I do for you folks?"

"We're thirsty," Henry informed him. "Do you have any lemonade?"

Dan chuckled again. "I haven't seen a lemon for some time now. But I got some apple cider."

"That would be fine."

270

Dan ladled out the cider from a large keg and into two tin cups. He handed one to each of them, but Melissa noticed that when Henry placed the coins in the man's hand, there was a small folded slip of paper with them. The man pocketed the coins and the paper.

"I feel sorry for them boys out in the field in this heat," Dan remarked. "And you can bet it'll get a sight hotter."

"I get a breeze from the river at my boardinghouse," Henry said.

"Say, ain't that Stonewall something! He was giving them Yankees fits out there in the valley!"

"They say if it wasn't for him making the Yankees keep an eye on what he was doing, they'd be here by now," Henry remarked.

"Ain't that the truth. You got any soldiers in the family, miss?"

"My cousin. He's with General Huger."

Dan made a face. "He ain't much in favor right now. No reflection on your cousin, miss."

"He wants to be transferred. At least, that's what he said in his last letter."

"Miss Armstrong's gentleman friend is with General Stuart," Henry told him.

"Is that a fact?"

Melissa put down her empty cup. "I saw Mr. McAllen go into the paper just now, Henry. I should be getting back."

"Me too. Well, thank you, Dan."

"Thank you, Henry."

Melissa and Henry went out into the sunshine and waited for several wagons from the Commissary Department to pass.

"What was that piece of paper you gave him?" Melissa asked.

"What paper?"

"I saw it, Henry. You slipped it to him when you paid him."

"You're very observant."

"And you're very careless, if that's what I think it was."

"I'm only careless around you," Henry smiled.

"Is he . . . like you?"

Henry just smiled and took her arm as they crossed the street. "You ask too many questions, Melissa."

When they returned to the paper, Melissa went back to Lewis's office and tapped on the door.

"What is it, Miss Armstrong?"

"I was wondering if you could have someone fix the windows?"

"What's the matter with them?"

"They're stuck. It's stifling out there."

"Oh, very well. I'll see if Bruce can fix them."

"I'm sorry to cause so much trouble."

Lewis looked at her, and his stern countenance vanished. "It's no trouble, Miss Armstrong. I should have thought of it myself. Is there anything else I can do for you?"

"No, thank you. I'll be getting back to work now." She turned to leave.

"Miss Armstrong?"

She looked at him. "What?"

"Nothing," he muttered, flushing. "Would you please ask Mr. Walkenfeldt to step back here?"

"Certainly."

When Henry entered the little office, Lewis motioned

for him to sit down.

"Mr. Walkenfeldt, I've got an assignment for you. I hope you don't mind taking a little trip?"

"A trip? Where?"

"We've had such good response from all over the South on your article about the Tredegar Iron Works, I've decided to send you to do the same thing with the Augusta Arsenal and the Columbus Armory."

"Are you sure they would allow it?"

"I've been in touch with the managers. They'll be happy to see you. Are you interested?"

"Of course, I'm interested."

"Good." Lewis smiled and took an envelope from his desk. "Here's money for your expenses. This should take care of it, but if it isn't enough, keep a record and we'll reimburse you."

"When do you want me to go?"

"Anytime."

"Well, in that case, I'll see about a passport and check the train schedules."

"Any other interesting stories you come across will be most welcome."

"Certainly. Thank you, Mr. McAllen."

Twelve hundred cavalry and selected artillery were camped at Kilby's Station on the Richmond, Fredericksburg, and Petersburg railroad. At two in the morning on June 12, Jeb Stuart awakened his staff.

"Gentlemen, in ten minutes, every man must be in the saddle."

Jackson gathered his equipment and saddled his horse. With no sounding of a bugle, the long column was soon in motion. Jackson supposed they were heading for the

Shenandoah Valley to reinforce Stonewall's brigade. Jeb had not spoken a word or given any indication as to where they might be going.

All that day, they rode along empty roads—past farms where women came out to wave or old men stared in admiration at the display of so much horseflesh. After covering twenty-two miles, they made camp at Winston Farm, near Taylorsville. Scouts were sent out and pickets posted, but the troop passed an uneventful night.

In the morning, again with no bugles sounding, the column got under way again. As soon as they turned toward the east, the men all down the line began to stir. They were not going to the valley. Their objective was McClellan's flank.

Riding along, with a poncho strapped on his pommel and a plaid blanket wrapped in oilcloth tied behind his saddle, Jackson knew better than to try to question Jeb. When he didn't wish to speak, he didn't; and this was obviously one of those times. Besides, it made it all the more dramatic, which was what Jeb liked. Jackson watched the woods and the fields of corn he was passing until they came in sight of Hanover Court House. The scouts reported that the enemy was there, but their strength was not known.

Hoping to cut the Federals off, Stuart sent Fitzhugh Lee, the general's nephew, to take his regiment around to the right, so that they could come up behind the courthouse. After sufficient time had passed for the men to get into position, Jeb gave the signal to advance. A few shots rang out, and the column rushed forward. But it was too late. The Yankees had fled under the cover of their own dust. They found nothing in the village but the few residents. Fitz Lee had managed to get his men slowed down in a marsh, allowing the Yankees enough time to escape.

Disgusted, the column continued on until they caught a glimpse of more bluecoats near Haw's Shop. Before they knew what was happening, the Federals rushed forward, fired a few shots and then veered off.

Stuart ordered the charge, but again it was to little purpose. Just a few dismounted men were captured. The only satisfaction the southerners had was in watching their captives. They were of the Fifth US Cavalry, in which Fitz Lee had served before the war. The scenes that took place were more like a reunion than those of opposing armies.

Stuart's column moved on at a trot toward the Totopotomoy Creek, where he believed the Federals might make a stand. Jackson waited while the squads of scouts went forward. He eased his tension by taking out the picture of Melissa and contemplating it. His apprehensions were unfounded, for the scouts reported the bridge was unguarded.

They started off once again toward Old Church. Jeb pulled back and rode beside Jackson for a while.

"Having a good time?" Jeb grinned.

"Lovely," he replied sarcastically.

"Cheer up. If I know my father-in-law, he wouldn't neglect the crossroad up ahead."

Brigadier General Philip St. George Cooke, the renowned Virginia trooper and father of Jeb's wife, was in charge of the Federals on the right wing of the Chickahominy River. The Union supply wagons had to pass through Piping Tree Ferry and New Castle Ferry at Old Church.

Word soon came that the Yankees were waiting. Stuart

gave the orders, and the leading squadron dashed forward, straight into the Federals. Swords and pistols clashed for a few minutes until the Yankees scattered. When it was over, one of Stuart's captains was dead, several Yankees killed and wounded, and some taken prisoner. But Jackson had himself a coveted prize—one of the guidons of the Fifth US Cavalry.

Fitz Lee wanted to push on to surprise his old regiment, and Jeb assented, warning him to return quickly. The First Virginia Cavalry went on and found the camp deserted of men but full of supplies. But, having no time to waste collecting the goods, the camp was set on fire, except for a keg of whiskey found in an ambulance.

Stuart had now accomplished what he had been sent to do—establish the fact that there was no large Federal force in the vicinity. He rode back to Jackson, who was talking to Rooney Lee, the general's son.

"What do you think of this?" Jeb asked, and he explained his idea. If he returned the way he had come, the Yankees would most certainly be waiting in force. "The York River Railroad is McClellan's main supply line. If we tore up the tracks at Tunstall's Station, they'd be cut off from their base. We'd be heroes!"

"But how would we escape?" Rooney asked.

"It wouldn't be impossible. Forge Bridge is only eleven miles south of there, and I think we'd be well beyond the left flank of the enemy. Once we got across the Chickahominy, your daddy could create a diversion."

"I don't know," Rooney sighed.

"The best reason for doing it," Jeb explained, "is that the Yankees won't expect us to do it."

Jackson watched Jeb ride off to find Fitz Lee. He grinned to himself. Jeb was relishing every moment of this drama he was creating.

They skirted the Pamukey River through a heavily populated area. Women and the old came out to greet the first gray-clad soldiers they had seen in weeks. Jackson was amazed at how often he would hear a delighted squeal, and one of the men would leap from his horse to embrace a mother, sister, or wife.

As the tired men and horses neared Hopewell Church, Jeb sent two squads to see what stores they could find and bring back any horses there might be while the main body continued on. They passed overturned wagons and loot of all description where the Yankees had abandoned it.

Jeb decided to be cautious and ordered the artillery to the front of the column. As he rode back to check on its progress, he found the howitzers stuck in the mud. As the men and horses pulled, the guns only sank deeper. Jeb finally told Captain Pelham to offer the tired men the prized keg of whiskey as a reward if they could get the guns out of the mud.

While Jeb was watching the men struggling with the guns, one of the scouts galloped up to him.

"There's one or two companies of Yankees guarding Tunstall's Station, General."

Jeb advanced to the head of the column and ordered a charge.

Drawing his saber and spurring his horse into a gallop, Jackson rode toward the station. He was too far away to see the expressions on the Federals' faces, but he could imagine what they were thinking as some one hundred men and horses thundered toward them. The Yankees scattered almost instantly, their numbers being too few to resist. Some fled into the woods, while others were captured.

Jeb gave orders immediately for some of the men to start tearing up the tracks. More men were set to work chopping down the two telegraph poles nearest the station, and the scouts went off to burn the bridge across Black Creek.

Jackson sat in his saddle, watching. It was a high moment for himself and his fellow cavalrymen. They were making a mess out of the Federal supply and communication lines. Then he thought he heard a whistle in the distance. A train was approaching— probably full of Yankees. He looked over at Jeb, who had also heard the whistle.

Jeb trotted over to him. "Get that switch, Jackson."

Jackson jumped from his horse and ran over to the switch. He tried to throw it to derail the train and make it run into the siding, but it was stuck fast. Even hammering on the lock with a piece of timber had no effect. Men began to throw any and all sorts of things onto the track, while others dashed off to wait in ambush if the train should stop or leave the track when it hit the barricade.

As Jackson was just getting behind cover, the train came into sight. The flatcars were loaded with men clad in blue. As the train began to slow, some of the soldiers hopped off the train to stretch their legs or get water.

The nervous youngster beside Jackson fired his pistol. "You idiot!" Jackson yelled.

The engineer must have heard the shot and sensed danger, for the train began to increase its speed. He was going to try to run through the barricade.

The Confederates opened fire on the train, and Jackson saw the Yankees throw themselves face down on the flatcars. One of the scouts raced alongside the locomotive and shot the engineer, but the train kept going, having successfully passed the poorly constructed obstruction.

"If only those damned howitzers hadn't been back there in the mud!" Jackson grumbled, watching the train pass from view. He was disappointed, but all he could do was watch the captives being rounded up.

Stuart looked perturbed as Jackson rode up to him.

"What now, old friend?" Jackson asked him.

"I'm thinking," Jeb smiled. "You know what I'd like to do is go after that base of supply. If we could destroy it, McClellan would have to retreat."

"And what happens when the train gets there? They'll be alerted and waiting. We don't know how many men they might have."

"I know. And we'll have to wait for the squads who went to burn the bridge."

"Here comes Pelham now," Jackson remarked, as the artillery came up the road. He noticed none of the men looked as if they had imbibed too much from the whiskey.

The two Lee cousins rode up and handed Jeb and Jackson a chunk of bread and a slab of ham they had found in some wagons.

"The longer we wait, the more chance we might be cut off," Jeb sighed. "As much as I'd like to do it, I think we'd better move on."

The men ate and then burned the stores, gathering up the mules. The bridge burners returned with twenty-five prisoners.

The column wound southeastward as the evening came upon them. They found a Federal hospital with 150 patients at Talleysville. Stuart didn't disturb them, but allowed his men to devour the contents of the nearby sutler's store.

The column was strung out and had to be closed again, and it was midnight by the time Pelham's artillery pieces arrived. Jeb wanted to reach Forge Bridge by dawn. To expedite the march, the prisoners were mounted on the captured mules and horses, and they started once again.

The men were exhausted. Jackson noticed Jeb nodding in his saddle, so he rode alongside him to keep him from lurching off the road or falling off his horse. Like everyone else, Jackson was tired. The horses staggered and the column dragged, but there was no sign of any pursuing Yankees.

It was beginning to get light when they halted at the ford. The scout was startled. Instead of the easy-flowing stream he had known, it was a swift torrent, overflowing its banks. Rooney Lee stripped off his clothes and dove in. As strong a swimmer as he was, the current nearly swept him away.

Totally discouraged and exhausted, the men got down from their mounts and sat down to eat the remnants of their food.

Jeb surveyed the scene, stroking his beard thoughtfully. Another of the men went into the water, succeeding in getting across with his horse. Encouraged by his success, some of the other men attempted it. But it was a slow process, and most of the men were not good enough swimmers. Besides, there was no way to get the guns across.

Jeb sent a courier with a message for General Lee, asking him to create a diversion of some sort. The only hope now lay in making some kind of bridge.

Men with axes set to work, chopping down trees. The men on the other bank proceeded to tear up a large abandoned warehouse, stripping it of its boards. An hour passed, and more. The only thing that kept the men going was the knowledge that the Union Army must surely be catching up to them quickly. The artillery got across, followed by the men and horses. Five men were left to set fire to the little makeshift bridge, and then they too swam across.

Jackson and Fitz Lee waited for the men to clamber out of the water, watching the crackling flames. Just as they were about to turn to join the column, a little group of Federal lancers appeared on the other shore.

Jackson grinned and waved, spurring his horse to catch up to the rest.

Jeb turned over command to Fitz Lee and left to report to General Lee himself. The men could rest and have something to eat before moving on to camp. The expedition had made Jeb famous, and it was very embarrassing to McClellan—the little brigade of Confederate cavalry had ridden completely around the Union Army without even getting into a serious fight.

Twelve

In Richmond, the whole city was buzzing about what Jeb Stuart had done. Melissa was keeping busy at the paper. The *Grasshopper* had docked at Wilmington safely, and George had arrived on the train with the cargo. Mahaley had gone back to her lint-scraping and bandage-rolling. Margaret and Nancy spent their days making the rounds of the hospitals. In no other way did they feel they could properly thank the soldiers who were risking their lives for the safety of the women of the South. All day long they would sit amid the sickening hospital odors, wiping a fevered brow, changing dressings, reading or writing letters.

Melissa was working in the office when she heard a great deal of commotion out in the street. Looking up from some copy he was reading, Lewis went over to the door and glanced down the street.

"It's Stuart."

Melissa got up from her desk and stepped outside with Lewis. Sure enough, the new hero of the Confederacy had returned. And such a reception he was receiving! Probably twenty of his men accompanied him, riding down the street. She recognized the two Lee boys, young

John Pelham, captain of the horse artillery, Major Heros Von Borcke, John S. Mosby, Major Will Martin, John Esten Cooke, Captain Will Farley,. and of course, Jackson.

It was a riotous welcome. Men cheered, women waved, and there were some girls strewing flowers in their path. One girl even ran forward and hung a garland of flowers about the neck of Jeb's horse.

"Jackson!" Melissa called, waving.

He took off his plumed hat and waved it at her. "I'll see you later, Melissa!"

Lewis and Melissa watched the procession turn the corner and ride down Main Street.

"Perhaps I should print that poem I was just reading," Lewis said.

"What poem?"

"Some woman brought it in this morning. It's called 'The Ride Round McClellan.'"

While Jeb was busy meeting with the president and Lee, the other members of his troop dispersed to do whatever they pleased for the day. Jackson went first to take a bath and have a shave and a haircut. Then he stopped by several shops to try to purchase some new shirts and socks. He then left his horse to be newly shod and groomed at the livery.

He stepped inside the office of the *Journal* near closing time.

"Are you ready to leave yet?" he asked, smiling at Melissa.

She smiled back at him. "Almost. Just let me finish up."

Jackson wasn't bored while he waited, for two of the reporters questioned him about the now-famous ride.

"Do you want me to get a carriage?" Jackson asked, as he and Melissa left the office.

"We can walk. It's not far. Besides, it's not easy to find a carriage." She looked at him questioningly. "There's something different . . . your beard! You shaved it off!"

"I know. It was too hot." He didn't like to tell her that the real reason he had shaved it off was because he was sick and tired of picking lice out of it. "Do you mind?"

"No. I didn't really like that old beard anyway. It scratched."

He grinned at her and squeezed her arm. "Would you like to stop for an ice cream?"

"Oh, I'd love it. It's been so hot. But I don't want to spoil my supper."

"Oh, come on. A little ice cream never hurt anybody."

"Well, all right. Uncle Edward's been getting home later than usual anyway, so we won't be eating for a while."

Jackson and Melissa walked to Pizzini's. When they entered, Jackson started to lead Melissa to a table, but he saw one of his company sitting alone in the corner.

"There's one of my friends," he said. "I'd like to introduce you to him."

The two of them went over to the table where the young man was reading a newspaper. He looked up, his blue eyes smiling.

"Jackson!" he greeted, standing up and eyeing Melissa.

"John, I'd like you to meet Miss Melissa Armstrong. Melissa, may I present Captain John Pelham?"

They shook hands. "I've heard a great deal about you," John said. "Jackson speaks of you often. Won't

284

you two join me?"

"Are you waiting for someone?" Melissa asked.

"Just Mr. Pizzini. And I'd love the company."

"Thank you, Captain."

Melissa and Jackson seated themselves while John folded up his paper. Melissa was surprised at how young he looked, with his handsome clean-shaven face and blond hair.

"I don't know many people in Richmond," John said as Mr. Pizzini came over to them.

"Three ice creams, please," Jackson told him, "and make mine extra big."

"Mine too," John added.

Pizzini looked questioningly at Melissa. She shook her head. "Just a little one."

Mr. Pizzini disappeared and soon returned with the ice cream.

"I never got ice cream at home," John remarked.

"Where are you from, Captain?" Melissa inquired.

"Alabama."

"When was the last time you were home?"

"Not since before the war."

"Did you find a place to stay tonight?" Jackson asked.

"Not yet. And I don't expect I'll have much luck."

Knowing her family were such staunch supporters of the cause, Melissa felt sure they would want her to at least offer him dinner.

"Captain Pelham, would you care to join us for supper?"

"Oh, really, I couldn't impose."

"It's not an imposition. There's always plenty to eat, and I know my family would love to have you. Please say you'll come."

He smiled. "All right. Thank you, I will."

Jackson smiled to himself, thinking John didn't know what he was getting himself into when he met Mahaley.

"How's Margaret doing?" Jackson asked, turning to Melissa.

"Very well. She's suddenly decided to get out. She's been helping out at the hospitals." Melissa looked at John. "Margaret is my cousin. Her husband was killed at Shiloh."

After finishing their ice cream, they walked to the Armstrong home. Nancy was just coming along the street from the opposite direction. She greeted Jackson warmly and was introduced to Captain Pelham.

"You two gentlemen are the talk of the town," Nancy told them.

"Not us, ma'am, it was Jeb's doing," John smiled.

"You were part of it. Come along inside. My daughters should be home now. And my husband will be home soon. We'll have a little celebration."

The men followed Nancy and Melissa into the house.

"I've asked Captain Pelham to join us for supper," Melissa said.

"I'm glad you did. We'll be very happy to have you, Captain. Just set your haversack down there by the hall tree. And go on into the drawing room and make yourself comfortable. Fix yourself a drink if you like. I think I'll just run into the kitchen for a moment. Melissa, why don't you take Jackson upstairs and get him settled in his room? And tell the girls we have guests."

Melissa and Jackson went up the stairs. Mahaley was just coming out of Margaret's room with little Jeff.

"Oh, Major Vaughn!" she exclaimed. "Welcome back!"

"Thank you."

"I saw all the to-do you made this afternoon when you rode in."

"That was really something, wasn't it?"

"We have another guest for supper," Melissa told her. "He's down in the parlor."

"A guest? Who?"

"Why don't you go down and keep him company?" Jackson suggested. "He's all alone and probably feeling very self-conscious."

"Oh, all right." She looked at the baby and then took him back into Margaret's room. "Here. You bring him down yourself . . . I have to go entertain a guest."

Melissa looked at Jackson out of the corner of her eye and smiled as they walked to his room.

"I'd like to see the expression on her face when she sees him," Melissa chuckled.

"Why?"

"He's so good-looking."

They reached the room and went inside.

"What about me?" he asked.

Melissa put her arms around his neck. "Oh, you'll do," she teased, kissing him warmly.

"I don't know why I even bother to bring my things in here," he murmured, nuzzling her neck. "It's such a waste of time."

"Yes. But we have to keep up appearances."

"So we do," he smiled, kissing her again. "I brought you a present."

"What is it?"

"I'll give it to you later."

She appraised him thoughtfully and grinned. "I imagine you will."

Jackson laughed and drew her closer to him. "That too."

Nancy was in the kitchen making sure that Tunia had prepared enough for supper.

"Yessum. I cooks a big chicken. Mas' Edward, he come home at dinner time to tell me dat he bringin' dat Englishmans home wif him fo' supper."

"Do we have plenty of food?"

"Fo' tonight, Miss Nancy. But I usin' de last of de eggs, and dere ain't but a little bit of flour and sugar lef'."

"I'll see about it tomorrow. I don't understand it. Edward bought so much."

"Yes, ma'am. But yo' ain't been buyin' no more neither. And, beggin' yo' pardon, ma'am, but yo' been so busy at de hospitals 'n such like, yo' ain't been checkin' de larder."

When Mahaley went into the drawing room, she saw the back of a gray uniform bending over several daguerreotypes on the table.

"Hello," she said.

John straightened up and turned around. "Hello."

"I'm Mahaley Armstrong," she said, stepping toward him and extending her hand.

"I'm Captain John Pelham."

They shook hands, and Mahaley was entranced by his merry, laughing eyes.

"I saw you in the parade today," she said, "but I didn't know who you were."

"It wasn't really a parade."

"It certainly seemed like it. Won't you sit down? Can I get you something to drink?"

"No, thank you. I'm fine."

Mahaley seated herself across from him, and for the first time in her life, found herself completely tongue-tied. She had never seen such a gorgeous man before.

"Have you been with the cavalry long?" she finally asked.

"Since the beginning. But I'm no cavalryman. I'm with the horse artillery."

"Oh, of course. How silly of me not to notice the red collar and cuffs on your uniform."

Melissa told Jackson to go on into the parlor while she went out to the kitchen.

"We runnin' low on salt too," Tunia was saying.

She saw her aunt looked perplexed. "Did you get Jackson settled in his room?"

"Yes," Melissa said. "I didn't like to say anything until I spoke to you, but apparently Captain Pelham hasn't been able to find any lodgings in town for tonight. I was wondering . . ."

"Say no more. He's welcome to Andrew's room."

Cindy had come in with a basket of laundry.

As Nancy and Melissa left the kitchen, Nancy was saying, "Our home is open to any soldier friends of yours who need a place to sleep. Even if they have to sleep on the sofa."

Cindy looked at Tunia and rolled her eyes. "Jes' so long as dey ain't buggy. I swear, some of dese here white soldier boys jes' give me de itch!"

Tunia laughed. "I think dey gives Miss Mahaley de itch too!"

Edward and George arrived shortly after everyone had

289

gotten acquainted.

"Brilliant!" Edward congratulated Jackson, pumping his hand. "Everyone's talking about it!"

"It was Jeb's doing."

"Whoever's doing it was, I think this calls for some of that champagne the *Grasshopper* brought in."

Melissa excused herself and went to tell Tunia to fetch the champagne from the cellar. While she was out of the room, Jackson had gone upstairs to get the present.

"Where's Jackson?" she asked.

"He went upstairs to get something," Margaret told her.

Melissa sat back down and noticed George staring at her. He made her feel uneasy. When she thought about it, she felt a certain tension whenever he was around. She didn't know why—only that it was there.

"Has it been hot enough for you lately, Mr. Ainsworth?" she finally asked.

"Yes. Quite."

She was relieved to see Jackson return. He handed her a rolled-up piece of blue satin with a gold-fringed border.

"What's this?" she asked him.

"A little souvenir from General McClellan."

Melissa unrolled it to reveal the guidon with a gold eagle and the words "Fifth Pa. Cav." embroidered on it. She just sat staring at it while Nancy and Mahaley came over to examine it, bubbling over with excitement.

"Did you kill the man who was carrying it?" Melissa asked him.

"Why, no," Jackson replied, surprised at her attitude. "It got caught on a tree when he was riding away. The staff broke, so I just picked it up."

"Why, Melissa, aren't you pleased?" Nancy asked.

"Jackson's done you a great honor."

"I know." She looked at Jackson. "Thank you. I do appreciate it. It's just that I'm very tired of this war. And seeing that this flag is from Pennsylvania made me think of my brother."

"The war will be over soon," Mahaley said cheerfully. "Pretty soon, the Yankees will give up and go home and leave us alone."

"Not according to my information," Jackson smiled. "Perhaps we didn't run into a large group of them, but they are massing. And Rooney says we don't have near enough men."

"Stonewall's sending his troops over here from the valley," John told them.

"You mean they're going to try to get into the city again?" Margaret asked.

"Rooney says his father knows they're going to attack," Jackson said. "And if McClellan only knew how small a force we have, he wouldn't hesitate for a moment. The war would be over by the Fourth of July."

"But Richmond isn't the whole Confederacy," George remarked.

"It's the heart of it."

"How many men do we have here to defend the city?" Edward inquired.

"General Lee hopes by the time Stonewall's men get here, perhaps eighty thousand."

"McClellan could have two times that many—and probably does," John added. "But Lee's a gambler. And we'll come out of this all right."

Melissa folded the little guidon very carefully while the others were discussing Lee's merits, tucking away the information she had heard. Jackson's words echoed in her mind: "If McClellan only knew, the war would be over by the Fourth of July." She picked up her champagne and patted Jackson's hand.

"I really do thank you for the flag."

"I wouldn't have given it to you if I'd killed the man." He leaned close to her and said quietly. "Just between you and me, I haven't killed anybody yet, and I hope I don't have to."

Mahaley waited until she was certain the household had settled down for the night; then she crept down the hall to Andrew's room. She opened the door quietly and stepped inside.

"Who's there?"

"It's Mahaley, Captain Pelham."

He sat up in bed in surprise, the covers gathering at his waist, and the moonlight illuminated his finely muscled chest. Mahaley stepped closer to the bed.

"I was wondering if you were comfortable, Captain?"

"Just fine, Miss Mahaley."

She sat down on the bed, and her wrapper fell open slightly, revealing her small but well-formed breasts. She leaned toward him, running her fingers over his shoulder and down his chest.

She smiled invitingly. "Are you sure there's nothing I can do for you, Captain?"

Melissa had gotten out of bed and gone over to catch the breeze from the open window, her lithesome figure silhouetted against the night sky.

Jackson watched her from the bed. "You seem upset about something," he said.

"It's all this fighting. I'm tired of it."

"So am I."

"Maybe it wouldn't be so bad if I were far away from it. But it's right here. Every time you turn around, the Yankees are ready to march right into Richmond."

Jackson got up and went over to stand beside her. "It must be hard living here. Maybe it's easier being a soldier."

"No. I'm sure it's not. But it's very depressing. I just wish it would soon end—one way or the other."

"I understand how you feel, but you'd best not let your Aunt Nancy hear you talking like that. She'd have you arrested for a traitor," he chuckled, pulling her into his arms. "The sooner it's over, the happier I'll be. Then we can think about getting married."

As soon as Jackson and John left after breakfast, Melissa left the house. Henry was in Georgia. She fervently prayed she hadn't been mistaken about Dan as she entered his store.

"Ah, Miss Armstrong, isn't it?"

"Yes." She was thankful the store was devoid of patrons.

"How are you today?"

"Very well, thank you." She looked at the man nervously. She didn't know what to say next, so she finally asked, her voice cracking, "Do you have any pins?"

"No. I'm sorry. Sold the last ones a couple weeks ago."

"Oh . . . how about some thread?"

"I've got a little. Here, let me get it." Dan put a rather empty box of thread on the counter. "Not much selection, I fear. The Yankees have managed to ruin my business. Appears they're going to try to get into the city again."

Trying to sound very casual, she said, "I understand when Stonewall Jackson's men arrive, Lee will have eighty thousand men here."

"Is that a fact? And where, might I ask, did you hear that?"

"From my gentleman friend."

"Oh, yes. The one with Stuart."

"You have a very good memory."

He smiled. "I have to."

Satisfied that she had done the best she could without incriminating herself, she said, "I'll take this blue thread."

"That'll be thirty-five cents."

"Thirty-five cents for a spool of thread? Lordy, what's the world coming to?"

In the next few days, the streets of Richmond were filled with soldiers passing through on their way to the front. With the army assembled along the eastern border, the city had become a vast camp. Regiments, wagons, and orderlies kicked up· the dust of the road in the hot summer sun.

Along with many of the families, Nancy had set up a table in the front yard, where she, Margaret, and Mahaley passed out food. The men marched on, with ham and bread speared on their bayonets.

The city battalion, under the supervision of Major Elliot, was working hard to throw up breastworks around the city. A home guard was organized for protection against raids by hostile cavalry. Outfitted with rifles and ammunition, the uniforms to be furnished at a later date, they were the object of ridicule by the women. Generally made up from the extremely old and very young, the ladies felt that they could do a better job defending the city and themselves. Indeed, any man who was not in uniform was now subject to scorn.

George was one of these, and he dearly wished he were somewhere else, for a variety of reasons. It was not uncommon for a woman to accost him on the street and ask him why he was not in uniform. When he gave his occupation, he was thanked or praised or blessed, or all three, but he still received suspicious looks from those ladies who didn't know. Another reason was Melissa. He had been immediately attracted to her when he first met her. Not so much by her beauty as by her warmth and honesty. After seeing her with Jackson, he felt any attentions he might give her would be fruitless. She seemed very taken with Jackson, and she had never shown the least bit of interest in George.

After working for several days, Andrew was finally ensconced in the breastworks at Harrison's Landing, on the James River. The heat was intense, and the men were miserable. He had been scratching a letter to Ellen on a scrap of wrapping paper he had found when a commotion down the line distracted him.

"Hey, Andrew! Come take a look here!" one of the men called.

Tucking his letter under his haversack to keep it from blowing away, although there was little wind, Andrew climbed over the top of the earthworks and onto the little rise. The group of men were watching the progress of a barge being towed up the river. Moored to the barge was the Confederacy's first observation balloon, and probably the most colorful one ever constructed. The women of the South had been called upon for the ultimate sacrifice—to donate their silk dresses. The ladies responded, and the result was a fantastic multicolored patchwork. It had been inflated in Richmond and was now en route to be put to use.

"That's my mother's dress!" Andrew exclaimed.

"Which one?" his friend asked.

"That purple one there—up by the top. I'd know that color anywhere!"

The men cheered and waved, grateful for a little release from the tedium and hard work of the last few days. As they watched the progression, the tide went out, and the balloon became stuck on a sandbar. And there it would remain, for the fighting soon began. The balloon would not be recovered until the Federals captured it, and with it, some of the last silk dresses in the Confederacy.

On June 25, a war council had been held in Richmond. It was attended by Generals Lee, A. P. Hill, D. H. Hill, Wise, Magruder, Ripley, Anderson, Longstreet, Whiting, and President Davis. Lee was ready to strike while McClellan was still smarting from Stuart's humiliating raid and off balance from Union efforts to get into Richmond in May.

Still, McClellan very nearly beat Lee to it. While the conference was taking place in Richmond, he moved his lines south of the Chickahominy. Some sharp fighting took place, and the Confederates gave way. A Confederate deserter had told him Stonewall Jackson was only a day's march away, which gave McClellan cause to ponder longer the idea of an attack. Meanwhile, the man Dan had sent out with Melissa's information never arrived. His

296

horse had bolted at a snake, throwing its rider and breaking his neck. The message he carried died with him.

The sounds of battle could once more be heard in the city. On June 26, Lee took the initiative and crossed the Chickahominy, heading toward Mechanicsville.

Melissa was just finishing her day at the paper when Lewis called her into his office.

"Miss Armstrong, do you have anything planned for this evening?"

"Why, no."

"Then I'd like to ask you to do a favor for me and the cause."

"What is it?"

"That notice we printed in today's paper—the one asking for all speculators to release their supplies to the hospitals for this emergency . . ."

"Yes?"

"I'm afraid your uncle and I are guilty of holding back. But with your help, I hope to remedy that."

"What do you want me to do?"

"You're very good at organizing. And right now, all our medicine is in big crates. What I want to do is break those down into smaller packages to go to each of the city's fifty hospitals. Mr. Ainsworth will take care of the records, but I'd like you to help me sort and package the supplies. Will you help?"

"Yes, of course."

"I think we'll have time to make our money off the rich women who insist on frippery. Right now, the men need the medicine."

"I'm glad to hear you say that, Mr. McAllen. If you'll pardon me for speaking so freely, I thought you had very little compassion."

"I'm not as hard as I appear, Miss Armstrong. Actually, I'm a very lonely man. If I had a good wife . . ."

There was a tap on the door, and George entered the little office, carrying his briefcase. "Good afternoon, Miss Armstrong. Mr. McAllen."

"Good afternoon, Mr. Ainsworth," Melissa said. She looked at Lewis. "I should go home first and let my family know where I'll be. And have a bite to eat."

"There's no need. We can send Ish with a note. And I thought we could all dine at the Columbian Hotel. It's nearby."

"But I'm not dressed for dining. I've been working in this dress all day."

Lewis smiled. "Miss Armstrong, you would look lovely in anything. Besides, have you taken a good look at what most of the women have to wear these days? Your clothes are in fine shape compared to most."

Ish disappeared with the note for Edward, and the three of them got into Lewis's little buggy and drove to the Columbian Hotel. Melissa had to agree, most of the women looked a little patched, thanks to the Union blockade. There were very few people dining out.

"Be sure to pick up some fine dress goods this time out," Lewis told George.

He nodded. "I've been expecting the ship for over a week now. I hope nothing happened. I'm anxious to get back home and see my family."

"Are you going to England this time?" Melissa asked him.

"Yes. We'll stop in Nassau on our way back, though." He grinned. "My mum will be surprised to see me—a rich man."

"And richer every time the ship docks," Lewis agreed.

"I've put all my money into bonds. It's just another small way in which I can help the cause. What about you, Mr. Ainsworth?"

"I do have a few bonds and some gold in the Trader's Bank here in town. But most of my savings are in the bank in Nassau. I expect I'll put some more away in Liverpool."

"A lot of people are beginning to doubt the Confederate dollar, but I hold it's solid," Lewis said.

"It's not worth as much anymore," Melissa said.

"Because we're a new country. It'll be worth its weight by December."

"Speaking of December," George said, turning to Melissa. "If you'd like, I'll be happy to pick up anything you might want to give as Christmas gifts."

"But it's only June. Besides, I don't want to put you to any trouble."

"It's no trouble. I rather like it. Makes me feel sort of like Father Christmas."

"Who?"

George smiled. "I believe you call him Santa Claus."

"How many more runs do you think you can make before Christmas?" Lewis asked.

"I imagine it depends on a lot of things—like weather and luck. Probably three, perhaps more."

After the food arrived, they ate in relative silence. The dining room was quiet, but there was a great deal of activity out on the street.

"I think when I return, I'll see about getting myself a horse," George said. "It's getting harder and harder to find a hack anymore."

"Good horses aren't easy to come by," Lewis remarked. "The army's buying them all up."

"I don't particularly care how good the horse is. I'm not much of a rider anyway."

"I brought my brother's horse with me when I came to the city," Melissa said. "Our coachman rides him occasionally, but he doesn't get enough exercise. You'd be welcome to use him, Mr. Ainsworth."

"How much do you want for him?"

"Oh, he's not for sale. But you can use him while you're in town."

"You must let me pay you something."

"In that case, you could pay my uncle for his upkeep. He's a very good horse and my brother loved him dearly. I trust you'll be gentle with him?"

"Oh, yes. I'm very good with animals."

Lewis had been observing this exchange. George was obviously very much enamored of Melissa, although she seemed to be treating him as she would any man. If he wasn't so set in his ways, Lewis thought, he might be able to win her over. After all, what were a few years? He was wealthy, was respected to a certain degree in the community, and most of all, he wanted her. The real fly in the ointment seemed to be Major Vaughn—him and his flashy good looks and youthful energy. Lewis wanted a wife, a young one who could bear children and entertain him on dull evenings. He smiled. Melissa could well do that, he imagined.

The small warehouse was full of crates and piles of material and blankets. George noted everything down in the ledger while Melissa and Lewis selected the most necessary medical supplies. They divided these evenly into fifty potato sacks. Lewis asked Melissa if she would help him make the deliveries in the morning. He wanted someone in authority from each hospital to sign for them, and he felt Melissa's presence might make the overworked doctors more inclined to comply. He could collect his money from the government later.

"You wanted me to work on that food-donation article to be ready for Monday."

"So I did. I really did want to have a woman along, though."

"Perhaps Mahaley could go."

Lewis picked Mahaley up early, and they began their rounds of the various hospitals. When they arrived at Richmond General, a very tired-looking Nathaniel came out to sign for the supplies.

"Nathaniel, you look awful!" Mahaley exclaimed.

"I don't look as bad as my patients. Mr. McAllen, you would be doing me a great favor if you could take me and some of this medicine to the St. Charles Hotel. We just received word that a whole load of wounded were sent there for lack of a better place to put them."

"Of course."

"I'll get my bag."

Nathaniel disappeared but returned shortly with his medical kit.

"There just simply aren't enough doctors or nurses," he sighed.

"Couldn't I help?" Mahaley asked. "I'd be proud to help you."

"I don't know," he replied. "I certainly could use you, but it's so . . . so unpleasant."

"I wouldn't mind."

"You don't know what it's like. Besides, you're young and unmarried. It's not proper."

"Who cares about that?" If I'm needed, it doesn't

matter. I don't care what people think of me."

"You go ahead with the doctor, Mahaley," Lewis told her. "I can finish up myself."

Nathaniel helped Mahaley down out of the carriage and picked up his bag and the supplies. The two of them walked into the hotel lobby.

Mahaley looked around her in disbelief. Every amount of available floor space was taken by the broken and bleeding bodies of soldiers. Some moaning, some crying, some silent—all miserable in the heat and discomfort of the bare floorboards. The only ones ministering to them were several soldiers who were wounded only slightly and two nuns.

Upon seeing Nathaniel, one of the nuns hurried over to him. "Oh, Doctor, I'm so thankful you're here. There's another doctor in the dining room. They're turning it into an operating room."

"I'll go right in. Thank you, Sister." He looked at Mahaley, who was staring in horror at the rows of men. "Will you be all right?"

"Yes." She stood a little straighter and looked at the nun. "What do you want me to do?"

Mahaley was given a flask of water, a cloth, and a basin of water. She bent down beside the first man and wiped the dirt and sweat from his face.

"Do you want a drink of water?"

"No, miss. I reckon it'd pour right out of this hole in my belly. But I thank you anyway. Leastways, if I'm goin' to meet my Maker, I got to see a pretty gal before it's time."

With only two bouts of nausea, Mahaley got through the morning. The worst part was the screams emanating from the dining room. The scant supply of chloroform had run out after the first ten men. After that, Nathaniel had to rely upon liquor, of which, at least, the hotel had plenty.

While the wounded kept pouring into Richmond, Jackson and the cavalry were very busy. They had destroyed a bridge, disrupting the Union supply line on the Pamukey River. For the most part, their duties had been to act as reserve for Lee and Stonewall. As the day drew to a close, they came upon several abandoned sutler's shops. They had been living on salt meat and crackers for days and were ready to appreciate the delicacies they found—sugar; millions of lemons; cases of wine, brandy, and other liquors; confections; canned meats, fruits, and vegetables. Some of the men proceeded to drink up the liquor.

Jeb scanned the men carefully and realized drunken soldiers were a hazard. Jackson was smoking a fine Havana cigar and sipping some brandy when Jeb approached the men.

"I've just had information that the Yankees poisoned all this liquor and left it as a trap," he announced.

The tin cup dropped from Jackson's hand. The men who were already drunk sobered up quickly. Jeb was satisfied.

"General, I ain't gonna die, am I?" one of the man asked. "I don't feel sick."

"Not all of it's been poisoned," Jeb said. "But there's no way of telling which is which. It's best not to drink any of it."

Jackson had caught on by now, and was enjoying Jeb's little joke. He didn't blame the men for wanting to drink, but he knew how easily they could be caught if they let their guard down. Jeb disliked liquor himself and wouldn't allow it in camp. For all the stories circulating about Jeb's wild streak and his fondness for the ladies, Jackson knew he was a deeply religious man who loved his wife and children more than anything in the world.

"Jackson, get a detail together and load this stuff into that wagon over there," Jeb told him. "If we can get it down to Lee, his men can use it."

As he drove along the streets in his secondhand buggy, Henry could not believe the confusion he saw. The train service was a mess, so he had purchased the buggy in Greensboro to get back to Richmond. As he was passing the St. Charles Hotel, he saw a familiar figure leaning against one of the balcony pillars. He stopped the buggy and got down.

"Mahaley! What are you doing?"

She raised her head and looked at him. "Oh, Mr. Walkenfeldt. I was just about to walk home. I was just resting for a minute."

He noticed the bloodstains on her dress, her dirty face and tangled hair. A stretcher was being carried from the hotel and then he knew what she had been doing.

"You're exhausted," he said gently. "Let me drive you home."

Henry assisted her into the buggy and they started toward Franklin Street.

"I'm glad you came along when you did," she said. "I'm so tired. I just don't think I could have walked home."

Henry was anxious to know all about what had been happening in his absence, but Mahaley was obviously too tired to talk. She leaned her head against his shoulder, and he felt this was probably the first time he had ever been around Mahaley when she had nothing to say.

Bobo came out to take the horse.

"What wrong wif de li'l missy?"

"She's been working at the hospital all day."

With his arm around her waist, Henry helped Mahaley into the house. Cindy came out of the kitchen.

"Laws! What de matter? Yo' looks like yo' been out fightin' de Yankees all by yo'self!"

"I've been at the hospital, Cindy. I want to take a bath and go to bed."

"Yessum. I help yo'."

"Is anyone else home?"

"No, missy. But dey all be along soon, I 'spect."

Mahaley turned to Henry. "Thank you for seeing me home. Why don't you go on into the drawing room and make yourself comfortable?"

When Melissa got home, she took off her bonnet and hung it on the hall tree. The house was hot, and more than anything she wanted a cool drink. She peeked into the drawing room to see if anyone was home and saw Henry sitting on the settee.

"Henry!" she exclaimed, rushing into the room. Henry stood up and suddenly found Melissa with her arms around him. "Oh, Henry, I'm so glad you're back and safe! I've worried about you."

He stroked her hair. "You did?"

"Of course I did."

"You don't know how glad I am to hear you say that."

He was about to attempt to kiss her when she drew back and gave him that mischievous smile of hers. "I did something while you were gone."

305

"What?"

"I gave a message to Dan." The horrified look on Henry's face caused Melissa to panic. "Don't tell me he's not . . . ?" she moaned.

"Yes. It's all right. You did the right thing."

Melissa heaved a sigh of relief. "For a minute there, you scared me."

"Maybe I should put it differently. You didn't do the right thing—but you did see the right man. Melissa, I told you not to get involved in this."

"I got involved when this war started. I believe in the same things you do."

"That's fine. But leave it there. You're a woman."

"So are Rose Greenhow and Belle Boyd. They're spies for the Confederacy."

"That's different."

"What's different about it?"

"Well, I don't know. It just is."

"That's the most ridiculous thing I've ever heard you say, Henry Walkenfeldt."

He touched her cheek gently with his fingers. "I just don't want anything to happen to you. I care too much for you."

The sound of the front door opening caused Henry to back away from Melissa. Nancy peeked into the room.

"Mr. Walkenfeldt, what a pleasant surprise. I want to hear all about your trip, but first I must freshen up."

Melissa sat down and waited until her aunt and Margaret had gone upstairs, wondering what Henry might have said if he had not been interrupted.

Henry decided it was better to let the matter of his feelings for Melissa rest. "What did you tell Dan?" he asked.

306

"The troop strength of the entire army around Richmond."

Henry whistled. "I must say, that was quite a tidbit of information. What did he say?"

"Well, I didn't really come right out and tell him exactly why I was giving him the information. I went into his store and pretended to be interested in some thread and just sort of mentioned it casually in conversation."

As upset as he was with Melissa, Henry couldn't help but smile. She saw his smile and grinned back at him.

"You aren't mad at me anymore then?" she asked.

"I'm furious."

"You weren't here!"

"I know. But from now on, tell it to me first."

"I don't know about you, but I'm thirsty. Can I get you something?"

"I don't suppose you have any lemonade?"

"No. But Tunia's invented a little something Aunt Nancy calls Confederate lemonade. It's not bad."

Melissa went out to the kitchen and got a pitcher and glasses from Tunia.

"Miss Mahaley, she worked at de hospital today."

"Mahaley?"

"Yessum. Cindy say she mighty tired."

Margaret had joined Henry when Melissa returned with the tray.

"What's all this about Mahaley working in a hospital?" Melissa asked, while she was pouring them each a glass. "I thought she was going to help Mr. McAllen."

"Apparently she did for a while," Margaret told her. "And it wasn't a hospital. It was the lobby of the St. Charles Hotel."

"That was terrible. One of the reporters was over there

earlier today," Melissa said. "How come she wa
allowed? You know how they frown on unmarrie
women helping in the hospitals."

"I guess Dr. Aldrich needed her."

"I'm so proud of my baby," Nancy said, bustling int
the room.

"If they're willing to take unmarried women, perhaps
should volunteer for weekends," Melissa said.

"Just in this emergency." Nancy picked up the pitche
and poured herself a glass. "Isn't this refreshing, Mr
Walkenfeldt?"

"Yes. It's very tasty."

"You'll never guess what it is."

"No. What is it?"

"Pomegranates. And Maggie Howell says she's beer
making beer from persimmons and sassafras." Nancy sa
down. "Have you heard anything about Andrew
Melissa?"

"Nothing. But from what I've heard and Andrew say
in his letters, General Huger will manage to stay out of
fight."

"How are things at the paper?" Henry asked.

"About the same as usual," Melissa replied. "I thinl
Mr. McAllen is beginning to soften up. You know, h
actually told me he was lonely."

"I'm not surprised," Henry laughed. "He's so grump
all the time."

"I don't think it's funny," Margaret said. "It's no fu
to be lonely." She got up. "If you'll excuse me, I thinl
I'll go feed Jeff."

Henry watched her leave. "I'm sorry. I didn't mean t
say anything to upset her."

"Don't think anything of it," Nancy told him

"Margaret's still very upset about losing her husband. You'll stay for supper, won't you?"

"If it's no trouble."

"No trouble at all. You know you're always welcome here. I'll just go see how Tunia's doing."

Nancy left, and Henry got up and helped himself to another glass of "lemonade." "Forgive me if I seem to be prying," he said. "But I always got the impression that Margaret wasn't particularly devoted to her husband."

Melissa gave a sadistic laugh. "That's an understatement. I never told you all about what happened, and I won't go into it now. But I think Margaret feels she caused Joseph's death. The other day she was even asking me if I thought she was raising Jeff as Joseph would want. If she was providing well enough for him, and things like that. She didn't care one whit how Joseph felt about things before."

Edward came in, and Melissa dropped the discussion of Margaret. Edward seemed genuinely pleased to see Henry.

"And how's one of our staunchest believers in the cause doing?" Edward asked him.

"Very well, thank you."

"We've missed your stories. I didn't think you'd be back so soon, though."

"I decided against doing any sight-seeing. The country there is feeling the pinch harder than we are here. I saw many women going shoeless."

"In Atlanta?" Edward asked, amazed.

"No. In the country and in small villages. When I asked them about it, they said that as long as the weather was warm, they were saving their shoes for winter."

"That's awful," Melissa murmured. "Do they have

309

enough to eat?"

"The country people seem to. They can grow their own. But, of course, there's little sugar or salt."

While they were eating, Henry told them all about his experiences deep in the heart of the South. Melissa admired his gift for words. When Henry talked, he made everything come alive. She also admired his acting abilities. He had completely taken everyone in. If she didn't know the truth, she would never suspect him.

An ominous silence had fallen over the city at sundown. The guns in the distance were quiet, and the population of the city was very anxious. The men on the field at Gaines' Mills were beginning to hope the terrible fighting of the afternoon was over. But Lee was gathering his men, and the Confederates rushed forward in an all-out desperate-effort charge at the Yankees. The Union line broke in places, whole regiments were taken prisoner, and Lee captured thousands of small arms and fifty-two pieces of artillery.

When the roaring of the guns started up again, Edward rose from his chair and began to pace. Mahaley was awakened and went over to look out her window. In the darkness, the flashes of light could be plainly seen. She put on her robe and went downstairs.

"It's like fireworks," she said. "Come up and look."

The entire group went up to the third floor and into Cindy's little room. When the sky was lighted for a moment, the balloons of the enemy could be seen hovering over the battlefield. The tops of the Exchange and Ballard Hotels, the Capitol, and every other tall building were covered with people witnessing the display. The president and his aides had gone up on one of the

310

surrounding hills to observe.

"I can't watch," Nancy sighed, leaving the room. "My son is out there somewhere."

Margaret, Edward, Melissa, Mahaley, and Henry watched for some time, fascinated by the brilliant bursts of light.

"It's beautiful," Melissa said. "But terrible."

"Reminds me of Fourth of July picnics," Edward remarked.

Henry's response was, "Those men out there are hardly on a picnic."

In the next days, the battles of Savage Station, White Oak Swamp, and Frazier's Farm were fought. While McClellan was retreating, Lee was preparing for a final blow. If all had gone as planned for Lee, the Union Army would have ceased to exist.

Andrew had been at work felling trees so that the artillery could advance, but tools were few and progress was slow. His unit was following the Yankees, who were working just as quickly to block their way. The strange spectacle presented a battle of rival axmen. It had taken them half a day to march five miles, but they had finally managed to get through, floudering through the woods toward the front.

Andrew could hear the steady fire of Union artillery, who were securely entrenched on the top of Malvern Hill. The guns were arranged hub to hub, where they could sweep every angle of approach. There was also a naval squadron on the river, where General McClellan was observing from the *Galena*.

The first attempts to charge the hill were a disaster. The few batteries in support of the Confederates were quickly put out of order. Andrew and his squad were trying to work up the western end of the hill. Stepping over the bodies of his comrades who had already fallen, Andrew rushed forward. The guns opened fire, and men fell all around him like tenpins. It was not war; it was mass murder. The broken butt of a rifle smacked against the side of Andrew's head, and he fell.

As night descended, the fields were covered with the bodies of dead and wounded. McClellan retreated, as he had done after every battle of this campaign. One-armed General Phil Kearney urged him to press on to Richmond, but McClellan refused. He still did not know the troop strength of the city. Lee, who had fought with all the odds against him, had won. McClellan, who had all the advantages but refused to take a risk, had lost.

A steady rain falling on his face brought Andrew back to consciousness. It was the dead of night, and he could see nothing. His head ached terribly, and when he touched it, it felt warm and sticky. He lay on his back, letting the rain wash the dirt and heat from his body, trying to organize his thoughts. The last thing he remembered was charging up the hill, men falling all around him, and the incessant roar of the Federal guns. He listened. The guns were silent. But now there was a different sound, more terrifying than the guns: the sobs, the moans, the screams, the delirious ramblings of the wounded.

Andrew struggled to sit up, and his foot brushed against something solid. Peering into the darkness, he saw a man lying faceup, his eyes staring wide at nothing, his face twisted into a grimace. Andrew scrambled to his feet and stumbled over the forms on the ground. He thought he could detect some movement at the edge of the trees. Were they his men or the Yankees? Anything would be better than spending the night in this graveyard.

"Help me," a voice called weakly.

Andrew stopped and glanced in the direction from where the voice had come. "Where are you?"

"Here. To your right."

Andrew took a few cautious steps, but could see nothing but bodies. He was ready to bolt and run, fearing some of Tunia's stories about "haunts" had been true, when the voice spoke again, this time very close.

"Please. I'm under this man. Please pull him off me. I can't move."

Andrew reached down and gingerly tugged at the arm of a huge man. The man must weigh three hundred pounds, Andrew thought as he struggled to drag the dead weight. He found himself becoming sick to his stomach, but he finally was able to get the body moved.

He squatted down beside the soldier who had spoken. "Are you hurt bad?"

"I can't move anything. But I thank you for movin' that feller. I couldn't breathe—my face was pushed into the grass."

"I don't think I can carry you," Andrew said. "But I'll send help." He glanced around and found a rifle. He planted the bayonet in the ground and placed a discarded cap on top of it. "Someone should see this. Do you know where the Yankees are?"

"They lit out. After sundown."

"I'll go get help," Andrew told him. "Try to hang on."

"Thanks again, soldier."

Andrew made his way toward the movement and found stretcher-bearers and orderlies collecting the wounded.

"There's a man out there," Andrew told one of them. "I stuck a rifle in the ground with a kepi on it by him. He's hurt real bad."

The orderly straightened up from the prone form he had been examining. "Might as well go now. This one ain't gonna need us."

The first faint streaks of light were beginning to touch the eastern horizon as Andrew wandered into the clearing where the field hospital was set up. It was a large tent with two canvas canopy shelters nearby. Both shelters were full of men lying on the ground. Andrew had never seen such a pitiful assemblage in all his life.

He wasn't aware how badly the gash in his head was bleeding until a passing orderly handed him a rag.

"Stanch it with this for a while. It'll have to do until we can get to you."

Andrew touched the cloth lightly to his face and winced. Upon examining it, he found that indeed he was bleeding. His head hurt, and he felt a little giddy, so he decided to get a drink of water and wait for a doctor to see him.

"Any drinking water around here, soldier?" he asked one of the men sitting on the ground by a tree.

"There's a barrel over that way."

Andrew nodded and made his way in the direction the man had indicated. He saw the barrel beside the tent and started toward it. As he stepped forward, he made a grisly discovery. Piled beside the barrel was an assortment of amputated limbs. Andrew's stomach turned, and he fainted.

Thirteen

Jeremiah had hurried home from the hospital to put his medical bag away before going to the park. His surgical instruments were his pride and joy. They had arrived last month rather mysteriously after he had received a letter from Melissa telling him that if things went as she hoped, he could expect a birthday present from her. After getting a notice that a package was waiting for him at the shipping office, he went to pick it up. It had come in on a steamer from Nassau. It was a black leather case with the surgical instruments nestled in green velvet. The instruments were of the finest Spanish steel, with pearl handles and his initials engraved on each blade. He had never been so pleased with anything in his life.

Jeremiah continued to marvel at his sister's ingenuity at moving letters and parcels through the lines. When her daguerreotype had arrived, he considered that quite an accomplishment, but surgical instruments surpassed even that. Sarah and Jim had made quite a fuss over Melissa's photograph after having heard so much about her.

Jeremiah didn't know how to break the news to Melissa

that he had joined the medical corps, and that he planned to leave as soon as he received his certificate next month. After a year of watching the mangled bodies arrive at the hospitals, he was sure he could do some good on the battlefield. He had already received his commission as captain in the Forty-sixth Pennsylvania infantry.

As he walked the two blocks to the park, Jeremiah hoped he would still be here when Sarah had her baby. It was due at the end of August, and he was anxious to see the child, for Sarah had become another sister to him. Sam was seldom home, and this was one of the rare times when he was. The tales Sam told him had helped to convince him that more doctors were needed in the field. Jim was going to stay on at the hospital. Sarah and his mother didn't want him to leave, and besides, he was courting Ben's daughter Caddie.

Allegheny City Park was filled with people enjoying themselves on this Fourth of July. Jeremiah spotted the little group, not far from the bandstand. There were blankets spread on the grass with baskets of food waiting to be opened. Besides Sarah and her brother were the widower, Benjamin Reno, and his three teenagers.

Jeremiah greeted his friends and sat down beside Sarah. In her late stages of pregnancy, Sarah's bulk made her look uncomfortable seated on the ground, but her impending motherhood seemed to enhance her pert, fair-haired attractiveness. "How are you feeling, Sarah?" Jeremiah asked.

"I'm fine." She noticed his little frown. "Jeremiah, it's perfectly all right for me to be out here having a good time. You're worse than a mother hen. When you have a wife who's expecting, I pity her."

Jeremiah grinned. "I can't help it."

Sarah patted his hand. "I appreciate your concern."

"I don't know about anyone else," Jim White said, "but I'm ready for some lemonade."

"I'll get it," Caddie offered.

"Then I'll help you," Jim told her.

Jeremiah felt Jim had found himself a fine girl. Caddie was a flaxen-haired beauty of nineteen. Her sister Amanda was equally as pretty, but she was only fifteen, although she had been giving Jeremiah the eye lately.

Jeremiah hadn't bothered to do much socializing. He wanted to get his schooling finished before he settled down to any serious courting. And now that he had joined the medical corps, romance seemed to be in the distant future for him. He wondered about Melissa and exactly what the situation was with her and the cavalry major of whom she had written. From what he had read of Jeb Stuart and his men, they appeared to be a wild lot.

"Are there going to be fireworks?" little Mary McClelland asked.

"Later tonight, dear, when it's dark," Sarah told her.

"Can we stay and watch?"

"We can see them from our front window."

Mary pouted. "But it's not the same."

Sam had been tossing a ball with his son Frank and came over to get some lemonade.

"Play more, Daddy!" Frank exclaimed.

"Daddy wants to sit for a while."

"I'll play," Jeremiah offered, standing up. "Come on, bring your ball."

Mary tagged along with Jeremiah and Frank.

Ben smiled. "He's grown into quite a man," he remarked. "It seems a long time ago that we brought him up the river. How's his sister doing? Is she married yet?"

317

"No, but she has a gentleman friend—a cavalryman," Sarah told him.

"You know she's working at a newspaper, don't you?" Sam asked, and Ben nodded. "And her uncle owns a blockade-runner."

"A blockade-runner!" thirteen-year-old Bart Reno exclaimed.

"Yep," Sam smiled. "Appears Jeremiah's family are all fire-eating Rebels. His cousin's in the army, the family's friendly with the Davises . . ."

"If Melissa had a mind to, she could be a very useful spy, I expect," Ben remarked.

While Jeremiah was playing ball, he noticed a familiar face approaching him.

"Charlie! How are you?" Jeremiah greeted, shaking hands with the stocky, bearded man. Charlie's whiskers concealed the good-humored turn to his mouth, but his gray eyes twinkled with friendliness.

"Jeremiah!" He turned to the slightly built woman with him. "Mattie, this is Dr. Armstrong. He took care of my hand for me last year. Jeremiah, this is my wife Mattie and my children here—Emma, Biney, and little Charles."

"Pleased to meet you, Mrs. Ahlborn," Jeremiah said.

"Charlie was so happy with the way his hand healed after you treated him," she said. Mattie appeared the exact opposite to Charlie, tall and willowy, with a rather disapproving look on her long features. Jeremiah thought she made the perfect picture of a strict schoolmistress, but her gentle voice belied her stern expression.

Charlie held out his left hand, showing two fingers missing at the joint. He had been injured at Bull Run. "Good as new, almost. So good, in fact, I reenlisted."

"What regiment?"

"The Forty-sixth."

Jeremiah clapped his shoulder. "Then we'll be camp mates. That's my unit."

"Well, it's good to know we'll have a decent doctor along," Charlie smiled. "You can patch 'em up, and I'll serenade 'em."

"I'm hungry," Emma complained.

"We'll be eating soon," her mother told her.

Jeremiah looked at the little girl holding the picnic basket. "Why don't you join us?" he suggested.

Frank and Mary approached them shyly, looking at the other children. Biney was eyeing the ball. "May I play with you?" she asked.

Mary grinned and handed her the ball.

"I think the children have decided for us," Charlie said.

Jeremiah introduced the Ahlborns to the group. The picnic baskets were opened, and the food was passed around. While they were eating, the band assembled in the bandbox and began to play.

"I don't think I could let my husband go off to war once he'd already been wounded, Mrs. Ahlborn," Sarah told her.

"Once Charlie has made up his mind about something, there's no changing it. He's a musician."

"That's relatively safer than anything else, I should imagine."

"I hope so. When are you expecting?"

"Next month."

Mattie Ahlborn leaned closer and said quietly, "Confidentially, so am I, but Charlie doesn't know it yet. As long as he had his heart set on going, I didn't want to make him feel obligated to stay."

"You're a very brave woman."

Charlie was talking with the men. "How did that little toy train work out I fixed for you?" Charlie asked Jeremiah. "Did the cowcatcher stay put?"

"So you're the one!" Sam exclaimed. "Jeremiah gave that to my kids for Christmas. I can't tell you how much enjoyment they've gotten from it."

"I'm glad to hear it," Charlie said. "I was a little strapped for money at the time I was seeing the doc here. I believe you treated my brother-in-law, too."

"Oh really?" Jeremiah asked. "Who?"

"Henry Walkenfeldt. He had a torn-up leg."

"Of course. I remember Henry. Don't you, Jim?"

Jim nodded. "How's he doing?"

"Well, now that's a funny thing," Charlie said. "As soon as he got to feeling pretty good, he just up and left. Said it was business."

"Haven't you heard from him?"

"Not much. Mattie," he called to his wife. "When's the last time you heard from your brother?"

"Christmas. Mama and Papa got a note from him."

"Where is he?" Jeremiah asked.

"He didn't say. Only that he was well and not to worry about him. The letter was postmarked from Alexandria, Virginia."

"See? I told you it was funny," Charlie remarked.

"If I remember correctly, he said he wanted to do some traveling," Jeremiah said. He caught himself in time before speaking remembering that Henry had asked that the matter of getting a letter through to Melissa be kept quiet.

"You don't suppose he's turned Reb, do you?" Ben asked.

"Henry?" Charlie laughed. "Not a chance!"

320

As they were finishing their meal, one of the city officials stepped up on the bandbox and made an announcement. "Ladies and gentlemen, we're going to have a few games now. Any of you men who would like to try your luck at winning a little prize for your ladies, step right over here and get ready for the three-legged race."

"Oh, Jim, go on," Caddie urged. "Win me a prize."

"But I . . ."

"Go on!" she laughed, getting up and trying to pull him to his feet.

"You too, Jeremiah!" Amanda said.

"All right," he grinned, standing up. "Come on, Jim."

"Daddy, I want the prize!" Mary exclaimed, pummeling Sam.

Sam glanced helplessly at Ben, who held up his hands. "I'm getting too old for that sort of thing," Ben said.

"You go, Papa," Biney told Charlie.

"Are you game, Sam?" Charlie asked.

"If you are."

The four men went over to where the contestants were assembling. Most of the entrants were teenage boys, too young to join the army. Each pair was given a length of rope with which to tie their legs together.

"I think we're too old for this, too," Sam muttered, tying his right leg to Charlie's left. Besides, he thought, Charlie was a good six inches shorter than he.

The official fired a pistol into the air, and the men were off. Jim and Jeremiah had a little trouble getting under way, but once they got synchronized, they took the lead. Sam was surprised at how well they were doing, but they crashed into a pair that had fallen, and went down in a tangle of arms and legs. Jeremiah and Jim crossed the finish line first, and each was rewarded with a small US flag.

Sam and Charlie were still getting untangled when the egg-in-spoon race was announced.

"Papa, I want a prize!" Biney squealed, running over to her father.

Charlie stood up. "All right," he sighed.

Jim and Jeremiah stood by to watch as Sam and Charlie adjusted the spoons holding an egg in their mouths. With the spoon clenched firmly between his teeth and his arms outstretched to the side for balance, Charlie made his way along the course. He glanced out of the corner of his eye and saw Sam approaching him on his right. Putting on an extra bit of speed, Charlie saw the egg was about to drop from the spoon. He lunged forward and fell face down on the grass. When he sat up, he discovered the egg had broken and was matted in his beard.

Mattie Ahlborn sighed and returned to where Sarah was sitting, shaking her head. "If this is any indication of the Union Army, we had better be prepared."

Charlie returned to the ladies to clean the egg out of his beard.

"Papa, we wanted you to win us a flag," Emma said petulantly.

"I'll tell you what I'll do. Since I didn't win you a flag here, I promise I'll capture a Rebel flag and send it to you."

Both children ran to hug their father. Mattie was holding one-year-old Charles on her lap and looked helplessly at Sarah and her mother.

"And we can also stay to watch the fireworks tonight," Charlie told them. "I know it's well past your bedtime, but we'll make an exception tonight."

"Charlie, you know I can't keep the baby out that long," his wife said.

"The Fourth of July only comes once a year."

"I agree," Sam said. "And I think, under the circumstances, we should all stay here for the show." He could see Sarah was about to protest, so he held up his hand. "The family's all together, we've made some new friends, so let's make the most of a pleasant day."

No one spoke it aloud, but they were all thinking the same thing: who knew what tomorrow would bring?

After the sun had gone down, everyone in the park assembled for the display. Sam had Mary on his shoulders, and Jim held Frank so that they could get a better view. As the colorful shower of sparks lit up the sky, the band played the strains of "The Star-Spangled Banner."

To be in Richmond in July was like living in an immense hospital. Death hung heavy over the city where every home was either a house of mourning or a private hospital. There was hardly a family who had not at least one in the field. As mothers nervously watched for someone to bring news of their boys, others received the bodies of their dead. The funeral processions seemed endless along the streets, and a cap or a sword resting on a coffin became a familiar sight.

The grave diggers couldn't dig the graves fast enough. Often bodies were buried in communal graves. Even worse, some were forced to be left out overnight. Sometimes the bodies would swell and burst the coffins, for they were so poorly constructed, and the grave diggers often caught diseases from the bodies. Hollywood Cemetery was full of new tenants, the fresh flowers

323

dotting the slopes.

The heat was intolerable, and the gangrene took its toll on the wounded. The hospitals were full of the bloated, disfigured victims of disease, as well as the wounded. The flow of men was too great for the fifty hospitals, and amputees were released only three days after their operations. There were so few doctors, the sick and wounded were attended by convalescing patients. There was not enough medicine, and the men suffered terribly in the blazing heat. The Baptist Female Institute was used as a hospital, as was the Young Men's Christian Association on Clay Street. Even the ladies of the bordellos made the transformation from prostitute to nurse. The citizens took their private carriages to the battlefield, piled in the injured, and brought them back to the city. Still, men lay for days unattended on the fields. There were simply too many of them. Tending to the wounded and burying the dead became the city's two leading professions. Strangers roamed the streets, mostly women searching for their loved ones.

Despite all this, the people were grateful to General Lee for repulsing the Yankees. Amid the sadness and hurt, there was celebration. The church bells did not peal, for they had been melted down for munitions. Even the antique Revolutionary War cannons, which for years had been embedded in the cement on certain street corners, had found their way to the Tredegar Iron Works. Besides the mourning, there was also rejoicing. There were ceremonies to present new colors to distinguished regiments. Bands played, and there was a general feeling of release.

Nancy spent long hours at the hospitals. Keeping busy was the only way in which she could try to blot out her anxiety over Andrew. She left the house early in the morning, and did not return again until late in the evening. Edward worried about her. The strain was beginning to show in the new lines that had appeared around her mouth, and her once-plump figure was slimming down.

Margaret also spent a great deal of time at the hospitals, while Mahaley went back to rolling bandages. Melissa knew that Jackson was safe, for there were complete lists on Stuart's men. She received a note by courier on the tenth, requesting that she and her family come to Stuart's camp on the seventeenth when a review was to be staged.

Melissa was the first to return home for the day, and to her surprise, found Andrew, dirty, disheveled, and patched, feasting on one of Tunia's chickens at the dining-room table. She was genuinely happy to see him and put her arms around him, placing a kiss on his forehead.

"Oh, Andrew, I'm so glad you're home safe. We've all been so worried about you. What happened to your head?"

"I'm not really sure," he replied, gingerly touching the stained bandage.

"When you finish eating, let me change those dressings. They're dirty."

"I'm dirty," he muttered, pausing to scratch his chest. "Damned little beggars!"

Melissa backed away from him and felt her skin crawl.

"Where is everyone?" he asked.

"Margaret and your mother are at the hospitals, and I guess Mahaley's helping out somewhere."

Andrew finished his meal and leaned back in his chair.

"Tunia's going to boil my uniform, and I'm going up to take a bath. Then I would appreciate your bandaging my head."

While Andrew was bathing, Melissa found a pillowcase and tore it up into strips, pausing occasionally to scratch an imaginary itch. She wondered how Andrew could stand it.

Clean-shaven, he soon reappeared in his dressing gown.

"I feel much better now," he said.

Melissa sat him down in the kitchen, and she and Tunia examined his wound. It was a laceration of about four inches, extending from his hairline down to his eyebrow.

"Did you see a doctor about this?" Melissa asked.

"Some assistant surgeon dressed it in a field hospital. I've been wandering all over, looking for my unit. They've probably got me missing in action. That Huger's a fool. I'm about ready to desert."

"You won't need to."

"What do you mean?"

"We got the news at the paper this morning. General Huger has been relieved of duty. He's been assigned the job of inspector of artillery and ordnance."

Andrew grinned. "That's a relief."

Tunia brought a small jar over to him. "Here, honey, yo' let Tunia put some of dis alderbark salve on yo' po' head."

Having received endless treatments of Tunia's mysterious remedies since childhood, Andrew allowed her to daub the sticky concoction on his wound.

"Dere now. It be fine as new in a couple of days."

Melissa proceeded to wrap his head in the strips of

326

clean linen. "Your mother had a new uniform made for you."

"I saw it. I hope it fits. I think I've lost some weight. You have a nice touch, Melissa."

"Thank you."

"Have you seen Ellen lately?"

"Not for a while."

"I think I'll change and go over to the Commissary Department and see if I can meet her. Maybe I could buy her supper."

"But what about your mother? She's been worried about you."

"I won't be late." He stood up. "I think I might ask Ellen to have her photograph taken for me. Is that studio still open on Main Street?"

"Parker's? I think so."

"Good. Minnis and Cowell charge too much money."

Andrew went upstairs to put on his new uniform, only to discover that indeed, he had lost some weight. He cinched the belt around his waist a little tighter, and, after splashing a little bay rum on his cheeks, left the house.

The family was greatly relieved to know Andrew was home and relatively unharmed. Nancy's feelings were hurt that her son had chosen to see his girlfriend before the family, but Edward pointed out that he was a young man of nearly twenty-four who had been away for a long while.

When Melissa told them of the invitation to visit Stuart's headquarters, everyone was excited, but no one could go.

"I can't possibly leave work," Edward told her.

"I feel I should stay at the hospital where I'm needed,"

327

Nancy said.

"What about you, Margaret?"

"I'd rather not. Going to a camp might bring unpleasant memories."

"There's no reason why Melissa and I can't go," Mahaley said.

"Oh, yes, there is, young lady," Edward told her. "I'm very fond of both Jackson and General Stuart, but I can't let the two of you go unchaperoned."

Melissa's heart sank. She had been surprised at how much she was looking forward to seeing Jackson again.

"But, Father . . ." Mahaley protested.

"I'm sorry. The answer is no, and that's final."

Andrew returned earlier than anyone had really expected. Nancy fussed over him terribly, and Edward opened a bottle of brandy.

"Did you see Ellen?" Melissa asked.

"Yes. Nathaniel checked my head for me when he got home. He says I'll live. But I might have a scar. I'm seeing Ellen tomorrow. She's going to try to get away at dinner."

"Hadn't you better see about your new regiment?" Edward asked.

"What new regiment?"

"Now that Huger's out, you're serving under Dick Anderson."

"What's left of us, you mean."

Margaret excused herself and left the room.

"I'm sorry," Andrew muttered. "Father, do you think you could pull a few strings and get me transferred?"

"Transferred where?"

"I don't know. Perhaps to the West."

328

"But Andrew, it's so far away," Nancy frowned.

"I know. But I had a lot of time to think on my way home. And it hurts me to see our homeland being torn up so much. Could you find out for me how I might go about doing it?"

"I'll see what I can do, son."

Before she went to bed, Melissa braided her hair and decided to sit down and pen a note to Jackson, informing him that she would be unable to attend the festivities. There was a tap on her door, and Mahaley entered.

"I saw the light under the door, so I didn't think you were asleep."

"No, I'm writing to Jackson."

"That's what I wanted to talk to you about. I think I've figured out a way you and I can go next week."

"How? You heard what your papa said."

Mahaley plopped herself down on the bed, her rag curlers on her blond locks sticking out crazily. "I know. But his only objection is the fact that we don't have a chaperone."

"Yes?"

"Well, you know Mrs. Stuart, don't you?"

"I've met her."

"So, why don't you see if we couldn't go with her? I'm sure she'll be going."

"But I hardly know her. I can't impose like that."

"How can it possibly be an imposition? Really, all we need to do is say she's going along. She certainly doesn't have to be a chaperone. It would just look like it to Father."

Melissa began to smile. "You may have an idea there. I'll see if I can get a little time tomorrow to call on her. Of

329

course, first I'll have to ask Mr. McAllen if he'll let me have some time off next week."

"We can talk to Father about it at breakfast."

Edward seemed agreeable to the idea, so Melissa went into Lewis's office to talk to him as soon as she came in. He looked up from the ledgers scattered on his desk and ran his hand through his thinning black hair. His face brightened a little as he saw it was Melissa.

"Mr. McAllen, I was wondering if I could have next Thursday and Friday off?"

"What for?"

"General Stuart is planning a review on the seventeenth, and Mahaley and I would like to attend."

"I see." Lewis frowned, knowing full well she was going to see her major friend. An article in the paper about it would be helpful for circulation though. "I'll give you the time off on one condition—that when you return, you write a story about it for Monday's edition."

"But I'm not a writer."

"Nonsense. If you do have any trouble, I'm sure Mr. Walkenfeldt would be glad to help you."

"Well, all right," she agreed, thinking she might pick up some valuable information for Henry. "I'll try."

"I'm sure you'll be able to do it."

"Thank you very much, Mr. McAllen."

At one o'clock sharp, Andrew met Ellen outside the Commissary Department.

"I can only be gone for a little while, Andrew. Does it take long to have your photograph taken?"

"No, not very. Here's the carriage. I thought we could save time by riding."

Andrew helped Ellen into the carriage, and Bobo drove off. Andrew leaned over and kissed her.

"You look very nice today," he smiled at her.

"Thank you. I wore my best dress. I'm afraid my clothes are in a very sad state. Remember my green gown?"

"Yes?"

"It's gone."

"Gone? Gone where?"

"Nathaniel needed the silk for a certain kind of dressing."

"That's a shame. When's your birthday?"

"In October. Why?"

"Oh, nothing," he smiled, thinking about the access he had to all the fine materials the *Grasshopper* brought in.

"I'm kind of frightened about having my picture taken," Ellen admitted. "I know everyone has it done nowadays, but all the same . . ."

"Well, we're here now. There's no getting out of it now."

Andrew helped Ellen down from the carriage and gave Bobo ten cents, telling him to find himself a cold drink somewhere. The bell on the door tinkled as they entered the photography studio. Ellen gazed around at all the pictures covering the walls.

A dark-haired woman, whom Andrew judged to be in her early thirties, appeared from a room at the back of the shop.

"May I help you?" she asked.

"Yes. This young lady would like to have her photograph taken. Is that possible?"

"Yes. Do you want a full figure or just the bust?"

Andrew had to keep from laughing. "The bust, I think, ma'am."

"Then just have a seat in that chair, miss," the woman told her. "I'll get the camera set up."

Andrew looked puzzled. "Where is Mr. Parker?"

"He's off somewhere with the army," the woman called, heading for the little room at the back. "The last I heard from him, his what's-it wagon broke down."

"Andrew," Ellen said quietly. "I don't know if I like this. What if she doesn't know what she's doing? I'm scared enough as it is."

"Shhh!" he warned, as Mrs. Parker returned with the copper plate which she inserted into the camera. "Ma'am, are you—er—qualified to be a photographer?"

"Oh, yes. I've been helping my husband for years." She lifted up the black cotton curtain and peered through the lens. "Hold your chin up a little more. That's it." She stood up and frowned at Andrew. "Sir, you're in the way."

"Oh," Andrew muttered, backing away.

"Now smile and sit very still," Mrs. Parker told Ellen.

Ellen tried to force her smile as the powder flash exploded. Little rivulets of perspiration trickled down the back of her neck and down her spine, as she feared the worst.

"There now. It's all finished," Mrs. Parker smiled. "You can move now."

Ellen let out a long breath and watched the woman remove the plate from the camera box and take it to the back room.

"Do you want a daguerreotype or a carte-de-vista?" Mrs. Parker asked Andrew.

"Could I have one of each?"

"Yes."

"You mean you can make more than one picture from that?" Ellen looked surprised and relieved.

"Yes."

"Oh, maybe I should get one for Nathaniel too."

"I'll take two daguerreotypes and two cartes-de-vistas," Andrew smiled. "And could you put the daguerreotypes in frames?"

"Yes. But I'm afraid if you'd come a day or two later, you couldn't get a frame. We simply can't find any more."

Andrew paid Mrs. Parker a deposit and told her he would return Monday for the photographs.

"That wasn't so bad, was it?" he smiled, as they stepped out into the bright sunlight.

"I was scared to death. And when that flash thing went off, I thought surely my heart would stop."

Andrew grinned and took her hand. "Then let's go have an ice cream."

An ambulance rattled by, and Ellen stared after it. "I feel guilty. When so many are suffering."

"You can't stop living just because there's suffering in the world. Besides, I'm sure I'll have to go back to the field next week, and I'd like an ice cream."

"Very well," she smiled.

Lewis left the office in the afternoon, saying he would be back in two hours. As soon as he was gone, Melissa told Henry she wanted to slip out for a while but would return soon. She climbed on the streetcar and rode through the dusty streets to the outskirts of town. She got off at the corner of Broad and Twenty-first Streets and walked the block to the little cottage owned by the Stuarts. It seemed much cooler, and the flowers in the garden were a riot of colors.

She tapped on the door, and a dark-eyed little girl opened it.

"Yes, ma'am?"

"Is your mother at home?"

"Yes, ma'am. She's knitting some socks for my pa. Won't you come in, please?"

Melissa stepped inside and found herself in the small parlor. Mrs. Stuart looked up from her knitting.

"Ma, this lady came to see you," the child told her.

Flora Stuart put down her sewing and came over to Melissa. She was a small woman with dark hair and eyes, several years older than Melissa.

"I know you. You're Melissa Armstrong, aren't you?"

"Yes. So good of you to remember me. I hope I'm not interrupting anything."

"No, of course not. I'm always glad to have callers. Won't you come in and sit down?"

Melissa seated herself and Flora sent her daughter out to get a pitcher of apricot cider. Three-year-old Jemmie was sitting on the floor, looking at drawings in a magazine, apparently unconcerned with the guest.

"This is a very lovely home," Melissa remarked.

"It's convenient. There's not much to it, but I can pack up the children and take them to see their father when I want."

"That's what I came to see you about. Major Vaughn sent me an invitation to come out to camp next week, and I thought if you were going, would it be too much of an imposition if my cousin and I came along?"

"Of course not. I'd love the company."

Five-year-old Flora returned with the cider and passed

334

it to her mother and Melissa.

"This is very good," Melissa smiled.

"Flora and I made it from the fruit off our own trees."

"It's delicious."

"It will be nice to have someone to talk to on the train."

"I'm so glad it's no trouble. You see, Jackson invited the whole family but, unfortunately, my cousin and I are the only ones who can go. And my uncle didn't want us to go without a chaperone. That doesn't mean you have to watch over us."

Mrs. Stuart smiled. "I understand completely. My father was the same way with my sister and me when we were at Fort Leavenworth, Kansas."

"Is that where you met Jeb?"

"Yes. He was a lieutenant in the dragoons. My father was a colonel there."

Melissa saw a slight touch of sadness in Mrs. Stuart's eyes. She remembered Jackson telling her about the falling-out the Stuarts had with her father when Jeb decided to go with the Confederacy. Even little Jemmie, now napping on the floor, had not escaped the trouble. He had been christened Philip St. George Cooke Stuart, after his grandfather, but his name was changed to James Ewell Brown Stuart, Jr. when the family split apart.

"Jeb's so fond of Jackson," Flora continued. "I've known him for years. He's such a nice man. And I know he simply adores you. Do you have any plans for marriage?"

"No. Not until the war's over."

"I know how you feel. I fret so about Jeb. Sometimes I think I'll go out of my head with worry, but I wouldn't have it any other way."

335

Melissa left Mrs. Stuart, telling her they would meet at the depot at seven o'clock Thursday morning. After seeing the anguish in the woman's eyes as she spoke of her husband, Melissa strengthened her resolve not to marry Jackson until the war was ended.

Andrew mentioned the lack of daguerreotype frames to his father, and, knowing it would be a high-profit item, Edward had his son take an order from Mrs. Parker when he went to pick up the photographs. With a new uniform and spare socks and drawers, Andrew left once again for camp on Tuesday.

Bobo drove Melissa and Mahaley to the Virginia Central depot Thursday morning. Mrs. Stuart and her children soon arrived and were introduced to Mahaley. The ten-mile train ride north to Atlee's Station was a short and uneventful one, but the Armstrong girls were able to see their first glimpse of the countryside's destruction.

Jeb and Jackson were among the men at the station to greet the ladies. Jackson lifted Melissa off the ground and twirled her around, hugging her.

"I'm so glad you could come!" he laughed.

"Jackson, put me down!" she giggled.

They gathered up their luggage and made their way to the camp. Jeb had made his headquarters in the Timberlake farm, whose owner had two sons in the cavalry. Jeb and Jackson settled the ladies in a nearby plantation, belonging to a very elderly couple who were glad of the company.

"Is Captain Pelham in camp?" Mahaley asked.

"Indeed he is," Jackson replied. "But it's Major Pelham now." He cleared his throat. "Ah—don't you

336

notice anything different about me?"

Melissa studied him carefully until her eyes caught the extra braids on his uniform jacket. "You're a lieutenant colonel now!" she hugged him. "I'm so happy for you."

"Come on. Let's go visit the camp. The men are anxious to see some pretty faces."

The camp was neatly set up, for Jeb was a stickler for cleanliness when it was possible. There were already quite a few women and children there. The white tents were pitched under the trees nearby the plantation. The grass was green and full, the birds were singing, and war seemed very far removed. Mahaley was scanning the men for John Pelham, but didn't see him anywhere.

A smiling bearded man approached them. "You're not playing fair, Jackson. You've got two girls."

Jackson laughed. "I'm not that lucky. Ladies, may I present Major General Fitzhugh Lee, the general's nephew. Fitz, this is Miss Melissa Armstrong and her cousin Miss Mahaley Armstrong."

"Pleasure to meet you, ladies," he said, bowing in a courtly manner. "But I'm afraid I'm going to have to take Jackson away from you for a while."

"Oh, is it that time already?" Jackson exclaimed. He turned to Melissa. "I never know what time it is anymore. I lost my watch in Turkey Creek. I see the ladies are heading toward the Timberlake house. Why don't you go on over and get yourself a seat?"

"What's going on?" Mahaley asked.

"We're going to have a little parade. And then some good things to eat." He gave Melissa's hand a little squeeze. "I'll see you later, honey."

Melissa and Mahaley started toward the farmhouse, where benches had been set up in the yard.

"Honey!" Mahaley laughed.

Melissa blushed and, grinning, shrugged her shoulders.

The two girls found a seat on the bench with Flora Stuart and her children.

"The men are all looking well and happy," Flora remarked.

"It appears so."

A bugle sounded and the men paraded past the ladies, dressed in their best, shabby as that might be. Sabers clanking, spurs jingling, the officers of the Virginia Cavalry saluted the women as they passed. The flags and sashes and plumes all fluttered in the breeze. Jackson's jacket was torn at the elbow, but he had polished his boots with lard and soot, his buttons gleamed, and Melissa noticed his gauntlets still appeared spotless. His sorrel mare, Gypsy, had been curried and groomed until her coat shone.

Sitting on his horse ahead of his beloved howitzers came John Pelham. His eyes sparkled as he saw Mahaley, and he took off his cap, saluting her.

After the parade, the brigade went through a series of drills. Melissa saw how proud Flora Stuart was of her husband who, only a little more than a year ago, had been a lieutenant and now commanded the cavalry of the whole army.

Fitz Lee and Heros Von Borcke hurried back to the house to round up the slaves who were waiting with the food. The blacks quickly set up plank boards for tables and brought out the refreshments.

Jeb had alighted from Skylark, his chestnut mare, who was now cropping grass, and came over to his family. He picked up little Flora.

"I have a surprise for you."

"What, Pa?"

"I'll show you later. After we eat." He smiled fondly at his wife. "I think the three prettiest girls in Virginia are sitting right here."

"What about me, Pa?" little Flora asked.

"You, little gal, are the prettiest in the whole South."

Jackson jogged over to them. "Let's get over there and eat," he suggested. "I'm hungry."

The group found their way over to the tables, selecting their food and taking it over to the shade of a tree. John Pelham joined them, his plate piled high.

"I'm very glad you ladies could come," he said.

"We wouldn't have missed it for anything," Mahaley told him. "I see you're a major now."

John smiled. "Jeb here was mighty busy handing out promotions."

"I only do it when they're deserved," he grinned, and his white teeth sparkled. "Lord this is fine food! Heros and Sweeny went hunting. Caught the fattest lot of quail and grouse you'd ever like to see."

"What's going on in Richmond?" Jackson wondered.

"It's very sad," Melissa replied. "And I think the saddest thing is all the women who've come to the city to search the hospitals for their men."

"It's that bad, then?" John asked.

"It's very bad," Mahaley replied. "I swear, if I roll another bandage, I'll go out of my head."

Jeb and Jackson laughed. "Would you like to trade places with us?"

"I'd love to," Mahaley said. "I'd take care of those Yankees!"

"You'd bowl them over with your charms," Jackson teased.

"Maybe we have the answer to all our problems," Jeb grinned. "Just send all our fair young ladies into the Yankees' camps, and they'd be too tired to fight."

"Jeb!" Flora giggled. "Watch what you're saying. I'm supposed to be these girls' chaperone."

Jeb sobered, but the laughter was still in his eyes. "Ladies, I beg your pardon."

After everyone had eaten their fill, Jeb called for Sam Sweeny to get out his banjo. Several fiddles appeared, and Jackson brought out his harmonica. Bob, the mulatto servant, gathered up his bones to beat out a rhythm to the music.

Soon, the soldiers were laughing and swinging the ladies around on the lawn to the music.

Merry Heros Von Borcke twirled Melissa to the strains of "Dixie." He was a large man, with a great curling blond mustache. Melissa wondered how the giant Prussian could be so light on his feet.

"You like to dance?" he asked her.

"Yes," she gasped, out of breath.

"You get tired too fast. In my country, women dance for hours."

"I imagine they must be too tired to do anything else."

"Not so," he smiled. "But they have more fat on them to give them energy."

Melissa wondered how they ever managed to be fat with all this exercise. When the dance was through, Heros took her over to where Jeb and his family were sitting. Heros bowed low to Melissa. "I thank you kindly for the dance, miss."

"Thank you," Melissa smiled, sitting down, out of breath.

Both Jeb and Heros eyed her heaving bosom appreciatively.

"Sit down and join us, old friend," Jeb told him. "We'll try very hard to understand you."

Heros sat down and smiled. "He always makes fun of my English."

"Don't pay him any mind," Flora said. "You speak very good English."

Jackson, John, and Mahaley rejoined the group. As Mahaley sat down, a big furry raccoon hopped out at her from behind the tree trunk. Mahaley squealed and jumped away. The enormous animal looked at her, his fur glistening, and scrambled over to Jeb, who Mahaley noticed was holding the end of the chain attached to a collar on the raccoon. The children were giggling at Mahaley.

"Don't worry. He won't hurt you," Jeb told her.

"Where did it come from?"

"He just appeared the day we set up camp, begging food," Jeb replied. "Sort of adopted me."

Little Flora gave the animal a crust of bread and delighted at the way he took it in his two paws.

"Every regiment needs a mascot," John smiled.

The musicians broke into "The Dew Is on the Blossom," and Jeb began to sing. Melissa was surprised at his clear, true voice.

With the sun shining, the breeze sighing through the trees, the soldiers laughing and dancing, the afternoon passed pleasantly. Remembering the scenes in Richmond, Melissa shuddered at whatever fate these happy, carefree, simple men might meet tomorrow.

Jackson and John walked with the girls back to the

plantation at dusk.

"I have a needle and some thread if you want me to fix that sleeve," Melissa told Jackson.

"I'd be grateful."

Melissa went into the house and to the room she was sharing with Mahaley. Jackson took off his jacket and settled himself on the porch steps.

"Would you like to take a little walk?" John asked Mahaley.

"I'd love to."

"Don't get picked off by any Yankees," Jackson called.

Mahaley's eyes widened. "Are there Yankees around here?"

"I certainly hope not," John grinned.

Jackson was chuckling to himself when Melissa returned with a kerosene lamp she had borrowed from the woman of the house.

"What are you smiling about?" she asked, sitting down beside him.

"Your cousin. She's a caution!"

"That she is."

Melissa adjusted the light and set about her mending.

"I'm mighty glad you could get out to see me," Jackson said, watching her as she worked.

"So am I. Uncle Edward wasn't going to let us come, but he figured Mrs. Stuart could act as chaperone."

"No need for that."

"No. Not as long as Mahaley and I are sharing a bed. I doubt there's enough room for another."

Jackson laughed. "I do believe you've broadened your outlook since you met me."

She stopped sewing and looked at him. "Why, Jackson, you don't think I've become a loose woman,

342

do you?"

He grinned. "'Course not. My intentions are honorable. I don't see anything wrong with enjoying life. And you surely do make it enjoyable." He leaned over and kissed her warmly.

"I think we'd better change the subject," she smiled. "Else I'll never get your jacket sewed up."

Jackson settled back against the post and stretched his long legs. Melissa glanced over at him, and he gave her a roguish grin and winked. His black eyes studied her with appreciation.

"Can't keep your mind on your work with me around, can you?" he teased.

"You make it very hard for me."

He chuckled. "Not as hard as you make it for me."

She feigned embarrassment, but it was touched with amusement. "Why, Jackson Vaughn!"

He shrugged, still chuckling, and took out a cheroot from his pocket. He bit off the end and struck a sulphur match. "Thank your uncle for sending me these," he said. "Tell me, what all's been going on? How's the rest of the family?"

"Fine. Andrew was home for a few days. He hurt his head at Malvern Hill, but he's all right. He doesn't like fighting in Virginia, though. He wants a transfer."

"That's too bad. For me, I'm glad I'm close by so I can come see you when I get time off. The cavalry isn't as bad as the infantry. Is Andrew much of a horseman?"

"Oh, he rides, but I wouldn't say he was outstanding at it. He's lived in the city all of his life."

"Now that you've been living in the city for a while, how do you like it?"

"That's a hard question. When I was home in Shady

Run, I couldn't wait to get out of there. I used to see the same people day after day and do the same things. But now, I don't know. The city's so big and full of people. I like it, I guess. It's my life now."

"Have you heard from your brother lately?"

"Not for a while. He's almost through with his schooling. I expect he's busy with that."

"Do you think he'll come home then?"

"To Virginia? I don't know. Do you ever hear from your brother?"

"Once in a while. He's with Phil Sheridan's cavalry."

Melissa sighed. "It's strange how brothers and sons can be on different sides. You remember Nathaniel—Dr. Aldrich?"

"Yes."

"He was telling us he met a Dr. George Todd. Do you know who he is?"

"No."

"He's Mary Lincoln's brother, and a surgeon in the Confederate Army."

"Well, Jeb's chief of staff, Henry McClellan's brother is none other than 'Little Mac' himself."

"That's amazing. I wonder how many other people have kin fighting on opposite sides?"

"Too many to count, I expect."

Melissa sighed again. "Where will you go next?"

"I don't know."

"You don't have any idea?"

Jackson grinned at her. "Why are you so interested? Have you suddenly become a strategist?"

"No, of course not." She bit the thread and handed him back his jacket. "I'm just interested in what you're doing."

"Well," he drawled. "I really don't know. Personally, I'd like to just take a little vacation. Maybe do some fishing. You like to fish?"

Melissa and Jackson sat on the porch for hours, talking and listening to the crickets. When Mahaley and John finally returned, everyone decided it was time to turn in for the night. Jackson gave Melissa a shrug and kissed her on the cheek.

"We'll see you in the morning," he said. "And take you over to the camp for breakfast before the train leaves." He squeezed her hand. "Sleep well."

"You too."

Fourteen

While sitting at the little table in his room, Jeremiah was concentrating on the letter he was writing to Melissa. He wanted to minimize the risks involved in being a surgeon in the field. At least he could say he didn't have to worry about being taken prisoner. Before the battle of Winchester in May, surgeons were liable to capture and imprisonment as well as the soldiers themselves. This resulted in many doctors abandoning the wounded when capture was imminent. When General Jackson captured a Federal hospital, he ordered that the surgeons be treated as neutrals. They did not make war, so therefore they should not suffer the penalties. This stand was immediately adopted by both North and South.

Nevertheless, he knew she would worry. He looked at his uniform, pressed and new, hanging on the door of the little armoire, a dark-blue frock coat with the letters MS in old English style embroidered on the epaulet straps. The light-blue trousers were hung over a chair. His black felt hat with its yellow hat cord was sitting on the chair. A brass laurel wreath was pinned to its front.

Tomorrow he would be leaving this little room that had been his home for three years. Last night he had supper with the Renos. Tonight he was going to have supper with Sarah. This afternoon he had gone out to visit his friends who lived in the Hill District: Nick and Pearl and their four children, and Corky and his new wife Kitty. Tomorrow morning Mrs. Oliver was going to prepare him a fine breakfast before he left on the train to Washington City with his regiment.

He dipped his pen into the ink and once more began to write when suddenly there was a frantic pounding on the door. Wondering who could be wanting him with such urgency, he quickly got up and opened the door.

Mary McClelland was standing there, wide-eyed with fright. "Jeremiah, Gramma says to come quick! It's Mama!"

"I'll get my bag."

Jeremiah dashed over and picked up his bag, bumping the table. The ink bottle spilled, blotting out the letter to Melissa.

"Hurry, Jeremiah! Mama's hurt awful bad!"

"Did she fall?" he asked, closing the door and starting down the stairs.

"No. Gramma says it's the new baby."

But it's not due for another two weeks, he thought. Mary was too slow negotiating the stairs, so Jeremiah picked her up. With the child in one arm and his bag gripped in his other hand, he hurried along the street. The block to the McClellands' seemed like a mile. He had pulled teeth, lanced boils, amputated limbs, and treated other sundry ills, but delivering a baby was something new to him.

Jeremiah dashed inside the house and set Mary down. Then he hurried up the stairs where Mrs. White came out of the bedroom.

"What is it?"

"It's the baby. It's too soon. She's in a terrible way. I've had three myself and she's had two, but there's something wrong this time."

"I'll go in and see."

Sarah was lying on the bed, bathed in sweat. She turned her head as he entered.

"Oh, Jeremiah, help me. I know there's something wrong!"

She gave out a moan as another labor pain struck.

"Get me some hot water and towels, Gramma White," Jeremiah called, rolling up his sleeves and opening his bag. "How long have you been in labor, Sarah?"

"Only about half an hour. I thought there'd be plenty of time for Jim to get home from work. I haven't felt well all day. I stayed in bed."

Jeremiah pulled up Sarah's nightgown and felt her huge belly. "It's moving. Have your other children been difficult births?"

Sarah shook her head and let out another wail. . . . Jeremiah wiped her forehead with a corner of the sheet.

"Don't worry, as soon as your mother gets . . . ah, here she is now." Jeremiah washed his hands and proceeded to examine Sarah. "I can feel the baby. He's right there, but I'm afraid he's going to come out feet first." He turned to Mrs. White. "Is there a neighbor you can leave the children with? I don't want them to be frightened, so I think it's better if they aren't here. I'm going to need you."

"I'll take them next door."

While Elizabeth White was gone, Jeremiah got out his instruments, finding little of anything that would be of any use.

"Jeremiah," Sarah said, "if anything should happen to me, tell Sam to marry again."

"Nothing's going to happen to you."

"But if it should . . . he's a good man. He needs a wife."

Jeremiah swallowed hard, trying to concentrate on all he had ever read about childbirth. Sarah let out another agonizing moan, and he turned to take her hands.

"Yell all you want, Sarah."

Less than an hour later, Jeremiah handed the newly washed pink baby boy wrapped in a blanket to Sarah. Cuddling the infant in the crook of her arm, she peeked under the folds of the cover at the tiny face.

"He looks just like Sam," she mumbled, drifting off to sleep.

Jeremiah had gone over to the window to get several deep breaths of air. Now that it was all over, his hands were trembling and he felt a little giddy.

"I think I'll go downstairs for a while," he told Mrs. White.

Jeremiah went straight to Sam's whiskey and poured himself a strong shot. He swallowed it in one gulp and felt the fiery liquid reach his stomach. Then he smiled. The enormity of his accomplishment pleased him. Perhaps if Sarah had not been so dear to him, he could have performed his work less emotionally. But just the same, he did a good job. Now that it was over, he felt a great relief. Sarah had come out of it fine, and the child appeared healthy.

The front door opened, and Jim entered.

"Congratulations," Jeremiah told him. "You're an

uncle again."

The relief of Richmond was tempered with some anxiety, for Lincoln had called for 300,000 new men for a three-year service. But the new Confederate conscription was beginning to bear fruit as well. Volunteers were pouring into the army from all parts of the South. With the men leaving their jobs for war, opportunities were beginning to appear for women. Mahaley felt she had seen the last of her bandage-rolling sessions, for, with her knowledge of arithmetic and fractions, she had gotten a job at the War Department at a salary of fifty dollars a month. Edward had received a raise as well, and he was now earning two thousand dollars a year. Everyone was getting their salaries raised. But the increased earnings were not much use as long as the prices continued to rise and the Confederate money decreased in value.

The Confederacy was beginning to run a little more efficiently though. From out of almost nothing, Davis had set up a chemical laboratory at Charlotte; foundries and rolling mills, smelting works, powder mills; and he had opened up new iron and lead mines. Following the Seven Days' Battles, the Confederacy became stronger and was nearing its high point of the war. The Federal campaign in Virginia had been pushed all the way back to Washington City, the late-summer harvest in the Shenandoah Valley was in Confederate possession, the Kanawha Valley had been regained and there was once again enough salt, and Lee was contemplating an invasion into Northern lands.

True, the streets were filled with amputees and bandaged men, but Richmond had returned to its old gay self. The railroads were repaired, and travel was easy once again. There was no lack of groceries except for imports. Mrs. Davis was soon to return from Raleigh, and a ball was being planned for her.

Henry strolled into the paper one afternoon with a very smug expression on his face. Melissa had come to know that particular expression and knew he had evidently just picked up some useful information.

"Where have you been?" she asked.

"Over at Rocketts. I thought I might do a piece on the ironclads that are being built at the navy yard there."

"I see," she said, her mouth turning up a little at the corners. "That ought to be very interesting."

"Indeed."

Melissa turned over a page of her advertising and scanned the message. Personally, she felt it was a fine thing to put in the paper, but knowing Lewis's aversion to printing anything that might be considered pro-Union, she decided to ask him about this request for aid for the prisoners. Taking the sheet of paper with her, she went to his office. Her dress was sticking to her back from perspiration where she had been leaning against her chair. She wondered how much longer this heat wave would last. For her own comfort, she had forsaken her crinolines for the plain dresses she had worn back home in the country.

Lewis smiled at her as she entered his office.

"You look warm," he said.

"Very," she replied. "I thought I should ask you about this before placing it in tomorrow's edition."

"What is it?"

"It's from a number of clergymen here in the city. They're requesting donations of blankets and soap and

351

such articles to better the living conditions at Libby and Belle Isle for the prisoners."

Libby had once been a warehouse on the river. It was a large four-story building containing eight rooms. The Union officers were housed here, where there were bathing facilities and a well-managed hospital on the ground floor. However, there was no furniture, and the men slept on the floor. Visitors seldom were allowed to go upstairs, for the vermin abounded amid the tattered blankets on which the men slept. Food was usually brought by boat and deposited at the dock at the rear of the building. Enlisted men were kept at Belle Isle in the James River. They were housed in tents, however scarce, and water was abundant and the drainage generally good. The men were allowed to bathe in the river, and the food was adequate.

Despite the efforts of the commandant of both prisons, Major Thomas P. Turner, the facilities were sadly lacking.

"I see," Lewis said, after reading it. "What do you think?"

"You're asking my opinion?"

Lewis nodded.

"I think it's a fine idea. After all, wouldn't we want the same treatment for our men?"

"Then go ahead and place it in the paper."

"I'll go get it ready right now."

"Miss Armstrong, before you go, I wonder if I could ask you to dine with me tonight?"

Melissa had to struggle to keep her mouth from falling open in amazement.

"There's something I'd like to talk to you about," he added.

"All right."

Lewis smiled. "Then I'll be by for you around seven."

Afraid she was going to be fired, Melissa went back to her desk. But that didn't make sense. Lewis seemed pleased with her, and hadn't he just given her a raise in salary? She hoped he didn't suspect Henry and want to get information about him from her.

After Melissa had dressed, she waited in the drawing room for Lewis to call for her. Edward and Mahaley returned from work, and her uncle came in to see her.

"You're very dressed up," he said. "A special occasion?"

"Mr. McAllen asked me to have supper with him."

Edward raised his eyebrows and was about to inquire further when there was a knock at the door. Cindy ushered Lewis into the room.

"Good evening, Lewis," Edward said.

"Good evening, Edward. Miss Armstrong, you look lovely as usual."

Edward frowned. "I understand you're taking my niece to supper." He emphasized the word 'niece.'

"Yes. I had some things I wanted to talk to her about. And I thought it would be a pleasant diversion from the heat." He turned to Melissa. "Are you ready?"

"Yes."

Lewis put Melissa into the buggy and they drove off, leaving Edward standing at the window, still frowning.

After some idle chatter, Lewis decided to get finally to the reason he had asked Melissa to dine.

"You do look very lovely tonight, Miss Armstrong."

"Thank you, Mr. McAllen."

"But you always look lovely. Would you think me too

353

forward if I say I admire you a great deal, and in the time I've known you, I've grown very fond of you?''

Melissa looked up from her plate of venison and stared across the table at Lewis.

He continued. ''I know I'm considerably older than you, but do you think you could ever consider marriage to me?''

Melissa was dumbfounded. ''Mr. McAllen!''

''I told you once that I was a very lonely man. I've never met a woman who, I thought, could make me happy until I met you. And I'm sure I could make you happy. I'm a very rich man, and I could give you anything you wanted.''

''Mr. McAllen, I had no idea you felt this way about me.''

''I've tried to keep my feelings to myself. But I can't hide them any longer. I want a wife who can give me children and make me happy.''

Melissa didn't know what to say or do. She felt like crawling underneath the table in her embarrassment for both of them.

''Mr. McAllen, I don't love you.''

''I know. But perhaps you will, in time.''

''I love Jackson Vaughn.'' She even surprised herself with this declaration.

''You do?''

''Yes. And when the war is over, we plan to marry.''

''I see,'' Lewis sighed. ''I had no idea. I thought, since you hadn't married him yet or at least declared your intentions . . .''

''Mr. McAllen, I don't know what to say.''

He gave her a sad smile. ''There's nothing you can say, my dear. It was just a foolish notion of mine.''

"I'm sure you'd have no trouble finding yourself a good wife. You just happened to ask the wrong girl."

Lewis smiled again, but inside he was hurting. He had spent long hours fantasizing about a life with Melissa. She was everything a man wanted—beautiful, intelligent, kind. And most of all, she was young and healthy enough to bear children. Since he had begun to accumulate a small fortune, he had become almost obsessed with the idea of having an heir to whom to leave it all. Now, as he realized his error tonight, he made up his mind to seek a wife elsewhere. Melissa was right; he shouldn't have too much trouble finding one. True, whoever she was, she wouldn't be Melissa, but he could always close his eyes at night and pretend. There were plenty of women in Richmond now, especially widows. A young widow might not be a bad idea.

"I hope this won't cause any problems with our relationship at work," Melissa said.

"Of course not. I think the best thing is just to forget I ever mentioned it."

A Federal blunder had left General John Pope in an exposed position north of the Rapidan River, and General Lee planned to make use of this error. If the cavalry could attack his rear and burn the railroad bridges on the Rappahannock, the Confederates could cut him off and gain a great victory.

On the night of August 16, Jeb Stuart sent Fitz Lee and his command to meet him at Verdiersville, while he and a few staff officers boarded a train bound for Gordonsville. Their horses were put in a stock car, but, as the train was already packed with troops, Jeb and his men sat on the logs in the tender behind engine. It was daybreak when they reached their destination, and as they stepped off the train, they began to laugh.

"If dem Yankees sees us, dey's liable to set us free!" Jackson grinned, peering into the soot-blackened faces of his friends.

After a thorough washing, Jeb reported to Lee at his headquarters at Orange Court House, and then the men rode on to Verdiersville.

A family living near the town had been ransacked recently by a Union cavalry column on reconnaissance, but the Yankees hadn't been seen in the vicinity for two days. Jeb was welcomed, but he didn't get the answers which he wanted to his questions. The family had not seen any Confederate cavalry in the area either. Jeb was concerned as to Fitz Lee's whereabouts, so he sent a scout out to hasten his march.

The weather was warm, and the men decided to spend the night on the porch of the old house. Not wanting to light a fire to cook their meal, they dined on salt beef and crackers.

"Do you think the Yankees are close by?" Jackson wondered.

"Probably across the river. But I'm not going to worry about them tonight," Jeb said. "I'm sleepy."

Jeb turned in, using his haversack as a pillow, his cloak for a bed, and placing his plumed hat to his side. He was very proud of this particular hat, for on the day of truce for burying the dead at Cedar Mountain, Jeb had met two of his comrades from before the war who were in the Union Army. There was much jesting about which side had won the battle, and later that day, the hat arrived at his outpost as a gift from his old friends.

Jackson stretched out a few feet away, his sword and

gun belt still around his waist. Despite Jeb's nonchalance about the whereabouts of the Yankees, the horses were still saddled and grazing close by. Jackson wiggled his toes in his boots. He had no socks, and the boots were beginning to wear. He wished he had asked Melissa to send him a pair of socks. Perhaps he could get into Richmond to see her and purchase some new boots and socks soon.

The scout who had been sent out to look for Fitz Lee sent no messages back to Jeb for a very good reason; he had been captured. He had ridden right into the waiting arms of the First Michigan and the Fifth New York cavalries. They took him back to their camp and proceeded to go through his papers, which contained Lee's full plans for the destruction of Pope.

As the gray mist of dawn covered the farmhouse, Jeb and his men stirred. Jackson looked over at Jeb, for they had both heard the same thing—the clatter of cavalry coming, from the east.

"Fitz Lee, I reckon," Jeb said, standing up and stretching. "It's about time. Mosby, you and Gibson ride out and meet them."

Jeb started to stroll down toward the fence that fronted the road. Picking up his hat and jamming it on his head, Jackson started after him. Through the mist, he could see troopers moving across the main road.

"Fitz better have a good excuse," Jeb remarked. "Twelve hours late on a thirty-two-mile march!"

Suddenly there was a spattering of pistol shots, and Mosby and Gibson raced back into the yard, low on their horses' necks.

"Yankee cavalry!"

Jackson ran for his horse, with Jeb close behind him.

They vaulted into their saddles and jumped the garden fence, heading for the woods behind the house. Von Borcke galloped through the gate and across a field with a squad of Yankees in pursuit. He managed to outride them, for despite the large target he presented, his horse was fresh while the Yankees' mounts were not.

The little group assembled again, safe in the woods. Stuart watched while the Yankees looted the gear left behind on the porch. One of the men waved Jeb's red-lined cloak about and rifled his haversack. Another man tried on his hat and rode away, the plume bobbing in the breeze.

Out of breath but unwounded, the men looked at each other. Jackson was trying to suppress a grin, but Jeb wasn't amused. Among the items in the haversack were more important plans and maps.

Disgusted, the men started off until they came upon Longstreet's infantry and a Georgia regiment's well-stocked sutler's store. Jeb purchased a plain wool hat, such as the lowliest private might wear. The story spread through the soldiers' grapevine, and all day Jeb had to endure the shouts of the infantry:

"Hey, General, where's your hat?"

Jackson rode along beside him, watching Jeb bear the brunt of the jokes with increasing difficulty.

"I intend to make the Yankees pay dearly for that hat!"

Fifteen

The South was planning to strike a triple offensive while the North was disheartened. Lincoln's army was in a sorry state as far as morale was concerned. After the second Bull Run late in August, General Pope had been relieved of duty and sent west to watch over the Indians. General Buell was heading the army of the Cumberland near Chattanooga, General Halleck was at Corinth, Sherman was at Memphis, Grant was in western Tennessee. Lincoln once again turned to McClellan to lead the army of the Potomac, against the wishes of Congress.

Lee planned to invade Maryland, where the land was rich in food and forage. From there, he could move into Pennsylvania, and a victory there might bring England and France to recognize the South officially.

Lee hated to divide his forces, but when he learned that Harper's Ferry was weakly guarded, he decided to capture the garrison of some ten thousand Yankees and make use of its supplies. Special Order 191 sent two rebel forces to take Harper's Ferry, and among the men was Andrew. Another force was stationed at Boonsborough, and still another was to proceed north to Hagerstown.

It was at this time McClellan was given a godsend. Somehow, Special Order 191 had been found on the ground wrapped around three cigars. Two Indiana privates found it and turned it over to the command. McClellan now knew Lee's complete plans and saw that the Confederate Army was split four ways. Even with all this, McClellan hesitated. He delayed for twenty-four hours, which was all Lee needed to pull his forces back together.

As his battleground, Lee picked the little town of Sharpsburg, where Antietam Creek made a natural barrier to the Federals. Taking advantage of the forests, orchards, and gently rolling hills, the Confederates were strung out all along the creek.

Along with the other new members of the regiment, Jeremiah had marched from Washington City to join the veteran Forty-sixth Pennsylvania. The many losses in earlier battles had depleted the ranks severely, and on the sixteenth of September, Jeremiah met his superior officer. He was Dr. Sidney Miltenberger, who had been out with the unit since the war began. Besides Jeremiah, there was Dr. Alfred Nichols, also a newly graduated surgeon. The entire medical unit of the Forty-sixth was composed of Dr. Miltenberger, surgeon in charge; Jeremiah, assistant surgeon; Dr. Nichols, second assistant surgeon; six orderlies; three ambulances; and two supply wagons.

Jeremiah gazed around at all the activities going on nearby. Batteries were being placed in position, with men moving here and there.

"I haven't picked out a site for the field hospital yet," Dr. Miltenberger said. He was a middle-aged man with a great red beard. "I'm waiting for orders from General

Mansfield. Apparently there's some delay at McClellan's headquarters. While we have the opportunity, I'd like to go over my routine with you. I've found some things helpful in battles."

The delay was again due to McClellan's hesitancy. Not about to make a mistake by hasty action, he bided his time studying, calculating, and attending to details. Due to faulty reports, he estimated Lee's strength at over 100,000 men, when he actually had only about 25,000, still awaiting the arrival of the troops from Harper's Ferry. So McClellan was fighting an imaginary army.

By late in the afternoon, there was still no order to move, and Jeremiah saw that Dr. Miltenberger was getting very nervous. Jeremiah glanced over the hills of Maryland, lush and green, to the stream. He wondered if the cousin he hadn't seen since he was nine years old was somewhere on the other side, or Melissa's cavalry friend. He sighed and turned, preparing to return to check his equipment. There were several bursts of artillery, and Jeremiah looked around to see if the battle was beginning. No one seemed concerned, so evidently it was only an overanxious captain somewhere.

Andrew was preparing to leave Harper's Ferry with another brigade. He had been amazed at how many new faces had replaced his old friends when he returned after Malvern Hill. And after the second battle of Bull Run, some of the new faces were replaced by still newer ones. He had discarded his cumbersome knapsack for a more convenient blanket roll slung over his left shoulder and under his right arm. With his toothbrush stuck in a buttonhole, a frying pan attached to his rifle barrel, and a coffeepot swinging on his belt, Andrew began the seventeen-mile march to Sharpsburg.

Jackson was getting himself settled for the night and feeling quite snug. Some of the men had returned to report to Lee the successful capture of Harper's Ferry, and with them they had brought buttermilk, bread, and meat. He intended to sleep on a full belly, for he never could be sure when he would eat another good meal.

Dr. Miltenberger finally received his orders, and shortly after dusk, the medical caravan crossed the Antietam and made its way past a cornfield and into a little wooded area. An abandoned storage barn was selected for the field hospital, and the men worked into the night getting it ready. A detail of privates swept the floors and set up tables from the supply wagons. Clean straw was gathered from the countryside and spread on the floor.

Jeremiah turned in for the night in his tent, listening to the occasional bursts of artillery or creaking wagon wheels. Sometime after midnight, it began to drizzle, and the patter on the canvas finally lulled him to sleep.

The fields were enveloped in a heavy mist when Jeremiah awoke in the morning, but the rain had stopped. During the night, Mansfield's corps had come up and were camped a little closer to the intended line of battle. Jeremiah sat down on his campstool and opened up his surgeon's kit to check his supplies once again. The fine instruments that Melissa had given him were still in Pittsburgh; these had been issued from the government. Among his tools were scalpels, a small amputating knife, straight and curved scissors, a variety of forceps, a dozen needles, a metacarpal saw, catheters, and miscellaneous

362

ourniquets. Most of his equipment was in his knapsack, o which an orderly attended.

He had started to see about some breakfast when Charlie came over to him. Jeremiah had to smile at the vay Charlie seemed to strut in his uniform, the buttons hining. And he never let his precious straight brass horn ut of his sight.

"Well, here we are," Charlie remarked, as Dr. Nichols oined them. He was tall and blond, a little older than eremiah but lacking six months training. "You all ready or the day?"

"I expect as ready as I'll ever be," Jeremiah said. "How bout you?"

"Naturally."

Jeremiah personally felt it was ridiculous to have a egimental band along during a battle, but the soldiers vere heartened if they knew music was close at hand. Music inspired the soldiers as much as the generals.

"Had breakfast yet?" Charlie asked.

"Not yet."

"Come on over to our mess. We got fresh milk. Somebody stole a cow last night."

Jeremiah and Al grinned, and taking their mess kits vith them, the two doctors followed Charlie over to his ness. As the fog lifted, thousands of men could be seen, ll preparing for the day. During the night, guns had been brought up to the low heights bordering the east side of he river, most of them long-range parrotts. Safely in the cover of the valleys behind the guns, were the dense nasses of infantry.

After filling their cups from the pail of milk, the urgeons seated themselves and were soon given some bacon and bread.

"Not a bad little hospital you got set up over there," a burly Irishman remarked. "I've seen 'em set up with nothing but a tree for shade."

"From what I've been told, it's fair," Jeremiah said.

"This your first fight, then?"

"Yes."

The Irishman grinned. "It appears to be a good one, anyway."

A soldier hurried over to the Irishman. "Come along with you, Patrick. Doubleday's going to move us up the road."

The Irishman put down his food and picked up his rifle. "Good luck to you, lads," he called, trotting after his companion.

"New Yorkers," Charlie muttered. "Always looking for a free meal."

"Do you think this will really be a big battle?" Al asked.

"I don't know. I was only at Bull Run, and that was before we really got organized," Charlie replied. "But I don't think there was as much equipment or as many men there."

Some of the veterans of the Twenty-seventh Indiana were mercilessly teasing the new recruits who were too nervous to eat their breakfasts. Before Jeremiah and Al could finish eating, they had amassed quite a collection of trinkets and valuables the men gave them and other noncombatants for safekeeping.

A volley of fire began in earnest off to the right, and the men began to stir. From one end of the camp to the other, bivouacs were littered with discarded decks of cards, frying pans, and blankets.

"I guess this is it," Charlie remarked, standing up and

cradling his horn under his arm. He shook hands with Jeremiah and Al. "I'll see you later. Hopefully not on a professional basis."

The fighting began early in the morning, and after a little over an hour, the hospital was beginning to fill up. There must have been at least a dozen other such hospitals on the field, and Jeremiah wondered at the incredible carnage. His adrenaline was flowing, and he worked as if possessed. He glanced over at Dr. Miltenberger who was using both hands to tie off an artery, his scalpel clenched between his teeth. Jeremiah shuddered. He realized that in this situation, things like that could not be prevented, but the unsanitary way in which he was forced to work caused him some concern. Sterilization and antiseptic techniques were still unknown, but Jim had always believed in keeping things as clean as possible. As one patient was removed from the table, an orderly threw a bucket of water on it, and another patient took his place. Jeremiah's apron and forearms were covered with blood, and the bucket of water in which he rinsed his hands and arms soon turned red. There was just not enough time or enough help to change the water.

The Union lines began to fall back under the crush of the Confederates, men falling by the hundreds. The Federals rallied, and pushed forward once again, General Mansfield riding his horse through the cornfield. A volley was fired, and his horse was hit. As the old trooper tried to climb over the fence and back to safety, a bullet struck him in the stomach. Some rookies made a crude litter of muskets and coats and carried him out of the line of fire. They had only been soldiers for a month and were uncertain what to do with a wounded general, but three men from the Tenth Maine arrived to carry the commander to the rear of the lines. Shells crashing all around and bullets whizzing through the air, the Maine men finally got the general back to the field hospital.

Jeremiah goggled at the general and watched as Al put a flask of whiskey to the injured man's lips, almost strangling him. Between the wound and the clumsy handling, the old general died. He had only been in charge of the corps for a few days, but the men liked and respected him.

Al and the orderlies covered him carefully with a blanket and continued their work. The saving of life could not be interrupted merely because a general had been killed.

Jackson was floundering in the brush, having lost his horse. A bullet had neatly severed his saddle cinch, and he had been unseated in the west woods near Dunker Church. The Federals were heading straight toward him and, knowing he had nowhere to run and only his saber and pistol as weapons, he promptly climbed a tree and waited for them to pass.

General Hood and his Texans were trying desperately to hold their ground but the Federals pushed him back and took the high ground near the Dunker Church. Jeb Stuart and D. H. Hill managed to hold off any further advance, but Jackson found himself in a nest of Yankees.

An hour passed, and then he saw the Yankees pulling back. The fresh troops from Harper's Ferry had arrived to aid General Walker. The Federals fled and took cover behind their artillery.

Andrew was reloading his rifle when he heard something behind him. He whirled, prepared to use his bayonet and found Jackson grinning at him.

"Jackson, where did you come from?"

Jackson pointed up in the trees. "I know how a frightened coon feels with a pack of dogs on his heels."

During a lull in the fighting, John Pelham and Heros Von Borcke saw Jackson's riderless horse straggling back toward their position. Heros caught the reins and brought it back behind the guns.

"Do you suppose he's . . . ?" Heros wondered.

"I don't know. But where's the saddle?"

Jackson had been able to capture a stray horse, and when he appeared at Stuart's position, he was greeted like a hero.

"We thought you were dead!" John laughed.

"Not me," Jackson grinned.

Jeb appeared with John Mosby. "Come on, Jackson. We've got some inspections to make for Stonewall."

"Be right with you."

Jackson took the saddle from the captured horse and put it on Gypsy. He caught up with Jeb, heading toward the batteries of Stonewall Jackson. As they passed some of the artillery positions, the ground was so strewn with the dying and the dead, the horses had to cautiously pick their way through the bodies. Jackson glanced off toward a farm road that apeared to be piled fifteen feet high with bodies.

They guarded the rear of the lines, where the tired and frightened men were trying to sneak off with the wounded. Every man who was not bleeding was sent back into the fight. Jackson hated his mission, for it was a ragged, barefoot infantry who comprised this last pitiful reserve.

By midafternoon, General Burnside had his Union troops in position to charge past the old church, but the remainder of the men from Harper's Ferry succeeded in pushing the Yankees into another retreat. As the sun went down, the battle remained at a stalemate.

Lee's men had done as much fighting as they could for the day. He hoped to pull them all together during the night to be ready if the battle should resume in the morning.

Andrew helped a detail carry the wounded back to the safety of the orange hospital flag of the Confederates. It was hateful work, but he was in better condition than most to assist. As he was making his way through the bodies, he heard, through the darkness, a young boy sobbing bitterly. Andrew started toward the sound to help but a man reached the boy first.

"Is that you, son?" the man asked, bending down.

"Yes, Pa. I'm glad you found me. I think my leg's broke, but I don't want you to think that's why I'm crying. I fell in a yellow jackets' nest."

Andrew tried to help the man pull his son away from the insects, but the combination of his wounds and the stings was too much, and the boy died in his father's arms.

Andrew turned away, gritting his teeth. "I'm getting out of this army," he thought. "I want to go where nothing's familiar."

Jeremiah had had his first taste of being a surgeon on the battlefield. He didn't like it, but he knew many of the men might have died had he not been there. In the distance, he heard the band playing a dirge as General

Mansfield and the other dead officers were being taken from the camp. He wondered how many more would die before it was all over.

Ever since Melissa had received Jeremiah's letter telling her that he had joined the medical corps, she had been very upset. He was her last link to the past and the person she cared for most in this world. Now, he was subjecting himself to all sorts of danger, not only from the battlefield, but from the many diseases. When the letter had arrived a week ago, she had delayed telling the family, and when she finally did, they received the news with mixed emotions. It wasn't until George, who had been in the house for supper, pointed out that Jeremiah would be helping the Confederate wounded as well, that the family relented in their feelings. After all, Jeremiah was there to save lives, not take them.

George had arrived in mid-August, laden with delicacies, silks and supplies. Melissa still felt a strain when they were alone together, one she couldn't understand, but as they were seldom alone, she didn't give it too much thought. When she had first met George, she hadn't been sure if she cared for him, but as she came to know him better, her liking for him grew. He had left for Wilmington and another cargo a week ago.

President Davis had been in constant communication with Lee, and on September 18, he declared a day of Thanksgiving for deliverance from the enemy and to pray for the army. All private businesses were closed, and Melissa attended church with Margaret, Jeff, and Nancy. The thought passed through her mind as she looked around at all the women sitting quietly and praying: How many of their sons and fathers and husbands still live? These women don't know. They may not know for days, yet they go on.

After the services, Varina Davis approached the family. Melissa had only seen her in church since her return in August.

"Ladies, I'd like to ask you over to tea this afternoon if you could arrange it," Varina said. "We're forming a larger hospital committee and I'd appreciate it if you could attend."

The women left little Jeff in the care of Cindy and went off to the executive mansion. Several women were gathered at the house, and the president looked in to greet them.

"Mrs. Armstrong, it's so good to see you," he said, taking her hand. "I have something for you. It came the other day, but I'm afraid I've been too busy to send it over." He took an envelope from his breast pocket. "It's your son's transfer."

"Oh, thank you, Mr. President! It was so good of you to intercede for us."

"What are friends for? Besides, they'll be happy to have a man who has some experience out west."

Margaret had taken the envelope and was reading the commission and transfer: "Second Lieutenant Andrew Armstrong of the Twelfth Virginia infantry transferred to command of General John C. Pemberton, department of the Mississippi. Promoted to first lieutenant."

"General Pemberton?" Melissa asked.

"Yes, he's a good man. I have a lot of respect for him," Davis said. "You know, Mrs. Armstrong, I'm planning on taking a little inspection tour out west in a month or two. Perhaps I'll take Andrew along as an aide until we reach his command. In the meantime, he could have a little furlough."

"Oh, Mr. Davis, I'd be so grateful!" Nancy exclaimed.

"Then consider it done, Mrs. Armstrong."

Melissa didn't think the president looked at all well. She knew he had been ailing, but he seemed even thinner than usual.

"Now if you ladies will excuse me, I'll let you get on with your meeting."

Varina didn't attend to the men in the hospitals personally, for she thought the men would feel too much restraint in her presence. But she visited regularly with supplies to be distributed to the soldiers. Now that Chimborazo Hospital was becoming so large, a new committee was needed to take care of all the incidentals.

Chimborazo Hospital, which had opened October 11, 1861, was the largest military hospital on the continent. It was situated on a hill with a commanding view of the James, an abundant supply of water and fresh air. It was actually five separate hospitals, each divided into thirty buildings or wards, and each accommodating forty to sixty patients, with bunks arranged in several rows. There were plenty of windows and doors for ventilation, with wide alleys separating the buildings. Tents were pitched on the surrounding slopes for convalescing patients, and it even had its own cemetery. Besides the nursing facilities, there were five soup kitchens, five ice-houses, a Russian bathhouse, a brewery, and a bakery capable of producing ten thousand loaves of bread a day. Tree Hill, a nearby farm, was available for pasturage. The surgeon in chief was Dr. James B. McCaw, and Phoebe Yates Pember was the superintendant of nursing.

Nancy and Margaret were more than happy to join the committee and help organize a bazaar. Melissa said she would do all she could to help, but her time was not as readily available as theirs.

"Of course we want to collect donations of blankets and shoes and all those things," Mrs. Davis said. "But I thought if we could collect some money, and with your husband's help, Mrs. Armstrong, we could purchase coats for the coming winter. Do you think he and his partners would consent to bring in a special order on their ship?"

"I know they would."

Maggie Howell smiled and nodded to her sister. "I knew we could count on the Armstrongs," she said.

"I'm sure Mr. McAllen would run a small notice in the paper," Melissa ventured.

"That's another thing I was sure we could count on."

"You know, before the war, my husband didn't particularly care for the *Journal*," Varina confessed. "But with the support it's given him, and Mr. Walkenfeldt's brilliant writing, Jeff's changed his opinion."

"Mr. Walkenfeldt's a wonderful man," Nancy said.

"I think he should run for congress," Maggie added.

Melissa smiled to herself and continued to listen to the discussion.

Henry was watching Melissa prepare the coffee of ground nuts for the office on the morning of September 23. They both knew Lewis had access to real coffee, as did Edward, but Lewis liked to keep up appearances. And as long as nobody else in the city had coffee, he wouldn't either.

Henry had been contemplating strengthening his facade of being a staunch Confederate by joining the Richmond Ambulance Committee. It had been organized in the spring by men who were exempt from military duty. It was headed by John Enders and had a membership of some one hundred men, most of whom were all prominent citizens. They attempted, at their own expense, to attend, feed, and transport the wounded. So far, they had been able to obtain some forty vehicles for ambulances. Both Lewis and Edward were members.

"I think you should join if you want to," Melissa was saying.

"So do I. It wouldn't be going against my basic principles. And, God knows, they could use some new ambulances. Some of those carts barely move. If I were to do a series of articles, some nice blacksmith or coach manufacturer might become generous."

The telegraph began clicking, and the operator let out a low whistle. Lewis walked into the office just as the message had been transcribed.

Lewis, Melissa, and Henry peered at the news. Yesterday, Lincoln had proclaimed all the slaves free. In essence, it stated "That on the first day of January, AD 1863, all persons held as slaves within any state or designated part of a state . . . the people whereof shall then be in rebellion against the United States . . . shall then be, thenceforward and forever free . . ."

Henry's eyes met Melissa's.

"Hogwash!" Lewis exclaimed. "It's nothing but a worthless piece of trash! How can he expect to enforce it? The damned fool! Henry, I want you to write a piece telling the people that. No, never mind—I'll write an editorial!" Lewis waved to the errand boy. "Ish, tell them to stop the presses!"

"Yessuh!" And Ish hurried off to the press operators.

"Now we know what kind of deceit we're dealing

373

with!" Lewis went on. "When Lincoln started this, he said over and over again he wouldn't interfere with our way of life; his only aim was saving the Union! Saving the Union—bah! Now look what he's done!"

Lewis continued on with his diatribe as he went into his office and slammed the door. Melissa and Henry looked at each other again.

"He's right, you know," Henry admitted. "Lincoln did say slavery wasn't the real issue. Now I'm afraid it is."

Melissa followed Henry back to his desk where he was gathering up his notebook.

"What will happen now?" she asked.

"God knows," Henry said. "I think I'll go over to the Capitol and see what I can find out. I'll see you later."

Late in the day, Henry was admitted to the president's office. Henry thought the man looked as if the entire weight of the world was upon his shoulders.

"Mr. Walkenfeldt, it's been quite a day," Davis said, shaking his hand.

"Yes, sir, it has. It's very good of you to take the time to see me."

"I'll always have time for you, Mr. Walkenfeldt. Now, what can I do for you?"

"I wondered how you felt about Lincoln's proclamation?"

Davis gave a tired smile. "That was the last thing I needed to hear today. I've got enough on my mind with Bragg's operations in Kentucky and Van Dorn in Mississippi. I hoped perhaps Bragg could get into Cincinnati or St. Louis."

"Really?"

"Yes. But that may be just another dream—like

Maryland. We've got to make some headway in the North. We've got men moving toward Corinth now." Davis smiled weakly again. "About Mr. Lincoln's statement . . ."

Henry was more interested in the information he had received about the army's intentions than how Davis felt about the Emancipation Proclamation. Henry went back to the paper and copied his notes from his chat with the president. Dan had already closed his store for the day, so Henry ate a bite of supper and went to his room.

Henry was both sad and happy, and he felt very lonely right now. He was glad that the rebel drive into the North had thus far been thwarted and his homeland of Pennsylvania was for the present safe from invasion, but he was saddened that he had such little correspondence with his family. He had the means to send letters home, but what could he tell them? He couldn't very well say what he was doing. And without letting his family know he was in Richmond, he could receive no letters from them. He missed his family and knew his father and mother would be worrying about him, being their only son and the only one to carry on their name in this country. He wondered how his brother-in-law was faring in the army. Henry didn't even know if he was still alive.

At times like this, he wondered if he had made the right decision when he had chosen to become a United States agent. He had had no conception that he would actually become fond of these people who were tearing apart the country. Sometimes, like today, when he looked at Jefferson Davis—a man burdened with a tremendous responsibility—he felt very guilty about his deception. Davis was a humane and kind man, one who had accepted Henry as a friend and loyal patriot. He was thankful he had Melissa to share his secret. At least, she believed what he was doing was right, and when he felt depressed as he did now, he could remember that. But what a lonely life!

Going over and sitting down at his desk, Henry took out a sheet of paper and prepared to write to his family. He had to let them know he was thinking of them. But most of all, he needed to hear news from home. He would tell them he was here on business for a while. He hated the idea of anyone at the post office seeing his name on a letter from Pittsburgh. Everyone knew Melissa had a brother who corresponded with her from the North, so Henry decided to have his mother address his letter to her. As he began to write, he prayed his loneliness would not be his undoing.

Margaret, too, was writing a letter. With all the acreage for pasture the hospital had, there were unfortunately very few animals to populate it. Her father-in-law, old Thaddeus Boone, had plenty of cows and chickens on his farm. If he hadn't already sold them to the government, Margaret hoped she could persuade him to sell or donate some to the hospital. She sealed the envelope with wax and went downstairs, surprised to find Lewis chatting with the family in the parlor. Actually, he wasn't chatting, he was still spouting off about Lincoln.

He calmed down when she entered. "Good evening, Margaret."

"Hello, Mr. McAllen. Father, would you take this letter to the post office on your way to work in the morning?"

"Of course," Edward said, taking the envelope and putting it in his pocket.

"I decided rather than just asking him by letter, I'd take the baby for a visit and ask in person. They've never seen their grandson."

"Is it safe for you to travel alone, dear?" Nancy wondered.

"What's this all about?" Lewis asked.

"Margaret is going to ask her father-in-law for some stock for the Chimborazo farm," Edward told him.

"Admirable," Lewis remarked.

"I don't know if you should be traveling all alone with the baby," Nancy said. "There might be Yankees hiding somewhere."

"Aunt Nancy," Melissa giggled.

"It's true! The Boones don't live all that far from Washington City."

"Jeff and I will be all right, Mother."

"You can't be too careful—a young widow traveling alone with her son. . . ."

The words hit Lewis like a slap in the face. A young widow! This might be the answer to his dilemma, and it had been here all along. He had known Margaret since she was a child and had never considered her anything other than Edward's daughter. But she was no longer a child, and she was available. She was young and healthy, and she certainly came from a good background. The Boones were quite well-to-do and would probably leave everything to their grandson, who he could raise as his own. He glanced from Margaret to Melissa. They were cousins, after all. Margaret might be a very acceptable wife. He knew there had been some kind of marital trouble before Joseph had joined the army, but he had no idea what it had been. Yes, Margaret might be the answer.

"If you'll permit me to make a suggestion," Lewis said.

"I've been thinking of getting out of the city for a few days for a little rest. I'd be happy to accompany Margaret and Jeff."

"Thank you, Lewis," Edward said. He looked at Nancy and Margaret. "Does that satisfy both of you?"

"Yes," Nancy replied.

Margaret nodded. "Thank you Mr. McAllen. I do feel it's time they met their grandson."

"You're quite right. When did you plan to go?"

"Next week."

"I'll make arrangements at the paper. I might even turn it over to Mr. Walkenfeldt for the time." He looked at Melissa. "Do you think you can get along without me?"

"We'll try," she smiled.

"It's very good of you to do this, Lewis," Edward told him.

"It'll be a pleasure. I've always been very fond of Margaret, and besides, I'm doing this with a very selfish motive."

Edward laughed. "I must admit, you could use a little vacation. Forget about Lincoln for a while. Relax."

Mahaley enjoyed her job at the War Department, for it was something to do. And all the men paid her compliments, even if they were all old or crippled. But it was cutting into her social life. She still managed to see a soldier on the weekends, but it wasn't the same. And Nathaniel caused her no end of exasperation. He was so dedicated to his work! That was all very admirable, but not much fun. She would have given up on him long ago, except that she was genuinely fond of him.

Since the wounded from Sharpsburg had begun to

come into the city, the hospitals filled up, and the doctor's time was spent among the sick and injured. Mahaley decided to pack some cold chicken and peach cobbler and take it to Nathaniel on Saturday. She found him busy, as usual, but glad to see her. He took a few minutes to sit in the gardens with her and eat his lunch.

"Nathaniel, I believe you look ten years older than when I first met you."

He gave a tired smile. "I'm only twenty-three years old but sometimes I feel like fifty."

Mahaley wondered if that was why he never got familiar with her like the other men. She had heard sometimes that people lost interest in such things as they grew older.

"There's an outbreak of smallpox. A lot of the men have it. They must have caught it in Maryland." He sighed. "It only adds to the problems."

Mahaley nodded and patted his hand. "Poor Nathaniel."

"Have you been vaccinated?"

"When I was a little girl. Why?"

"I wouldn't want you to catch it. Most of the cases are isolated at the Smallpox Hospital, but it's impossible to tell how many more might have it."

"I understand it's a terrible thing."

"Yes, it is. The surgeon general tried to have most of the men vaccinated at the beginning of the war, but we couldn't get to them all. Especially the men from the country. We're going to try to get more vaccine."

"Will that cure the men?"

"No. Not the ones who already have it. But if we can get enough men vaccinated, it may prevent another outbreak. Do you know if your slaves have ever been vaccinated?"

"I don't know. I don't think so."

"I'd like to come over this evening and take a look at them. If they haven't been vaccinated, I'd like to do it. Then we can use them to get more vaccine."

"How do you do that?"

"From the scabs."

Mahaley shuddered. "Oh, how terrible!"

Nathaniel grinned at her. "That's how it's done."

"It's sickening."

"Nevertheless, that's the way it is. Do you think your parents would mind if I vaccinated your people?"

"I don't think so." She looked at him very solemnly. "If a white person were vaccinated from the slaves, would they turn black then?"

Nathaniel laughed, partly from the ludicrousness of the question and partly from the seriousness with which Mahaley asked it. He took her hand in both of his. "Mahaley, you're a true gem. But I must get back to work now."

"Do you have to?"

"Yes, I do. But I'll see you this evening."

As Mahaley was walking back toward her house, two ragged soldiers accosted her while she was waiting to cross the street.

"Howdy, miss. I'd be happy to carry that basket for you, if it's too heavy," the one man said.

"It's empty, Corporal."

"Well, maybe we could just sort of walk along with you for a spell?" the other asked. "It's been a right long time since we kept company with a pretty gal."

"We just got paid too. Maybe we could buy you something cold to drink, some lemonade maybe?"

380

Mahaley studied the two anxious faces, young and yet very old at the same time. "You just got into town, did you?"

"Yes, ma'am. We're with the Second Florida at Sharpsburg. We had to escort some bodies into town on the train."

"We surely would appreciate your company, ma'am."

Mahaley smiled. "I'm afraid there's not a drop of lemonade in the city. But I will allow you to buy me an ice cream."

Melissa had gathered up two cakes of soap and a pair of socks she was wrapping to send to Jackson. A letter had arrived from him, telling her about his adventures in the tree and running into Andrew. He didn't know when he would be able to get into Richmond, but he would be grateful if she could send him some socks and soap. She eyed the tin of coffee sitting on the shelf in the kitchen. She knew there was more in the pantry, and Jackson probably hadn't tasted coffee for months. The keys were hanging on the peg by the door, so she opened the lock and stepped into the large pantry. She seldom entered there and her eyes widened as she gazed at the piled sacks of salt, sugar, and flour. She wondered what the poor people would think if they could see all this—especially at a time when sugar was selling at the unheard-of price of twenty dollars a pound and flour at sixteen dollars a barrel.

Melissa knew her Uncle Edward was doing some good with his blockade-runner but he was unquestionably one of the men the press called "profiteers." The war was making him a rich man, but his ship was bringing in the necessary medicines and supplies the army needed. After selecting a tin of coffee, Melissa left the pantry and packed this luxury in with the soap and socks for Jackson.

When Mahaley had returned home just in time for supper, she told her parents about Nathaniel's request to vaccinate the slaves in order to obtain the needed serum. They were more than willing to donate the arms of their slaves.

After Nathaniel arrived, Edward assembled Bobo, Tunia, and Cindy around the kitchen table.

"You three can do a great service to the country," Nathaniel told them.

"You wants us to fight de Yankees, suh?" Bobo asked.

"No—to fight disease."

"Who dat?"

"It's not a who, it's a what. Sickness," Nathaniel said. "I want to vaccinate you. Then in a week, I'll come back and see you again."

"I won't gets me a baby wif dis, will I?" Cindy wondered.

Nathaniel smiled. "No. Now roll up your sleeves, and I'll get on with it." He took a vial and needle from his bag. The three blacks hadn't made a move. They were staring wide-eyed at the needle.

"No suh! You ain't gonna stick me wif dat!" Tunia announced. "Mas' Edward, I been wif yo' since yo' come to de city, and I been a good slave, but I ain't gettin' poked wif no needles!"

"Now Tunia, it's for your own good," Edward told her.

"No suh. I ain't never been sick yet."

"I'm not going to stick you," Nathaniel told her. "Only make a little scratch."

Mahaley stepped forward and rolled up her sleeve,

showing Tunia her own arm. "See that mark? I was vaccinated when I was a little girl."

The three black faces peered at the vaccination mark on Mahaley's arm.

"We've all had it done," Edward said.

"I don't care," Tunia said.

"Tunia, I'm beginning to lose my patience with you," Edward told her. "I've never whipped any of you yet, but there can always be a first time."

"Tunia," Melissa said, "remember last May when the doctor came and vaccinated little Jeff? Remember you wondered how he got that little scab on his arm?"

"Yessum, I remembers."

"That's all this is. If it didn't hurt a little boy, it certainly won't hurt you."

"Humph!" Tunia grunted. She gave Edward a dirty look and proceeded to roll up her sleeve, holding out her arm to Nathaniel. "Go ahead, do yo' thing."

In order that Lewis would be absent from the paper as little as possible, Margaret agreed to leave for the Boones' on Thursday, October 2. They would take the train, leaving at seven in the morning on the Richmond, Fredericksburg, and Potomac railroad, and hopefully arrive in the afternoon. The evening before, she was upstairs packing the baby's things when she heard a great deal of commotion from below.

When Cindy had answered the knock at the door, she found Andrew standing on the porch.

"It's Mas' Andrew!" she called.

Nancy dropped the sewing off her lap and hurried out into the hall, hugging her son. She wrinkled her nose and looked at his dirty, bearded, and torn countenance. By this time, the rest of the family had come up behind them.

"Oh Andrew!" Nancy laughed, hugging him again. "Are you well?" You're not hurt, are you?"

"No, Mother, I'm fine. But I warn you not to get too close to me until I've bathed." He shook his father's hand and gave Melissa and Mahaley each a peck on the cheek. "I'm very tired, but I think I better wash first before I sit down anywhere. I don't want to dirty up the house." He grinned at Tunia, who was peeking out of the dining room. "I know how fussy Tunia is about finding lice around the house."

Tunia grinned back at him and nodded her head. "I put de water on to bile now, Massa Andrew."

Margaret came downstairs and greeted her brother. He was surprised at how much she seemed to have aged in the few months he had been away. He sipped the whiskey his father had given him and studied Margaret. Little worry lines had begun to crease her forehead, there were dark circles under her eyes, and he thought he detected some gray hairs, even though she had just turned twenty-seven. Something was definitely bothering her, for he had never known her to concern herself, and the only time he could remember her distraught about anything was when she had been afraid she would grow up to be an old maid. Surely all this couldn't be because of Joseph's death. He felt her mourning was mostly all show.

"I got de water, Massa Andrew," Tunia told him. "Cindy be up wif it in a minute."

Andrew handed his empty glass to his father. "I'll be down in a little while. You'd best tell Tunia to boil my blanket too," he said, prodding the blanket roll with the toe of his shoe.

"We'll throw it away and get you a new one," Edward told him.

Andrew went upstairs and found he could almost fall asleep, even as cramped as his legs were in the shallow tub.

"Do all soldiers get so dirty?" Nancy wondered.

"They hardly have the time or the means for taking baths," Edward smiled.

Mahaley silently agreed and situated herself more comfortably in her chair. She knew firsthand now, after managing to pick up some of the lice from the two Florida soldiers with whom she had spent last Saturday afternoon. After a day of unbearable and very unladylike itching, she had finally gotten rid of them by using some of Tunia's strong lye soap. The chafing which the soap had caused was as bad as the lice. From now on, she was going to be more particular with whom she associated.

"Are you all packed and ready for tomorrow, dear?" Nancy asked Margaret.

She nodded. "It was very nice of Mr. McAllen to offer to come along. The more I thought about going alone, the more it concerned me. You're right—Fairfax County is awfully close to Washington City."

"Lewis isn't all bad," Edward smiled.

"Frankly, I'll be glad to have him out of the office for a while," Melissa grinned. "He's still fussing about Lincoln. And now that there's talk that the Yankees might allow blacks to join the army . . ."

"Disgusting," Edward remarked. "Bobo would cringe at the sight of a gun."

"What's Bobo doing with a gun?" Andrew asked, entering the room.

"Nothing, dear," Nancy replied. "We were just

talking about the possibility of blacks in the Union Army."

"Oh," Andrew poured himself another drink and sat down. "They'll never do it."

"I hope not," Mahaley murmured.

"Andrew dear," Nancy began. "President Davis arranged your transfer for you."

"He did? Where is it?"

"It's in my desk," Edward said. "I'll get it."

"And he says you can have a leave of absence for a month or two," Nancy went on. "He's going to have you as an aide when he goes on inspection of the troops. Isn't it exciting?"

"He wants me to be an aide? The president!" Andrew began to laugh.

"See, Andrew?" Mahaley said. "I told you when you first enlisted you might become a general."

"You've already been promoted to first lieutenant," Edward told him, returning and handing his son the document.

"Wait till I tell Ellen!" Andrew laughed. "Has anyone seen her?"

"She's fine," Nancy told him. "We've had Nathaniel and her over to supper several times."

"Did the silk material I asked you to get come in?"

"Mr. Ainsworth brought it last trip out," Edward said.

"It's the loveliest shade of green," Nancy told him. "It'll go so nicely with her green eyes. Andrew, I'm so glad you like her. She's such a sweet girl. I'd like to see you settle down with someone like her."

"I think I might too—someday."

Margaret bit her lip. Everyone had someone but her. She had tried to keep herself busy by spending long hours at the hospitals and with charities, but it wasn't enough—she wanted to be loved. Not physically, but just to have someone who cared for her. She could probably find a man if she tried, but she didn't really want another soldier for a husband. And she most definitely didn't want one who would be too demanding in bed. With these two prerequisites, her selection was very limited.

"I saw Jackson briefly at Sharpsburg," Andrew told Melissa. "Seems the Yankees had him cornered up a tree."

"Yes, I know. He wrote me about it."

"I'm beginning to think Jeb Stuart's bunch are invincible," Andrew remarked. "They never seem to sustain too many losses. 'Course, they rush in and get the hell out of there before the Yankees know what's happening."

"I guess you don't know," Melissa told him. "Jeremiah's in the army."

"He is? When did he come back home."

"He didn't," Nancy said. "He's a Yankee."

"A Yankee!"

"Now, Aunt Nancy, that really isn't fair," Melissa said. "He's in the medical corps."

"Of the Union Army!" Nancy sniffed.

Her aunt's derogatory comments hurt Melissa, for Jeremiah's conclusion to side with the Union came from his beliefs, as Nancy's choice for the Confederacy had been hers. He was as much a part of the family as she, and she was sure his decision had not been an easy one to make.

"They're not so bad," Andrew told his mother. "One fellow from our brigade was wounded and taken to their field hospital. When he said he had seven kids back home, the doc wrote out a pass for him to get back to our lines. Was Jeremiah at Sharpsburg?"

"I don't know."

"I'd like to have seen him. I bet at least he had good clothes and plenty to eat."

Charlie was sitting outside the hospital tent with Jeremiah.

"Damn my luck," Charlie muttered, tracing patterns in the dirt with a stick. "I find myself a nice little Rebel battle flag lying in the dirt to send home to my kids, and now I'm afraid to. I don't want to send them anything that might have Reb smallpox on it."

"Maybe you'll get another someplace."

The smallpox epidemic had struck the Federal camp as well as the Confederates. The Yankees thought it was Rebel smallpox, and the Southerners thought it was Yankee smallpox. Regardless of whose it was, it was causing a delay. The main body of the army had moved a few miles away, while isolation tents were filled with the sick men. Jeremiah had stayed behind along with two orderlies and several members of the band who had already been vaccinated. It was their job to nurse the men back to health if possible, but so far, luck had not been too good. A small detail of pickets posted around the camp also served as a burial party when it was necessary. There had been no concentrated effort to vaccinate the Union soldiers, as the Confederates had done, and consequently the disease was rampant. About all that could be done for the stricken men was to give them plenty of fresh air and cover their sores with an ointment made from linseed oil and limewater.

"How long do you figure we'll be stuck at this pesthouse?" Charlie wondered.

"There's no telling. I think maybe it's run its course. Anyway, at least we haven't had any new cases brought in yesterday or today. I'm going to need more opium, though. And I was thinking about giving the patients who were past their delirium regular doses of wine."

Charlie grinned. "Maybe I should get sick too."

Jeremiah grinned back at him. "Are you sure you don't have any stationery that doesn't have flags and patriotic pictures all over it?"

"I told you—no. Mattie gave me a whole stack of it so's I'd be sure to write to her."

Jeremiah grunted. He wanted to write Melissa, but he didn't want to send it in an envelope with "The Union Forever" printed across the front. He stood up. "I think I'll see if I can't borrow a horse and go pick up that morphine. Maybe somebody at the main camp has some plain writing paper—or at least an envelope."

"I'll go with you."

Charlie and Jeremiah borrowed two horses from the pickets and started off toward the main body of the army, Charlie's ornamental musician's sword their only weapon. They were amazed at how tidy the camp appeared and how none of the men seemed to be idling around. Stopping near the large hospital tent of Dr. Miltenberger, they tethered their horses and stepped inside.

Charlie stopped short, goggling at the tall dark man shaking hands with one of the patients. Charlie nudged Jeremiah in the side as the man straightened up, his stovepipe hat clutched in his hand.

"I think, under the circumstances, Dr. Miltenberger, you and your staff have done wonders," the man said. "I

389

shall try to persuade congress to appropriate more funds for ambulances."

"Thank you, Mr. President." Miltenberger's eyes fell on Jeremiah. "Here's one of my staff now."

Lincoln turned and looked at Charlie and Jeremiah. Charlie felt his legs turn to jelly.

"Mr. President, this is Dr. Armstrong," Miltenberger said.

Jeremiah shook hands with the man and gazed up at his somewhat sad face.

"I'm honored, sir," Jeremiah said, his voice cracking with emotion. His fingers seemed to tingle from their contact with this awe-inspiring man.

"You doctors do our country a great service," Lincoln said. He smiled slightly as he noticed the ornamental braid on Charlie's uniform. He extended his hand to Charlie. "And so does the band."

Charlie took the firm grip of the President. "Thank you, sir."

"Dr. Armstrong is attending to the smallpox cases," Miltenberger explained.

"And how are they doing?"

"Fair to middling, sir."

Lincoln smiled again. "I haven't heard that expression used in a long while. You must be a country boy, like myself."

General McClellan was scowling in the background. He knew Lincoln had come to see him, not socialize with the musicians and doctors. Even though the army of the Potomac was in need of everything from shoes to horses, the Confederates were in far worse shape, and Lincoln wanted an offensive. McClellan wanted to wait a month or two to get his army back into fighting strength.

"As soon as I get back to Washington City, I shall endorse your proposal to vaccinate all new recruits, Dr. Miltenberger," Lincoln said.

"Thank you, sir."

The President nodded pleasantly to Charlie and Jeremiah and left the tent, followed by Dr. Miltenberger and General McClellan.

"Wait till I write Mattie and the kids about this!" Charlie exclaimed. "They won't give a hoot about that old flag now!"

Margaret stood by the porch railing, gazing out into the fields, watching as three of the Boones' slaves herded the cows in from the pasture. Two little pickaninnies were playing in the driveway as the sunset shaded the horizon in beautiful tones of pink and orange. She felt she had accomplished much on her visit. The Boones were delighted with their grandson and hadn't dwelt too much on Joseph's memory. They had generously given her four cows, a bull, two roosters, a dozen chickens, and eight sheep. The Boones hadn't nearly the fine stock they once had—soldiers from both armies had seen to that. But they had been fortunate up to now, despite the fact that much of the surrounding countryside had been made desolate by the battles fought so near. Thaddeus Boone was glad to have some of his stock go to the hospital, for he doubted if he could hold on to it much longer. The county had been in the possession of both the Federals and Confederates, and he felt it would change hands at least a few times more before this war was ended. For his own protection, the old man had buried some gold and the family silver in the yard.

Lewis had been very helpful, and Margaret was grateful to him. He had made arrangements for the stock to be shipped to Richmond, and he would arrange for its delivery to the hospital. In the four days they had been here, he had been very attentive and solicitous of her, and it made her feel much better about things. She knew he was only being kind because he was her father's friend, but his attentions were appreciated.

"It's lovely," Lewis remarked, coming out of the house and standing beside her. "I wish we had sunsets like these in the city."

"Yes."

"I think I shall miss this place," he said. "I wish I didn't have to go back to the paper."

"You could leave the paper, now that you're doing so well with the ship."

"Leave the paper? The newspaper's my life. If I didn't have that to think about, I would have nothing."

Margaret smiled at him. "I sometimes feel that way about my work at the hospital."

"You have your son and your family. I have no one."

"You have friends."

"But friends aren't always enough." Lewis put his hand over Margaret's, resting on the porch railing. She looked at him in surprise. "Perhaps we two lonely people should see more of each other when we return to the city?"

"Mr. McAllen, I . . ."

"Call me Lewis. Mr. McAllen makes me feel like I'm just one of your father's friends. And I wish you wouldn't think of me as that."

Margaret looked at him and wondered if Lewis might not be a way out of her loneliness. He wasn't exactly what she had in mind for a man, but he wasn't a soldier; neither did she feel he would be a sex fiend. She smiled at him. "All right, Lewis."

Sixteen

Jeb had been conferring and visiting Lee a great deal in the last few days, and Jackson knew some sort of campaign was about to begin. And when Jeb was as secretive as he had been, the men knew it was something big.

On the evening of October 8, Jeb selected 1,800 troopers, putting 600 men each under the commands of Wade Hampton, Rooney Lee, and W. E. Jones, with John Pelham taking four of his guns. After checking Gypsy's harness and cleaning his gun, Jackson turned in for the night, sorry he would be leaving before he heard from Melissa. He had hoped he could get away from camp long enough for a visit, but evidently that was not to be.

The next morning, the troops assembled, and Jeb read them an order. They were about to undertake an expedition into the enemy's country, where property of the United States was to be seized, chiefly horses. Each brigade commander was to have one third of his men engaged in gathering and leading horses. All horses were to be paid for by receipt of the Confederate Government, whereby the owners could seek recourse with the United States Government. There was to be no individual plundering, and no property, except government property, was to be touched. As ransom for previously abducted Virginians, public officials were to be taken prisoner and treated kindly.

"I repeat, soldiers—no straggling, no looting, and no foraging off the line of march. The destination and extent of this expedition had best be kept to myself for the time being. We will leave at midnight."

Jackson managed to find a scrap of paper to dash off a note to Melissa and tell her he was leaving on another expedition, and from Jeb's attitude, he felt it would be every bit as dramatic and exciting as their ride around McClellan.

Jackson slept a little, and then joined Jeb at eleven o'clock, finding him sitting on his horse, contemplating the stars.

"We're going to Pennsylvania, aren't we?" Jackson asked.

Jeb looked at him and smiled. "Reckon we are."

The column moved out, under a star-filled sky, leather creaking and sabers jingling against the stirrup irons.

As they crossed the Maryland border into Pennsylvania, detachments were sent out to scour the countryside for horses. Despite Jeb's orders, the men came back to the column with hams, turkeys, and beef strapped to their saddles, while haversacks bulged with bread, butter, and crocks of thick cream. Most of the day was spent impressing horses, except for those driven by ladies.

At noon, they rode into Mercersburg. As the column clattered down the main street, startled Pennsylvanians came out of their houses and shops to stare at the gray troopers. Jackson spotted a shoe store and reined in his horse. He stepped inside the shop, to find the owner and his daughter stuffing their money into a bag, evidently attempting to hide it before the Confederates tore the town apart.

"Howdy, folks," Jackson smiled, doffing his hat to them. "I wouldn't like to inconvenience you any, seeing as how you were about to close up shop, but I was wondering if you might have a pair of boots—size eleven."

The little shoemaker swallowed and glanced at his daughter. "Take whatever you want and leave," he told Jackson.

John Pelham entered the shop, and the fright on the man's face increased.

"Hello, Johnny," Jackson said. "I've been trying to get myself a new pair of boots, but all this here feller can do is stare at me."

"I need a pair too," John remarked. "Not very hospitable, is he?"

"He surely isn't, and that's a fact," Jackson said, reaching inside his jacket. The man pushed his daughter behind him, certain Jackson was reaching for a hidden gun. Instead, Jackson pulled out a handful of crumpled Confederate notes. He set them on the counter and looked at the man. "I expect that ought to cover the price of a pair of boots. So if you'll kindly find my size, I'll be on my way and won't trouble you anymore—that's size eleven, remember?"

The little man's eyes widened as he looked at the notes. John took out some money and placed it next to Jackson's.

"I wear size ten and a half."

"Papa," the girl said, "do what they want so they'll leave."

"Thank you, miss," John remarked. "We're in a bit of a hurry."

The little man seemed to visibly relax after the money had been picked up by his daughter. He checked through his stock for the proper sizes.

"This money isn't any good here," the girl said.

"Your government will take care of it for you," Jackson told her.

The man handed a pair of finely crafted boots to Jackson. "I'm still looking for yours," he told John.

John nodded politely. "I'm Major John Pelham of the horse artillery, and this is Lieutenant Colonel Jackson Vaughn of the First Virginia cavalry."

"Pleased to meet you," Jackson told the man, extending his hand.

The little Pennsylvanian took the proffered hand and shook it cautiously. Then he took John's hand, amazed at how courteous these men were. He had expected them to be near-barbarians. Both southerners were enjoying the little man's trepidation immensely.

"I'm Albert Hudson, and this is my daughter Hester," the man said.

John smiled politely at the girl. "Pleased to meet you, miss."

Jackson sat down and proceeded to try on his new boots while Albert Hudson found a pair for John. The leather was soft and pliant, and Jackson couldn't remember when his feet had felt so comfortable in a new pair of boots.

"Our soldiers will be out looking for you," Hester said.

"I don't expect they even know we're here."

"Oh, yes, they do," Albert stated, handing the boots to John. "It came over the telegraph early this morning."

Jackson looked up from fastening his spurs to his new boots. "What do they know?"

"The whole army knows you're here. Appears a signal post spotted you in Maryland."

Indeed, it was true. At five-thirty that morning, a party of the Twelfth Illinois cavalry had seen them crossing the Potomac River. A courier was sent out, and soon telegraph keys were chattering to a dozen Federal posts.

Jackson stood up. "Much obliged, Mr. Hudson. I'll see you later, Johnny."

Jackson found Jeb sitting on the sidewalk, drinking milk and eating ham. He offered some to Jackson.

"The Yankees know we're here," Jackson told him, sitting down.

"I know."

Jackson admired Jeb's coolness and seeming unconcern. He took a chunk of ham and gnawed on it. "What are you going to do about it?"

"Go on," Jeb replied. "We've still got a bridge to burn at Chambersburg."

Many of the men had availed themselves of the merchants in Mercersburg, and as the column left the town, there were many new shirts and boots and belts among the cavalry. They stopped to feed the horses in a cornfield a few miles above the city, while the details went out and surprised the rich Dutch farmers working in their barns.

It began to rain as they approached the outskirts of Chambersburg, and Jackson pulled on his oilcloth poncho. From the hilltop, he could see the lights of the town. Jeb had John Pelham set up his guns, commanding the town in case of any resistance, and then Wade Hampton took nine men with him into town, demanding its surrender.

Jackson pulled his poncho closer around his shoulders and watched as a small party returned. Union Colonel A. K. McClure was with them and told Jeb the town was undefended.

"Resistance would be futile," Jeb told him. "We wish to avoid the loss of life and property. We'll take only what we need and only United States property will be seized and destroyed."

As the column moved into town, the local provost marshal managed to get off a message before the wires were cut by two of Jeb's men. Jeb ordered the vault of the town's bank emptied, but the money had already been taken to safety. The courtly manner of the raiders so impressed the bank's cashier, he had his wife and servants bring them food.

Jones had taken a detail out to destroy the Cumberland Valley railroad bridge, the major objective of the expedition. They returned to report failure, for the bridge was made of iron, and their torches and axes did no damage.

Jeb and Jackson settled in a house at the edge of town, studying maps and making plans with Rooney Lee and Wade Hampton. The men behaved with the utmost courtesy toward the citizens of Chambersburg during the night. A group of wounded Federals were taken prisoner and immediately paroled. One group of Jeb's men who needed fuel for their campfire asked permission of the owner of a house if they could use his picket fence.

The next morning, most of the town's stores were closed, and the cavalry did no looting except to break into a government warehouse where some uniforms were stored. They replaced their old patched jackets and pants with new ones before leaving the town. Jackson had not worn a blue jacket for a year and a half, and he wondered what Melissa would think if she could see him now.

As the rear guard left Chambersburg, they set fire to the train depot, a machine shop, and several government warehouses. Jackson turned in his saddle and watched the smoke, wondering if this would be the last time he ever spent a night in Pennsylvania.

To confuse pursuit by the Yankees, Jeb had made it a point to let the people of the town think he was heading toward Gettysburg. But instead he led his men within seven miles of that soon-to-be-famous town. They turned at the village of Cashtown and headed back toward Hagerstown in Maryland. Once they crossed the border, Jeb ordered the horse details to be brought up to prevent straggling.

One trooper, a gaunt, disheveled-looking man with two huge pistols tucked in his waistband, rode beside Jackson for a while, leading his captive horses. He grinned at Jackson, revealing several missing teeth.

"You look happy, Corporal," Jackson remarked.

"I was just thinkin' about that farmhouse I stopped at a ways back. I was hungry, so I went up and knocked on the door and asked if they could give me somethin' to eat. I reckon the menfolk had all run off 'cause there was just two women and some babies. They told me they didn't have no food—nary a scrap." The trooper bit off a chaw of tobacco and worked on it for a moment before continuing. "Well, Colonel, I looked at them little pink Pennsylvania babies and said to the woman, 'Ma'am, I ain't never et baby meat before, but it looks like I'm goin' to have to try it now.' I like to tell you, them women set out food so fast, it'd make your head spin!"

When the column reached Emmetsburg, they were fed buttermilk, bread, and meat by the citizens, who thought they were Federals, dressed in their new blue coats. It was nearly sundown when one of Jeb's scouts captured a Union courier, just a frightened boy. He told them the Philadelphia Lancers and some New York artillery were lying in wait for the Confederates at Frederick.

The force in Frederick had to be avoided, so Jeb turned his column east for an all-night ride. To keep from falling asleep, Jackson would dismount, lead Gypsy for a few miles, and then ride again. After midnight, Jeb and several others left the column and rode six miles out of their way to create a small diversion. However, that was not his only reason, for he knew a family whose sympathies were with the South, and stopped at their plantation. Whatever information he gained about the enemy's movements, he did not disclose to the others.

At the town of Hyattstown, Jackson was glad to see Jeb return to rejoin the cavalry. Twelve miles away lay safety, but Sugar Loaf Moutain was still ahead, where Jeb was sure the Yankees would, by now, have moved guns to block their escape. In Barnesville, they learned that the Federals were closing in on them. The area was thick with Yankees, and they were practically surrounded.

Captain White, one of Jeb's scouts, was now in the territory of his boyhood home and knew the area well, and he proposed a plan. After much show that they were still headed in the same direction, the column left the main road and started moving through a weed-grown cart track. They rode almost two miles until they reached a road parallel to the Potomac, still wearing the blue uniform coats they had gotten in Chambersburg.

It was there they saw the Federal riders.

Jeb led his men forward, and Jackson watched the Union leaders hesitate. With the mistaken identity working for him, Jeb raised his saber.

"Charge!" he shouted, galloping forward.

Jackson spurred Gypsy and charged toward the Federal cavalry. The Yankees fired a quick volley and fled. Jackson chased them for nearly a mile until he reached the top of a ridge. From there, he could look down on the enemy across the Little Monocacy River. Pelham brought up his guns and fired at the Yankees, who were digging in on the far bank. Rooney Lee took the main column over a farm road to approach the river crossing while Jeb stayed behind with several artillerymen to hold off the Yankees approaching from behind.

Jackson sat in his saddle as Rooney Lee peered through his glasses at the Yankee riflemen waiting for them. As a last effort to fool the Federals, Rooney scratched out a note demanding the Yankees' surrender. There was an anxious wait, as the Federals pondered the note, wondering how outnumbered they might be. Finally, Rooney fired upon them, and the Yankees retreated, assuming the risks were too great.

Pelham and his guns crossed the river, followed by the cavalry, and captured horses and mules. As the enemy was closing in from behind, Jeb managed to get his guns down the hill and safely across the river.

Jeb Stuart had done it again, and once more General McClellan was the source of embarrassment for the Union Army. From their trip into Pennsylvania, they had captured 1,200 strong horses, and some thirty mayors, postmasters, and various officials for exchange. In gratitude for his feat, Jeb received a pair of golden spurs from some lady admirers in Baltimore.

The women's committee organizing the charity function for the soldiers had decided to hold a dance instead of a bazaar. Because of the many shortages the citizens were now experiencing, no one really had the means to make trinkets and delicacies to sell. Nancy had suggested the dance instead, and the idea had been accepted. There were many attractive young girls in the city with whom the men would almost certainly be willing to pay fifty cents to dance. The money collected could then go toward the purchase of supplies for the soldiers. Varina Davis succeeded in obtaining the services of the small orchestra which always entertained at the executive mansion. The ladies of the committee each planned to donate some cakes or beverages for refreshment.

Margaret had dined with Lewis twice since they had returned to the city, and she had abandoned wearing the black mourning clothes. She, along with Mahaley and Melissa, had selected material from Edward's supply and had Sabina make them new gowns for the affair.

Saturday afternoon, the family left for Richmond Hall.

"Which one of us do you think will collect more money, Father?" Mahaley asked.

"I don't know."

"What makes you think any of you will?" Andrew teased. "There's lots of pretty girls in Richmond."

"I don't get tired easily," Mahaley said. "I'll outdance everybody there."

Edward looked at his three girls and smiled. He had to admit they were three of the most attractive women in the city. He then looked at Nancy. He realized much time had passed since she was a girl, but the years had been kind to her. The little lines at the corners of her eyes and the extra flesh under her chin only seemed to make her more charming to him. Had they not moved to the city, she would have undoubtedly fallen prey to the strain of hard work, but their comfortable life had kept Nancy attractive, and beauty was one thing which Edward enjoyed. He patted his wife's hand. "Will you save a dance for me, my dear?"

Nancy blushed. "Why, Edward, I hadn't planned on dancing for money. Who'd want to dance with an old woman like me?"

"I would," Edward told her. "You're not old."

"I'll be forty-six in December."

"And you've got it all over these young girls."

There was already a goodly crowd at the hall when they arrived. The price of admission was a donation for either the soldiers or the families of soldiers who had been killed—soap, candles, crockery, cooking utensils, shoes, blankets, clothes for children.

Varina Davis greeted the family. "You young ladies all look so lovely. It reminds me of the days before the war, when everybody had new dresses. You're very lucky to have access to the blockade-runner."

"You know you're welcome to anything the ship brings in, Mrs. Davis," Edward told her.

"That's very kind of you, Mr. Armstrong. But I feel we should live as Spartan a life as everyone else." She saw the expression on Edward's face. "That isn't to say you shouldn't reap the benefits of your enterprise, Mr. Armstrong. Without ships like yours, the South would surely have to surrender."

Robert E. Lee and Jefferson Davis joined the little group, greeting the Armstrong family.

"It's good to see so many people turning out today,"

Lee remarked. "I hope we can realize enough money to buy some proper overcoats for my boys." The band was beginning to tune up for the first dance. Lee held out his hand to Melissa. "Miss Armstrong, if you'll do me the honor, shall we get the dancing started?"

"Of course, General Lee," Melissa smiled, taking his hand and following him onto the dance floor.

Melissa enjoyed dancing with the courtly gentleman who stood nearly six feet, his broad shoulders accentuated by his uniform.

"I understand your beau is one of General Stuart's staff," Lee said.

"Yes, Lieutenant Colonel Jackson Vaughn."

"You must be very proud of him and the rest of General Stuart's staff, as we all are."

"Yes, I am."

The news of the Chambersburg raid had spread throughout the South, and the papers praised Jeb and his men for their daring and ingenuity.

While Melissa was dancing with General Lee, Henry entered the hall. He scanned the group of dancers until he spotted Melissa. He smiled to himself. "I wonder if she's finding anything out?" He wandered over to say hello to the president.

"I'm very proud of what the cavalry has done," Lee said. "When the war started, we had no cavalry. Now it's surpassed that of the Yankees."

"What do you plan to do next?" Melissa asked.

"Next?" Lee gave a little laugh, possibly reflecting on the Confederacy's recent losses out west. "Wait. Wait for the Yankees to make a move, and in the meantime, try to get ourselves better equipped."

"Are we really in that bad a shape?"

405

Lee smiled. "Let's talk of more pleasant things than war. It's not often that I have the opportunity to dance with a beautiful young woman."

After taking a bath and changing his clothes, George left the flat he occupied while in Richmond. He had arrived at Wilmington two days ago and had spent a miserable thirty-four hours on the train. He wished the tracks could be repaired properly and stay that way, but he realized what little iron there was in the South had to be stretched to accommodate many things. Tired, but too tense to sleep, he decided to pay a visit to the Armstrongs and make his report to Edward. That part of it could certainly wait, but he was looking forward to seeing Melissa.

George wondered if the nervousness he experienced when he was near her was noticeable to anyone else. He had no explanation for it, other than he wanted her more than he had ever wanted a woman in his life. He assumed his frustration stemmed from the fact that Melissa was unattainable. He knew he was gone for long periods and was too unsure of himself to try to hold on to a woman from whom he would be absent for so much of the time. He had been hurt once with his unhappy marriage, and he didn't want to be hurt again. Besides, Melissa was obviously devoted to her cavalryman. Nevertheless, George wanted to see her.

After walking the few blocks to the Armstrong house, he stepped up on the porch and let the brass knocker fall against the door.

Cindy answered, always somewhat impressed when she saw the lean, impeccably dressed foreigner. "Hello Mista Ainsworth."

"Hello Cindy. Is Mr. Armstrong in?"

"Nossuh. He and de family all gone to de dance."

"Dance?"

"Yessuh. I reckon de whole town's dere."

"I see. Do you think it would be all right if I took the horse?"

"Yessuh, I reckon it would. Masta Edward, he say yo' kin use him while you's here. Yo' come in, and I'll send Bobo to put on de saddle."

George stepped inside. "I'll go with him."

George followed Bobo out to the stable and carriage house where tack and equipment hung neatly on the walls. The two grays which pulled the carriage, Edward's black stallion and Andrew's mare, were in their stalls, along with Jeremiah's roan. George stroked his nose and gave him a lump of sugar, even more a delicacy for horses than humans, nowadays.

"I brought five whole pounds of sugar from Nassau especially for you, Bax."

"Dat hawse, he sho' do like sugar," Bobo remarked, leading the animal out of its stall. "Miss Melissa, she spoilt him afore sugar was so hard to git."

"Bobo, do you know if Miss Melissa's going to marry that cavalryman?"

"Cunnel Vaughn? I don' rightly know, suh. He ain't been here fo' a while."

"He hasn't?"

"Nossuh. Not fo' a long time." Grinning, Bobo looked up from tightening the cinch, his white teeth gleaming. "Yo' like Miss Melissa?"

George cleared his throat, reddening. "Why, yes, I like her." He hoped he wasn't as transparent as Bobo led him to believe. He decided to change the subject. "Where is

407

this dance?"

When George arrived at the hall, he discovered he had nothing to donate, so he gave the woman at the door a twenty-dollar gold eagle. Her eyes widened as she thanked him, for here was twenty dollars that really was twenty dollars. George made his way through the people to where Edward was sipping punch with Nancy.

"Mr. Ainsworth!" Edward said in surprise. "I didn't expect to see you here."

George shook hands with Edward and turned to Nancy. "Hello, Mrs. Armstrong. The ship got in the day before yesterday. We had a very easy time of it."

"How did you do with the cotton?" Edward wondered.

George grinned. "Very well, indeed, sir."

"Lewis will be pleased to know that. He's dancing out there somewhere with my daughter now."

George's eyes traveled over the dancers, failing to find Lewis and Margaret but falling on Melissa and Henry. At that moment, she glanced in his direction and waved. George waved back.

"Who were you waving to?" Henry wondered.

"Mr. Ainsworth," Melissa replied. "I didn't even know he was in town. Henry, you haven't told any of your—whoever they are—about Uncle Edward's ship, have you?"

"No. I told you I wouldn't." He contemplated the creamy skin of her well-rounded bosom against the pale lavender of her gown. "Besides, if the ship can bring in material to make you dresses like this, I'm all for it."

Melissa smiled. "Thank you, Henry."

"Anyway, I like Mr. Ainsworth, from the little I've seen of him. I'd hate to have him sitting in jail someplace—or worse."

"Worse?"

"Well, you know, those patrols don't take kindly to blockade-runners. Sometimes they have to use their guns."

Melissa and Henry joined the others when the dance was finished.

"Hello, Mr. Ainsworth," Melissa said.

"Hello Miss Armstrong, Mr. Walkenfeldt."

"You made the trip safe and sound?" Henry asked him.

"Not a problem. I'm beginning to think those patrols are all asleep out there," George said. "But I'm more inclined to think it's due to the talents of our pilot."

Andrew was talking to President Davis while another man had claimed Ellen for a dance.

"I want to tell you how much I appreciate what you've done for me and how honored I am to be your aide," Andrew told him.

"I don't want to be accused of playing favorites," Davis said. "But your family's done a lot for the South, and you've earned a little rest. I understand you were injured at Malvern Hill."

"Oh, it was just a scratch." Andrew unconsciously touched the scar on his forehead, marring his otherwise good looks.

"It appears now you'll have a longer furlough than I'd planned," Davis told him. "I won't be leaving for the West until around Christmas."

"Well, if there's anything I can do in the meantime . . ."

"Not a thing. Just enjoy that pretty little girl of yours."

*   *   *

Meanwhile, George had asked Melissa to dance.

"I warn you, it'll cost you fifty cents," she said.

"It would be cheap at twice the price."

Melissa smiled, and they joined the other dancers on the floor. For the first time since she had known him, Melissa felt relaxed with George.

"That dress is from some of the material I brought in last time, isn't it?" he asked.

"Yes it is. Did you pick out all the material yourself?"

"Some of it. The shipping agent's daughter helped with most of it. I don't have much feel for that sort of thing. I know what looks nice, but I'm not too certain of good quality."

"Well, this is certainly very good quality. What's this shipping agent's daughter like?"

"Charlotte? Oh, she's all right, I suppose."

Melissa found herself becoming curious as to just how well George knew this Charlotte, and then wondered why it should be of any interest to her.

"You're on a first-name basis with her, then?" Melissa remarked.

"Well, I spend a good deal of time at their house when I'm in town."

"Is she pretty?"

"Sort of. She's engaged to a chap who's captain on another blockade-runner."

"Oh." Melissa chided herself for being so inquisitive. If she didn't watch herself, she was liable to become as meddlesome as Mahaley. "Do you like Nassau?"

George smiled a little. "Yes and no. It's a bit too wild for my tastes."

*   *   *

The dance was a great success, and the ladies were able to place an order for five hundred overcoats with Edward. Besides the money, they collected a variety of useful things for the soldiers' widows and children.

On Monday, the owners of the *Grasshopper* pored over the books late into the night, and all of them left feeling considerably more prosperous than before. Lewis decided to look around to see if there were any little cottages for sale, hoping Margaret's friendliness toward him was an encouraging sign.

While riches flowed into the pockets of these men, most of the city was finding it harder to stretch their ever-decreasing dollars to meet the rising prices. Every week, a red auction flag was waving somewhere along the street, signaling the sale of fine goods in order that their owners might eat or be well clothed. Jewelers' stores were full of merchandise, and the most spectacular collections of diamonds and pearls were displayed in their windows. Their owners, too, had sold them to purchase the necessities to live.

On the last afternoon of October, before going to the Armstrong house for supper, George was strolling along Main Street, when he stopped to gaze at the window of one such jeweler's shop. The dazzling gems caught his eye, especially one particular diamond tiara. Not really knowing why, he entered the shop and inquired its price. George had never seen such magnificent jewelry before, and when he realized these precious stones could be purchased with Confederate money, he decided it might be a very wise investment. After examining the merchandise carefully, he decided on his original selection of the tiara. He really had no idea what he would do with it, for he couldn't quite picture it sitting atop his

411

mother's gray head, but bargains and opportunities like this had come seldom in his life.

Melissa was just coming out of the post office as George was passing.

"I hope I'll have some company on my way to your house," George said, touching the wide brim of his felt hat.

Melissa had been intent on studying the envelope in her hand, and looked at George, startled, "Oh, Mr. Ainsworth, it's you."

"I hope you don't mind if I walk along with you?"

"Not at all. I'd be glad of the company."

Melissa pulled her shawl a little tighter around her shoulders, against the bite of the fall air, and dropped the letter into her reticule.

"A letter from your sweetheart?" George asked.

"No. From my brother. And I'm very glad to get it. I haven't heard from him since August, and I've been worried about him."

"He's the only family you have, then? Besides your family here, I mean."

"Yes, and I miss him very much."

"Perhaps you could go visit him."

"In a Yankee camp? How could I?"

"You know the president. Surely you could get some sort of pass. I'm sure they wouldn't think you were carrying information to the enemy."

"Oh, Mr. Ainsworth, do you think I could?"

George grinned at her. "Don't ask me; I'm only a stranger here."

"Oh, but I don't even know where he is. I don't even know how this letter got here. Besides, Mr. McAllen

412

would never give me time off to do that."

George smiled. "You might have a point there."

Nancy, Margaret and Andrew were gathered in the drawing room when George and Melissa arrived. Andrew served them all some port while Melissa hurried to read the letter aloud:

26 September, 1862

Dear Melissa,

I hope this letter reaches you. I was told to send it to a man in Alexandria who would get it through the lines. I had my first taste of battle, and I can tell you it is such a waste of life. Our hospital was so full of wounded, we ran out of places to put them. My commanding general, Joseph Mansfield, was shot, and he was brought in too late to save him. I am now under command of General Henry Slocum. My superior is Dr. Sidney Miltenberger of Pittsburgh, and he is a fine fellow. The only other doctor for our brigade besides myself is Dr. Alfred Nichols. He is a little older than I, but I am above him, as I have more medical training.

Right now, I am not with the main body of the army. There has been a smallpox epidemic in the army, and I am in charge of the isolation camp. There are two orderlies to help, and six members of the band. I must tell you about one of them, for he has become my best friend here. His name is Charlie Ahlborn, and he is from Allegheny City, too. He is a lot of fun and always joking, and he never lets his brass horn out of his sight. I would be very lonely

413

here without him to talk to. He was injured at Bull Run, and I treated him while I was still in school. I also treated his brother-in-law for a laceration in the leg. In fact, he was the first patient I ever operated on.

Charlie and I had some excitement the other day. We had to go into the main camp, and guess who we met? President Abraham Lincoln! He even shook my hand. He was there visiting patients in the hospital and talking with General McClellan. Rumor has it that he's going to be replaced. . . .

"We can thank Jeb Stuart for that," Andrew laughed. Melissa continued:

We are all getting fat here, for all the farmers send in their food for us and for the patients. I am feeling fine, and hope you are too. I hope Uncle Edward didn't get too upset when you told him what I had done. I am certainly not an enemy, nor do I think most of these men are. They want this war to end so they can get home to their families. . . .

"Humph!" Nancy exclaimed. "Then why don't they just go home and leave us alone!"

"Go on, Melissa," Margaret urged.

Melissa once again felt hurt at Nancy's anger at Jeremiah. She found her place and continued:

I just don't know where I will be for you to send my mail to me, but perhaps it will reach me if you send it to me at Army Medical Corps, Army of the Potomac, Twelfth Corps. I hope to hear from you soon, for letters bring a little warmth to this otherwise terrible job I must do.

Your loving brother,
Jeremiah.

"So he met Lincoln," Andrew remarked.

Nancy was still smarting over the fact that Jeremiah had joined with the enemy. Andrew, from the little contact he had had with the Yankees, felt the Union soldiers were in basically the same predicament as he; he was there simply because there was a war going on, and he happened to live below the Mason-Dixon Line, while his cousin made his home above it.

Margaret surprised everyone by saying, "I think it's a fine thing he's doing." The corners of her mouth turned up a little in a rare smile. "The thing I find hard to comprehend is the fact that he's a grown man. I can only remember him as a little boy more interested in pulling Mahaley's pigtails than anything else."

Margaret's comment made Nancy soften, as she recalled the two bright-eyed happy children of Edward's brother who had filled their house with laughter so many years ago. She looked at Melissa, who was carefully folding the letter to put back into its envelope. "I'm very glad he's well and safe, Melissa. He was a dear little boy."

"Thank you, Aunt Nancy."

Melissa hoped in the future whenever Jeremiah's name was mentioned that her aunt would remember him thusly, instead of as an enemy.

George had been quietly taking all this in and sipping his port. He thought about a magnificent diamond necklace in the jeweler's shop and wished he had the right to present it to Melissa. The gems would look so lovely on her, and he knew she was the only woman who could do them justice. Regardless of whether he ever had the opportunity to give it to her, George made up his mind to cash in some of his gold for Confederate notes and return to the jeweler's shop in the morning. Even if the necklace never left his possession, it would still be a good investment.

Andrew stood up to refill his and George's glasses. "You know, Melissa," he said, while he was pouring the liquor, "it's too bad Jeremiah isn't a little more closely associated with the high brass. You might be able to learn some very useful information from him. And then I could sort of pass that information on to my superiors, and I might earn myself another promotion."

Melissa's eyes widened. She had been deep in thought about Jeremiah's reference to whom she believed to be Henry, and was thankful that no names had been mentioned. "Why, Andrew, you aren't suggesting . . . ?"

"I'm not suggesting anything," he said, handing George his glass. "Jeremiah's only a doctor."

Edward and Mahaley came in from work at the War Department. Edward shook George's hand and gave each of his ladies a kiss on the cheek.

"Father, tell them about the funny little boat," Mahaley urged.

"Let me sit down and relax first," Edward said, getting himself a drink.

"It's the strangest thing," Mahaley told them. "And it's top secret, but Father saw the plans, and he showed them to me. Oh, I'm so excited! I got to see the thing that's in the Federal Navy!"

"What is it?" Andrew asked.

"It's an underwater ship," Edward said. "Apparently,

416

it can move underneath the surface of the water with a crew inside."

"How would they breathe?" George wondered.

"I don't know. But they're building it at Mobile right now."

The first submarine was to be made from an old twenty-five-foot-long boiler. Two hatches rose from the top, and there was an air box which could admit fresh air, provided the craft was very near the surface of the water. Crude ballast tanks could be filled and emptied from inside by hand pumps. Eight crew members could propel the boat by turning the shaft like a crank. The weapon was a torpedo, towed behind and intended to smash against the hull of an enemy ship.

"The whole thing sounds crazy," Andrew laughed. "You couldn't get me into one of those."

"But if it works . . ." Edward smiled.

"Might help us with the blockade," George remarked.

"That's something I wanted to talk to you about," Andrew said. "I haven't mentioned it to anyone yet, but I'd like to go along on your next trip."

"Andrew!" Nancy exclaimed.

"It's all right with me," George replied.

"Father?" Andrew asked.

"I don't know. What about your army duties?"

"President Davis said he wouldn't be leaving till about Christmas. I figure I can be back in time. And I would like to see what it's like—meet the people you're dealing with overseas."

"I trust Mr. Ainsworth's judgment on that."

"Please, Father."

"When do you figure the *Grasshopper* will be back for you?" Edward asked George.

"In a week or so, I should imagine. And I'm sure Captain Bubb wouldn't mind if Andrew came along—after all, it's your ship."

"Let me give it some thought."

Jackson was sitting in Jeb's tent one evening in the first week of November, playing chess. The snow had begun to fall lightly outside, and he could hear Sweeny's banjo in the distance.

"I wish I could get away to Richmond," Jackson said.

Jeb smiled. "You really miss that little gal of yours?"

"Yes."

"Quite a turnabout for you—settling down to just one woman."

Jackson shrugged.

"Well, I'd like to be able to say go in and see her," Jeb said. "But I can't. We have to stay close till we figure out what the Yankees are up to. Darned if I can figure 'em out. Now that they've got Harper's Ferry again, they keep moving troops around here and there. . . ."

Heros Von Borcke entered the tent.

"Howdy, Heros," Jeb grinned.

"Hello, mein General. A telegram came for you." Heros handed Jeb the paper and left the tent.

Jackson watched Jeb read it, and then his head slumped over the table, burying his face in his arms, a great sob shaking his shoulders. Jackson picked up the telegram and read it. Little Flora Stuart had died that morning.

Jackson felt tears well up in his own eyes as he stood and touched his friend's shoulder. He knew Jeb's little daughter had been ailing, but Jeb couldn't leave the camp to go visit her. He had no idea how serious it had been.

"I'll never see her laughing little face again," Jeb moaned. "Not in this world at least."

Jackson gave him another pat and left the tent, knowing it best to leave his old friend alone with his grief. He sat down on a log by the now-extinguished camp fire and felt a warm tear roll down his cheek and begin to turn to ice. "Will it never end? When a man can't go to visit his dying child or see his sweetheart—families separated for years—it has gone too far." Jackson held his head in his hands and let the snow fall on his shoulders and melt down the back of his neck.

Seventeen

The docks of Nassau were looming over the bow of the *Grasshopper* as Andrew stood on the deck, watching the bright sunshine reflect off the sails in the harbor. After the first day out, Andrew had found his sea legs, and it had been a relatively easy voyage—until yesterday. While leaving the North Carolina coast, they had had to outrace a Federal cruiser, and during the chase had apparently scraped a piece of coral. They thought no damage had been done, but yesterday the *Grasshopper* sprang a leak. Captain Bubb had crept slowly toward the Bahamas, trying to keep as much strain off the hull as possible. Now, watching the gulls circling above him, Andrew at least knew he could swim to shore if needed.

And what a shore, he thought. Such greenery with occasional bursts of color along the low slopes. A few wispy clouds floated on a blue sky, whose color was mirrored by the clear waters.

"Quite a sight, isn't it?" George remarked, joining him at the rail.

"I've never seen anything like it before in my life. I used to think our Shenandoah Valley was beautiful, but this is beyond my imagination. I wish Ellen could see it."

"So it's Ellen now? And wasn't it just the other day you were asking me about the shipping agent's daughter?"

"A man's got to have a little fun while he's away from home, doesn't he?" Andrew grinned.

"If it's a lively time you want, you'll find it here. But I warn you, stay out of the waterfront taverns and brothels. They'll slit your throat for a penny, the same as a fortune."

The cargo was unloaded, and George paid off the crew—one hundred dollars in gold and fifty dollars in bounty. Joe Majors made the arrangements for repairs to the ship. The docks were lined with warehouses full of crates marked NAILS, COMBUSTIBLES, AND MERCHANDISE, all ready to be shipped to the South. In a hired carriage, George, Andrew, Will, and Jacob drove through the busy streets to the Royal Victoria Hotel. The proprietors welcomed them as if they were royalty, for in a way, they were. Blockade-running had given this tiny island undreamed-of prosperity.

A black boy dressed in a clean white jacket carried Andrew's luggage to his room, an elegant suite with a balcony overlooking the lush green slopes. He ordered a bath to be sent up and gave the clothes he had been wearing to the boy to have them cleaned and pressed. After his bath, Andrew poured himself some rum from the decanter on the table and stepped out onto the balcony.

"What a paradise! And what a fool I was to join the army when I could have spent the war here."

The next day, Andrew accompanied George to the office of the Colon Trading Company, with whom he did business on the island. He was surprised at how sumptuous the office was compared to the dingy little export company's office where his father had worked before the war. Along with George, he was ushered into a private office, where he was introduced to the owner, Sir Thomas Lacey, a stocky middle-aged man who bore the appearance of overindulgence in too much food and drink. He wore a neatly-trimmed beard to try to cover his pockmarked cheeks, and Andrew felt sure the man used shoeblack on his hair.

The man rose from his desk and came around to pump George's hand. "George, my lad, it's good to see you."

"It's good to be back—especially this time."

"I can well imagine. One of my boys went down to the dock to see the cotton and told me about the damage to the ship."

"Sir Thomas, I'd like you to meet Andrew Armstrong of Richmond, Virginia."

Sir Thomas extended his hand. "You're very young to be part owner of a ship."

"That's my father, sir," Andrew said, accepting his hand.

"Of course, of course. Glad you could come along. Sit down. I'll pour you a glass of wine and we can get down to business."

Andrew sat down and studied the man as he poured the wine.

"The price of cotton's rising again," Sir Thomas said. "Probably in anticipation of the winter months. Those nine hundred bales should bring a nice price."

"There was a little water damage to about fifty of them," George told him. "We were able to get most of the ones closest to the leak up on deck." He opened his case and slid a sheet of paper across the desk to Sir Thomas. "There's the list of things we'll want to take back with us."

Sir Thomas put on his spectacles and scanned the list. "I don't think there should be any problem with any of this. I'll have my boys gather some of this up and put it in one of our warehouses for your inspection. We'll get some of this business out of the way this morning." He looked at Andrew. "I'd like you and George to dine at our house tonight—meet my wife and girls. We'd all love to hear how the war's going."

"Thank you, sir."

Andrew was very bored while he waited for George and Sir Thomas to conclude their business. He had to give George credit for trying to get the best deal for his father's money. He had been wondering just how honest George was, but he felt now that he could report to his father that George was their biggest asset—perhaps even more important than the ship itself. For without an honest man to look out for their interests, the enterprise might well be a disaster.

After leaving the offices of Sir Thomas, they drove down to the dock to see how long the repairs might delay their return. Andrew was relieved to learn it would only be three to four days, for he had visions of missing his trip to the west with the president. Now it appeared he would have plenty of time to explore this tropical paradise.

"I need to find a good watchmaker," Andrew said.

"I think that can be arranged," George replied. "I know a fine watchmaker here. I bought myself one the first time out."

"And a gunsmith."

"I think I can help you out there too. Do you want to do it this afternoon?"

"I don't have anything better to do."

George and Andrew went first to the watchmaker, where Andrew selected a fine pocket watch, amazed at how cheaply it could be purchased.

"Did those surgeon's instruments arrive in America safely, Mr. Ainsworth?" the watchmaker asked.

"Yes. And the party was apparently very much pleased with them."

"Surgeon's instruments?" Andrew asked.

"Yes. Your cousin asked me to see if I could send them to her brother in Pittsburgh for his birthday."

Andrew raised his eyebrows. "It seems Melissa's doing quite a lot of business here." He turned to the man. "Do you do engraving here?"

"Yes sir."

"In that case, I should like to have an inscription put inside this watch." Andrew took a folded piece of paper from his pocket and gave it to the man. "With that on it."

The man studied it. "To Jackson from Melissa—Christmas 1862."

George clenched his fist and cursed himself for a fool, wishing he had never met Melissa Armstrong. Why did he have the ill fortune to fall in love with someone who already belonged to another?

Andrew purchased four small derringers at the gunsmiths, making sure that each fired true. He then bought himself a double-barreled, .44-caliber, 9-shot French Le Mat revolver, the upper barrel firing bullets and the lower barrel firing a .60-caliber shotgun charge. He also bought a brand-new Enfield carbine—both deadly weapons.

Although he knew nothing about firearms and personally disliked guns, George had been examining the pistols while Andrew was busy with his purchases. Remembering the last time he was here when he had nearly been mugged one night, he wondered if it might not be prudent to carry a small gun. Only his agility and swift speed had prevented him from spending the night in an alley and waking up with a headache and empty pockets, or possibly not waking up at all.

"Could you teach me how to shoot, Andrew?"

"I guess so. Don't you know how?"

"I've never fired a gun in my life."

"I thought everybody knew how to shoot."

George shrugged. "I'm pretty good at fisticuffs."

With Andrew's assistance, George selected a .32-caliber four-barreled derringer.

As they drove back to the hotel, Andrew said, "I'll make a deal with you George. We'll go out and find a nice deserted place where I'll teach you to shoot, if you'll take me to one of those fancy gambling and whorehouses I've heard so much about."

"Where'd you hear about them? Not from me."

"Joe Majors."

George smiled. "And I imagine Ernest, too. They don't miss much."

"Is it a deal?"

"It's a deal."

Late in the afternoon, the two men left for the villa of Sir Thomas Lacey.

"I want to warn you," George said, as they approached the wrought-iron gates. "Sir Thomas is looking for a husband for his daughter. One's already been spoken for, but he'd like them to both marry money. I don't think he was doing too well in business until the war came along. Just between you and me. I don't think he's any more of a 'sir' than you or I."

The wrought-iron gate opened on to a tiled patio, shaded from the sun by a veritable jungle of tropical plants. A strange sound startled Andrew, and he looked around to discover a colorful long-beaked bird squawking at him from a tree. They were greeted at the door by a towering black, looking very incongruous in red satin breeches and white knee stockings.

"Mr. Ainsworth, sir. So good to see you again."

"Thank you, Arthur."

The black nodded pleasantly to Andrew as the two men entered. Andrew had to look twice when the servant spoke again with his very cultured British accent.

"The family is expecting you in the library, sir."

Andrew smiled to himself, thinking, I never heard any darkies in Virginia talk like that. And wouldn't Bobo just die if we dressed him up in a monkey suit like that!

The family greeted George like one of their own, and Andrew was introduced to them. Jane Lacey was a very pale and thin woman who looked as if she never saw sunlight, but Andrew found her to be pleasant enough. Charlotte was an auburn-haired beauty, but Hannah seemed to be a younger version of her mother, straight as a stick and very shy.

"You must tell us all about how the war is doing over there," Mrs. Lacey said. "We'd like to hear it firsthand."

Arthur appeared with a tray of frosty glasses, filled with a delightful-looking beverage with fruit floating on top, and Andrew found it to be most refreshing.

"What would you like to know?" Andrew asked.

426

"Everything," Charlotte said.

"Well, it appears to be going very well for us right now. We've had some very good victories and some losses as well. General Lee and President Davis seem hopeful."

"You aren't in the army, are you?" Sir Thomas asked.

"Yes, I am. Right now I'm on furlough."

"Did you ever fight in a real battle?" Charlotte asked him.

Andrew spent most of the afternoon telling these Britishers about America. He was beginning to wonder if Hannah even had a tongue in her head, especially when he was seated beside her at the supper table and was faced with the problem of trying to make conversation with her. He could well understand why her father was trying to marry her off, if for no other reason than to get her out of the house. If these three females represented English womanhood, Andrew decided he would stick to the girls from the South. He felt the evening would never end, and when they finally left the villa, he heaved a sigh of relief.

"How do you stand it, George?"

"It's my job to be nice to these people. Besides, I get along pretty well with most people. You're lucky, though. At least Sir Thomas didn't try too hard to push Hannah off on you. I went through that myself until he decided I didn't have good enough breeding. He's very big on that sort of thing, you know—appearances and good family backgrounds."

George and Andrew rented two horses and, taking their guns with them, followed a cart track into the green hills. Andrew found George to be an apt pupil and as he spent more time with him, found the Englishman to be a very likable person.

"Would you mind telling me why you bought all those

427

derringers?" George asked.

"Father wanted me to get them. He's going to give them to Mother and my sisters and Melissa for Christmas. He thinks it would be a good idea, in case the blacks get out of hand or the Yankees get into the city. Of course, that won't ever happen."

"Can they shoot?"

"Mother can. I don't think my sisters know how. I don't know about Melissa."

George took Andrew to the gambling casino as he had promised and spent the evening playing cards and quietly piling up a sizable amount of winnings while Andrew availed himself of the various pleasures. George decided to stay away from the women, for no matter how high-class they seemed to be, they spelled nothing but trouble.

Andrew spent most of his days sleeping while George went about his business for the owners of the *Grasshopper*. They spent one more evening with Sir Thomas and his family, but Andrew was anxious to leave and get back to the casino to try to recoup his heavy losses at the roulette wheel and poker table.

George spent their last afternoon browsing through the open-air market in the square. He loved haggling over prices and examining the trinkets the natives brought down from their homes in the hills to sell.

"You buy magic pearl," one old woman told him, showing him a display of black pearls. "Will bring you much love and happiness."

The shiny pearls caught George's eye, and he picked one up to inspect it. "Why will it bring me those things?"

"Because I am the daughter of the greatest mamalois on this island—perhaps on all these islands. And when my son dives for the pearls and brings them to her hut, she puts a spell on them."

"Mamalois?"

"Voodoo priestess. You keep one and give one to the woman you desire most, and she will be yours."

George didn't believe in all this island mumbo jumbo, but he decided to humor the old woman and buy two of her pearls. At least they were pretty. As he paid her, she pressed a tiny carved figure in his hand. "This is our god, Damballah. He will protect you on your journey across the water. Carry him with you always."

Late in the afternoon, George learned that the *Grasshopper* would be sailing at six the next morning and hoped Andrew would be in condition to travel if, indeed, he was even back at the hotel. After worrying about it for some time, George finally decided to go in search of him.

He found Andrew at the casino, where every conceivable vice was readily available. There, the men wagered, drank, wenched, and seemed almost crazy to get rid of their money. George saw that Andrew had a considerable pile of winnings in front of him at the poker table, so he stood back to observe, knowing Andrew had been worried about losing so much of his father's money.

The three men playing with Andrew were not the most savory fellows, especially after consuming as much liquor as they evidently had. Andrew, on the other hand, seemed to be fairly sober and was winning constantly. When one of the men bowed out, they asked George to join them.

"No thanks, I'm not in the mood. But I wanted to tell you, Andrew, we sail first thing in the morning."

"I'll play one more hand and then I'll leave."

George got himself a beer and leaned against the wall to

watch. Hoping to make a killing, the two men raised the stakes first to $1,000 and then to $1,500. Andrew smiled and laid his cards on the table—two sevens and three nines, a full house.

He picked up his money and stood up. "Thank you gentlemen. Better luck next time."

Pocketing his money, he turned to George. "Just one drink, and then we'll go." He grinned at him. "Pretty lucky tonight, wasn't I?"

George was still standing near the card table when one of the men stood up. "Cheating pup!"

George turned and saw the man taking a pistol from his coat pocket and leveling it at Andrew's back. George jumped forward and kicked the man's arm. The shot went wild and shattered the mirror over the bar. Regaining his balance, George took out his new derringer and aimed it at the man.

"I didn't see any cheating," George said. "And I was watching very closely."

His one shot spent, the man eyed George's hand holding the gun and slowly set his pistol on the table.

George looked at the other man. "I would appreciate it if you'd hand that pistol you've got in your coat over to me," George told him.

A tense silence followed until the man finally took his gun from his coat pocket and handed it to George. Andrew was standing wide-eyed by the bar as George came over to him.

"Come on, let's get out of here," George said quietly. "Before anybody else gets any ideas."

As they were leaving, they heard someone say, "Who's going to pay for my mirror?"

Outside and safely around the corner, George found

his hands were shaking. He pocketed his own pistol and threw the other one into the gutter.

"What can I say but thank you?" Andrew asked. "You saved my life."

George didn't reply, for he was thinking about the situation in which he had just been. He, a man who detested violence.

"I got through Manassas and Malvern Hill and Sharpsburg relatively unhurt," Andrew was saying. "And it takes a fight over cards to nearly do me in. I'll never forget this, George. If there's ever anything you want . . ."

*   *   *

Melissa was in the kitchen with Cindy and Tunia, teaching them how to make butter. One afternoon, on her way home from work, she had seen a butter churn at the pawnshop's entrance. Knowing how hard it was to obtain butter at any price, she went in and bought it, sending Bobo to the shop to pick it up after she got home. She knew a neighbor who owned a cow had been giving milk to little Jeff and the Davis children, and Melissa decided to contribute her talents by supplying butter to the three supper tables.

Both Cindy and Tunia had been born in the city, and this was a new experience to them.

"Laws, Miss Melissa, yo' goin' to git arms as big as a man's doin' dat!" Cindy remarked.

"Oh fiddle. A little exercise never hurt anyone." She stepped aside. "You try it for a while, Tunia."

Tunia spat in the palms of her hands and rubbed them together, preparing to take up the churn handle. Melissa smiled and winked at Henry, who was sitting at the kitchen table, taking all this in. He had written to the

431

Navy Department in Mobile, asking permission to come down and observe the new secret weapon they were building, but even his fine reputation could not gain his admission.

Melissa sat down. "Tomorrow, if I can find some cheesecloth, I'll teach you how to make cottage cheese."

"You amaze me, Melissa," Henry remarked. "How can one woman seem to have so many talents as you. I bet only a handful of women in this city know how to make butter and cottage cheese."

"Mama taught me when I was a little girl. We used to have a cow."

"I suppose you even knew how to milk it?"

"Of course. Who do you think did all the milking? Mama used to make the sweetest cream I've ever tasted. In the summertime, we used to pour that over fresh-sliced peaches from our tree every morning with our breakfast. I be that's one thing Jeremiah's missed these past few years."

"But he got to shake hands with Lincoln."

This was a bit of information neither Cindy nor Tunia had heard before. "Yo' brother shook hands wif Linkum?" Cindy asked.

"Yes."

"What we gonna do if'n he sets us all free?" Tunia wondered. "I's belonged to somebody all my life. It all I knows."

"I don't wants to be free," Cindy said. "I likes it right here. I got good food and a nice bed to sleeps in."

Henry looked at Melissa, knowing full well this was the attitude of over half the slaves in the South.

"I hope I'll be able to make a good batch of jellies before Christmas," Melissa said, deciding to change

432

the subject.

"I hope I'll get a jar or two," Henry smiled. "My mother used to make a pretty fair batch of preserves every year."

Bobo came in, patting Tunia's fanny as he passed.

"Cut dat out, boy! Can't yo' see I'm workin'!"

"Miss Melissa, I got all de metal took off'n dem things and loaded dem in de wagon," Bobo said. "Does yo' know what Masta Edward wants me to do wif 'em?"

"No. He should be back soon, though."

"What are you talking about?" Henry wondered.

"Uncle Edward's giving anything we can spare that's made of leather to the shoemaker who's contracting for the government to make shoes for the soldiers. What did you find, Bobo?"

"Well, dey's de old buggy top and an extry seat, and some harnesses and Masta Andrew's pony saddle. I goin' up to de attic now to strip de leather off'n dem two trunks."

Bobo left the kitchen, and Melissa got up to see how Tunia was doing.

"How much longer do I got to do dis, missy?"

"Oh, it takes quite a while."

"Laws! De war's liable to be over by de time dis butter's ready!"

* * *

It had been a rough voyage, due to a storm at sea, and Andrew was thankful when Jacob took the wheel to guide the *Grasshopper* toward the mouth of the Cape Fear River. He was in George's cabin, and the two of them were playing checkers and drinking hot coffee.

"No more checkers tonight," George said, standing up and reaching for the overhead lantern. "Lights out."

Andrew drained the contents of his mug. "It's just as well. I was getting tired of just sitting here."

"I'm going up to the pilothouse to see what's happening."

George and Andrew made their way along the darkened companionway, knowing the way well by this time, and up the stairs to the pilothouse. There had been no activity spotted by the watchman who received one hundred dollars for every sail he spotted, and all seemed peaceful. Jacob was standing at the wheel, chewing his tobacco and constantly scanning the dark waters all around them.

"How far are we from land?" Andrew wondered.

"About ten miles," Captain Bubb replied, lifting the cover on the binnacle and shielding the dim light with his hand as he read the compass.

The men in the wheelhouse were silent for the next half hour, all eyes peering into the darkness. Andrew began to hear a faint noise besides that of the engine.

"What's that noise?"

"The surf hitting the rocks," Jacob replied.

Andrew listened carefully. "I don't see any shore yet."

"That's the trick to all this," Jacob smiled.

"And a neat bit of piloting it is," Will said. "To get this ship safely up a half-mile-wide piece of water with no lights to guide us."

The purring of the engines and the sound of the crashing waves against the rocks were suddenly broken by Joe Majors's clattering up the steps and into the pilothouse.

"Two ships off to port! Another off to starboard bow!"

Andrew's eyes followed the other men's gazes. Sure enough, there they were, but now there were at least five ships. The *Grasshopper* had found itself amidst a blockading squadron, without any warning.

A cry rose up from one of the ships. "Heave to, or I'll sink you!"

"I'm not going to lose this ship!" Jacob exclaimed. "Joe, get those guns manned!"

Joe raced back down the steps as Jacob rang for speed. The Yankee guns opened up as the *Grasshopper* lurched forward, lighted by the blinding glare of Federal rockets. Andrew and George looked at each other, as, under an unrelenting hail of shot and shell from every direction, the *Grasshopper* raced full speed ahead. Andrew let out a cheer as he saw one of their own shells explode the boilers on one of the Union gunboats. Every rivet in the *Grasshopper* was straining while Jacob dodged her in and out through a maze of smoke and bursting shells. Fort Fisher was still more than a mile away, but neither Will nor Jacob thought of surrender.

Shells screamed across the decks, and the foremast exploded in a shower of splinters. The ship's carpenter quickly cut away the spar while another shell ripped away a dinghy. Below, Ernest, black with sweat and grease, drove his coal heavers as hard as they could work, satisfied as the needle on the pressure gauge crept upward.

A shell exploded overhead, smashing part of the wheelhouse. A piece of glass slashed Jacob's cheek, and George was thrown against the big metal first-aid box, cracking his kneecap. Andrew held out his hand to help George to his feet as another Union boat caught fire. Still, the *Grasshopper* raced toward shore.

A sudden roar from Fort Fisher's artillery warned the pursuers that they had reached their limits. Gradually, the *Grasshopper* began to draw away from the Federal ships, and in a few minutes she had crossed the bar, soon to be anchored under the protection of Confederate guns.

George put his hand in his pocket and squeezed the little carved voodoo god.

Eighteen

Jeremiah's unit had marched to Harper's Ferry, where they planned to spend the winter months. The smallpox epidemic had run its course, so now all he had to contend with were the usual cases of bronchial and chest infections. Charlie had received a letter from his wife telling him that the family had finally heard from her brother Henry, and, although he was well and safe, he hadn't given them any details about where he was or what he was doing.

Jackson had watched Jeb take the loss of his daughter as only a true friend could see it. From his outward appearance, he bore up well, but Jackson knew how deeply he was hurting. Flora and little Jemmie had come to camp shortly after the tragedy, and Heros and Jackson had entertained the little boy by taking him riding and squirrel hunting. Jackson noted that Flora had seemed composed, but her eyes betrayed her grief.

The cavalry suffered from a loss of mounts, due to the poor forage for the animals and such diseases as sore tongue and greased heel. Most of the men were insufficiently clothed, wearing every variety of blankets like shawls or ponchos for protection against the cold.

Nevertheless, the cavalry was called upon to assist Lee. In November, Lincoln had removed McClellan from command of the army of the Potomac and replaced him with General Ambrose Burnside. Burnside was a man who did not believe in delays, and on the morning of December 13, in a heavy fog, he attacked the Confederates at Fredericksburg. The fight raged all day and until after darkness fell, Lee repulsing the Federals at every point, inflicting severe punishment. The Yankees made six charges across the plain between Fredericksburg and the hills where the Confederates were entrenched, and each time they were mowed down with deadly effect. Union casualties were double the Confederate losses, and Lee had captured over ten thousand weapons, and quantities of food and clothing.

Lee had something of a shock when he came out of his tent one morning and found that the dead Yankees lying between the lines were no longer wearing blue. He peered through his field glasses and saw that they were naked. During the night, his half-frozen men had crept forward and relieved the dead men of overcoats, jackets, shoes, shirts, and long underwear.

Andrew was with Jefferson Davis when the president received dispatches of the battle. On the ninth of December, only two days after his return from Nassau, Andrew had left Richmond by train with the president and two other aides, Custis Lee and Joseph R. Davis. Custis was Lee's eldest son, and Davis was the president's nephew, both of whom had been with him since the outset of the war. The party went to Chattanooga, and then to Murfreesboro, where Davis inspected the troops, talked with officers, and gave a speech which was accepted enthusiastically.

Davis had placed General Joseph E. Johnston in command of the western department and hoped his visit would prompt men who were not already in the service to enlist.

The president was staying in a farmhouse, and Custis and Andrew were with him while he was going over the news from Virginia.

Davis smiled with almost fatherly affection at one particular dispatch.

"It seems the South has a new hero," he remarked.

"Who?" Custis asked.

"Listen to this dispatch from General Jackson," Davis said, rereading the paper aloud. "Major John Pelham of the cavalry's horse artillery is credited with holding an entire brigade of General George C. Meade at bay with a single gun for almost an hour, firing up the road into the blue masses with devastating effect. Whenever the Federals got his range, he would change his position so swiftly that the confused Yankees thought there was a full battery on the hill. I asked Pelham to direct the fortifications of my line for the second day of the battle. He arranged the strongest possible defenses, almost as if by magic. I said to General Stuart that if he had another Pelham I wished he would give him to me. Stuart has dubbed him 'The Gallant Pelham.'"

Davis knew the young planter's son from Alabama was already idolized by his men and his chief. Now it seemed the boy major was loved by all.

"My sister knows him," Andrew remarked. "I believe he stayed at our house."

"General Stuart has recommended his promotion to lieutenant colonel. I concur with that wholeheartedly."

439

Richmond received the victory at Fredericksburg with little show except for the enthusiastic applause for young John Pelham, for the South had never doubted that they would be victorious at Fredericksburg. The people were busy preparing for the holidays and entertaining soldiers on leave or visiting foreign dignitaries, many of whom were appalled at the shabbiness of people's clothing, the high prices, and squalid streets.

Nancy and Margaret had returned to their nursing duties. After the battle, the wounded came in so fast it was impossible to examine them and dress their wounds. They lay upon the floors of the receiving wards, rows of ghastly forms, covered with blood and dirt, their uniforms stiff with mud and gravel from the little streams in which they fell. Margaret and her mother passed among them with pails of milk, water, and sponges, trying to comfort them as best they could.

On the Sunday afternoon before Christmas, Melissa and Mahaley walked through the several inches of snow lying on the ground to the Davis home. They were greeted at the door by five-year-old Jeff.

"Mama and Aunt Maggie are in the kitchen," he said. "Cook's been busy all morning getting things ready."

After removing their wraps, Melissa and Mahaley followed Jeff into the large kitchen. Varina and her sister had decided to make taffy for the children at the orphans' home, and, thanks to Edward's sugar and the resourcefulness of the women, the ingredients for the candy had been gathered.

"You must be chilled to the bone," Varina remarked.

"It's not too bad out today," Mahaley said.

Melissa gave Mrs. Davis a fresh crock of butter, the

consistency of which was improving now that Tunia was getting the hang of it.

"Oh, thank you, Melissa. You don't know how much we enjoy this," Varina said. "I haven't tasted really fresh butter since moving here."

Melissa and Mahaley had never pulled taffy, so they watched with the Davis children while Maggie showed them how. Before long, the women were giggling and laughing right along with the children as they pulled and twisted the sticky confection.

"I wish we could do more for everyone this year," Varina said. "But some things just can't be done."

"I think you've done quite enough already, considering," Melissa told her.

Varina had made no plans for entertaining as long as her husband was away. Her main interests were the children, the soldiers, and the wounded. The Soldiers' Aid Society had collected boxes of clothing of all description—cotton shirts, flannel shirts, drawers, and socks—for distribution among the wounded in the hospitals. In a statement Varina had made and Henry had written in the *Journal*, she publicly advocated the women of Richmond going to the hospitals to read the Bible or write letters for the soldiers. She had also suggested writing cheerful letters to soldiers in the field, and a list of names had been provided for this purpose. In defiance of official red tape, the women had collected five thousand pairs of shoes, made from their donated remnants of leather, and sent them to the soldiers, after having observed them marching barefooted through the snow-covered Richmond streets. The committee had petitioned the quartermaster general for blankets and overcoats to go to the field. As more refugees crowded into Richmond, accommodations grew harder to find, but the people were in good spirits this holiday season.

"Have you heard from your husband lately, Mrs. Davis?" Mahaley asked.

"Mahaley Armstrong, how many times have I told you to call me Varina?" she chided. "Yes, I received a letter Friday. He was in Chattanooga."

"Did he mention my brother?"

"No. But I know if there had been any kind of trouble, he would have mentioned it."

"Andrew's not one for writing letters. Most of our information we have to learn from his girl. He writes to her a lot."

"I understand you've had several letters from your brother, Melissa," Varina said.

Melissa looked at her in surprise. "How did you know?"

Varina smiled. "Word travels fast."

"I hope you don't think any less of me because I have a brother in the Union Army."

Varina laughed and hugged Melissa. "Don't be foolish, dear. These things happen. Jeff and I know you're as much a daughter of the South as I am."

Little Jeff Davis stopped pulling taffy and looked at Melissa, scrutinizing her carefully. "Your brother's a Yankee?"

"He's a doctor with the medical corps."

"General Lee will fix him," Jeff muttered, going back to his taffy pulling.

On December 23, Henry finished up late at the paper and decided to stop at the Spotswood to have some supper and see if he could pick up any newsworthy information.

442

Upon entering, he saw George sitting alone at a table, so he went over to speak to him.

"Well, Mr. Ainsworth, it's nice to see you. I trust your knee is feeling a little better?"

George's crooked grin appeared. "So you heard about that, eh?"

"Melissa told me."

"Won't you join me?"

"Don't mind if I do," Henry said, sitting down. "I hate eating alone."

"The knee's a little sore still," George said. "The ship's doctor took a look at it, and then I had Dr. Aldrich check it as soon as I got into town. I thought I'd broken it, but he says it was just badly bruised."

"That must have been some chase the Yankees gave you. Old McAllen was strutting around the office for days boasting how his ship could hold off the whole Federal Navy if it had to."

"It took quite a beating, I'm afraid. It won't be ready to put out again until after the new year. I think I'll head back down to Wilmington after Christmas."

"Melissa's also told me you saved Andrew's life."

George reddened a little. "Oh, it wasn't quite like that. I don't know that the chap would really have shot."

"What are your plans for Christmas?"

"The Armstrongs have asked me to dinner."

"Me too. I was there last year. It was good to have a home to go to and friends to spend the day with. I haven't had any luck finding any suitable presents, so I told Melissa that I'd supply the tree this year. I thought I'd go out tomorrow and see what I can find."

"Would you mind if I went with you? I haven't got anything to do around here, and I get very bored."

"I'd be glad to have the company. Besides, I might need some help. I suppose between the two of us, we might be able to muster up at least two good legs."

"Thank you, Mr. Walkenfeldt."

"Call me Henry."

"Well, then, Henry, do you happen to know if Colonel Vaughn will be at the Armstrongs' for Christmas dinner?"

"No, he won't. Melissa says he's got to stay with the cavalry. Why?"

"Just curious."

Henry and George took Henry's little secondhand buggy out through the snow and found a suitable tree. It wasn't an easy task strapping it to the small buggy, but after a good deal of engineering, the chore was accomplished, and they deposited it with Bobo, who carried it into the house. They then returned to their respective lodgings to dress for the evening. George asked Henry if he would mind picking him up, as he had too many parcels to carry on horseback.

Mahaley insisted on having mistletoe this year, so, bundled in their warmest clothes, she and Melissa drove to the edge of town in search of some. By the time they had located any, the snow had begun to fall very hard, and both were cold and wet when they returned home. Mahaley had already begun to sniffle, so she spent a good hour soaking in a hot tub.

When Melissa came downstairs, Edward was mixing the hot punch.

"No eggnog this year, I'm afraid," he smiled apologetically. "But maybe we'll have it again next year."

"Nearly no turkey either," Nancy said, arranging a

spray of poinsettias on the table. "I spent all day yesterday looking for one, and when I finally found one, it cost me eleven dollars. Can you imagine! And it's a scrawny little thing too!"

"You're not that fond of turkey anyway," Edward remarked. "I can remember you used to get pretty tired of them when we first got married."

"Well, we had them running all over the yard. I'm just glad we have plenty of ham and sweet potatoes."

"And Melissa's plum pudding," Edward grinned.

"Uncle Edward, do you think you could hang this mistletoe over the punch bowl? I can't reach."

"Be glad to."

"And anywhere else you think it would be appropriate."

"Mahaley's idea, no doubt?" he smiled.

"How's she feeling?" Nancy asked.

"All right, I guess. She's still in the tub. I think her feet got even wetter than mine."

Edward exchanged a little smile with Nancy and went on with hanging the mistletoe. Melissa took some and went into the drawing room. For the occasion, Edward had Bobo light a fire, but wood was scarce, and Edward's fireplace was usually just as empty as everyone else's, except that he had the money to pay for the wood, even at the ridiculous price of eighteen dollars a cord.

Margaret brought Jeff downstairs in his nightclothes at about the same time Lewis arrived, followed closely by Henry and George, carrying a load of parcels. While everyone was greeting the men, Jeff toddled over to the bare tree and was fingering the fragrant needles. He began chewing on them when Lewis went over and picked him up.

"Now, my boy, you mustn't eat the Christmas tree. How else will Santa Claus know where to come?"

Jeff stared at Lewis, not comprehending his words.

"You don't know about Santa Claus?" Lewis asked him, as Margaret came over to them.

"I'm afraid he's still too young to understand such things."

"Perhaps next year."

"Yes. And maybe next year it will seem more like a real Christmas," Margaret said, glancing at the meager pile of bows and candles that had been saved from last year with which to decorate the tree. "Not even any candies or sugarplums to hang on the tree."

"Next year I might even have my own tree," Lewis said. "I bought a little cottage this week."

"A cottage? Why Lewis, what on earth will you do with a cottage?"

"Live in it. It was such a good bargain, I couldn't pass it up. Besides, with all the people coming into town, the boardinghouse was becoming very noisy. There's two or three families in some of the rooms. I'll need help furnishing it. I wonder if I could impose on you for your help?"

"It wouldn't be an imposition at all."

After Mahaley had come downstairs and the Aldriches arrived, they got down to the business of trimming the tree. Nancy held her grandson on her lap and he watched every movement with fascination.

After the tree was finished, the presents were passed around. Melissa gave everyone her tasty jellies and preserves; Edward and Nancy gave each of the three girls a pair of fur-lined boots. The derringers all of the Armstrong women received came as quite a surprise to all

446

of them. Lewis gave Margaret a tortoiseshell comb with three tiny rubies set in the crown. George's presents caused the most speculation, and when they were opened they were received with pleasure. For Edward and Lewis there were fine cigars, for Nancy and Mahaley, scented soaps, for Margaret there was candy. Melissa received some perfume and he even gave Jeff a little toy drum.

Lewis produced a big bundle wrapped in heavy paper and presented it to Margaret. "These are for you and Jeff."

Everyone watched expectantly as Margaret opened the package, careful to save the string and the paper. It was books.

"They just came off the presses last week," Lewis said.

Margaret read the titles. *"Les Misérables, Great Expectations, Robinson Crusoe, The Dixie Speller, The Confederate Reader,* and the *Virginia Primer."*

While everyone was looking at the books, Melissa remembered they had forgotten to set out Tunia's cornbread-molasses cakes, so she excused herself to go into the kitchen to get them. George followed her with his eyes and decided this would be a good time to refill his punch cup, for he wanted an opportunity to present the pearl to Melissa in private.

When Melissa came out of the kitchen with the tray of cakes, George was busy at the punch bowl.

"I took the liberty of refilling your cup as well, Miss Armstrong," he said, setting the glasses down.

"Thank you, Mr. Ainsworth."

He took the tray from her and set it down beside the punch bowl. "I have another little present for you," he said, reaching into his pocket.

"Oh, Mr. Ainsworth, you shouldn't have. All I have for you are the few jars of preserves."

"Believe me, I appreciate them. If you'd like to do something for me, you could call me George instead of Mr. Ainsworth."

She smiled at him. "Then you must call me Melissa."

He smiled back at her. "Very well, Melissa. Now hold out your hand."

Melissa did as she was told, and George dropped the shiny pearl into her hand.

"It's lovely," she said. "But what is it?"

"It's a black pearl. According to some legends in the islands—a magic black pearl."

"Why, I've never seen a black pearl before," she said, holding it up to the light to get a better look at it.

"I would have put it in some sort of setting, but I felt you might consider it too presumptuous of me," he said. "I had mine made into a stickpin."

Melissa peered at his cravat and fingered the stickpin, her hair brushing his cheek. "Is yours magic too?"

"Supposedly. It will bring you happiness."

"Well, I'm certainly very happy with it," she smiled. "I'll keep it as a sort of good-luck piece." She glanced up, her eyes falling on the mistletoe hanging above them, and she hesitated for a moment, pondering the propriety of a Christmas kiss. To keep in the spirit of the holidays and thank George for his gift, she stood on tiptoe and kissed his cheek. "Thank you very much, George."

"You're welcome," he murmured, gazing at her with longing.

They went back into the parlor to find Mahaley convulsed in a fit of sneezing. The fresh ink from the books had irritated her already sensitive nose.

"Mahaley, you're sick," Nancy said. "I think you should go to bed."

"I'll be all right, Mother."

"Perhaps Nathaniel should look at you while he's here."

This idea appealed to Mahaley, so she suggested they go into Edward's study where he could feel her pulse.

"You're warm," he said, touching her forehead. "Stick out your tongue. . . . That looks all right. Do you have a headache?"

"No. But I have a pain in my chest."

"In your chest?"

"Yes." She began to unfasten several of the delicate pearl buttons on the bodice of her gown. "Maybe you better look and see."

Back in the drawing room, Lewis was saying, "I realize Jeff's a little young for schoolbooks, but they'll soon come in handy."

"It's never too soon to start teaching children to read and write," Nancy remarked. "I think we still have Andrew's old slate up in the attic."

Melissa had picked up the elementary arithmetic book and flipped through the pages, Henry and George peering at it too. She giggled and began to read one of the problems: "A Confederate soldier captured eight Yankees each day for nine successive days; how many did he capture in all?"

Ellen laughed. "He must be quite a man!"

"Oh, he's nothing compared to the next one," Melissa grinned. "If one Confederate soldier can whip seven Yankees, how many soldiers can whip forty-nine Yankees?"

"Seven," George replied.

"Very good," Melissa applauded. "You may go to the head of the class."

Margaret was munching on her cake and smiled at Lewis. "Thank you, Lewis. I know Jeff will now have a proper education."

Henry nudged Melissa in the side.

Nathaniel followed Mahaley out of the study, and he was blushing furiously.

"How is she, Nathaniel?" Nancy asked.

"Fine, ma'am. Just a little case of the sniffles." He sat down and finished his punch in one gulp.

Nancy went over to the piano and sat down. Jeff clapped his hands. "Nana, sing!"

"Yes, dear, it's time for Christmas carols."

Christmas Eve at cavalry headquarters was full of good cheer. Mrs. Stuart had come up from Richmond to spend the holidays with her husband. Wagons had been sent out and slipped through the Federal cavalry fringe, returning with hams, eggs, and a few turkeys, which Hood's Texans who were camped nearby had managed to steal. Von Borcke provided music and the enormous buckets of eggnog. But the revelry had to be cut short, for they were leaving in the morning to see what Burnside was doing.

Bundled in his warmest overcoat, Jeremiah was sitting on a log outside his tent, the warm scarf Sarah had knitted and sent to him as a Christmas gift wrapped around his neck. Joining him, Al sat down and handed him a steaming mug of hot buttered rum. They listened together, sipping the steamy brew, while the band played Christmas carols, reminding all the men of homes and loved ones far away.

George surprised the Armstrongs by sitting down beside Melissa in their pew Christmas morning before the service began.

"Why, Mr. Ainsworth, what a pleasant surprise," Nancy remarked.

"I hope you don't mind my squeezing in here with you. I didn't know the church would be this crowded."

"There's always a big turnout on Christmas day," Nancy told him. "And we're glad to have you."

"I always attended services with my mother at home."

George spent more time thinking about his close proximity to Melissa than what the Reverend Dr. Minnegrode was saying in his sermon. He so wanted to reach over and take one of her hands folded in her lap, but he resigned himself to just letting his shoulder brush hers.

The family stopped by the Davises' after church to share holiday greetings and give the first family a few small gifts—five pounds each of cocoa, coffee, and tea. By the time they arrived back home, it was snowing again, and Tunia had the Christmas feast ready.

On December 26, the cavalry, with 1,800 men and four guns, started north from their base near Fredericksburg. Their objective was Burke's Station, very near Alexandria, where they planned to take possession of Telegraph Road and capture any prisoners or supplies they might find.

Jackson rode quietly beside Jeb, and both of them were so cold they did little talking. Jackson couldn't remember when he had been this cold. The wind whipped against his face, even protected slightly as it was by the beard he had grown again, and his long underwear was so worn and full of holes, he might have not been wearing any at all. The only part of his body that felt halfway warm was his feet, for the socks Melissa had sent him and the boots he had bought in Chambersburg were still like new.

Fitz Lee attacked a few straggling wagon trains and herded them north to meet his cousin Rooney who had been doing some skirmishing, taking about seventy prisoners and driving out the garrison. When Jeb's group met them, he was so disappointed with their results thus far, he had half a mind to call the whole thing off and return to camp. Instead, he sent the wagons and prisoners back with a party of men.

The next day, they met some Union cavalry ahead in the woods. Jeb ordered a charge, and the Yankees greeted them with scattered pistol fire before fleeing. Rooney rounded up the prisoners while the rest raced after the running Federals. On stronger horses, the Yankees reached a ford and dashed through the chilled waters of the Occoquan River.

Jeb hesitated, not sure whether to follow through the narrow and difficult ford, but Jackson dashed across, and soon the column was right behind him. They plunged across, greeted by a halfhearted firing from the Yankees, but no saddles were emptied. Pelham, to everyone's amazement, succeeded in crossing with his guns, even though the ford had always been considered impassable for vehicles.

They crashed through the brush and into a deserted Federal camp. Jackson was astounded at how comfortably furnished the Yankee camp was, and, as the others went through the tents to look for anything of value, he found himself a pair of fairly decent longjohns and a straight razor. Some mules were gathered up, and whatever could not be carried off was burned.

Jeb decided to do as he had done before and not return by the same route, where enemy forces might be gathering. The column turned west and approached Burke's Station, on the Orange and Alexandria Railroad, after dark. Deeper than ever in Federal lines, Jeb still felt confident that they could get safely away.

Jeb sent Jackson and Fitz ahead to pounce on the telegraph operator at the station before he could sound the alarm. Jackson strolled into the little office and smiled pleasantly at the soldier, his pistol pointed at the little man's head.

"Now, if I were you, I'd get up off that chair, Yank, and not do anything foolish."

Fitz stepped inside with a rope with which to bind the soldier's hands and feet while Jackson went back outside and waved his hat for Jeb to come on.

Jeb soon entered the office with Sheppard, the cavalry's own operator, who sat down and read off the messages that Union commanders were transmitting about ways and means of catching the Rebel raiders. Jeb grinned and picked up paper and pencil, drafting a message. He handed it to Sheppard. "Send this right off."

Sheppard's eyes widened as he read the communication:

Quartermaster General Meigs, United States Army:
   Quality of the mules lately furnished me very poor. Interferes seriously with movement of captured wagons. J. E. B. Stuart.

After the message had been sent, the men cut the wires, burned a bridge, and started for Fairfax Courthouse. Jackson was still chuckling with Jeb as they neared the village.

Suddenly Federal ambushers opened fire on the column, and Jeb ordered his men to withdraw. Jackson felt a sharp thump against his chest and looked down to discover a bullet hole in the left breast of his uniform. But he didn't feel like he had been shot. Once he reached the safety of the trees, he examined the bullet hole more closely. There was no blood and he felt fine, so what had happened? He reached inside his jacket, and his fingers closed over the daguerreotype case. As he pulled it out, the cover fell off in his lap, and he found the ball embedded in the metal and leather.

"Oh, Melissa, you don't know how much I appreciate you right now."

Jeb trotted over to him. "Talking to yourself again?"

Jackson handed him the broken cover of the case. "Look."

Jeb whistled. "Looks like your little gal just saved your life. I reckon you owe her your thanks. I think you ought to skedaddle on into Richmond and thank her in person."

"When?"

"As soon as we get out of this mess."

The black denseness of Jackson's bearded face was broken with a broad grin. "Then let's get out of this nest of Yankees!"

Jeb was picking briars out of his hat. "We will, in time. I haven't gotten us caught, have I?" He appeared to be deep in thought for a moment and then looked over at his friend. "Did you ever notice how many questions Melissa asks about what we're doing, or is it just my imagination?"

"The cavalry, you mean?" Jackson scratched his whiskers in reflection. "Come to think of it, she is a might inquisitive. Why?"

"I just think it's strange. Most women care more about—well, you know—women things."

Jackson smiled. "But Melissa isn't like most women. She's one of a kind."

Puzzled because the Confederates had not fired back, the Yankees sent out a flag of truce. Were they friend or foe? The flag would be answered in the morning. In the meantime, Jeb had his men light enormous campfires and sneak out during the night.

Jackson left Gypsy at headquarters and took the train into Richmond, sleeping most of the way as the car clattered over the tracks in the moonlight. He was embarrassed over his untidy appearance, but there was no helping it.

Mahaley was helping Melissa coat pecans with cinnamon and molasses in the kitchen when Cindy announced the caller.

"Miss Melissa, you got a visitor," she grinned.

"Who is it, Cindy? I'm busy right now."

"Too busy to see me?" Jackson grinned, stepping into the kitchen.

"Jackson!" Melissa squealed, standing up so fast she overturned the bowl of nuts. Jackson gathered her in his arms and kissed her.

Tunia clucked her tongue and began picking up the pecans.

"Oh, Jackson, I'm so glad you're back!"

"So am I," he grinned, hugging her. He peered over her shoulder. "'Lo, Mahaley. Tunia."

"Jackson," Mahaley nodded, wishing someone would make such a fuss over her.

"Laws, Cunnel Vaughn, I ain't seen so much life in de li'l missy in a long while," Tunia remarked.

Cindy carried some hot water upstairs for Jackson's bath, of which everyone agreed he was sorely in need. Melissa found she couldn't concentrate on her work.

"I think I'll go upstairs and see what I can find of Andrew's that Jackson might wear until his uniform's clean and dry."

Tunia was examining the threadbare longjohns. "Land sakes, dis wouldn't even make a good cleanin' rag!"

Melissa found a pair of Andrew's trousers and a shirt, and, on second thought, a pair of drawers. She tapped on the door and entered the bedroom which Jackson always occupied. He was soaping himself with a bar of Nancy's scented soap and looked up, grinning when he saw Melissa.

"Did you come to scrub my back?" he asked.

She smiled. "I'd love to. But I wouldn't want Aunt Nancy to come home and find me in here. I brought you some of Andrew's clothes to wear."

"You're sure you won't stay?"

She shook her head and smiled. "I'd better not. Why don't I fix you something to eat? Are you hungry?"

"I'm starved. I haven't eaten anything except some moldy bacon yesterday afternoon."

Melissa returned downstairs and found Jeff had finished his nap and was sitting at the table watching Mahaley and Tunia coat the pecans. Melissa told Tunia not to bother getting up and reheated last night's stew.

"He didn't say anything about John Pelham, did he?" Mahaley asked.

"No. His name didn't come up." Melissa studied her cousin. "You liked him quite a bit, didn't you?"

"Yes. Almost as much as I like Nathaniel. I just wish Nathaniel was as exciting as John."

"Excitement!" Tunia sniffed. "Child, yo' livin' in de middle of a war! Ain't dat excitin' enough fo' yo'?"

"Oh, Tunia, you don't understand."

"I understands. I ain't dat old!" She began to laugh. "An' I hopes I never gits dat old!"

Nancy and Margaret came in the front door as Jackson was coming down the stairs, Andrew's pants well above his ankles, his sleeves too short to be fastened. The women greeted him as if he were one of their own. Melissa fixed him a bowl of stew and corn bread, and he listened as the women told him all the news, including Andrew's trip to Nassau and out west with the president.

"I saw Maggie Howell today; the president's due back tonight," Nancy said. "Varina's so glad he'll be here to bring in the new year."

"I'm curious about those derringers you ladies all got for Christmas," Jackson smiled. "Do any of you know know how to shoot?"

"I do," Nancy replied. "And Melissa knows how to fire a rifle."

Jackson looked at Melissa with new interest. "You wouldn't care to join the cavalry, would you? That reminds me," he said, reaching into his pants pocket. "I wanted to thank you for saving my life."

Melissa took the broken daguerreotype case, gasping when she saw the bullet embedded in the lid.

457

"Oh, my dear!" Nancy exclaimed.

"Luckiest thing I ever did—meeting you," Jackson told Melissa.

"Maybe Mrs. Parker could replace the case," Margaret suggested.

"I think I'd like to keep it just the way it is, without the lid."

Melissa looked at him and smiled, her fingers tightened on the case.

Nancy stood up. "I'd better go see how Tunia's doing in the kitchen. I'm sure Mr. Walkenfeldt will be glad to hear all about your adventures when he comes by this evening, Jackson."

Melissa and Jackson spent the afternoon chatting, until she decided it was time for her to go upstairs and get ready for the evening. Jackson was glad when his uniform was dry, for even though Andrew's fine lawn shirt felt good next to his skin, he was used to his old uniform.

Nancy was at her dressing table when Edward came in. "Cindy tells me Jackson's back," he said.

"Yes." Something had been gnawing at Nancy all afternoon, ever since she had gone with Margaret to inspect Lewis's cottage. "Edward, don't you think Lewis has taken an abnormal interest in Margaret lately?"

Edward looked up from removing his boots. "Yes, I do."

Their eyes met for a moment. "What do you make of it?" Nancy asked.

"I don't know. At first, I thought he was just trying to keep her mind off losing Joseph. Now, I'm not so sure. Lewis has never had any use for children, and yet he treats Jeff like his own son."

"And now this little house."

458

"Has Margaret said anything to you?"

"No. And I haven't liked to ask. You know what a private person she is."

"Well, I think I might have a little talk with Lewis tonight. Whatever's going on, it seems to be good for Margaret, but Lewis is twenty years older than she is."

Melissa found Jackson warming his hands by the fire in the drawing room. He looked up and, after making sure no one was around, took her in his arms.

"I wish I'd had you to hold close when I was so cold out there," he whispered.

"I can't imagine you ever being cold."

"You'd be surprised. Nothing was warm out there."

"Nothing?"

He grinned at her. "Nothing," he laughed, hugging her.

"I've got your Christmas present," she said, handing him a small box.

Jackson opened it anxiously, finding the inscribed pocket watch Andrew had purchased in Nassau.

"Oh, Melissa, it's the finest watch I've ever seen." He kissed her. "Thank you so much. You know, I didn't have any time or any place to do any shopping for you. But I planned to give you this." He reached into his pocket and gave her a large gold ring with a blue sapphire set in the center.

"Why, Jackson, it's your class ring from West Point! Don't you want to keep it with you?"

"I can't wear it in the field. It gets in the way. Besides, I'll make a bargain with you."

"What?"

459

"Someday we'll trade this ring back for a wedding ring."

She put her arms around his neck and smiled up at him. "Someday we will."

When Lewis arrived, Edward asked him to come into his study, supposedly to discuss business.

"What I really want to talk to you about is Margaret," Edward said. "Just what is going on here?"

"I plan to ask her to marry me."

Edward raised his heavy eyebrows. "Lewis, we've been friends for many years, but do you think that's wise?"

"Do you have any objections?"

"Well . . . you're much older. And does she want to marry you?"

"I haven't mentioned it yet. I wanted to wait a little longer—give her a decent amount of time after Joseph's death. I'd make a fine home for her and young Jeff. I'm a rich man. Every bit of my profits from the nail company and the *Grasshopper* is sitting in the bank in Confederate notes. I'll provide very well for her, you know that. She'll never want for anything."

"But do you love her?"

Lewis flinched for a moment, knowing what his answer must be in order to satisfy Edward. "Yes, I love her."

"In that case, I'll say no more. Margaret's a grown woman and knows her own mind."

Henry was full of questions for Jackson, and Melissa hoped everyone would think it was just his reporter's curiosity. At midnight, they toasted the new year with champagne, all hoping for an end to the war in 1863.

Nineteen

The Union Army was bivouacked not far from the Confederate camps—one north and one south of the Rappahannock River near Fredericksburg. On January 25, Lincoln had replaced Ambrose Burnside with General Joseph Hooker, and the men were taking bets as to how long he would stay around.

On a crisp sunny day in March, Jeremiah found Charlie giving the finishing touches to something he had been carving last night and this morning. It looked like nothing but a rather fat, smoothed hickory limb, about thirty inches long, and a little wider at one end than the other.

"What is it, Charlie?"

"You'll see," he grinned, closing his whittling knife and putting it in his pocket. "General Doubleday asked me to fix it up for him." Charlie stood up. "Can you spare some time to go over to his camp with me?"

"I think so. Al's with the men now."

Jeremiah had been inundated with an outbreak of typhus, or "Chickahominy fever" as the men called it. The inclement weather and sameness of diet had contributed to the disease.

461

Jeremiah followed Charlie about one quarter of a mile to a small rise, and when they came out of the trees, he found himself overlooking a barren cornfield. There were some of General Abner Doubleday's men, arranged in the strangest formation he had ever seen for any army squad. Four men composed what appeared to be a large square about seventy-five feet apart, while five more men fanned out some ten to twenty yards behind them. There was another man standing directly in the center of the square, and as Jeremiah and Charlie approached this strange spectacle, the soldier in the middle threw something. It was then that Jeremiah noticed a soldier standing at one of the corners, armed with a fence post. He swung at the object, missed it and walked away, dejected. Another man took his place.

The general saw Charlie and hurried over to him.

"Here it is, General," Charlie said.

The general took the object and examined it with admiration. Jeremiah had never met Abner Doubleday before, and saw that he was a man in his middle forties with a mustache and dark curly hair, and cheeks that puffed slightly like a squirrel storing nuts.

"Corporal Ahlborn, this is just what we needed."

By this time, some of the men who had been standing along the sidelines took the places of those who had been arranged on the field. Upon closer inspection, Jeremiah saw that there was a knapsack lying on the ground by each of the four corners, for what reason, he had no idea.

"Thank you again, Corporal," Doubleday said, handing the wooden stick to one of his men.

Jeremiah gazed in fascination as the man with Charlie's hickory limb swung at the object the man in the middle threw at him. The object sailed through the air

462

past the men in the field while the soldier dropped the stick and ran to the first knapsack on his right.

"Charlie, what's going on here?"

"It's a new game General Doubleday's invented."

Jeremiah continued to watch as another soldier swung at the object that had been thrown at him. This time, the first man raced around to the other knapsacks until he came back to the original spot from where he had hit the object in the first place. Some of the men cheered, and Doubleday scratched a mark on a piece of wood with some chalk. He then returned to Charlie and Jeremiah.

"It works fine, Corporal," he said, clapping Charlie on the back. "Tomorrow perhaps we'll have a game with you Pennsylvanians."

"General," Jeremiah began, "just what is this game?"

"I call it Base-Ball." And Abner Doubleday explained the object of the game to Jeremiah. "We seem to have the problem of the hitting stick solved, thanks to our carpenter friend here. Now the problem is the ball. It's just a walnut with yarn wrapped around it, but the yarn unravels."

Jeremiah watched the rest of the afternoon, and came to the conclusion that he thought it really was a rather good game. At least it was a change from leapfrog or wrestling.

That night, he lay wrapped in his blankets in his tent, thinking about Abner Doubleday's game and the problem of the yarn-wrapped walnut. An idea came to him, and he got up and lit the lantern in his tent. Rummaging through his possessions, he found a torn sock. He put on his boots and, taking his knife, went over to one of the sutler's wagons, where he cut a square of canvas from the top. He then found a walnut tree, and after identifying himself to the picket on duty, returned to his tent. He first wrapped the sock around the walnut, and then carefully sewed the canvas cover over it with his surgical needle and thread. He tossed the ball in the air several times and, satisfied with his handiwork, crawled back into his blanket and fell asleep.

When the soldiers from Pennsylvania met the New Yorkers at the playing field the next morning, Jeremiah presented Abner Doubleday with his new ball. For their efforts, the surgeon and the carpenter were elected co-captains of their team. And as the month of March progressed, it was this way in which the Union Army entertained itself.

Stuart's headquarters during the winter had been the center of gaiety among the Confederate camps. Despite the poor clothing and sporadic cases of scurvy, the men's spirits were high—Jeb made them so. The South had celebrated the new year with General John Magruder's capture of Galveston, which opened up a valuable port for blockade-running. Richmond seemed secure, and the Federal Army was somewhere beyond the Rappahannock, disorganized and sunk in gloom. Morale in the Mississippi Valley had been stirred by President Davis's visit to his home soil, and since Lee had taken charge of the army, the Confederacy had won many victories. The future looked optimistic for the South.

Jeb held songfests and musicales in camp, entertained visitors, organized snowball fights, and tried to keep his men happy. There were fox hunts, and the men shot squirrels and blackbirds to vary their diet of rancid bacon and beef that was so tough that nobody could chew it. An admirer had sent Jeb a barrel of oysters for Christmas,

464

but there was no salt with which to season it. Many critics thought Jeb frivolous, but he was hardworking and attended closely to business. Every Sunday, religious services were held in the grove, no matter what the weather might be, and they were well attended by all. Jeb was like a brother to his staff, and he wanted them to present a handsome soldierly appearance.

Jackson and Jeb were at Culpeper as witnesses in a court-martial proceeding when Jeb received word that Fitz Lee was after some Union cavalry and wanted his commander to join him. John Pelham had been visiting friends in the area when Jeb sent for him. He arrived at Culpeper on the night of March 16 and the next morning the three men borrowed horses and trotted off toward Fitz Lee's camp.

"If you've been off sparkin' with a pretty girl, Johnny, I know a little gal in Richmond who'll be jealous," Jackson grinned.

"Who?"

"Mahaley Armstrong."

John smiled. "She's a mighty nice girl, but Richmond's a sight farther than I wanted to travel."

When they reached Fitz Lee, they learned that Yankees were swarming all around the vicinity of Morrisville. They needed to protect the Orange and Alexandria Railroad, but the Confederate cavalry was in a sorry state to do so. Horses were so scarce, most of the men were on foot. Just as scarce were shoes and precious nails, and on more than one occasion, Jackson had seen men leading limping horses with the hooves of a dead horse which they had cut off for the sake of the shoes nailed to them, dangling over the saddle.

Fitz took dismounted sharpshooters toward the woods

in search of the Yankees while Pelham watched anxiously beside Jackson.

"I've never been in this type of combat before," John said, unconsciously touching his saber in its scabbard. "I've always had my guns."

"We've always had a cavalry before," Jackson muttered. "We look more like infantry now."

Jeb, Jackson, and John rode off toward Kelly's Ford where an advance guard had located the enemy. There was scattered firing, and Jeb and Jackson remained at the front to observe while John trotted around in his excitement. Never before had he been in the middle of the action, even in the some sixty-odd skirmishes and battles in which he had participated. It had always been reliable Pelham, supporting the cavalry with his guns. The Confederates fell back from the fire and began to run. Jeb and Jackson raced forward toward the stone fence from where the Federals were shooting, trying to rally the men.

A shell burst near the fence, killing several of the men, but Jeb had succeeded in rallying his men, and they dashed forward. Firing at the Yankees, the cavalry rushed ahead.

John Pelham drew his saber, the joy of battle shining in his eyes, and galloped after Jeb. "Forward!" he shouted, approaching the gap in the fence where the men were streaming in upon the Yankees. John drew rein and, standing in his stirrups, shouted encouragement to his comrades.

There was a roar as a shell exploded. The horse leaped, and John fell. He lay on his back, the smile still on his face, looking as if he would rise and shake off the dirt and again shout "Forward!" But a shell fragment had entered the back of his head.

The column had already passed before Pelham fell, and up ahead sabers clashed and pistol shots rang out. One lone rider recognized John; it was Captain Gilmor, and he jumped off his horse and bent over the boy, trying to minister to him. It looked as if the Yankees were preparing to countercharge, and he knew Pelham must be moved or he would become a prisoner. He managed to lift John up and over the withers of a horse, but he couldn't take the time to see if he was still alive. Gilmor rode to the rear and saw two men whom he ordered to take John to the nearest ambulance while he returned to report to Jeb.

Almost from the time Pelham had been hit, the battle lost its menacing character. It became nothing more than a military exercise. Jackson was with Jeb when Gilmor galloped up to them, blood on his hands and jacket.

"You're hurt," Jeb told him.

"Not me—it's Pelham. I think he's dead. I sent two men off with him a minute ago, to find an ambulance."

Jackson would never forget the look of anguish and horror on Jeb's face.

"Are you certain he's dead?" Jeb asked.

"He appeared to be to me."

"Tell me what happened."

Jackson spurred his horse and rode to the rear, skirting the road to avoid the photographer's little rickety wagon rambling toward the scene of the action, finally overtaking the two men with Pelham's body. Jackson stopped the men and got down from his horse. He carefully lifted John's head, his face and hair matted with mud and blood, and Jackson was astonished to find Pelham was still breathing. With the assistance of the

467

two men, Jackson lay John's body on the grass.

"Why didn't you look for an ambulance?" Jackson shouted, looking around frantically. His eyes fell on the rear of the photographer's wagon. "Go take that wagon!"

The two soldiers chased after the wagon and commandeered it, leaving the dismayed photographer standing by the roadside, his equipment lying at his feet where the soldiers had dumped it.

Jackson put John in the wagon and drove it himself to the nearby home of Judge Shackleford in Culpeper, where he was immediately put in bed. Three surgeons arrived and worked over the boy, finding the fragment of shell. Although it had done no harm to the brain, it had severely damaged the nerves.

At one o'clock, Pelham opened his eyes, gave Jackson an unconscious look, heaved a great sigh, and died. Jackson bowed his head and left the room just as Jeb arrived at the house. Jeb went into the bedroom and gazed at the lifeless body of the handsome boy major for a few moments, and then bent down and kissed his forehead.

"The noble, chivalric, the gallant Pelham is no more."

The news spread throughout the Confederacy that one of its brightest stars had fallen. Jackson and Von Borcke accompanied the body to Richmond, where they arrived late at night and found no hearse was waiting to meet the train as had been ordered. They hired a common dray and went to the home of Governor Letcher, who offered a room in one of the senate halls for the body.

It was after one in the morning when the two weary men left the governor. Jackson hated to disturb the Armstrongs at this hour, even though he was sure he

468

would be welcomed, so he and Heros went to the Spotswood Hotel. There was not a vacant room in the building, so they curled up in the overstuffed chairs in the lobby and slept there.

While Heros went to make final arrangements for Pelham's body to be returned to Alabama, Jackson walked over to the public baths, where he cleaned up and had his beard shaved off again. He then ate some breakfast and walked over to the Armstrong house, having told Heros to join him there later. The black arm band Jeb had ordered the entire cavalry to wear in tribute to their comrade wrapped around his sleeve, Jackson met Cindy at the door and learned the family was out. He sat in the drawing room, reflecting sadly about what had happened.

After the Armstrong women had delivered to the hospital some items which the *Grasshopper* had brought back, they stopped to pay their respects to the memory of John Pelham, whose body lay in state in the Senate Hall. Von Borcke had arranged for a small window to be left in the casket and Mahaley thought John looked for all the world like a little boy asleep. She had been truly saddened, for John Pelham had personified all that southern manhood should be.

When Melissa saw Jackson sitting in the drawing room, she ran into his arms. "Oh, Jackson, I'm so sorry about John!"

As he held her against his chest, he realized how very much he needed Melissa. She was the one strong thread that had helped him to keep his sanity for the past two years in this nation gone mad.

Nancy came over and kissed his cheek. "He was a fine boy, Jackson."

Edward returned late in the afternoon from his meeting with Lewis. When Von Borcke arrived, his presence seemed to put a little life back into everyone's hearts, for despite his own grief, the jovial Prussian always managed to make things come alive.

Jackson and Heros took Melissa and Mahaley to the Varieties that evening, a diversion the men needed more than the women. Jackson was disappointed, for not only had the seats cost five dollars apiece, he felt the men in camp could have staged a better performance. More importantly, he was looking forward to getting back to the house and visiting Melissa in her room.

Under the warmth of the blankets, Jackson leaned on his elbow and traced his fingers over Melissa's lips.

"I spent a lot of time thinking about things on the train coming down here," he said.

"What things?"

"Oh, lots of things. You and me mostly."

"That's a nice subject," she murmured, curling his hair around her fingers.

"I joined up for three years, and two of those years will be over next month. Johnny's death really got to me—how senseless all this is. I still think we can whip the Yankees, but how much longer is it going to take? It's not fair for us to have our happiness taken away from us like this. I'm not going to reenlist when my time runs out, if the war's still going on. I'm leaving the cavalry. I want a home and babies."

"So do I."

He kissed her in the moonlight. "I don't know what I'll do when I get out. All I know is the army. But I'd like to get a little place in the country somewhere. Maybe do a little farming. What I'd really like to do is raise some fine

470

horses. How does all this sound to you?"

"It sounds wonderful."

"A year's a long time, though. I was wondering if maybe we couldn't cut that down some. Like, say—if we were to get married in the fall. The army never sees much action in the winter, anyway. Maybe Jeb could get away and come into town and be my best man. . . ."

"Is this a proposal?"

"'Course it is. What did you think it was?"

She chuckled. "Well, you never came right out and asked me before."

"Well, I'm asking you now. Will you marry me?"

"Yes."

"In the fall?"

Her eyes reflected her happiness. "Yes," she whispered, kissing him. "Oh, yes."

As they made love once more, Melissa knew finally that her commitment to Jackson was total, and that there could never be another man to take his place.

At the breakfast table before leaving for camp, Jackson announced his intentions to marry Melissa in the autumn. He looked at Edward. "If it's all right with you, sir?"

"You have my blessings."

"Oh, I'm so excited!" Nancy bubbled over. "A wedding in the family! Oh, we'll have such fun planning it. Perhaps we could have the ship bring in some white satin and lace for a gown . . . and cases of champagne and caviar. Oh, what a thing to look forward to!"

"Please, Aunt Nancy, I don't want you to go to all that trouble and expense."

"What other pleasures do we have these days?"

471

"Melissa Vaughn," Edward mused. "I rather like the sound of it."

Jackson grinned. "So do I."

One morning in early April, Henry was sitting at his desk, staring out the front window. He was debating what to do with the information he had gathered that Jefferson Davis was sending Josiah Gorgas, his chief of ordnance, to open a foundry and furnaces on the Trinity River in Texas. He didn't really know what value it would be to the Union and besides, he was becoming very wary. Rumors of spies abounded in Richmond, but due to the inefficiency of the military police, few had been apprehended and brought to trial. Nevertheless, he was being especially careful.

While he was staring out the window, he noticed a crowd passing by the office of the *Journal*. It was more than a crowd; it appeared to be a mob. Henry got up from his desk and found that more people were joining the group. After feeling in his pocket to make sure he had his notebook with him, he turned to Melissa.

"Tell McAllen I'll be back later. This looks like a story here."

Henry left the office and followed the mob. They were led by a pistol-toting giant of a woman carrying a bowie knife, a white feather sticking out of her shabby hat. By the time they reached the corner, there must have been several hundred people, mostly women and teenage boys.

"What's going on here?" Henry asked.

A small, thin woman carrying a broom smiled pleasantly at him. "We're going to find something to eat."

As the mob turned the corner, Henry hurried along as

472

best he could with his bad leg, trying to reach the head of the column. As they marched, small groups of citizens joined, some armed with hatchets and knives.

"Bread! Bread!" they chanted.

The mob moved along Ninth Street, nearing the War Department. Inside, the workers heard the commotion. Some of the clerks got up from their desks and stepped outside.

"What is it, Father?" Mahaley asked, trying to see past and through the men standing in front of her.

"It looks like a riot. By God, I believe that's Henry with them!"

Still trying to ask questions, Henry's leg was beginning to pain him from the exertion. He spotted Edward and paused to catch his breath.

"Henry, what's happening here?" Edward asked.

"They want food," Henry explained, rubbing his leg. "They can't afford the high prices anymore. They say they're starving."

"That Amazon leading them hardly looked like she was starving."

The ever-growing mob turned down Cary Street, where most of the speculators' stores were located. The women rushed into the various stores and proceeded to clean them out, carrying out great amounts of food and putting it into wagons or carts they had impressed along the way.

The owners barred their doors almost immediately, but this was not to deter the angry mob. They smashed the glass windows as well as the doors.

"Our children are starving while the rich roll in wealth!"

"Down with the aristocrats!"

"Give us food—not our dead sons and husbands!"

The mob had grown to more than one thousand people, all shouting and becoming uglier with every step. Not satisfied with the necessities, they stormed jewelry shops and pillaged general stores, taking anything they could find. Still limping after the mob, Henry saw a youth come out of a store, his hat filled with Confederate bank notes.

By the time they approached Capitol Square, Mayor Mayo had called out the fire brigades, among them a new steam engine which had been presented to the city just last month, and the hoses were turned on the mob. The drenched rioters fled to join another mob approaching from another street. Governor Letcher called out the militia and had the mayor read them the Riot Act, telling them that if they did not disperse in five minutes, they would be dealt with by military force. Some slunk away, but the rest defiantly stood their ground, loaded with spoils.

President Davis had learned of the demonstration, and with armed guards to accompany him, went to the scene of the commotion. He climbed up on a dry-goods dray and confronted the crowd; a few crusts of bread were thrown at him as the utmost insult. The military police stood ready as he spoke to them.

"Citizens of Richmond, listen to me!" he called. "I know times are hard. But you have taken jewelry and finery as well as food. Return to your homes so that the bayonets now menacing you might be sent against the enemy. This demonstration might well bring famine, for the country people might hesitate to bring their produce to the city."

Henry stood back, watching the president, his admiration for the man growing. Did he not already have enough troubles? His wife had just returned from burying her father, General Lee was ailing, the president himself was having troubles with his glaucoma, and he was trying to direct an undersupplied army to defeat a much superior force. Guiltily, Henry remembered he was also one of Davis's worries. Straightening his shoulders, he listened to what the president was saying.

"I would gladly share my own loaf of bread with people in need. I trust everyone to bear the current privations with fortitude and remain united against the northern invaders, the authors of all our sufferings."

Impressed by his fearlessness and sincerity, the crowd had listened in awed silence. The president paused, and an angry growl came from several of them, the sunlight glinting off a butcher knife.

Davis changed his manner and signaled to his military escort. They aimed and cocked their rifles, and Davis turned back to the crowd.

"My friends, I will give you five minutes to disperse. If, at the expiration of that time, you remain here, I will order this command to fire on you."

Davis surveyed the scene and took out his watch. A few tense minutes passed until the mob began to drift away. He got down from the dray and, after telling the police to arrest the ringleaders, he walked back to his office.

Several days after the bread riot, Davis asked everyone to plant food, especially the large plantations. The next Saturday, Melissa, Cindy, and little Jeff spent the afternoon planting a garden of beets, sweet potatoes, strawberries, string beans, and carrots.

Melissa found much pleasure digging in her little

475

garden, and even though it was yet too early to have any results, she enjoyed pulling the weeds in the bright sunshine, Jeff usually building imaginary fortresses in the dirt by her side. It was in this way that George found Melissa when he arrived at the house on the first day of May.

"I see you're keeping yourself busy, even when you aren't working at the paper," he smiled.

She looked up, her battered straw sunbonnet shading her features. "George, how nice to see you. You're overdue. We've been concerned about you."

George held out his hand and helped her to her feet. "We had some problems in Nassau." He smiled when he saw a big smudge of dirt on Melissa's cheek. He took out his handkerchief and wiped it off. "You seemed to be wearing a little of your garden."

"Oh."

He studied the little sprouts in the ground. "Any luck yet?"

"Not yet. But I think my beans should be coming out soon. I find it relaxing to dig out here in the garden."

"I bet it makes you thirsty."

"Why, yes. I suppose it does."

"Then come along with me into the house. I gave Tunia a little something I brought for all of you."

He picked up Jeff and the three of them went into the house.

With great anticipation, Margaret was watching as Tunia squeezed every drop of lemon juice into a pitcher. There was a basket of lemons on the table, sitting beside a five-pound tin of sugar.

"Lemons!" Melissa exclaimed. "And real sugar! Why we haven't seen any sugar since before Christmas."

476

George set Jeff down on his feet, and he gripped the edge of the table, wide-eyed as he watched Tunia.

"I didn't think the soldiers and hospitals would miss a dozen lemons," George said. "The rest should be on their way tomorrow to wherever it is they're going."

"Oh, I'm so glad you brought lemons—for us and the soldiers," Melissa said. "Nathaniel says he's been getting a lot of men brought to him with scurvy."

Jeff picked up a fat yellow lemon and was examining it. He looked questioningly at his mother. "Ball?"

Margaret smiled. "No, dear, it's a lemon. It's something to eat. I don't suppose you've ever seen a lemon before."

"He's never seen a lemon?" George asked.

"No. He'll be two this month, and we haven't seen lemons in Richmond since right after the war started."

Tunia took the lemon from Jeff's hand and put it back in the basket. "I save de rest of dem fo' another time."

"That's a good idea, Tunia," Melissa said. "When you finish, would you please bring a tray with glasses into the parlor? And fix a glass for yourself."

Margaret sighed. She believed in keeping slaves in their places, and she found Melissa's attitude toward them most exasperating. Taking Jeff by the hand, she followed George and Melissa into the drawing room.

"You said you had some sort of trouble in Nassau?" Melissa asked.

"Well, I didn't, but a couple of our men did." He smiled a little. "I don't know if you remember Ernest and Joe, but they got into a little set-to at a . . . er . . . ah . . . a brothel."

Margaret gasped. "Oh dear!"

"I hope I didn't say anything offensive."

"No, of course you didn't," Melissa said. "Go on."

"Well, the long and the short of it is, they got thrown in jail, and the authorities wouldn't let them out right away, so we had to wait. We couldn't very well sail without a first mate or an engineer."

"How awful," Margaret remarked.

"Sailors are a rough lot," George said.

"You're not."

"I'm not a sailor either," he smiled.

"Did you tell George about your engagement, Melissa?" Margaret asked.

"No."

"Engagement?" George inquired, fearing the worst.

"Yes. Colonel Vaughn and I are to be married sometime this fall."

George stood up and held out his hand to Melissa. "I wish you all the best. I'm afraid you'll have to excuse me now. I forgot something very pressing I have to do."

After George had left, Margaret looked at Melissa. "That was very strange."

"Yes, wasn't it?" Melissa remarked.

That same day a battle was being fought at Chancellorsville. Hooker was caught off balance and Lee and Jackson took advantage of this the next day. Against terrific odds, the Confederates split their forces and maneuvered around to attack Hooker from the rear. The Union Army collapsed, but Lee's jubilation quickly died. Stonewall Jackson had been mistakenly shot by his own men, and he lay mortally wounded.

On May 4, while the city waited for news of Stonewall Jackson's condition, the alarm bell began ringing in the tower on Capitol Hill. Melissa looked up from her desk as the telegraph began chattering. Lewis had been talking to George in his office, and the two men came out to learn what was happening. Hostile cavalry were on the outskirts of Richmond, and the city was practically defenseless. Wise's brigade were the only regular troops at hand, besides the home guard and the city battalion. The breastworks around the city were still in good shape, but there was no one to man them. The employees of the War Department were released from their work to go out and defend the city.

Mahaley hurried along after Edward. "I'm going with you, Father."

"You're a woman."

"Yes, and those are Yankees out there. This is my home, too, you know. I have as much right to defend it as you."

Edward looked at his daughter and smiled. "Come on, then."

Mahaley dashed upstairs to get her derringer, while Edward took his fowling piece from the pegs where it was hanging in his study.

Half of the men cleared the office of the *Journal*, shouting oaths against the Yankees.

"Everyone out!" Lewis exclaimed. "Go out and protect the city!"

The rest of the office cleared, leaving Henry, Melissa, George, and Lewis staring at each other. The thought of seeing blue uniforms after so much gray and butternut all these months thrilled Melissa. Perhaps the end had finally come, and she wanted to be there to see the Union Army when it arrived. Remembering the rifle she had brought with her from her home, she decided to use it as a ruse to get out to the earthworks surrounding the city.

"I'm going too," she announced, heading for the door.

George hurried after her. "What can you do?"

"I can shoot!"

George grinned. "So can I," he said, unhitching the horse. "I'll give you a ride. Get on." He boosted Melissa up onto the saddle and climbed up behind her. Unladylike as it seemed, Melissa figured no one was paying attention anyway. George put his arms around her waist as they rode off.

Lewis turned to Henry. "Well, Walkenfeldt?"

"Yes, sir. I'm going."

When they reached the Armstrong house, Melissa hurried up to her room and took her father's rifle out of the armoire where it had been for two years. She didn't even bother to load and prime it, knowing full well she had no intentions of using it. George was waiting in the entry hall for her and they hurried out the door.

From behind the sandbags at the edge of town, Mahaley spotted George and Melissa when they rode up, and she waved frantically to them. George helped Melissa down from the horse and joined them.

"Did you see any Yankees yet?" Melissa asked.

"Nothing," Mahaley grumbled.

"I don't suppose there's any sense in my asking either of you girls to go back home?" Edward asked.

"Not a chance," Melissa replied, peeping over the tops of the sandbags.

George glanced around at the odd assortment of defenders: an old man with a blunderbuss, a foppish young man with a dueling pistol, a boy of about ten clutching his slingshot. Sighing, George sat down and leaned against the barrier.

"I don't think this bunch will do much good," he remarked.

"We won't give up without a fight," Mahaley said.

After several hours had passed, six lone riders carrying the Confederate flag approached from the woods to report the whole thing had been a false alarm. Union General Stoneman's cavalry had unexpectedly turned back.

"Oh, fiddle," Melissa sighed.

For a week the people of the South awaited news of Stonewall Jackson. He had contracted pneumonia and on Sunday May 10, General Thomas Jonathan Jackson expired. His body arrived in Richmond that night, and Jefferson Davis asked for the handsomest Confederate flag in the capital to cover the body.

Business was suspended on Monday and the citizens lined the streets to watch the funeral procession. The Armstrong family gathered at the western gate of Capitol Square with a throng of mourners.

At the signal of a gun, the procession started from the statue of George Washington in Capitol Square. The hearse was preceded by two regiments of Pickett's division, their arms reversed, then followed by the Fayette artillery and Warren's cavalry company. A groom led Jackson's horse, his boots placed across the saddle. Next came his staff officers and the remaining members of the Stonewall brigade, mostly invalids and wounded. A vast array of officials came next, including the president, the cabinet, the mayor, city authorities, and a cavalcade of carriages and friends. The procession moved along Governor Street to Main Street, then returned to the western gate of Capitol Square.

His fellow generals acting as pallbearers, Stonewall Jackson's casket was taken up the steps to lie in state in the house of representatives before returning home to Lexington.

Of the South's truly great military geniuses—Robert E. Lee, Albert Sidney Johnston, and Stonewall Jackson— only Lee remained to guide the Confederacy through the trying times that were to come.

Twenty

Andrew and his friend Sergeant Luke Randolph were posted behind some rocks on the crest of Champion's Hill in Mississippi, where a battle had been raging for several hours. General Pemberton had selected his position well, crowning it with artillery, and his 18,000 men commanded all the ground in range. General Joe Johnston was supposedly on his way from Chattanooga to take command in person, but in the meantime, the Confederates found themselves facing Generals Grant, Sherman, McPherson, and McClernand. At least the terrain was conducive to the defense of the hill, for it was one of the highest points in the area, and the large trees and dense undergrowth made it difficult to penetrate with troops.

Andrew had proven himself a fine marksman and had been delegated to command the sharpshooter's unit, which he found exasperating when working with the newly enlisted troops. In this first engagement for the new men, Andrew was disgusted with them. The unconscious excitement caused the soldiers to yell constantly, throw away equipment, and forget to bite off the end of the paper cartridge, which resulted in the spark not setting off the powder. They would rush forward, fire, and then retreat behind bushes and trees to reload. The new men, suffering from thirst and hunger in the fight, had stopped in the middle of the battle to pick blackberries.

Andrew and Luke had finally given up trying to direct the new men and settled back to pick off any Yankees who might be trying to sneak up the hill.

"I'm almost out of ammunition," Luke remarked.

Andrew checked his own supply and then looked at his friend. Luke was a blond, muscular farm boy from Kentucky who had proven himself as a fighter early in the month when they had struggled to dodge Grant in the creeks and swamps. "So am I, Luke." He gazed down at the lazy Mississippi River below them. "All we can do is hold out as long as we can."

But it was not to be for long. Recognizing their plight due to the dwindling supply of ammunition, General Pemberton ordered the troops to withdraw. While the artillery was being carted down the back of the hill, Andrew and the other sharpshooters stayed to hold off the Federals.

It was nearing twilight when Andrew finally tugged at Luke's shoulder. "Come on, Luke. We've got to go."

Luke had spotted a small party of Union soldiers making their way up the hill. "One last shot." Luke raised his rifle and took aim at one of the blue-coated soldiers carrying the guidon of the Fifth Iowa. "Just a little closer, Yank . . . that's it." Luke squeezed the trigger, and the soldier fell. The guidon snagged on a bramble bush, while his companions tried to drag him to cover.

Luke and Andrew scrambled down the hill after the retreating army.

"Where are we going?" Luke wondered.

"Pemberton says Vicksburg."

The city of Vicksburg was located on a bluff overlooking the Mississippi. For two years, the city had been under bombardment of one kind or another from the nearby river, and the citizens had grown accustomed to almost anything—except this seemingly never-ending flow of soldiers streaming into the city on the night of May 17.

Pemberton had ordered the soldiers in the rear to disrupt Grant's army from following, for the Federals were close behind. Andrew and Luke, with some other men, had smeared a bridge with turpentine and set it afire, delaying the Federals a whole day and preventing them from entering Vicksburg with the Rebels. After the battle of Champion's Hill, General Sherman had blocked the only escape from Vicksburg, and as the tired men entered the city, it was no longer the unapproachable fortress, for Grant's lines stretched all around it.

Aware that he had an army to feed, Pemberton had his men herd all the cattle, sheep, and hogs from the surrounding countryside into the city. Vicksburg was well provisioned, but the army was bringing in an inordinate amount of mouths to feed.

All that evening an army in the last stage of endurance poured into the city. Wan, hollow-eyed, footsore, and ragged, the men limped into Vicksburg, followed by siege guns, ambulances, gun carriages, and wagons. Soon after sundown, a band assembled on Courthouse Hill and played patriotic songs. Families and slaves brought pails of water into the streets for the thirsty men to drink, while houses and sheds were taken for use as hospitals.

Andrew and Luke settled down on the porch of a general store and took off their shoes to rub their tired feet. Andrew passed his silver flask of whiskey to Luke.

"What a day," Andrew remarked.

"Hope we won't be here long."

"Me too."

Confusion slowly turned into relative order, and the tired minds and bodies of the soldiers sank into exhausted sleep. The city gradually became silent and only the clatter of hooves or the occasional rumbling of a wagon moving along the streets could be heard.

The next day it was learned that the city had absorbed some thirty thousand extra bodies. The army's mules and horses, plus all the livestock, caused the mayor to fear a stampede, so the men set to work building corrals. Late in the afternoon, Grant moved up to the edge of the city, and that night the sky was lighted by the glare of burning, abandoned farms on the outskirts.

At daybreak on the nineteenth, firing began from the Union Army. The attempt to get into the city was repulsed, and another effort failed on the twenty-second. After that, the Federal Army decided to settle down to a siege. Grant's army was too strong for Johnston to send reinforcements and, from that moment on, it was only a matter of time before Vicksburg fell.

There was no large-scale fighting—only the constant bombardment of shells thrown into the city. To escape the incessant shells, the inhabitants began to dig caves in the sides of the bluff to seek shelter. Soon, the bluff was honeycombed with subterranean vaults and passages. Some were more elaborate than others, and the caves which were favorably situated brought high rents.

*   *   *

The Armstrongs had received an invitation to attend another of Jeb Stuart's cavalry revues on June 5 at their newly dubbed Camp Pelham on Fleetwood Hill in Culpeper County. Anxious to get away from the overcrowded city, the family decided to attend. Nancy's cousin, Judge Oliver Sprague, had a home in the county seat from which he presided over the entire district, so there was no problem about where they might stay. Jeb had planned a ball for Friday night which Mahaley didn't want to miss, consequently she unexpectedly came down with a sore throat in order that she might miss a day of work. Edward planned to join them Saturday. Melissa had no problem obtaining a day off from the paper, for things at the *Journal* had not been going well. Owing to the acute paper shortage, Lewis knew he was going to have to cut his publication of the *Journal* down to three days a week. As it was, he had been printing their editions on half sheets for some time.

The cavalry had swelled to its largest number since the war began, with new recruits coming in from all over the South, bringing their own mounts with them. Forage was plentiful, for grass was thick on the rolling plains; the sickly horses were once again in good shape and the many mounts captured during the spring gave almost every man a horse to ride. There were nearly ten thousand riders in Jeb's command, the largest group the cavalry was ever to have.

Jeb planned to make it a great extravaganza. Hotels and homes for miles around were made ready, and people from far away flocked to see it. The stage for the pageant had been given to him by nature—a long wide field near Brandy Station, overlooked by a hillock. The Orange and

487

Alexandria Railroad was so near that a halted train would make excellent seats for spectators.

Jackson spent hours shining his saddle with hog fat and polishing the metal with wood ashes. Gypsy's coat gleamed, and he even planned to fasten a rose to her tail. Some of the men had been able to procure new uniforms, but the rest had to patch their old ones as best they could.

Jackson was so busy cleaning up, he almost missed meeting the train. By the time he arrived at the station, Nancy's cousin had already put them in his surrey. Melissa saw Jackson coming and waved her bonnet to him. He greeted the family, and followed behind as they drove to Judge Sprague's home.

It was a gracious but small home, for the judge had been a widower for seven years and there had been no children from the marriage. He resembled Nancy, in that he was rather short and stout. He had a great bushy blond beard peppered with gray and merry little eyes. Melissa thought he looked more like Santa Claus than a judge.

Jackson visited with the family for a while and then left them to get ready for the ball, promising to be back to pick them up. The three girls went upstairs to dress while Nancy visited with her cousin.

Mahaley was as excited as if she had never before been to a ball. Margaret tapped on the door and entered the room Melissa and Mahaley shared.

"I need help lacing my corset. You'd think Cousin Oliver could at least send that little black wench of his up here to help us dress."

"Maybe he didn't even think of it," Melissa said. "After all, there's nobody around here with corsets to lace."

"She was a haughty little darkie anyway."

"But she's very lovely," Melissa said, gripping the lacings. "Hold your breath."

Margaret let out a gasp as Melissa yanked the corset strings and tied them securely.

"Margaret, haven't you been seeing an awful lot of Mr. McAllen lately?" Mahaley asked.

"Yes. I suppose so. Why?"

"Do you think he's sweet on you?"

"Don't be ridiculous," Margaret sniffed, leaving the room. That comment had hurt. She was sure Lewis had planned on proposing marriage after he had bought his little house, but months had passed and nothing had come of it. Sometimes she found Lewis a bore, but he was better than nothing. She envied Melissa in catching a man like Jackson, but she wondered if Melissa knew what she was getting herself into. Jackson struck her as the type of man who would want to spend a great deal of time in bed, whereas she felt Lewis would be content counting his money.

When Melissa returned downstairs to wait for Jackson, the house was quiet. Nancy and Oliver had evidently gone upstairs, so she picked up a newspaper lying on the table. It was the *Washington Post,* and the headlines were about how Grant had herded Pemberton's army into Vicksburg. She read the article, wondering if Andrew was with them.

There was a knock at the door, and the little black girl let Jackson in.

"My, don't you look handsome!" Melissa remarked.

"Thank you kindly, ma'am," he grinned, bending down and kissing her. "I can honestly say you'll be the most beautiful girl there tonight."

"Thank you."

"I told Jeb all about us getting married. He says he'll make time to get into town for the wedding." Jackson took her hands in his and squeezed them. "Oh, Melissa. I'm so happy! We've got so many plans to make and so much to talk about."

Mahaley came downstairs, and Jackson drove her and Melissa to the county courthouse where the ball was to be held. Sweeny already had his little orchestra tuning up, and Jeb was chatting with some officers in the corner. He looked over and noticed Jackson, beckoning them to join him. Jackson took the girls over to the group, and Mahaley was terribly impressed by all the medals and epaulets surrounding her.

"Ladies, I'm so glad you could come," Jeb said. "I'd like to present General Hood, General Longstreet, and General Lee. Gentlemen, Miss Melissa Armstrong and Miss Mahaley Armstrong."

Lee took Melissa's hand. "We're old friends, aren't we, Miss Armstrong? And may I say you look exceptionally radiant tonight?"

"Why, thank you, General."

"I'd like to hope it's because of me," Jackson grinned. "Melissa and I are getting married in the fall."

"It's about time some of Jeb's wild bunch settled down," Hood remarked.

"You Texans aren't exactly saints," Jeb laughed.

Lee shook Jackson's hand. "You're a lucky man. She's one of the fairest flowers in the Confederacy. I want to wish you both much happiness."

"Thank you very much, General Lee," Melissa smiled.

"I know we'll be very happy," Jackson said, beaming at Melissa.

Heros joined them with Flora Stuart on his arm. He

pinched Mahaley's chin playfully. "Ah, my little liebchen, how good it is to see you again."

Flora put her arms around Melissa. "I'm so happy for you. Jeb told me all about you and Jackson."

Edward arrived at the train depot at seven in the morning. He barely had time to deposit his bag at Judge Sprague's house and have a bite to eat when it was time to assemble for the festivities.

The sun shone warmly down on the scene when the cavalcade rode triumphantly onto the field, the buglers heralding their approach. The line of horses extended for a mile and a half, and at the front rode Jeb Stuart and his staff—the Lees, Wade Hampton, William E. Jones, Jackson, and Von Borcke. Along the flank were the horse artillery commanded by R. F. Beckham who had replaced Pelham.

Melissa and her family were seated near the generals, and she noticed how proudly Lee observed the marching squadrons. Touching their swords to their hats, the men saluted Lee as they passed, and Jackson added an extra wink for Melissa.

Lordy, how handsome he is, she thought.

Jeb wheeled away from the flank and took his position beneath the Confederate flag, flying gallantly in the breeze. After the line had ridden the entire length of the field, they doubled back. As they neared the reviewing stands, they drew their sabers, spurred their horses into a gallop, and let out the Rebel yell. Beckham opened up with blank charges from his Napoleons, as if to repel the mock attack.

The thrill and excitement of this spectacle caused the onlookers to cheer. The ladies were overwhelmed and waved prettily embroidered hankies to the soldiers. Lee smiled, comparing this vast show of strength to the few mounted battalions who had fought at the first Manassas.

Two days earlier, Jackson had gone hunting and shot a big fat grouse and a turkey. The turkey, he presented to Judge Sprague for their supper, but he had carefully cooked the grouse and packed it away for a picnic lunch with Melissa. When she had mentioned her picnic plans at home, the judge told her to take his wife's old sidesaddle and put it to use. Mounted on a borrowed horse, Melissa rode along beside Jackson through the hillsides. Green clover covered the ground, spreading its perfume, and the flowers were bursting with color. They found a shady tree in the woods and spread their picnic on the ground.

"It's not much," Jackson apologized.

Melissa smiled at him. "We don't need much when we have each other."

He leaned across his haversack and kissed her. "I can hardly wait till fall."

"Me too."

He took a bottle of Madeira from his kit.

"Where did you get that?" she wondered.

"I've been carrying it around with me ever since your uncle gave it to me a year ago. In case of emergencies, I guess. But I think this is a fine time to open it."

While Jackson opened the bottle, Melissa spread out the cold grouse and some apples and carrots.

"I planted a garden back in Richmond," she remarked. "But my carrots aren't as big as these yet."

"What can't you do, Melissa?"

"Oh, there're lots of things."

"I haven't seen anything you can't do yet. Like riding that horse. You rode like you were born in the saddle."

"Well, I practically was. I used to ride a lot back home. Personally, I can't stand to ride sidesaddle. I never did before I came to Richmond."

"You didn't?"

"No. I used to wear Jeremiah's pants and an old hat, and nobody knew I was a girl."

"It would be pretty hard to disguise it now."

She smiled at him. "Speaking of disguises, is Flora Stuart pregnant, or was it my imagination?"

"She's pregnant. And Jeb says they're going to name the baby after Johnny."

"Even if it's a girl?"

"That's what he says." He chewed thoughtfully on his meat. "Who knows? Maybe this time next year we'll be picking out names for our baby. How many do you want?"

"Oh, Lordy. I don't know."

"A hundred of 'em!" he laughed. "And all the little girls looking just like you. Maybe we should name them after all the big Confederate victories."

She giggled. "Manassas Vaughn?"

"How about Fredericksburg Vaughn? Or Chancellorsville Vaughn?"

They both laughed. "I think I'd rather stick to plain old everyday names," she said.

"Jeb says he might give me a week off, if we aren't doing anything important. I thought around the first part of October would be a nice time. It's not too cold yet then and all the trees are just beginning to turn. Can you be ready by then?"

"Ready? What do I have to do?"

"Well, don't women always have a hundred silly things to do? You know—like picking out clothes."

"The selection's a little limited right now, I'd say."

"That's true. But at least maybe we can have a nice honeymoon trip. I was thinking about going west a little, away from all the hubbub. How about White Sulphur Springs? That's a pretty place."

Melissa felt an icy stab at her spine, and the color drained from her face. White Sulphur Springs, where such an unspeakable degradation had happened to her on her journey to Richmond. She had managed to push the incident to the back of her mind for all this time. In a detached way, she wondered what had become of that man's body, or if anyone had ever found it.

"No. I don't want to go there."

"Is anything the matter?"

She smiled. "No, I would just rather stay closer to civilization. After all, you're a Confederate soldier, and if some stray band of Yankees found you, you'd be sent to prison."

"That wouldn't be much of a honeymoon," he grinned. "Then where would you like to go?"

"Oh, anywhere would be fine, as long as I'm with you." She sipped some wine from the tin cup. "Aunt Nancy gave George specific instructions on what kind of material he was to bring back for my wedding dress. They are going to England this time, so he's bound to find something. And I might as well tell you now, my wedding present to you will be a new uniform. After all, I don't want my husband looking like a ragpicker," she teased.

"I wouldn't care if you didn't wear anything."

"Wouldn't that be a shock to the congregation at St. Paul's?"

He grinned. "I can't very well get a farm until the war's over. No sense having the government take half of everything. I thought maybe I could get a job as an aide or a liaison man. What do you think of that?"

"Whatever you want to do. Uncle Edward says we're welcome to live at his house if we want to."

Jackson frowned and studied his apple thoughtfully. "We might have to do just that. I haven't got much money. All the money I saved before the war went for buying equipment when I joined up with Jeb. And my pay now hardly gives me enough to live on."

"I've got some money saved."

"Oh, no, Melissa. That's yours. You worked for it, and you keep it."

"That's silly. What you make, you'll share with me. Why shouldn't I do the same for you? I've really got quite a lot saved—almost a thousand dollars. And after we're married and you're still finishing up your time, I'll go on working. If Mr. McAllen keeps the paper going."

Jackson wrapped the bones in a piece of cloth and put them back in his haversack. "I'll save these and boil the fat off them to make saddle polish or something." He refilled their cups with wine and leaned back against the tree. "Is the *Journal* going out of business?"

"No. But it's just so hard to get paper and ink anymore. He's thinking about publishing only three times a week instead of daily."

"What will you do with your time then?"

"Oh, I don't know. I suppose I'll help out at the hospitals."

"That's not a very pleasant business."

"Neither is this war. But I'll manage. I nursed you back to health, didn't I?"

"Indeed you did." The breeze was blowing a few wisps of Melissa's dark hair, and Jackson reached out and touched it with his fingers. "Oh, Melissa, I love you so much. I can't wait for us to be married."

She grinned mischievously at him. "We haven't waited."

He laughed, gently pushing her back onto the deep clover and kissing her. "Don't worry. I plan to make an honest woman out of you."

"I should certainly hope so," she grinned.

"I don't suppose anybody would be likely to stumble across us out here . . . ?"

"Why, Jackson, could you be trying to take advantage of me?" she teased.

He kissed her again and released some of her hairpins. "Let's just say I'm taking advantage of an opportunity."

"And who knows when we might have another one again?" she whispered as their lips met.

Jeb held another ball that evening, this time under the stars. The greensward echoed with laughter and music as Jackson and Melissa danced under the sparkling heavens.

"Oh, Jackson, I'm so happy."

"You mean you don't even care that the hem of your dress is probably getting ruined by the dew?" he laughed.

"How could I possibly care about anything like that when I'm in your arms?"

"When we're married, I'll buy you a hundred dresses."

"On your pay?" she grinned.

"Well, maybe after we get our little horse farm started," he admitted.

She laughed, her eyes shining. "I won't need any dresses there."

"Then I'll buy you a hundred pairs of overalls."

Edward had been talking to Lee and watching the dancers.

"I think it's good for the men to break loose once in a while," Lee remarked. "If they didn't, they would surely go mad."

"My daughter Mahaley seems to be having a fine time dancing with your son."

"I'm glad. Rooney was disappointed that his wife couldn't come up to see him. And they'll all be leaving again in a few days."

Out of breath, Jackson and Melissa joined the two men.

"You two make a very handsome couple," Lee said. "I hope I'll be invited to your wedding?"

"Of course, sir," Jackson replied. "It would be our honor."

"I'm afraid I'll have to take your husband-to-be away from you for a little while," Lee told Melissa. "But he'll be back before you know it."

"Jeb hasn't said anything. Where are we going?" Jackson asked.

"I'm starting Ewell and Longstreet for the Potomac. I'll need cavalry to cover the march."

Melissa thought what this information would mean to Henry, and then she looked at Jackson. Not this time. The Pinkerton agents would have to forgive her for not passing on this particular troop movement to them. The man she loved would no doubt be in the thick of it, and she would do nothing that might endanger his life.

She linked her arm through Jackson's. "I've learned to wait already, General. I can wait a little longer."

Jackson saw the family off on the train the next day, and Judge Sprague invited him to supper anytime he felt like dropping in. Melissa stood on the step of the train, face to face with Jackson.

"I'll miss you," she said. "So hurry back."

"I will." He kissed her lightly on the lips. "I love you."

"I love you too."

The engineer blew the train whistle, and Melissa hurried inside. She passed through the car and out onto the little platform. As the train began to roll south toward Richmond, Jackson grinned and waved his plumed hat at her, the feather dancing in the sunshine. Melissa remained on the platform until she could no longer make out Jackson's form in the distance. As she turned to reenter the car, she was suddenly overwhelmed with fear for his safety. She looked back once more, only to see the tiny depot of Brandy Station fading from view.

Several weeks later, Melissa was sitting in the drawing room with the family, making a list of guests to invite to the wedding.

"Do you think it would be proper to invite the Davises?" she wondered.

"I don't see why not," Nancy replied. "I hope Mr. Ainsworth selects some nice material for your gown."

"He seems to have very good taste," Mahaley remarked.

"We can hold the reception here, if it's not too large,"

Nancy said, "provided the ship brings in what we need."

"If it doesn't, we might end up serving the guests corn bread and water." Mahaley laughed.

Edward came into the room from his study and sat down.

"Uncle Edward, I really feel guilty about all this expense you'll be going to."

He smiled. "Don't. It's the only bright spot we've had to look forward to since the war started. Besides, it keeps my ladies out of mischief."

"I want you to know how much I appreciate it."

"I know you do, Melissa. I do have some rather bad news to tell you all. I just learned about it before I left the office."

"Well, what is it, Edward?" Nancy asked. "Don't keep us in suspense."

"The Union has another state. Yesterday, the new state of West Virginia was admitted to the Union."

"Oh, dear," Nancy sighed.

Melissa was dumbfounded. If she had stayed in Shady Run, she would now be a citizen of the United States. She would never have known this dilemma of being loyal to both the Union and her friends and family here in Richmond.

"Do you know what the capital is?" she asked.

"Charleston."

"I'm so glad you came here now," Nancy said. "It's bad enough having Jeremiah on the other side. I couldn't stand you being considered an enemy too."

"Besides, you'd never have met Jackson if you hadn't come here," Mahaley told her.

Melissa smiled. "Yes. That's very true. I'm glad I left

Shady Run."

Melissa meant what she said. Jackson had brought new meaning to her life. Besides, when the war was over, everyone would once again be on the same side. She only hoped it would be the Union side.

Special Preview of
RICHMOND VOLUME 2: THE FIRE
Coming in November

Stuart's cavalry had been galavanting all over the countryside, collecting captured supplies and engaging in small skirmishes. Lee was upset with him, for the Army of Northern Virginia had marched north into Pennsylvania and without Stuart's cavalry, the army was blind. To add to his other worries, Rooney had been captured while recuperating from his wound.

Part of the purpose of the invasion had been to gather supplies, and as General Pettigrew's men neared Gettysburg, they decided to check the town's stores for shoes. There they stumbled into the army of General George C. Meade, who had replaced Hooker as commander of the Army of the Potomac only three days earlier. The battlefield had been inadvertently selected in the sleepy little farm village which had no importance other than it was situated on a crossroads. Lee called his brigades back from their journey to Harrisburg and set up headquarters. The battle was about to begin.

About noon the next day, Stuart led his men along the York Pike. The artillery was booming in the distance behind them as they turned off the main road to a ridge with a commanding view. Below them was a barn and several outbuildings amid cultivated fields and a small forest nearby. Jackson went with Fitz Lee's brigade to the woods along with Hampton's brigade. Jenkin's men went forward on foot to the barn, but by some omission had only ten rounds of ammunition per man.

Jackson watched as the 1st New Jersey swooped down upon Jenkin's men. Stuart's batteries opened up and were answered by the Federal guns. There was much dodging in and out of trees and rifle fire until Jenkin's men were forced to withdraw.

Wade Hampton moved into the fray, and Jeb ordered all of his units in just as General Armstrong Custer placed himself at the head of his column of Michigan men.

The two columns drew nearer and nearer, and Jackson raised his saber, yelling like a demon. He wheeled Gypsy to the right just in time to avoid a Yankee sword, and a bullet ripped past him, tearing the braid on his sleeve.

The battle veered off toward the trees, men yelling, horses tumbling down, and pistol fire cracking. Jackson watched a Union officer fall from his saddle and get trampled by a hundred sharp hooves. Another Yankee struck his saber, knocking it from his grasp, but he pulled out his pistol and rushed on.

The fight raged for over two hours, and the Confederate cavalry began to get the upper hand until suddenly from the left came a fresh batch of Federals, the 3rd Pennsylvania. The gray troopers began to scatter as the Yankees chased after them. A few harmless bursts of artillery fire followed the riders.

Jackson spurred Gypsy after Jeb when something struck him in the shoulder. He fell forward out of his saddle and onto the ground. His right arm was useless, pinned under the weight of his body. As he raised his head to see the dust clouds of the riders passing from his view, another ball struck him in the thigh and the impact fairly lifted him off the ground. He was bleeding profusely but did not lose consciousness.

He listened as the sound of the caissons faded from his hearing range, and all was quiet except for a moan or a cry from the other men left on the field. Raising his head, Jackson looked in the direction in which the cavalry had left. Nothing was moving except for some smoke curling up from a charred outbuilding which had been struck by a shell.

A strangled cry stuck in his throat, "No!!!!!"

His head fell back to the ground, and a great sob shook his body.

"Reb?"

Jackson raised his head at the sound of a voice. It came from a Union cavalryman lying a few feet away.

"What?"

"Where you hit, Reb?"

"In the leg and the shoulder."

"If it was my bullet, I'm sorry."

"Do you think the cavalry's gone for good?"

"I don't know."

"Can you move, Yank?"

"No. Both my legs got blown clean off."

Jackson lifted his head again to look. The angle was bad for him to see the soldier to whom he had been speaking, but for the first time he noticed the incredible carnage all around him. The field that had once been full of wheat rippling in the sun was now trampled straw. Splintered trunks of trees dotted the orchards and all through them were the bodies of the dead and wounded, both men and beasts. Strewn among the bodies were broken wheels, abandoned muskets, canteens and haversacks spilling food which would never be eaten. The breeze blew open the pages of a lost Bible and a few scraps of paper danced in the air—letters to sweethearts which would never be read.

"Reb, if I'm dead before they find me, tell 'em I'm from Huntingdon County, Pennsylvania."

"What's your name?"

There was no reply and Jackson repeated his question, his own voice growing weak. The Pennsylvanian did not answer. Jackson lay his head back down and closed his eyes.

Lee was gathering his forces for the retreat back to Virginia. There were not enough men or ammunition for another day's fighting, and he needed to move fast before Meade could cut him off. The wagons and ambulances, loaded with wounded, fell in behind the soldiers, preparing for the march to the Potomac. The cavalry spread out to lead and guard the flanks and rear of the procession.

Jeb was husbanding an ambulance, and Wade Hampton rested inside, his arm nearly severed by a saber. As yet, he was unaware of what had befallen Jackson. It wasn't until they were miles away that he heard the report that his friend had fallen.

"Did you see him fall, Private?"

"Yes sir. I rode right past him. He was all bloodied up and not moving."

Jeb clenched his fist and struck his saddle. "Is there no end to this?"

*   *   *

Jackson opened his eyes and discovered that it was dark. He had no idea what time it was. The ground around him was silent. The loss of so much blood made him cold, and he shook with chills. He was so thirsty—just one drop of water might help, but he couldn't move. There had been a canteen lying not three feet from him but there was no response to the effort to make his arm reach out. He had little hope of seeing another day.

He thought of his childhood and how he loved to go riding through the hillsides with his brother. He wondered if he had been in the group of cavalry who had attacked them.

"Oh Melissa, I'm so sorry this had to happen. I wish I could see you just once more. I wonder if you'll ever know my fate—if anyone will ever know? Will Jeb or Fitz come back and find me? Or will I be buried in a common grave with all these other dead men scattered all around me? I'm so afraid of dying out here all alone."

Jackson prayed for a long time and wished it were daylight. At least then, someone might see him. His limbs were as cold as ice, and he had no feeling in them at all. Sometime after midnight, it began to rain, and as General Lee's cavalcade moved slowly South, Jackson lay alone in the field, the rain washing the blood from his clothes.

*   *   *

By midweek, all sorts of erroneous reports began to trickle into Richmond. Knowing that many wounded would be arriving the hospitals got ready.

On Saturday, Henry spent the day making the rounds of the government offices, gathering bits of information. He found President Davis about to hand out the first casualty lists to his secretary to be prepared for publication.

"Any news, sir?" Henry asked.

"Lee has reached the Potomac, but it's so swollen he can't cross. He's dug in at Williamsport. It's now a question of whether the river will subside or Meade will arrive—whichever happens first." Davis looked solemnly at Henry. "I'm glad you're here. You're probably the best person to pass on the information I received from General Stuart. Lieutenant Colonel Jackson Vaughn is missing in action. Someone saw him fall, and he's believed to be dead."

Henry was suddenly overcome with a rush of pity and grief for Melissa. "I see," he murmured. "Well, I suppose I should go tell Melissa now."

"Tell her how very sorry Mrs. Davis and I are."

While Nancy and Margaret were busy at the hospital, Melissa was working in her garden. She had just picked a basketful of strawberries and had given them to Tunia, telling her to make a special dessert with them. Cindy was outside doing the laundry when there was a knock at the door.

"I'll get it, Tunia," Melissa said. She went into the entry hall, wiping her hands on her apron, and opened the door to find Henry looking gravely at her. "Hello, Henry. I'm surprised to see you."

"May I come in for a minute?"

"Of course."

Henry hung his hat on the hall tree and followed Melissa into the drawing room.

"Would you like some fresh strawberries?" she asked. "I just picked them and they're ever so sweet."

"Melissa . . ."

506

He hesitated, and she turned and looked into his eyes, finding a combination of anguish and pity.

"What is it Henry?"

He put his hands on her shoulders. "It's Jackson, Melissa."

Her gaze was steady as she looked into his face. "He's dead, isn't he?"

"I don't know. Melissa, no one knows. He's been reported missing. So far, that's all anyone knows. Someone saw him fall from his horse."

Melissa fell against Henry's chest, and a silent sob shook her body. He put his arms around her, gently stroking her hair and swaying her in his arms.

"I know he's dead. I can feel it," she murmured.

"You don't know for sure, Melissa. He may have been taken prisoner, or maybe he's right now trying to catch up with the army."

Melissa shook her head against Henry's chest. "No. He's gone forever." She began to cry then, great racking sobs, while Henry held her in his arms.

FICTION FOR TODAY'S WOMAN

READ THESE ZEBRA BEST SELLERS

THE BIG NEEDLE   (512, $2.25)
by Ken Follett
Innocent people were being terrorized, homes were being destroyed—and all too often—because the most powerful organization in the world was thirsting for one man's blood. By the author of *The Eye of the Needle*.

NEW YORK ONE   (556, $2.25)
by Lawrence Levine
Buried deep within the tunnels of Grand Central Station lies the most powerful money center of the world. Only a handful of people knows it exists—and one of them wants it destroyed!

ERUPTION   (614, $2.75)
by Paul Patchick
For fifty years the volcano lay dorment, smoldering, bubbling, building. Now there was no stopping it from becoming the most destructive eruption ever to hit the western hemisphere—or anywhere else in the entire world!

DONAHUE!   (570, $2.25)
by Jason Bonderoff
The intimate and revealing biography of Americas #1 daytime TV host—his life, his loves, and the issues and answers behind the Donahue legend.

Available wherever paperbacks are sold, or order direct from the Publisher. Send cover price plus 50¢ per copy for mailing and handling to Zebra Books, 21 East 40th Street, New York, N.Y. 10016. DO NOT SEND CASH!

SENSATIONAL SAGAS

THE FRONTIER RAKERS   (633, $2.50)
by David Norman
With half their lives packed in their covered wagons and the other half staked on the future of the great frontier, these brave pioneers begin their arduous journey down the Oregon Trail.

THE FRONTIER RAKERS #2: THE FORTY-NINERS
by David Norman   (634, $2.50)
Lured by the promise of gold the pioneers journeyed west, coming face to face with hardship, struggling to survive. But their need for adventure, wide open spaces and new-found wealth led them to meet the challenge of taming the wild frontier.

THE FRONTIER RAKERS #3: GOLD FEVER
by David Norman   (621, $2.50)
The brave and determined forty-niners are blazing their way across the wilderness, heading toward California, the land of gold. Neither murder, thieves nor Indian attacks can deter them from staking their claims and fulfilling the great American dream.

WHITEWATER DYNASTY: HUDSON!   (607, $2.50)
by Helen Lee Poole
This is the first in a new historical-romantic-adventure epic that traces the growth of America by its magnificent and powerful waterways—and the proud, passionate people who built their lives around them.

Available wherever paperbacks are sold, or order direct from the Publisher. Send cover price plus 50¢ per copy for mailing and handling to Zebra Books, 21 East 40th Street, New York, N.Y. 10016. DO NOT SEND CASH!